THESAURIZE

The Completionist Chronicles Book Ten

DAKOTA KROUT

MOUNTAINDALE
PRESS

ACKNOWLEDGMENTS

Hello, my friends!

As per usual, this is the hardest part of the book to write, but only because there are so many blessings in my life I want to speak on.

First in my heart, and in life, to my wonderful wife Danielle. Your support is the foundation my dreams have been built on.

My kids, your love is my greatest treasure, and I'll cherish you forever.

To my amazing readers, and my Patreons Lilly Hawk and Mike Rylander, your enthusiasm and support is a continuing gift, and I'm so thankful for each and every one of you.

-Dakota Krout

PROLOGUE

"They're breaking through!"

"How's this happening? They're *Penguins,* for Ascetic's sake!"

Daniella looked on in horror as the once-serene Elven Camp was ruthlessly stomped flat by an onrushing horde of monsters. She had admired the Camp's strange, ethereal beauty, where the Elven craftsmanship had blended nature and tundra together into one scintillating whole. At the same time, as an Architect, she'd been cautioning against it since the first day she'd been exiled to Jotunheim.

"Aesthetics doesn't equal *defensibility.*" She let out a soft growl of frustration as she watched dozens of enormous Penguins bounce over the walls, squawking in what seemed to be mocking laughter to her ears. "I *told* them! Abyss, *Joe* warned me, and no one would listen! It would've been better not to have the walls in the first place, if they're just going to be blocking our vision and not helping us stay safe."

Daniella's heart was racing with a mix of fear and determination. She didn't have much in the way of combat skills, having always preferred to be an observer, to study and appreciate the world around her, to build up the skyline in a way that preserved natural wonders while offering functionality to the people living in the buildings. That was why she'd joined the Elves in the first place: she'd assumed that the sheer beauty of their creations would be what she'd been searching for her entire life.

"But look how useless it is." Letting out a final, frustrated grunt; Daniella turned and sprinted toward the Camp, her feet barely touching the ground as she raced to find some modicum of safety. Even so, compared to the Elves fleeing around her, she may as well have been running through a swimming pool filled with molasses.

Hwa-bam!

A tiny scream escaped her lips as chunks of glittering stone blasted through the air around her, small shards of stone digging into her exposed back. The Architect stumbled and barely managed to catch herself, throwing her weight forward and performing a small hop that put her just out of range of a hulking Penguin that *splatted* on the ground behind her. It was uninjured and quickly shook the dust off of its fluffy feathers. She turned her head, meeting its eyes, and it let out a squawk that would sound more fitting coming from the maw of a lion.

Adrenaline surging, she leaped over the crumbled ruins of the wall and sprinted toward the only building that was still standing. Unfortunately, even though it represented the best chance at safety, Daniella also understood that it was the main target of the incursion. The Treehouse, the Elven version of a Beginner-rank Village Hall, was acting as a lodestone for the hundreds of monsters boiling over—or through—the wall that had been meant to protect the Camp.

The Hoardlings—ice-coated gorilla-lizards—were lumbering through the Camp with satisfied grunts, going out of their way to attack anyone too slow to keep ahead of them. Their eyes were gleaming with hunger and greed as they ripped apart tents and smashed through stable structures, all the while being driven toward the Treehouse. Daniella quickly scanned the area, realizing that they were surrounded on all sides. She got closer to the Treehouse, noting that every single Elven defender had vanished from view. That could only mean one thing. "Those pompous brats left us out here to die!"

Already, she could see her fellow humans pounding on the entrance to the Treehouse, but no matter how they struggled, the door wouldn't budge. Desperately trying to find a way to escape the tide, Daniella turned off her original path and ran toward a structure that had already been mostly destroyed. She didn't care about that—in fact, all that mattered was that it had space among the rubble to hide. Daniella could only hope that it would suffice to keep her from danger long enough to make her escape.

She *would* escape, given the chance. Not just from the monsters of Jotunheim, but from the Elven Theocracy that had cut off her access to resources and study material while only giving her a pittance of food, unsanitary water, and a tarp thrown over a pole as a tent to sleep huddled with a dozen other people for warmth. "Abyss, now I won't even have *that*."

Not for the first time, she cursed at herself for not following along with Joe when she had the chance. She knew he was thriving, as was the community he'd built, and if she had just gone along… Daniella shook that thought off, remembering the circumstances she'd been in while Joe had been making his own escape. If she'd tried to run from the Elves while standing next to the Children of Light, she wouldn't have gotten the light rebuke of a few years in exile—she would've been tossed into a prison camp somewhere for 'reintegration'. "Which… this *is* kind of that. How did I not realize that 'til now?"

As she cowered among the rocks, her whirling thoughts latched onto a single question: what did she do to make the Theocracy so angry at her? Before she could search any deeper for an answer, vines erupting from the ground across the area caught her attention. The Elves were invoking their spells, growing plants and attempting to channel nature's wrath against the invaders.

Sadly, the vines were thin and pathetic, freezing in the air even as they grew. Even the weakest of the Penguins mostly ignored the lashing of the foliage as they threw themselves bodily at the Treehouse. Each *thud* drove home her resolve to get out of here and try again somewhere else, hopefully somewhere no one knew her. "Or maybe... I could find a way to get to–"

With a shriek of tortured wood, the Treehouse toppled to the side, collapsing on the Elves still within it. Most of them easily survived the blow, springing out of the rubble with swords and bows drawn. The leadership of the Camp, faces etched with determination, circled together and formed a defensive line, their weapons gleaming with reflected sunlight and bright enchantments. With practiced, coordinated precision, they threw everything they had against the onslaught, pushing the Penguins and Hoardlings back with each swing and thrust.

Settlement upgrade (Camp to Hamlet) failed!

"Well, isn't that just the icing on the cake." There was no more time to lose. Creeping along the ground, sprinting from chunks of stone to blasted detritus, Daniella quickly moved out to the very edge of the Elven-claimed space. A harrowing, beautiful voice let out a mournful cry that slowly faded instead of being abruptly cut off. "I don't know how they do that... *seriously*, they die as if they're in a Hollywood production."

She was certain that the last of their Elven chaperones had fallen, and with the destruction of the Treehouse, the monsters were already scattering and looking for any tasty morsels they could find. With a last burst of energy, she escaped through an enormous hole in the wall and started running out into the vast, snow-covered landscape.

For a few long minutes, she was certain she'd made it.

You have been slain by an Ancient Ice Salamander! Ooh, bad luck! Your spawn point has been destroyed, which means that you'll respawn at the nearest aligned settlement. Stay warm out there!

As a pair of blue eyes snapped open in front of her, and she was frozen solid, the ice statue of Daniella still had a smile on her face.

CHAPTER ONE

"Sixteen days." Joe was standing atop one of the tallest towers he'd made yet, matched only by its twin on the opposing entrance of the labyrinthian walls that surrounded Novusheim. Forty feet of open air loomed between the two stone defenses, even if *technically* they were a single serpentine superstructure. "No, I can't forget that 'days' means something completely different on Jotunheim... I believe it would be more accurate to say 'a little over four hundred hours'.

A tiny smile graced his lips as he thought of how annoyed the Dwarves had been that they needed to adjust their mindset on issuing quests and requests. Joe was glad of the small moment of levity, as he was extremely tense at the moment. Far into the distance, the Ritualist could see thousands of monsters scrambling across the open, frozen tundra toward his beautiful but untested setup. "Beautiful *and* defensible. Just how I like it."

Gently patting the ritual tower he'd just put the finishing touches on, Joe took a few moments to activate the ritual itself. Bubbles of acid had proven to be an effective opening volley against the densely-packed monsters, the heft of the attack enough to stagger most of the foes it hit. Once the ritual was active, in place, and ready to give the invading monsters a proper greeting, he turned and scanned the changes he and the Council of Masters had made over the last several hundred hours of work time.

The straight-edged stone palisades that had once surrounded their Town had been fully replaced, the Trash-tier stone having been broken down and almost entirely reduced to rubble during the assault by the Cyclops. To replace the protection and killing corridors, Joe had invested in sturdy city walls. To his amusement, all the resources he *technically* owed to the Council of Novusheim were instead dumped into the project.

He had finished ringing the innermost layer of the Town with Tier five, Journeyman-rarity walls. Even now, they were slowly being etched by the best Enchanters among the Dwarves and humans who had migrated here with them. "No shortage of Uncommon cores for enchanting, thank the celestials. They can always add a higher-tier layer to it later when more Rare cores are available."

From there, the wall swirled out around Novusheim in a whirlpool pattern. The Ritualist had maintained at least six inches between each hundred-foot section of stone, ensuring that no single attack would be able to take down the superstructure. Joe had to stop there: as much as he still wanted to check final details, it was time for the culmination of his efforts to be put to the test.

To his amusement, as soon as he stopped thinking about what they had done, his mind shifted to what they should be doing with the upcoming rewards. His attention hovered for a moment on the fact that, if the approaching Beast Wave was repulsed easily, it was highly probable that the Town would get a surge of morale, allowing them to quickly build a bunch of workshops and other necessary items for their Town.

The now-familiar enemies were approaching, and the time for daydreams had come to an end. Massive Penguins sprint-waddled forward with surprising speed, Ancient Ice Salamanders snuck along beneath the clouds of snow, four-limbed

Hoardlings thundered along, and… something new? "Uh-oh. I don't like *new* things. Not when they're coming to eat me. Scouts! New enemy, I need a report!"

"Councilman Joe!" came a sharp reply, a stark difference from the information blackout Joe had been contending with before he'd defeated the Cyclops. The Ritualist stood straighter as his newfound authority was recognized, and a Dwarven scout immediately began rattling off a report on the monster coming toward them. "It appears to be called a 'Verglas Leaping Leopard'. Initial observation shows only five percent of the horde is composed of this new type of creature. Most likely possibility: it was unable to attack settlements under the rank of Town. Going by the sheer numbers of attackers previously, there's a ninety-eight-point-two percent chance this is a correct estimate."

"New levels, new devils," Joe muttered to himself as he gave the scout a nod of appreciation. "I knew we were going to have to deal with new monsters eventually. I wonder how many per settlement rank? There were only Penguins, Salamanders, Hoardlings, and Boss monsters during the last rank, but we also skipped straight to 'Hamlet' in the middle of an upgrade to 'Village'. Was it just one per settlement rank? Or… no, no use speculating. I guess we'll just have to find out the hard way."

Another quick glance around revealed a startling fact: a huge number of the population of the Town were amassed along the tops of the walls, wanting to get a first-hand look at how well the defenses held up. Joe's neck and back started to itch as he was slammed with a bout of anxiety. Rolling his shoulders, he tried to ignore the onlookers as the monsters sprinted closer.

Hzzt… Fwizzz!

The Ritualist stood firm as his outermost duo of ritual towers spun up an enormous ball of acid and launched it at the onrushing creatures. Both impacted at nearly the same time, sending nearly fifty monsters tumbling as they ran into the creatures in front of them. That was when Joe's smile started cautiously growing. "Looks like the stopping power of the Double Bubble Trouble is much more effective than a single hit. Good, Ms. Mcshootypants was right about that."

A cheer erupted from the assembled townspeople as the bombardment of acid continued. In their mind, victory was already secured, and everyone was immediately starting to revel in the knowledge that they could settle down and build up toward a City without fear. So long as this Town could stand strong on its own against the otherwise relentless onslaught of wandering monsters, the path to a permanent society was clear... at least until they tried pushing to a higher rank and captured all of the benefits and hardships that came with it.

Monsters started to pour into the walls, sprinting along the killing corridors as rapidly as they could. Thankfully, the whirlpool layout ensured that they wouldn't be able to ever reach their top speed, keeping the beasts from crashing into the walls and damaging them at the same time. A tradeoff to this was the fact that the monsters were able to maintain a *constant* speed throughout the entire distance, so overall, it was a wash in terms of how long it would take them to get to the center of the labyrinth. Still, Joe took it as a win that they wouldn't have to deal with the constant maintenance of Penguin beaks embedding into stone.

"Leaping *Leopards!*" A warning was called out just in time, and Joe threw himself to the side as an icy cat pounced through the space he'd just been standing, directly bounding over the outermost wall. It spun in the air, claws flashing at him as it snarled but was unable to halt its momentum, and it dropped the remaining distance to the ground far below.

Joe took a few deep breaths, trying not to hyperventilate. He'd gotten used to being safe atop the walls, and this was a sharp reminder not to get complacent. Still, that had given him plenty of time to study the creature as it went past him. The beast was snow white with dark blue spots along it that would help it blend into this frozen tundra it called home. A quick guesstimate told him it would be nearly twenty feet long from tip to tail, and it stood eight feet tall from the bottom of its feet to the frosty spikes of its ears.

He hopped to his feet, finding out firsthand what the 'Verglas' part of its name was as his head *cracked* onto a transparent sheet of ice that had followed the beast on its jump.

"Ow!" Joe yelped in surprise, his Exquisite Shell ensuring that he took no damage from the strange terrain feature that had been created. He reached up and felt the odd parabola of ice that hung in the air, sliding his hand down it and realizing what was happening. "Hammers out! They create ice bridges after them when they jump! Smash 'em!"

His ritual orbs popped out of the bandolier on his chest, and he quickly began chipping away at the frozen surface, even as Penguins lined up to get on the ice bridge. As soon as the flightless birds had their stomachs touch the new path, they shot up it like they'd been launched from a slingshot. Over a dozen of them—separated from his bald head only by the incredibly thin surface—went up over Joe before he was able to destroy it. As soon as he knocked a small chunk of the ice out, the entire pathway shattered, dropping the remaining Penguins to the ground.

They didn't seem to mind, simply running to rejoin the line of beasts entering the walls of the Town. Joe watched the monsters, quite disgruntled over all of the surprises they were experiencing. "Gonna have to find the limits of that *real* quick. Those cats are dangerous."

The rest of the Beast Wave continued fairly normally, and no other Leopards ventured over the spot Joe was standing. Roughly a thousand monsters in total entered the killing corridors around the Town, but as the notification cheerfully informed them approximately an hour into the attack, none of them had been able to enter the Town itself.

Beast Wave Cleared! Congratulations! You have perfectly repelled a Beast Wave, not allowing a single creature to step foot into an area where civilians reside! You've earned a bonus!

Bonus 1: Morale boost! For the next 48 hours, or until a monster manages to damage a resident of Novusheim, current morale is multiplied by 2.5!

Bonus 2: Productivity boost! Your citizens feel safe and secure, allowing them to produce at a slightly higher rate. Production speed +10% for the next 48 hours, or until a civilian of Novusheim is threatened by monsters.

Amidst the cheers, applause, and laughter resonating from the center of the Town, Joe could hear other, more serious conversations. Plans for expansion and growth were already beginning to take shape. Artisans and Craftsmen were running toward their workshops or bitterly complaining about the lack thereof. The people of Novusheim had been plagued with the constant threat of war, destruction, and the loss of their homes for far too long. Joe hoped that now they could be filled with renewed hope and excitement for the Town they'd built together.

He would let them celebrate their first total victory and work to ensure that it was just one of many.

Joe took a deep breath and started toward the work he had waiting for him in Town Hall, both as a councilman and a Ritu-architect. His eyes flicked over to his new title, and he allowed a bit of excitement to fill him as he read over the most in-depth title he'd ever earned.

Councilman of Novusheim.

Privileges: While in the area controlled by the Town of Novusheim, you have the authority to declare a state of emergency, requisition resources for purposes of bettering the Town, order members of the Legion to action, and pass judgment on crimes.

Responsibilities: Abusing your privileges can lead to being removed from the council. You must work for the betterment of the citizens of Novusheim. You must be present for 8 of every 10 council meetings, if you are in the area.

Bonus: You are the first human on the council. All human citizens will be inclined to offer you discounts, work for or with you, and are much more likely to accept your orders without complaint.

All of it made sense to Joe except for the bonus, as he was uncertain how that would work without some kind of mind-bending. "You know… it's kinda like having a high reputation with humans. Maybe titles like this are why Dwarves were able to use reputation as currency? They could spend it all and still have the positive effects of a high reputation?"

The only way to know for sure was to keep the title for a long, *long* time. As the Ritualist looked around, his mind full to the brim with lists of things that needed to be done, he knew he'd be able to put the title to good use.

"It's going to be a *wild* year."

CHAPTER TWO

The Ritualist stumbled out of the council meeting, rubbing his eyes, greatly annoyed that the Dwarven Constitution allowed them to sit for nearly twenty hours at a time and make plans. "Seriously, they could just meet for an hour or two a day, instead of a whole day every other week. It's not like we have a whole lot of other things to do."

Still, he'd been able to create a full plan of action for building up the Town. With the area considered somewhat secure, everyone was fighting for the opportunity to have their own workshops set up in a favorable location—as well as jockeying for build order and priority placement. "I can't *believe* how resistant they were to having a greenhouse. Why wouldn't they want vegetables, herbs, and so forth? How are they even planning to get the supplies for half the other buildings, if they can't grow trees?"

Certainly, there was *minor* concern over creating a hunting ground within their city that would turn feral if the plants weren't harvested frequently enough. Yet, Joe didn't think that was going to be an issue with their population having soared back into the high sixty thousands. They'd lost a quarter of their people when Master Dreamstrider had led them off into the wilderness to create their own Dwarf-exclusive society, but a good number of them had trickled back when they recognized the challenges in creating a new settlement from scratch.

He tried not to let it get to his head, but Joe was proud of the fact that, without the interference of Master Stu, his value was recognized and lauded. "Still, being really great at your job always begets more work. The trick is seeing it as job security instead of a burden."

Staying productive was a good problem to have, but it *was* still a problem.

Scanning over his list of workshops and supply depots, Joe kept to himself as he casually evaded the 'Novusheim is secure' jamboree that was still raging. A glance upward told him that someone had been messing with his ritual to create a day-night cycle. The ritual tile of the false sky was now in a secure location instead of buried a couple inches below the surface, which made it even more odd that someone had managed to access it. "Lasers and strobe lights. Huh. Who knew Dwarves were into raves? Wait... is that the only one they're messing with?"

Each of the rituals he deemed necessary for the Town were locked up in his workshop instead of scattered around town to act as last-resort landmines. Even though it had worked out once, hoping that his enemies would blow their toes off as they ran at him was foolhardy.

Hurrying over to his workshop, the Ritualist threw the door open and watched with open shock as Havoc played with his ritual title like he was a DJ, his fingers swishing back and forth as his head bobbed to the music that was blasting in the area, each movement corresponding with the lights shifting in the sky.

They were interesting illusions with no substance, but they represented subtlety and a familiarity with power that Joe didn't have, so he simply watched carefully and studied the movements of not only the Dwarf, but the mana that he was massaging into the ritual itself. More than the party, *this* was what he wanted to be involved in.

Magic.

Not just for the sake of survival, but for *fun.* For interesting and exciting ways of bending the world to his will.

Eventually, the Grandmaster turned, his cigar hanging out of the left corner of his mouth as he offered Joe a half-grin. "I hear you're looking to learn some fire magic. I think I can help you out."

"Yeah..." Joe was barely able to hold himself back from asking about altering active rituals on the fly, as he was planning on working that out himself after studying what Havoc was doing. "You're a Grandmaster Enchanter, right? I don't particularly care about throwing fire around myself, but I want to be able to add it to the towers out there. It seems pretty effective against the local monsters."

"That it is." The Dwarf lifted his hand, adjusting his oversized cigar. For one long moment, as Havoc took a deep pull on the alchemical creation, Joe could see that the burning, glowing end was far more than a simple flame. It was constantly swirling and compressing. When it was pointed at the human, the Ritualist realized its heat was trapped within some kind of ever-collapsing magical field.

The Ritualist stared at the burning object, trying to figure out how to ask the question on the tip of his tongue. "Havoc... is that a miniature star on the end of your cigar?"

"No, no... You've got it all wrong. It only looks and *acts* like a cigar." With that evasive answer, the Dwarf's grin expanded out to show far too many teeth. "If you want the power of this red flower, I'll make a deal with you. The rituals you have right now are already working just fine for the wandering beasts of this world, so—"

"Wait, stop. I've changed my mind." Joe interrupted the Grandmaster, whose bright smile dimmed significantly. "Don't get me wrong, I still need to learn something very important from you. In fact, I want to learn about fire, too, but this definitely takes priority. I have the schematics to create a mana condenser, and I need to figure out the rest of the ritual or enchantment I need in order to refill batteries autonomously."

Havoc went silent for a few moments, eventually making a grumpy 'gimme' motion with his hand. The Ritualist passed over the diagram he'd earned as a quest reward, and the Dwarf inspected it for a few long minutes, his fingers tracing over the lines and iridescent three-dimensional imagery that was imbued in the blueprint.

"This is… interesting. I *like* interesting. Tell you what, I was going to make you seek out five Elven settlements and destroy them, but since you're giving me something interesting in exchange to look at and work on, let's call it three. I would've still made it four, but you gave me the diagram for the condenser, which was the only thing I haven't ever seen before. The rest of what you need is fairly common, thanks to our ability to craft War Golems, and I think I can shift it a bit to fit your needs."

Quest gained: This planet isn't big enough for both of us. Grandmaster Havoc has decided that this planet, Jotunheim, which is as large as the surface of Sol, Earth's sun, simply doesn't have the capacity to sustain both Dwarves and Elves. Ye~eah. Anyway, you are to venture into the frozen, treacherous lands of Jotunheim and destroy three Elven settlements. The settlements can be at any rank, but you will get a bonus for each settlement tier above 'Camp'. As this planet is vast beyond your comprehension, there is no time limit for completion.

Reward: Blueprints for a Mana Battery Recharge Station. This will be a combined enchantment of a:

1) Mana Collector: gather ambient magical energy.

2) Mana Condenser: store and concentrate mana for later use.

3) Mana Transfer Output: channel mana into devices or storage items.

"How am I supposed to find an Elven settlement?" Joe's aghast question was simply waved off by the Dwarf.

"Did you *not* see that there isn't a time requirement?" Havoc walked out of the door, shaking his head. "Some people just don't know how to read."

The Ritualist shook his head and shoved the notification to

the side. "Got it. I'll need to find a completely different method than relying on Havoc for this. Abyss, I'd refuse the quest outright, if I didn't think he'd come back here and taunt me for it until I accepted."

With a sigh of regret and a longing look at the ritual towers that he would now need to fill by hand—or pay a hundred Dwarves and humans to refill for him—Joe turned his attention back to the list of buildings in his hand. "All right... let's see what we've got here. Priority number one—thank you, me—the Evergrowth Greenhouse. That's a Special Rare, but I'll have to figure out how to set that up here without the plants immediately turning into monsters. What did the O'Baba tell me? Too much mana density makes the building go from a greenhouse to a dungeon?"

He swiped his hand through the air, practically *shoving* against the dense, chaotic energy that suffused the atmosphere of this planet. "Yep, this is basically monster soup. Gonna need to figure that one out."

The list was fairly exhaustive, but he'd cut the council off at ten buildings. "Millinery for hats and headwear, pretty important with the weather. Tannery or leatherworking workshop to supply *them*, so that goes first. I still need shoes, that means tannery goes second."

Joe wiggled his sock-clad toes, glad that his Exquisite Shell was keeping them from getting frostbitten. He had taken off his remaining shoe, as walking around with only one on was less comfortable than just going without. "Herbalism shop, but that needs the Greenhouse to matter, as does a brewing station and a carpenter. Hard to do carpentry without access to wood."

The last several were outside of his areas of specialization, including masonry, pottery, and glassblowing workshops. Down at the *very* bottom was a forge, as he already had created one version of it, no matter how subpar it ended up being. "Hmm... I feel like there should be a dedicated workshop for enchanting, but I haven't had any requests for that. Why?"

No answers were forthcoming, especially when he wasn't

having an actual conversation with anyone, so the Ritualist could only shrug and set off to work on the Greenhouse. As the building itself was fragile, it was slated to be built as far away from the entrance to Novusheim as possible, not *quite* pressed against the South wall, but close. They were going to put another several sturdy buildings around that, just in case some walls got smashed and sent rubble inward. Joe knew that it would eventually be indispensable to the Town, and he planned to treat it that way from the start.

Finally having more free time than he had since being on this world, Joe took his time leisurely strolling toward what would soon become the foundation for all of their plant matter. As he arrived, he found a man with a shovel digging out the space. "Hey! It's shovel guy! Still dig snow, bro?"

"You know it." The human Joe only knew as 'shovel guy' stretched and wiped some already-freezing sweat off of his forehead. "I do more than just dig, though. I've got a shovel for every occasion. Snow removal, dirt, bailing out sinking boats, even juggling. I'm the world's greatest shovel whisperer, able to communicate with snowflakes and convince them to make safe paths."

The Ritualist considered the man in front of him for a few long moments before finally deciding how he'd respond. "I feel like you're messing with me?"

"Yeah," the man chuckled as he finished clearing off the area Joe would be building. "Here you go, one council-approved plot of land for a greenhouse. They sent me the specifications so that you could move a little faster. Have a good one."

"Wait, what's your–" Joe didn't ask his question fast enough, as the shovel guy hopped in the air, swung his shovel up and under him like a skateboard, and shot into the distance as he landed. The bald magic user watched him go, utterly nonplussed. "What even *was* that? He's not telling, and I can't just see for myself. Bleh. This is the first time I'm really annoyed that I destroyed my Intrusive Scan skill."

Shaking off the confusion, Joe turned his mind toward

things he was good at. Stabilization cubes went down, ritual diagrams were set out, and the Rituarchitect survey tool ensured that everything was where it was meant to be. "Good. Now I just need to decide how to make this so it doesn't break or go feral."

CHAPTER THREE

Putting the finishing touches on his plans, Joe decided he'd incorporate the Special Aspect 'Scattering' and hope that would be enough to give the greenhouse some resistance to the chaotic nature of Jotunheim. "It's supposed to give items bonuses in damage against magical defenses, but it should work to repulse the chaotic energies here. In theory."

He didn't have much information on this aspect, as he hadn't had a chance to use it on anything other than a ritual in the past. That gave him pause, and he realized that the ritual he'd used it with, the Ritual of the Crawling Storm, would be an excellent addition to his ritual towers. "If I take out the Mage-hunting portion of it and just have it crawl around the killing corridors… yeah, I like that. It's probably going to have to wait until I figure out how to recharge the rituals without doing it myself, because that one was pretty mana-hungry, if I remember correctly."

Breaking out of his thoughts, Joe realized that the volunteers sent by the council to help him activate his ritual had arrived. He turned to them with a bright smile, clapping his hands before freezing in place. "Master Stu. I admit I'm confused as to why I'm seeing you. First off, why aren't you chained in a mine or something, turning big rocks into smaller rocks?"

The Dwarf simply glared at him, unable to speak around the thick leather muzzle he was wearing. A Legionnaire stepped forward, politely nodding at Joe. "Councilman Joe, please don't address the prisoner directly. He's paying for his crimes with community service but isn't allowed to speak to others during his period of house arrest, due to his propensity to create trouble with his words."

"Ah. I see." The Ritualist let out a heavy sigh and sized up the Dwarf, who was still glaring at him. "I certainly won't question the *wisdom* of this decision; I'm sure it was the best option available. Also, not speaking to anyone in particular, but after the Town has decided that you've paid for your crimes... I *will* try not to hold our personal history against you. I believe in rehabilitation, and I promise to give you that chance."

Most of the other people involved in the process *wanted* to be there, and that was good enough for Joe. After arranging everyone, he activated his ritual and let the aspects flood out of his storage. Joe couldn't help but feel great pleasure in seeing the metal framework of the greenhouse spring into existence, the glass appearing as if it were ice slowly creeping across the surface of a lake. "I can't believe how difficult it used to be to gather the resources required for this. How far have I come... how far will I go?"

In what felt like no time at all, the greenhouse was standing on its own, and the flow of mana and aspects vanished. The surface of the greenhouse refracted light, creating a scintillating display as if he were looking at a disco ball. "Kind of reminds me of my Exquisite Shell... makes me wonder if there's a way to push aspects into spells?"

"'Scuse me!" Joe hopped to the side as dozens of Dwarves pushing wheelbarrows caravanned over to the entrance of the greenhouse. The human looked around slightly wide-eyed; he hadn't seen or heard them coming, even with their bearded leader barking orders at the group. "Sandy soil all the way to the left and down! Anyone carrying seedlings for succulents, radishes, carrots, or the like, follow them. Clay to the right, get those roses, sunflowers, and broccoli moving right away! This place needs some color, and I'm sure *someone* can figure out how to keep a plant alive out there after we grow it."

The Dwarf clearly knew his soil and plants and was directing everything like a master logistician. Joe watched in awe as everything was smoothly brought into the greenhouse, with far more aplomb and efficiency than he'd seen in almost any industry so far.

"What do you have there? Loamy? Excellent! Front and center with the loam soil, we have vegetables to grow. You there, bald human! Thanks for the building. Now, stop standing around and help, or get out of the way!"

Joe decided that he'd pitch in and was quickly handed a tray of seedlings. Walking into the building, which was already starting to heat up from the magical influences of the world and the false daylight streaming down on them, he quickly found that the Dwarf in charge was walking alongside him. "Hey there, I'm Joe. Let me tell you a little bit about how this building works."

He went on to explain the issues of monsters that would be drawn to the potent vegetation, the fact that the flora would turn rabid if it weren't carefully managed, and his concerns over the general danger of the greenhouse. The Dwarf listened carefully, only asking questions at the end, and quickly showed that he had the situation under control. "Thank you for the information. Anytime you need fresh vegetation, let us know. In fact, you'll be hearing from me very soon... I'm an Expert herbalist on the cusp of Mastery, and I'll be coming for your position on the council. Keep an eye out for Herbie Thymebeard."

Joe froze in place, turning to look at the hard-eyed Dwarf in surprise at the sudden shift in conversation. "What? Why would you do that? What is it with Dwarves coming out of the wood-work to go after me? You wanna fight now and get it outta the way?"

"Huh? I bear you no ill will…?" Now Thymebeard was the one that seemed confused and off-put. "That's… how the council works. Every new Master gets a chance to challenge a standing member. It's not an attack; it's a way for us to showcase our skills and announce our newfound Mastery to our people."

"Oh." Joe thought about that for a few moments, realizing that the position on the council was going to be far more annoying than he'd thought it was. Long meetings, constant challenges now that there were new materials and product lines being created, all so that he could have a little bit of say in the community. The Ritualist weighed the different paths he could walk against each other and decided to maintain his position. He tried not to think about how close he was to tossing the new post out and being done with the drama it brought. "I look forward to being able to congratulate you on your Mastery in the near future. At least I know that, if you take my position, you'll be able to run things smoothly."

"Uhh. No. I don't *want* your position." The Dwarf shuddered at the thought. "Hold on… if I challenge you, you're not going to make me win, are you? How do I rig this so that I don't get the council position… maybe I'll have McPoundy–"

Joe chuckled as the Dwarf began muttering nearly the exact same arguments he'd been having in his own head moments prior. "Don't worry about it, friend. I'm thinking we'll have plenty of conversations in the near future. Here, have some seeds from Floodwater Grapes. Ah… be careful? There's a human noble house on Midgard that would eviscerate you for growing these."

Tossing over a sachet of seeds that would eventually be able to turn into some of the best wine in three worlds, Joe casually waved and walked out of the greenhouse. He was filled with purpose. The Ritualist had meticulously planned and laid the foundation for the next surge of construction, and it was time to get additional workshops ready for use.

Over the next several scores of hours, between Beast Waves every forty-eight hours and careful selection and construction of the buildings commissioned by the council, time flew by. Resources and—more importantly to Joe—aspects flooded into the Town, sparking a huge wave of industry. Most notably for the Ritualist, the very first product made by the leatherworkers was a brand new pair of shoes, allowing Joe to march around the frozen tundra much more confidently from that point forward.

The greenhouse was already starting to tamp down the supply limitations for several of the newer and original shops, such as already growing flowers that would be used to scent the luxury soaps Joe had an investor's stake in. Thanks to the plants' rapid growth in the mana-rich environment, there was even a breakthrough for Jake the Alchemist, who proudly displayed a Grandmaster-ranked Injection able to permanently offer immunity to the cold environment of Jotunheim, as well as a massive reduction in any damage taken from cold-based attacks.

There were three deaths at the auction for the Injection, and Joe didn't even know who won the bidding war for it. He was only glad he hadn't attended.

Woodworkers were already putting in orders for the saplings growing deep in the new Greenhouse, Brewers had started their first batch of Novusheim Special Ale, and fur hats were churning out of the Millinery. Joe was especially glad for the last one, as he'd been mostly clothed in his robe of Liquid Darkness, relying on his Exquisite Shell to deal with the elemental terrain damage. He'd already commissioned fur-lined clothes, as well as a new cloak that would blend in with the environment, but he was number two hundred in line.

Metal and stone were flowing into the Town from the mine and quarry that had been placed to the east—outside of the walls, to ensure that no burrowing monsters would rear their ugly heads due to the carelessness of the citizens. Frankly, Joe thought it was hilarious to watch a bubble float over the walls three times a day, filled with ores and enormous chunks of stone. Part of him was still thinking about trying to convince the council to exile Master Stu to one of those locations. "If we're gonna have paved roads in the future, we're gonna need a lot of gravel. Plus, smashing rocks builds character."

The high-quality materials were put to use immediately, and ever-so-slowly, the Dwarven craftsmen began to outpace Joe in the creation of new walls. Individually, they were all slower than Joe, but there were nearly eight thousand stone workers among the Oligarchy—the craft had been known as a noble profession of their race for millennia. Even with all of the embellishments, artistry, mosaics, and the like that were added to show where the stones were coming from, the walls began to grow outward at a ridiculously rapid pace.

It wasn't long ago that nearly everyone living here had assumed that this Town was doomed, and now it had evolved into a thriving hub of industry. Above all else, it was a fortified bastion that practically *stank* of security and prosperity. Even their diet was slowly balancing out, thanks to the addition of fresh greens and alchemical multivitamins. People were working harder, staying happier, and becoming stronger.

With the basic needs met, people had even begun venturing out into the wilderness to start the hunt for opportunities offered by Jotunheim.

"This has been a nice few weeks." Feeling calm and composed, thanks to the relaxed and consistent schedule he had been keeping, Joe entered the Town Hall in preparation of another meeting—only to flinch backward as a letter appeared in his inbox, flashing with bright red lights that indicated someone had sent it with extreme urgency and paid a huge price to make it interrupt his vision.

Subject: Joe! Help!

Joe, I hate having to write you this letter, but I find that I'm in desperate need of help. I've been sent to respawn nearly a half-dozen times. Our Camp was destroyed by monsters when we tried to upgrade to a Hamlet, and I've been bounced around Jotunheim every time I run into so much as a Penguin. I got to test the respawn mechanic for you. If there's no affiliated settlement within about a hundred miles, it just drops you randomly across the world. Zero out of five, do not recommend.

I got dropped in a Hamlet working toward becoming a Village, but guess what? Now I'm stuck here with a human leader that's <u>really</u> into Elves, we are talking crazy levels of zealotry. Turns out I wasn't wrong; I was being targeted by the Theocracy. Where they just played dumb, he directly has been calling me a traitor and is making me shovel snow for fifteen hours at a time as 'penance' for 'corresponding with the enemy', whatever that means.

I need to get out of here, and if you have any ideas, I'd love to hear them.

-Daniella

"Well, abyss." Joe closed his eyes and rubbed the back of his head, conflicted about what his next course of action should be. "What do we have to do to stop people from reading our mail? Do we need to boobytrap it? Someone *has* to have a skill that does that."

CHAPTER FOUR

"Why yes, of *course* I would love to venture out into the bone-white wilderness with you!" Jaxon clapped the tops of his hands multiple times, though his palms never moved apart. "I would be positively elated to sally forth, finding new and interesting bones to shift into place. Why, imagine if I'd been able to take that Cyclops on as a customer instead of having to help you bring him down? The prices I could've charged! The information I could've gained! The skill levels! Oh, Joe, the *skill* levels! Why did we have to slay that giant?"

"I'm glad you're coming with us, but Jaxon, he was trying to… destroy the entire town, wipe out the Dwarves, and scatter us to the wind?" Joe explained gently, knowing that his sound reasoning didn't particularly matter to the Chiropractor. "Did you at least learn some new things from that fight?"

Thinking it over, Jaxon eventually nodded sharply with a bright smile on his face. "In fact, I did! I was finally able to push higher into the Master ranks for my Chiropractic Services, and I'm looking forward to seeing what I'll be able to accomplish as I attain further Mastery, Grandmastery, then Sagehood. I found that, when I attempted to imbue my attacks with a concept, beyond simply twisting bones, I was able to attain a new record of motion for myself."

Joe went very still when he heard that information, then he leaned forward slightly, his eyes intently locked on his friend's face. "You can imbue your attack with a concept?"

"It was fairly straightforward, youngster! All I needed to do was have my mana extend around the point of contact, twisting away not only the bone as intended, but the blood, flesh, nerves, fat tissue, epidermis—"

The Ritualist cut him off, knowing that Jaxon would continue onward until he'd fully explained everything that had been on his mind at that point. "I see. So you went a step beyond what you're typically aiming for, to deal additional damage."

"What? No, not at all! The intent of Chiropractic Services is *never* to damage your patient! I was trying to *Adjust* his perspective." Jaxon shook his head sadly as he saw that Joe wasn't understanding his meaning. "He meant to do us harm, so I wanted to adjust his mindset, similar to when I adjusted a rafter of turkeys to follow my commands via the principles of stockholm syndrome. If you recall, during the battle, I didn't attack him, I tried to force him to turn the other cheek. I thought that, perhaps, if he took his eyes off his intended goal, the destruction of the Town Hall, he could see that there was a better option. Alas, it was not to be, and in no time flat, you were swimming in his aqueous humor."

Gagging slightly at the reminder, Joe decided it was time to end the conversation and move on. "I want to hear more about those turkeys—pretty sure that's a crime against animals—but for now… do you have any other recommendations for who we should bring with us? I've met a few nice people here. There's a Formations expert who thinks he's a wizard, Socar, but his cat is actually the magic user. Also, I feel like having the eyes and range of Heartpiercer Mcshootypants would be a good option for us."

"Ah, yes, your classic go-to of putting together a ragtag

band of misfits." Jaxon sighed in contentment as he tried to think if there was anyone he would want to bring along. "You know, Major Cleave is always welcome to ride along with me. Anywhere she wants. Anywhere at all. She's been wanting to learn about my… *flexibility*."

Joe was shaking his head by the time the Dwarf's name was mentioned. "I remember that conversation on wanting to learn your movement techniques, but unfortunately for us, she's been assigned command of the Legion at the wall. That makes her the person responsible if a monster manages to break through into the Town itself. There's no way we're going to be able to get her away from here, and trying is just going to get her annoyed with us."

A moment later, he realized that he'd just been off-handedly insulted by the Chiropractor and squinted at him as he tried to determine if it was intentional or not. "Also, I don't get together a group of misfits. I make a party of the people I think are best for the task at hand."

"And they all just so happen to be bizarre outcasts." Jaxon nodded and winked 'knowingly' at his friend, much to Joe's annoyance.

In an attempt to defend himself, the Ritualist tried to explain his reasoning one last time. "That's not an intentional choice on my part, it just happens to be that the people who're best at what they do tend to have something that sets them apart from the average warrior or archer or whatever. Again, I want the best, not the most team-friendly. You do realize you'd be included in that list, don't you?"

"Oh, if only! Sadly no, I'm the most boring, run of the mill Chiropractor you've met in your entire life. I must say, my boy, I'm absolutely *tickled* by this amusing misunderstanding. *Me*, a misfit, that would be a most marvelous compliment indeed! Imagine it: me! A free spirit, a non-conformist, dancing to the beat of my own drum!" Jaxon reared back in laughter so hard his head nearly touched the ground, with his hands remaining on his hips. "Ahh. All jokes aside, we should probably get going.

Based on what you told me about that letter, if things had gone well for her, I'm sure she would've sent another message by now."

"By now? What do you…?" Joe looked at the timestamp on the letter he'd shared with Jaxon, realizing that it had come in nearly two hundred hours previously. The fact that Daniella hadn't sent any follow-up messages meant that she either couldn't or was being so carefully watched that she didn't dare risk it. He could only hope that she'd figured out the Elves were reading her mail, or perhaps the loudmouth who was having her do menial manual labor had directly told her that as proof of her crimes. "Yeah, we should probably get going."

Over the next few hours, the duo worked to gather additional people for their cause. Unfortunately, they couldn't convince a single Dwarf to part with the security of the thick stone walls, and Socar had to beg off for at least a few days while he worked on his current project. Heartpiercer Mcshootypants was on board immediately, and so the trio began sprinting along the tops of the walls, where temporary bridges were strung across the openings to allow for rapid movement whenever there were no Beast Waves attacking the city.

Something about the team composition made Joe deeply uncomfortable, and he tried to feel out what his intuition was telling him. Eventually, he decided it was just the fact that he'd almost always been able to go out with an extremely well-balanced team. A tank, both a long and close-range damage dealer, some form of combination buffing or debuffing, and finally himself as healing, utility, and magic damage. Going out with a party of three felt… strange.

Only a few minutes passed before they were fully outside the defensive walls and running along to the east of the Town. They'd decided to scout out approximately one day's travel in each of the cardinal directions before making a final decision on which way they would explore further. By choosing to go east, they'd also have the benefit of running into the Dwarven mining camp and quarry.

This would allow them to assess the travel conditions, as well as what gear they were lacking for long-term travel on Jotunheim, without leaving them stranded in the dark, unknown world without a plan.

They sprinted along, none of them wasting their breath on conversation. As they continued to run, minutes ticking by, Joe started to feel a slight mental strain. Not because of the act of running, nor was he overly anxious about monster attacks. No, it was the simple fact that, outside of the city, the tundra was absolutely *featureless*. Every hint of elevation had been stomped flat by enormous monsters, and the wind howling over his body was an annoying, constant irritant.

Every once in a while, he'd been looking over his shoulder at the walls of the city in the distance, which were lit up both by the false sky he had created, as well as the slowly brightening sunlight stretching across the entirety of Jotunheim. Joe forced himself to stop checking, for the simple reason that it made all of their progress feel pointless. The city was the only terrain feature, and no matter how fast they ran, it seemed to grow smaller only very slowly. Just out of a desire to see something different, Joe took a look at his status.

Name: Joe 'Tatum's Chosen Legend' Class: Reductionist
Profession I: Arcanologist (Max)
Profession II: Ritualistic Alchemist (4/20)
Profession III: Grandmaster's Apprentice (14/25)
Profession IV: None
Character Level: 27 Exp: 404,907 Exp to next level: 1,093
Rituarchitect Level: 11 Exp: 65,950 Exp to next level: 50
Reductionist Level: 6 Exp: 26,891 Exp to next level: 1,109
Hit Points: 2,496/2,496
Mana: 6,078/8,327
Mana regen: 72.68/sec
Stamina:1,925/1,925
Stamina regen: 6.68/sec

Characteristic: Raw score

Strength (bound): 182
Dexterity: 183 → 184
Constitution (bound): 177 → 179
Intelligence (bound): 190
Wisdom: 178 → 180
Dark Charisma: 141 →142
Perception: 178 → 180
Luck: 115 → 116
Karmic Luck: 23

Over the last several hundred hours of work, his Constitution was ever so slowly increasing, thanks to his Artisan Body skill. He was especially thankful for that skill, since increasing any of his Characteristics was becoming treacherously slow. The other Characteristics that had increased were a result of stopping misplaced rituals just in time to keep from blowing himself and his helpers up. Twice. He could only blame the cold for his inattention.

Joe grinned as he looked at how close he was to leveling up in all of his classes. The hard work and constant cycle of killing monsters, reducing them to aspects, then using those aspects to build walls and towers to kill more monsters had been *phenomenal* for his overall experience gain. "I haven't grown this fast in... well, not for a long time."

A bubble filled with ore or stone zipped over their heads, and the Ritualist slightly adjusted his heading after flinching and tracing the bubble back to its source. Heartpiercer watched the frozen orb travel above them with slight annoyance in her eyes. "Is there a reason we aren't riding comfortably along in a bubble like that right now? This enormous, flat landscape should be perfect for that kind of travel, shouldn't it?"

"It should, yes. But that's a trap." Joe explained brightly. "Remember, the point of today isn't about making the best distance we possibly can. Today's all about figuring out what else we need while we're exploring this massive world."

Jaxon made a sound indicating he was intrigued and joined the conversation. "Oh! I know! How about, instead of a bubble that moves us around, Joe sets up a ton of rituals that slowly raise the ambient temperature of this planet to a livable, comfortable position? What would you call that? The Ritual of Aerosol Cans? Grandmaster Ritual of Global Warming? I could use me some warming right now."

"I have no interest in messing with the climate of a super-massive planet." Even thinking about it caused an ethereal shiver to crawl along his skin. "I bet if I started setting that up, I'd bring down the World Boss on us even faster than if I'd built an Ecumenopolis that completely covered every surface of the planet in buildings."

"Ha! An Ecumenopolis?" Heartpiercer shook her head at that thought. "With a planet this size, you'd be more likely to build a Dyson sphere than anything else."

"Well, that would just be pointless." Jaxon's brow furrowed as he lifted his right hand to his chin in thought, all while sprinting at top speed. "The point of a Dyson sphere is to gather sunlight, and there's none to be had here."

The Archer shook her head in slight annoyance, "No, I mean, it would be easier to make a sphere around the planet made out of metal than to build a... you know what, forget I asked anything about bubble travel. Let's go back to being quiet while running."

"No need, no need!" Joe pointed into the distance, where another landmark was finally appearing. "There's the mining camp. When we get there, let's review what we think we're going to need."

"I vote for *music*." Heartpiercer muttered loud enough to be heard by the others, while being able to maintain the fiction that she was trying to be quiet. "Something tells me we're going to need to drown out some... prattling."

"I like music, too! I'll get us started." Jaxon cleared his

throat and started warbling above the protests of the other members of his small party. "I'm a Barbie girl, on a giant world–"

"No!" came the instantaneous shutdown.

"Hey! I'm making it relevant to our situation! I said 'giant world', not 'Barbie world'! I'm hip, I'm fly. I'm with the times, ye ken?"

CHAPTER FIVE

As they strolled into the mining camp, Joe looked at his team with a smile that chattered even as he maintained it. "I think that was approximately fifty miles; how do we all feel?"

"Cold," Heartpiercer grumbled at the two of them as she rubbed her arms. "The chilled debuff is way worse outside of the walls. Jotunheim is insane; how are we supposed to get anything done? Building and expanding in the ice and snow would've been incredibly difficult and tedious without your help."

Jaxon spoke up, "I have a few suggestions! Joe, firstly, I think you should upgrade your wardrobe. Running around in leather shoes, a blanket, and a metal codpiece probably aren't the best options in a world that slowly freezes you to death. Think of touching your tongue to a metal post, then extrapolate that else-where. Secondly, each of us should be holding an emergency ritual bubble that will allow us to create a temporary camp wherever we are. Lastly, let's be done with all of this running and travel through the air in bubbles, please."

"What kind of supplies do we need, rations, water, thank

you for the mention of gear." Joe firmly ignored the whining as he tried to extract the information he was after.

"No. Hear me out!" Jaxon slithered over to stand next to Joe, wrapping one arm around his shoulders and pulling him close. "Here's what we do. Fly all day in a bubble, keeping an eye out for anything interesting. When we're at the maximum range that they can connect to each other, you drop one of your little shrines that lets us fast travel between them. Then, that way, we can still go back to the city for any supplies or housing as needed. Less to carry; home by dinner."

Joe went silent for a few minutes as he contemplated what his ever-more-serpentine friend was telling him, going pale as he realized how much time he'd been wasting by not doing exactly what Jaxon had just said. "Wow, yeah, that makes… really good sense. I guess sometimes I forget that we don't have to walk everywhere. We're not playing with the same physics we used to be subject to, and every once in a while, I completely forget that fact."

Heartpiercer let out a long sigh of annoyance, "Did we seriously just run fifty miles so that you could have an epiphany? It's *cold* out here, Joe, and now my legs are tired. Add that to the fact that my fingers are freezing, meaning I'll likely have less damage output and accuracy if we get attacked by monsters."

"You can't rush art." Joe tossed his head back, as though he had a long mane of flowing hair. "The muse arrives whenever she decides, not when I need a breakthrough."

Jaxon nudged Heartpiercer. "Hear that? I'm his *muse*."

The grumbles coming out of the Archer on the team took on a much more dark, calculative air. The Ritualist did his best to ignore them, even when they became very specific, such as how she'd be able to use his hamstring as an impressive new bow string. The bald man looked around, taking in the bustling mining camp and the odd looks being thrown their way. "While we're here, might as well look around, right?"

"That's a great idea, Joe! Why don't we interrupt everyone's schedule so we can, with our inexperienced eyes, judge how *they* are doing." Jaxon didn't wait for any further words, walking directly toward the entrance to the mine. Just before he entered, a Dwarf with the frizziest beard and most barrel-shaped chest stepped out, legs shaking as he moved forward one foot at a time.

"Get outta the way, ya half-pint giant!" the Dwarf bellowed at the Chiropractor, who slid to the side with a simple sway of his hips, his feet not moving whatsoever. "Stay away from my shaft!"

"I beg your *pardon!*" Jaxon gasped sharply, recoiling in horror.

"There's no room in my mineshaft for someone of your height! You're going to block the flow of traffic and get in the way of every swinging pick in the room." Throughout his tirade, the Dwarf had never stopped walking forward ever-so-slowly.

Joe looked at where the Dwarf was going, his eyes picking out the shimmer of a ritual circle hanging in the air. "Hey, *this* is where that got off to? That's not good... this ritual is designed for personal transport. Hang on there, something tells me you're not heading back to Novusheim."

"Do I... look like... I need walls around me all the time?" the straining Dwarf grunted out between each laborious step.

"No, you look constipated," Heartpiercer snarked back at the Dwarf, who finally came to a standstill.

A deep grunt of frustration escaped from deep in his chest, and Joe could see him straining to lift one of his legs back into the air. "Do you need a hand there?"

The Dwarf stopped straining, sucking in a few deep breaths before turning his head to glare at the trio. "Do ye have any idea how difficult it is to walk when over-encumbered with three tons of Uncommon metals? Every time I stop, it takes twice the amount of effort to get going again!"

"Perhaps you should wear lighter gear?" Jaxon offered gently, reaching over and knocking on the thick metal plate armor that the Dwarf was decked out in. "I can't imagine being this slow is useful in combat."

The Dwarf considered them for a few minutes, apparently coming to the realization that he was talking with absolute imbeciles. "Let me guess, you have big, fancy storage devices that reduce the weight of the things inside of them? Unbelievable."

"I don't have a storage device," Heartpiercer called out, mirrored a moment later by Jaxon simply nodding to agree with her. Joe decided against informing those that didn't already know that he was wearing a Legendary spatial storage codpiece, simply focusing on the ritual. Somehow, he just figured the information on his gear wouldn't be met with a cheerful smile at the moment, especially when the Archer continued thinking aloud. "You know what, I should actually go get one. If I remember correctly, they aren't nearly as hard to get."

"Pah." The Dwarf shook his head in disgust at her attitude. "Maybe they weren't so hard to get back when the city that focused on building them was still standing. Now you're going to have to murder someone to get one of these, even the basic Uncommon porters' pack I'm wearing. Abyss, all this one does is let you put everything inside without adjusting its weight or how quickly it degrades."

He paused for a moment, realizing exactly what he'd just said. Now a teeny bit nervous, the Dwarf licked his lips as his eyes darted between Jaxon and Heartpiercer. "Of course, my bag is registered with the council and easily traceable. Actually murdering someone for their device is *highly* not recommended."

"There we go! I knew I had a couple of spares on hand." Joe dusted his hands off in a clapping motion, then reached forward and tapped the shimmer in the air with a single finger. The ritual popped like a soap bubble, particles of mana floating out before dissipating. Joe turned as the Dwarf let out a strangled scream of fury, confusion in his eyes. "What? What's the matter?"

"Do you have any idea how difficult it is going to be to walk my heavy rear all the way to the Town to drop these off? Get over here so I can sit on you!" The Dwarf took a mightily struggling step forward, then continued building his momentum, ever so gradually reaching a slow walking pace.

Joe brushed off the Dwarf's concerns, turning and setting down the ritual tile he had in his codpiece. "I knew I had a couple of practice ones from when we were getting ready to set up the escape plan from Town, and I bet, if I adjust the power output to be single bubbles at a time instead of a stream of them... here we go. There! Now, this should better handle the transport of the metals or stone you're all putting in here."

Dropping his hand onto the tile, the Ritualist pumped some mana into the diagram and allowed the rituals to swirl out and around him. By the time the Dwarf was halfway to him, Joe was already standing up and studying the dense, cycling power. The rings of the ritual were now substantial enough to be mistaken for wood or metal at first glance. "Wait, wait. Let me adjust the heading a little bit... there we go. That should match up with where the last one was depositing the goods you were sending. Go ahead and drop your stuff anywhere within the outer ring, and it'll all be collected."

"You..." the Dwarf didn't slow down, but the expression on his face was nearly comical as his attitude adjusted itself at top speed. "You made it *better*? Ah... then you must be Councilman Joe. sorry, I didn't recognize your title. I was... distracted."

"No problem! I hope this does better for you, I take my responsibility to better the lives of our citizens extremely seriously. Also, now you won't have to worry about getting caught up in the bubble; it'll only take cargo."

"That's more helpful than you might know." The Dwarf was picking up speed again, and a rueful smile showed above his beard. "As you can imagine, it can be hard to slow down without falling and having to dig myself out of the resulting crater. I always get chewed out when I need to run back for the next load."

As he got closer to the outer ring, the Dwarf lifted his hands out in front of him, as if in supplication. As soon as his palms crossed the energetic line, stone began spewing out of empty air like a landslide. With every second that passed, the Dwarf was clearly under less strain, though he was still working to push his feet into the ground to stop himself from stumbling forward. When the last bit of unrefined ore had dropped to the ground, a massive bubble encapsulated the space, lifting into the air and *slurping* all of the loose material into the air before rolling through the air off into the distance.

"Looks a little slower than usual," the Dwarf commented offhandedly.

Joe had to agree with that, but he was able to offer up an easy explanation. "It is, but now the likelihood of the ritual failing and dropping all of that across the landscape for you to go and play hide and seek with is a lot lower. It'll also be able to fly higher, keeping it out of range of jumping monsters and... I was going to say archers, but I'm pretty sure Heartpiercer here could still get it at its maximum altitude."

"You bet your frigid butt I could." She'd clearly still not forgiven Joe for making them run all the way out here.

The Ritualist rolled his eyes and offered a hand to the Dwarf. "With introductions and pleasantries out of the way, would you mind pointing me to a space that'd be good for a small shrine?"

"Yea." The Dwarf waved a hand at Joe in a let's go motion. "Let's introduce religion to this world. It's always worked out for everyone in the past."

Joe let out a soft sigh at how poorly all of the interactions with this Dwarf had gone, and apparently would continue to go. "You weren't in Dawnesha's faction about the Deities, huh? Oh, abyss... I haven't seen her since we got to Jotunheim–"

"No, I was *not* on her side of the issue. Yes, she's fine, her guards have been keeping her away from danger and... ah, people of *interest*, I'm told. I'm sure she'll seek ya out as soon as a shrine appears in a nice, comfy, safe Town like Novusheim," the Dwarf grumped as he plodded along. Then a small smile tugged at the corners of his mouth. "But, if *we* have to be in this godforsaken frozen wasteland, we may as well put *them* to work. Then it'll only be a frozen wasteland."

Only Jaxon laughed along at the odd joke, Joe and Heart-piercer exchanging droll glances and rolling their eyes.

CHAPTER SIX

The creation of the shrine went smoothly, no issues arising as the book-shaped magical structure appeared on the flat, frozen landscape. As the ambient energies of the world settled into their usual chaotic format, Joe realized that the building was actually fairly well-hidden, even if it was out in the open.

Coloration-wise, it was a slate gray that blended well with the ice and snow. To his magical senses, unless he was extremely close to the shrine itself, he couldn't locate it over the static 'noise' of mana Jotunheim constantly produced. Obviously, it had no scent, so the only real way of finding it was to get close to the ground and look for anything that was above 'perfectly level'.

"Finally, it's time to get the reward for the quest I turned in a while ago." Joe placed his hands on the shrine and offered a cheerful greeting to Tatum.

Zone notification! The deities have come to the World of Giants! Joe 'Tatum's Chosen Legend' has created the first shrine to a Pantheon on Jotunheim! As a reward, for one full day, anyone aligned with this Pantheon will see a rapid boost in skill acquisition and growth. Caution! The denizens of this world may take great umbrage to this fact. While your reward is active, the time between Beast Waves is halved.

"All right, not exactly the notification I was here to get, Tatum." Joe tried not to gulp nervously as he read over that message once more. "Pretty sure people are going to be a little grumpy with me now that I'm sending monsters at them... wait a second! I can find a diamond in this pigsty; if we have enhanced skill growth, having a ton more enemies to practice our skills on can be considered a second reward!"

As the Ritualist drew his hand back and away from the altar, black lightning flashed from the ever-present clouds in the sky, impacting him from eight directions at the same time. Instead of injuring him, Joe was suffused with power. He let out an unbridled cry of euphoria as the overabundant energy lashed out into the environment around him.

Delayed Quest reward granted!

Skill upgraded: Resurrection (Beginner 0) → Mass Resurrection Aura (Apprentice V)!

Mass Resurrection Aura: Once per standard week (168 hours), you can channel the divine energies of Occultatum, bringing back to life any slain entities within n+5 meters that are within n+class level levels of you, within n+class level minutes of being killed. This spell will last n seconds upon casting. Upon activation, you will lose access to all mana for 60-n minutes; where n = skill level.

Please note, Occultatum is a Neutral Deity, so this spell will not distinguish between friend or foe.

Breathing heavily, Joe looked over his upgraded skill in absolute awe. "Celestials, you weren't kidding when you told me you'd give me something overpowered. Oh no, does this remove my ability to resurrect individuals?"

Even with his hand on the altar directly, Joe didn't get an answer to his question. He could only shrug and assume that was the case. Frankly, Joe was completely fine with that. He used this spell so irregularly that it had barely managed to move above Novice rank since he got it. Taking a deep breath and letting out a sigh of contentment, Joe hoped he wouldn't need to use this far more powerful version very often, if at all.

"That was neat!" Jaxon enthused, rushing over to touch the stone book. "What just happened? Can I be hit by lightning as well? It seemed fun when you did it!"

"I think my skill Rarity got upgraded? Or it got combined with other spells that Tatum was going to give me...? Really, I'm not a hundred percent certain. Normally, with such a massive jump in my levels, I would've gotten the option for some other spells. So... the latter is seeming more probable." Joe quickly explained the spell that he had just gained, getting *oohs* and *ahhs* from his friend, as well as smiles tinged with envy from Heartpiercer.

As soon as his explanation was finished, the shivering Archer waved at the shrine. "Can we *please* get back to Novusheim now? We can even pretend it's for some reason other than me freezing my phalanges off. Yeah, I got it! We're only going back so you can make another one of these and test out the fast travel. Totally."

Seeing no reason to argue, the group quickly set up a Ritual of Bubble Travel and flew into the air over the empty land-scape. Even moving twice as quickly as they could run, it was still quite a while until the dot on the horizon expanded into Novusheim. They came down into the city, slightly off-course from where Joe had expected them to land. Instead of nestling down onto the ground and gently popping, the bubble slammed into the side of the Pyramid of Panacea and sent the trio tumbling through the air into the snowdrifts below.

Heartpiercer shot to her feet out of the snow, charging off into the distance while rubbing her arms and cursing loudly. Joe pulled himself out of the drift with ease, but he found that Jaxon had landed head-first and was stuck with his feet flailing wildly above the drift. Grabbing his friend, Joe yanked the Chiropractor onto solid ground.

Jaxon gasped for air, shaking off the melting ice crystals. "Thank goodness! You know, I feel like I'm becoming cold-blooded, because that made me lethargic as all get out. I'm off to take a nap; hope your shrine travel works well for you!"

Moments later, Joe was alone and walking toward the Town Hall. Completely used to solitude, the Ritualist took the group splitting up in stride. It took less than ten minutes to get confirmation as to where he could place a shrine, with the expectation that it would be upgraded into a Grand Temple at some point. From there, it was only a matter of spending the mana and resources to have a secondary shrine appear on the edge of what would eventually be the town square.

Reaching under the stone book, Joe activated the sigils that allowed him to control who could use the travel function. Lastly, he placed his hand on top of the altar and changed his location —returning to the mine in an instant.

Joe's eyes roved the area, landing on a shocked Dwarf who had come out of the mine moments previously. Waving the miner over, the Ritualist explained how to use the fast travel functionality and let him go off to spread the good news.

An instant later, the bald man was back in Town with a wide smile on his face. The rapid-fire transportation had drained his mana by a small amount, but it was already working to refill at a rapid pace. "I love it when things work out how I hope they would."

With the issue of travel across the enormous planet solved, if not yet put into place, Joe decided to knock a few additional tasks off his list. Working with the volunteers sent by the council, he created the last few buildings that had been requested, then he retreated into his workshop to make a plan to find and rescue Daniella.

He had thought about this issue for quite a while, eventually deciding that she'd done far more good for him than harm. Plus, the fact of the matter was, on the previous world, she was doing what she had to do to win the war between the unified and shattered races. Frankly, if he blamed her for making sure her side came out on top, he'd need to accept responsibility for all of the unfortunate things that had happened to anyone who aligned with the Wolfman on Midgard. "Can't have it both ways… either everyone is doing what they need to do, or the other side are evil, bad, no-good antagonists. I lost that battle, but Humanity needs each other for the war."

Now having a logical, fully justified reason to go rescue his ex-teammate, the Ritualist began working on a method to actually find her.

He considered sending out letters, asking for help from people on different planets, creating new technologies or spells that could find her, even going so far as to toy with the idea of making a ritual that could create drones to map out the planet from the air. There were a multitude of problems with all of these ideas, ranging from having to completely invent brand-new magical technology to having to deal with intense resistance from the Dwarves if he wanted them to participate in finding the lost Architect.

But, above all else, there was one resounding fact: any tracking spell needed a focus. If he wanted to be able to magically find her on this enormous planet, he needed something of hers, at the bare minimum. Seeing as there was no way to go back to the previous world and find a lost shoe, it seemed to be an impossibility. He let out a deep sigh as he collapsed in his chair, feeling as though the last several hours of contemplation were a complete waste.

"Haaa." Joe pulled AutoMate's cup off the carabiner that kept the mug attached to his belt, taking a sip of the daily special that his coffee elemental whipped up for him on the spot. "Thanks, Mate. It's always nice to have you by my side; you make my life better by leaps and bounds."

The elemental appeared in the cup, wiggling back and forth happily at the praise being heaped on it. The Ritualist watched the tiny coffee bean eyes staring at him happily, finding himself relaxing as he did so. "I don't suppose you'd have any ideas on how to find Daniella, would you? I know you can't speak, sorry. It's just I'm so completely lost on–"

AutoMate took on a red blush, and Joe stopped speaking,

wondering if he'd managed to make his elemental either embarrassed or furious. Then the coloration shifted even more, moving from red-tinted coffee, to coffee-tinted blood. Unsure of what was happening, the Ritualist amusedly held up a small glass vial as Mate waved at him to move.

The fluid poured out of the cup into the vial, and as soon as Joe corked it, a notification appeared.

Item gained: Vial of human blood (Daniella)

Staring at the item, Joe wasn't sure how to react at first. Finally, he tore his eyes away from the sight of the blood, looking over at the coffee cup where Mate was peeking out to make sure Joe was happy with the offering. "That's right! You're able to capture and contain any liquids that get poured into your cup. When did you get this…? No, never mind, I remember her getting slashed next to you. What else is in there? Wait, no, again, I don't need to know. Just, thank you."

Burble! the elemental cheerfully bubbled at him.

The Ritualist turned his eyes back to the vial of blood in his hand, his stare sharpening as he thought about how best to use it. "First things first, make a long-term tracking ritual with this. Then, we're going to start chasing her down. Hopefully, she doesn't die too much and mess with our trajectory."

He let out a huff of air, shaking his head in amazement. "Mate, I can't tell you how great this is. Sorry if I haven't been listening to you well enough recently. Any time I'm missing the point, feel free to smack me on the hand."

B-burble! Mate's head shook back and forth furiously.

"No, really! Please do. If I'm missing something, and I need to know, do it." Joe smiled gently at his summon. "After all, as they always say, 'in capulus, veritas'. I'd be more than happy to find my truth in the bottom of my coffee mug, partner."

The elemental didn't make any further noises, but he certainly seemed to enjoy the praise.

CHAPTER SEVEN

"Well, this is rather unfortunate," Joe grumbled as he looked over all of his various options for seeking out Daniella. After asking around, he hadn't found anyone willing to put their own expertise on the line to chase the Architect down. The Ritualist had truly thought he could convince some bored scout or tracker to work with him on this project, but as soon as he mentioned that he was going out into the frozen wastes, any flickers of interest in their eyes cooled immediately.

The fact of the matter was: he had no ability to create rituals that would *gently* show him where to find her; like a nice ritual-based compass that always pointed at her without a terrible side effect. To Joe's great chagrin, he *did* have one ritual that would last long enough to be useful. The only issue with the magical diagram was that it was found within the book of slightly twisted rituals he'd gained long ago.

"Let's see… Ritual of the Ghostly Army, Ritual of the Lonely Tree, Ritual of Argus…" Joe leafed through the dark grimoire, carefully only reading the names of the rituals and not studying the components necessary to use most of them. "Here it is. Ritual of the Insomniac Stalker. This ritual requires two targets; the first creature will target the second."

Confirming that he'd need to target himself first, Joe grimaced and took a deep breath before continuing. "The first creature will no longer receive the benefits of sleeping, beyond the absolute minimum to maintain health. Great, I didn't like to sleep anyway. Instead, that creature now has an intense animosity for the second target. Less great, kind of makes it hard to want to save someone when you have a deep hatred for them."

His eyes moved on to the next descriptor of the ritual, which was the only reason he was considering using this in the first place. "They will know the direction and distance to the target at all times. There it is. That's exactly what I needed. Then… when the first target encounters the second target, they must attack the target unless able to resist the compulsion. Maybe I can build a failsafe into this to turn this bad boy off? They must resist every minute the target is in sight; which will grow harder over time. Yep, a failsafe is going to be pretty important. This effect lasts until one of the two targets die. Requirements: blood-stained pillow-"

Glancing over at the vial of blood, Joe realized he had more than enough of the sanguine liquid available for that portion of the ritual. From there, he took his time to convert all of the other components over to aspects, finding himself somewhat amused that this was a Journeyman-rank ritual. "Makes sense to me, because I'm a man that'll have to go on a journey. Ahh… *yeah*. I'll need to activate this only when I'm sure I'm ready to go. Otherwise, with this ritual, I'll put the 'fun' in 'non*funct*ion-ing'. Or maybe 'dys*funct*ional'."

Now that he had an initial plan, there were many things Joe was going to need to do before actually setting out into the world and seeking out Daniella. The first among them was going to be taking advantage of the increased skill gain and growth making a shrine had afforded him.

It was time to seek Havoc.

Joe exited his workshop after spending… frankly, he wasn't certain how long he'd been holed up. He couldn't even give himself the ol' sniff test, as his Neutrality Aura only came off in the most dire of circumstances.

From the screams of monsters, bellowing of Dwarves, and rampant wagering going on, there was a Beast Wave currently testing their defenses. For the time being, the Ritualist ignored that fact and went over to the Town Hall to get a bead on the Grandmaster's location.

Surprisingly enough, the Dwarf was thought to be somewhere on the walls, watching the onslaught. Before Joe could escape and go search for his mentor, he was handed a thick stack of papers that detailed the overall state of the Town. Politely glancing at the sheaf of paper, Joe nearly choked as he saw what the first line detailed. "*Population* requirement? *That's* what's estimated to be the largest holdup on moving from a Town to a City? Abyss, we need one hundred *thousand* people? That's absolutely ridiculous. It's not like we can reproduce!"

The Ritualist paused for a moment as he considered his outburst, then shook his head. "Nope, sure can't. Dwarves are locked as a Shattered race, and I'm about ninety percent certain that humans traveling between planes can't have kids."

Now his plans to go out into the world and seek population centers had taken on a new flavor. Where originally he'd planned to do so only to bring Daniella back, now Joe was extremely pleased that his friends had brought up the idea of setting up a fast travel shrine system. "There's gotta be people out there willing to convert their allegiance over to the Dwarves to get out of here."

After storing the remainder of the papers in his codpiece, Joe hurried out to the walls and began looking for Havoc. It wasn't terribly difficult to find the Dwarf, as most people left a respectful distance around the powerful, unstable Grandmaster. He was also one of the very few Dwarves not actively attacking the onrushing beasts, simply content to observe and take notes on what was happening.

Havoc's head snapped to the side, his eyes locking with Joe's. The human didn't even get a word in before the Dwarf laid into him. "*You!* Just the human and I needed to see. Take a look at this mess. A single glance, and I can see fourteen areas I could waltz through to avoid every attack your towers can throw out. I want this rectified!"

"Oh. Yeah, I'll get on that." The Grandmaster was kind enough to hand over a hand-drawn map of the area, detailing the weak points he'd noted. Joe gave it a cursory glance before storing that away as well. "I was wondering if you can make time to teach me a fire spell or three? With the bonuses we're currently getting offered, I think now is the time to get them in my magical repertoire."

"You *sure* about that?" Havoc questioned him coyly. "I know you're seeking other answers that I know I have as well. A little bit of fire might be useful *here*, but who knows what it'll look like in a year or three?"

"Better something than nothing." Joe shrugged without giving it much thought. "Who knows where we'll be in a few years? We might not even be able to see each other, or even be on the same planet. Fire is primordial. It always has been useful; it always *will* be useful."

"Fair enough. Do you want a basic fire manipulation spell, or do you have something more… *specific* in mind?" At Havoc's question, Joe went silent. It was likely that this was some kind of a test, but he didn't particularly care at the moment.

Making his choice, Joe firmly replied, "I want some kind of a fireball spell or a variation thereof. Something that you think would be great to add to these towers and will help me kill the greatest number of monsters possible."

"But you still want to be able to harvest them?" Havoc's nonchalant question made the Ritualist realize that he had forgotten that aspect of things. "That rules out clouds of burning phosphorus, napalm hot enough to destroy the entire body… maybe a combination spell? How do you feel about dropping small meteors on your enemies?"

"Yes, please!" Joe replied with no hesitation.

"Well, too bad! That's a high-level spell; you can't handle it right now." The Dwarf scoffed as Joe's pleased expression faded away. "Did you actually think you could go straight to a meteor spell when you have no proper foundation in fire *nor* earth magics? Don't put the forge before the anvil. Hammer out your spells in the right order, or you'll end up with sparks in your beard. Ehh. Theoretically speaking."

The Dwarf waved at Joe's general facial shininess, then reached into a pocket and pulled out a thin strip of paper. "Here's how this is going to work, kid. I'm going to teach you a really *dark* spell, and you're not going to tell anyone where you got it. Even if you do, I'll deny it."

"Uh–" before Joe could say anything further, Havoc looked him in the eyes, and Joe's body froze in instant paralysis. Then the Dwarf held up a book, moving it in front of the Ritualist's frozen stare, line by line, until he was certain that the human had read every word. Then the book burst into flames for a long moment, releasing a high-pitched scream as it reduced itself to ash.

"Perfect." Havoc grinned triumphantly as he shook the last bit of powder off his hands. "That's how you know it's working."

Profession 3: Grandmaster's Apprentice. 15/25.

Spell learned: Infernal Conflagration (Novice VII). This is a super intense infernal fire spell that inflicts damage upon multiple enemies while preserving their corpses for processing. When unleashed, this spell creates a devastating blaze of flames with unique properties. Despite its overwhelming power, the spell's arcane nature ensures that it consumes only flesh and vital essence of enemies, leaving behind intact corpses suitable for processing or rituals.

This spell deals $30n$ damage, where n = skill level. Cooldown: $10-.5n$ seconds. Range: $.5+n$ meters.

Caution! Do not consume any part of a corpse that has been damaged by infernal energy.

"I've been waiting to find someone I could pass that on to.

It's a Unique-rank spell, so it'll start with fairly high damage compared to the other basic garbage you've been showing off. It's also *real* hard to level, so take advantage of the target-rich environment you have going on here. Oh… don't let any people aligned with Light deities see you using that, or they'll probably attack without warning." Havoc then attached the thin strip of paper he had pulled out to Joe's wrist, where it sank into his skin like a temporary tattoo.

"Actually, you shouldn't think of this as an evil spell. Instead, try and think of it as… steam damage. Yeah. You ever see someone get steam burns? How their flesh boils under their skin without seeming to do too much damage to the surface? It's kind of like that." The Dwarf lifted Joe and tossed him over the wall. "As payment, you're going to have to learn how to use this spell properly. Hope you figure it out."

All spells beyond 'Infernal Conflagration' have been locked for 3 hours!

As Joe approached the ground, dozens of rampaging, enormous monsters looked up to see him falling toward them like chum being tossed to sharks.

CHAPTER EIGHT

"Havoc, you madman! Novice spells don't *work* on Jotunheim!" Joe shouted just before he hit the ground. A small shockwave gave him some room as his 'Superhero Landing' title came into effect, the remaining damage being mitigated by his Omnivault skill. Realizing that not all of his skills were locked, only his spells, the Ritualist immediately launched himself toward the wall to get back up top.

As he pushed off, Havoc appeared above him, grabbing Joe's entire face with one hand and bodily hurling him at the ground. A passing Hoardling was kind enough to block him from impacting the packed ice of the ground, and Joe crunched through its icy outer shell with his breath getting knocked out of him. "No *cheating*!"

The Dwarf was gone, and the only thing keeping Joe alive for the moment was the fact that the enemy he'd landed on was as stunned as he was. Shoving himself forward, Joe used the monster as a kick pad, throwing himself out and away. "Someday, I'm going to figure out how to hurt you, Havoc! *Infernal Conflagration*!"

His hands were outstretched in the somatic component

required for the use of the spell. Mana gathered in front of him, but he was unable to force the spell itself to manifest. The sphere that was forming had a small hole torn in it, and power rushed out in a raspberry of sound. Joe would've found it funny, even going so far as to try to replicate it, if he didn't have to roll backward to avoid the ice-coated fangs of the Hoardling trying to chow down on his proffered arms.

Joe's heart raced as he immediately got to his feet and began sprinting down the twisting killing corridors of the labyrinth. Behind him, the closest monster howled in fury at its free meal getting away. A strange feeling came over the human at that moment as he tried to catch the line of Penguins in front of him: it was a bizarre knowledge that, as soon as he got in front of one of the other contestants in this marathon, he would immediately need to evade the attack that was sure to come at his heels. "Omnivault!"

Gaining some distance from the Hoardling allowed Joe to turn part of his attention on to his new spell. His lungs burned from the cold, sweat beaded on his brow, only to be frozen or whisked away by his passive auras, and he pushed his body to its absolute limits in sprinting and leaping over monsters when they came too close. He couldn't afford to slow down, though if he managed to make it to the Town without properly using the spell at least once, his mentor would simply chuck him back into the thick of it.

As he moved, focusing his mind on the spell, Joe tried everything he could to bridge the gap between his current knowledge and the intricate web of energy required for casting Infernal Conflagration. "Follow that mana channel; it should be bridging across this area… *Infernal Conflagration!*"

His tiny amount of study wasn't enough, and the spell backfired in his hands, the damage getting caught by his Exquisite Shell.

Exquisite Shell: 11,487/11,907 (210x2 damage. Infernal damage is twice as effective against magical shields!)

"Because of *course* it is, why *wouldn't* it be?" Joe grumpily spat as he dodged a clacking Penguin beak. Again, he tried to grasp the intricate, delicate design that needed to be passed through his body before being manifested in reality. Each time his foot slammed into the ground and sent him careening forward, he took the moment of being airborne to concentrate on unraveling the mysteries of this new power, searching for what he was missing about it that was keeping it in the Novice ranks.

The creatures pursuing him—as well as those he was chasing—began closing in, their snarls and discordant screeches echoing wildly along the hard surfaces surrounding them. He took a moment to try and estimate how far he'd run, quickly realizing he was only half—the Ritualist dodged sharply as a strike of black lightning slammed into the monster in front of him and sent it spinning across the ice. "Abyss! Now I have to avoid my own defenses?"

Joe's eyes narrowed as he suddenly recognized where he was. This was the exact space where the Grandmaster had pointed out the holes in the attack patterns of the towers. The paper appeared in his hand, and he flipped to the right as structured mana slammed into the ground like an artillery shell where he'd been standing. "The good thing is that they aren't directly targeting me. The bad thing is they won't *not* hit me. I can't believe Havoc read me so well that he gave me instructions on how to get through here while practicing the spell he was going to stuff in my head."

It was a deeply uncomfortable feeling to know that he was so predictable, but he got over it quickly with everything else going on. His Intelligence allowed him to remember the ways he needed to move, so he barely had to think about it as he twisted and turned among the monsters and bombardment of magic. "Infernal Conflagration!"

Sparks flew out from his outstretched hands, not a complete spell, but not a backlash, either.

Skill increase: Infernal Conflagration (Novice IX).

"I skipped Novice eight? Yes! Hooray for setting up shrines before doing this!" With renewed resolve, Joe continued to channel his magic and attempt to force the spell's progression. Each time he had to throw himself into the air, he attempted to create an unholy flame, limited only by the cooldown of the spell. Thanks to reaching Novice nine, he was able to attempt a casting of the potent magic once every five and a half seconds.

With an abundance of mana and almost nothing to spend it on, he was able to put all of his intense focus into casting. A stray thought crossed his mind, and Joe shook his bald head with a shiver. "I'm so glad whatever Havoc did to me didn't cancel my active spells. I probably would've frozen to death already without the elemental resistance my Exquisite Shell gives me!"

As quickly as he was moving, even while dodging monsters and practicing a spell he couldn't use, Novusheim was quickly approaching. The Ritualist was intimately familiar with the interior of the labyrinth, having built a good chunk of it with his own rituals. Hours and hours had been spent carefully and meticulously placing the walls, so even though there was a fresh coat of blood and several layers of snow, Joe would be seeing the Town in under three minutes at his current speed.

He forced the desperation away, since casting while in an improper frame of mind was going to cause a misfire of the spell. As truly neutral as he could cast—logically, coldly—he devoted every ounce of his being to the spell, leaping into the air as high as he could to have a moment of safety to focus. His mana surged through his channels, and he felt a breakthrough as the spell *boiled* through the barrier from Novice nine to Beginner zero.

A triumphant cry escaped his lips as he completed a flip, his feet perfectly perpendicular to the ground as he aimed the ramping-up spell at the stampeding creatures following him through the maze. Dark energy crackled around his outstretched hands, black wisps of flame leaping out of his palms and gathering into a swirling orb of staticky black and white energy.

"*Infernal Conflagration!*" He unleashed the wicked incantation, and the now-empowered spell shot forth with a faint hint of malevolent glee washing back and causing Joe a bit of concern. As the power roiled through the air at his target, it screamed like a mortar shell before erupting into a maelstrom of searing flame.

With a current range of eleven meters, the infernal fire caught several of the monsters in its initial detonation. But, to Joe's great concern, it hung in the air for several seconds, causing any of the following creatures to light up as they passed through, forced forward by their compulsion to destroy the Town Hall. Any affected monster screamed, and Joe's stomach churned as an additional high-pitched whistle sounded. It took him a long moment to realize that the sound was steam escaping through small tears in their skin as their flesh cooked under their hide.

"I can see why this would cause issues if a paladin or the like saw me use it," he whispered as he landed on the ground once more. He pushed that thought out of his head, grimly focusing on continuing his sprint towards safety. With the immediate threat on his heels diminished, but certainly not vanquished, Joe wasted no time in Omnivaulting along as fast as he could.

On his third leap forward, a Leopard caught him in midair, both of their trajectories impacted as they flew into the wall. A characteristic snarling erupted from the Leopard as it tried to maul the bald human with tooth and claw, getting in a good half-dozen attacks before they slid to the ground. The human felt his Exquisite Shell shatter, and the cat's natural weapons opened deep wounds in his abdomen.

Already knowing better than to use Infernal Conflagration at close range, Joe reared back and *slapped* down at the beast, hitting its nose as directly and forcefully as possible.

Very few creatures were immune to pain, even if it was unlikely he'd done much damage. The cat flinched back for an instant, and that was all Joe needed to throw himself into the air once more. He took a deep breath, slightly sickened by the spell but knowing it was his only good option for combat at the moment. "Infernal Conflagration!"

Once more, there was an approximate charge time of one and a half seconds before the malicious energy had coalesced enough to form the spell. Then it rocketed down, hitting the Leaping Leopard dead-on and engulfing three passing Penguins at the same moment.

Exquisite Shell: 0/11,907

Damage taken: 2,390 (Heavily bleeding, internal organs damaged! -30 health per second!)

Damage dealt: 300 Infernal Damage (six enemies burning at 50 infernal damage per second! Caution! Infernal damage debuffs continue until mitigated!)

Skill increase: Infernal Conflagration (Beginner IV)

Joe landed on unsteady feet, right at the entrance to Novusheim. He took one stumbling step in, toward the safety of the Town, just as the last of his health ticked away. Just before being sent to respawn, he hissed out a few final words. "Abyssal... Havoc! Where's my Neutrality Aura? I haven't died to damage over time... in ages."

You have died! Calculating... Experience lost: 28,080.

You have lost a level! Current level: 26.

CHAPTER NINE

Joe spent the hours of forced relaxation and recuperation sending messages to his guild, his mother, and even penning one out to Daniella in case she managed to get access to her mail in the near future. During that time, he stumbled upon what he thought might've been either a strange bug in the game or a mechanic he didn't fully understand the purpose of.

As far as he could tell, not nearly as much time had passed on Midgard as had passed for him on Alfheim and *especially* Jotunheim. Figuring this out had been fairly simple; the letter to his mother had included a portion apologizing for not writing more often during his adventures, and the reply—which came nearly instantly, as far as he was concerned—showed great confusion from her. Apparently, he was sending her messages fairly consistently, and she hadn't been worried. Not until now, at least.

Follow-up messages to Aten confirmed the disparity. Time was moving fastest on Jotunheim, medium on Alfheim, and slowly on Midgard. To top it off, being in the respawn room messed with all of his calculations.

"Great. I'm never gonna get rid of this abyssal 'Despised by

Humanity' title." Joe could only groan softly at the mess this was making for him. "Uuuhhhggg. I'm already terrible with time; this is just going to make everything so much worse. People on different worlds are moving at a different time dilation? Does that mean that the strongest will get even stronger, faster? Is it meant to separate out groups of people?"

He thought about that question for a few minutes, deciding that Eternium wanting them spaced out was the most likely answer. "That means, by the time someone currently on Midgard levels up high enough to go to Alfheim, then gets here, I'll likely be a world or two away, even if I spend a *lot* of time getting stronger here. Is it meant to partition off groups? Or is there a world coming up that will be at a much slower time dilation and mess with everything again?"

Having no way to test his hypothesis at the moment, Joe could only give up and decide to live in the moment, just like everyone else.

With nothing else to do beyond study for the next several hours, he pulled out the Mana Manipulation manual given to him by Grandmaster Snow. Even though he couldn't practice the incredibly intense methods, getting a better understanding before attempting to dive in was crucial to his eventual success.

Much later, the portal crackled open, and Joe was able to step out of his respawn room and into the Town Hall of Novusheim once more. Joe wasted no time in querying the receptionist that always hassled him. "How long was I gone?"

"Not *nearly* long enough," the bearded Dwarf rumbled instantly. "But the last time you stepped foot in here was approximately one hundred and twenty hours ago."

"*Five days?*" Joe gasped sharply, only calming down as he realized that getting furious wasn't going to help him in the slightest. "Okay… yeah. I'm back now, I just need to hurry."

As usual, the clouds were swirling in the sky, causing any warmth that the glowing sun could offer to be converted into an icy chill. As he hurried along toward his workshop, Joe's fur and leather cloak billowed in the stiff breeze, his face set in grim determination as he rushed along toward his goal. Waving down a messenger, he sent out a request for Socar, Heartpiercer, and Jaxon to be sent to meet with him, tipping the bored human with a bar of luxury soap to ensure that the missive would be delivered quickly.

Leaving the door slightly open behind him, the Ritualist hurried over to his table and got to work putting together the Ritual of the Insomniac Stalker. As far as he was concerned, it was time to get out into the wilderness and find his lost friend. Seeing as the ritual was only a Journeyman-rarity diagram, he was able to get it almost fully complete by the time the first of his chosen teammates arrived.

Continuing on with his work, he explained to them what he'd found about the time difference between this world and the previous ones. To Joe's consternation, they took it in stride. With a sigh, he reminded himself that *they* weren't bearing time-locked titles taking up a useful spot. Sure, they might be Excommunicated, but that wasn't something time alone could heal. "The reason I called all of you here is that I'm planning to start traveling into Jotunheim. If you want to go with me, I'd appreciate the company."

"I'm out." Heartpiercer immediately replied, turning on her heel and walking toward the door. "All you're going to do is spend all day in a bubble, touch down, build a shrine, and be back here, anyway. Find me when there's something interesting to do, someone to fight, or somewhere to explore."

"We'll *be* exploring—and she's gone." Joe grunted with annoyance as the bitter wind blew in from the open door. He walked over and secured it, turning around to see guilty expressions on the faces of the other two. "Oh, *come* on! You guys are going to sit out on it as well?"

"She had a point." Jaxon pointedly pointed out the point. "At least you're a class that can gain benefits from sitting and studying all day, casually glancing out at the horizon to see if there are landmarks. I would just need to sit in a cramped bubble, watching you do work and having my hand slapped anytime I tried to adjust your hunched form."

Joe turned pleading eyes to Socar, who let out a light groan and nodded, clearly showing that he was doing so under duress. "I can fly along with you every once in a while, but I have my own research to do. Don't expect me to come every day! *Rare!*"

"Yay!" the Ritualist cheerfully clapped, earning a few eyerolls for his effort. "I just need to gather a few supplies, activate this ritual that will let me stalk Daniella, and we'll be on our way. I'm just trying to figure out a way to have it automatically cancel when I get in range of her, otherwise I might accidentally detonate the entire camp she's staying in."

Jaxon and Socar exchanged glances, but it was the wizard who leaned forward. "Sorry, did you say you were going to stalk her? Joe, that seems a little—"

"No, no! All this ritual will do is let me know exactly how far away she is and the exact direction I need to go in order to get there. Sure, it makes it so sleep doesn't do much for me, and *technically* it'll make me want to, you know, kill her on sight…"

"Perhaps some alterations to the ritual are in order before you ever, *ever* activate that?" Socar offered with a wary smile. "You didn't come up with it yourself, right? You found that? Didn't make it?"

"Of course! But this is the fastest way to—"

Jaxon gently pulled the aspect inscriber out of Joe's hand, where it exploded into a brilliant shower of sparks that set his hand on fire. "Ow. Anyway, I'm certain that using it may be fast, but just go ahead and *don't.*"

With even the anti-Charismatic Chiropractor calling for a moratorium on the use of the ritual, Joe had no choice but to take a breather and rethink his plans. Ever so slowly, he came around to the idea of taking what he currently had and making it into something different, something far better.

The question was, who could he seek out for advice on changing or improving a ritual? Havoc was out of the running, as Joe was pretty miffed at him for causing his recent death.

Not to mention, he would likely throw Joe back into the scrum if he came back and was asking for more right away. To be fair, the training had been *effective*. Looking at how Infernal Conflagration had gone from Novice seven to Beginner zero in under twenty minutes? Yeah. That was impressive, even for Joe.

It was unlikely he could get someone like Grandmaster Snow to take the time with so much else going on, and it wasn't like there was another Master who was easily available for... Joe closed his eyes and shook his head, hoping he could come up with another, better solution. Thinking hard, nothing came to mind, and he let out a deep sigh of annoyance. "Thank you both for stopping me from activating that. I've got an idea of what to do now, I just... really don't want to."

Each of them stepped out into the blowing snow once more, and Joe began trudging to the Town Hall. Normally, he could get there in under a minute, but currently, he was fighting against himself every step of the way. When he finally entered the building, he marched over to the receptionist and cut off the snide comment coming his way with a sharp question. "Who's in charge of Master Stu's punishments and community service?"

The bearded Dwarf closed his mouth with an audible **click** and glared at the bald man in front of him. "Who wants to know?"

"What? Literally me." Joe rolled his eyes in contempt at the Dwarf who must've been a devoted student of Master Stu Sarcasm. "I thought of something he could do to help commute his sentence. Something that wouldn't be life-threatening to him and would show immediate returns on investment for the population."

Still looking at Joe with great suspicion, the receptionist leaned over and pressed a button on his desk. He didn't say another word, and Joe simply waited patiently until the door to the council room opened. Grandmaster Snow poked her head out, huffing in annoyance as she saw the situation. "Topher!

Master Joe is *on* the council. He can just walk in. Bother us with your inane pettiness again at the risk of your position."

"Bro. You literally could've just said the council is in charge of him." Joe walked past the annoying Dwarf, who had a name that matched his personality. "Abyssal *Topher*. Sitting out here being a *butt*."

Entering the council room, Joe noted that only three others were in attendance, which made sense for the time of day and lack of scheduled meetings. Giving a polite salute to Snow, Joe addressed the others heavily. "I need some assistance with the alteration and improvement of several of my rituals. I had a thought that perhaps Master Stu would be an acceptable teacher, or at least someone that could help to improve their quality. Please tell me that I'm out of my mind and should look for someone else."

Snow looked at Joe with a pensive stare, gently fondling her mustache as she thought about what the human had proposed. "No... in fact, Master Stu is likely the closest to my own skill in Mana Manipulation, of the Masters. Certainly, if you could get any of the Grandmasters to assist you, they'd be far better choices, but..."

"Surely you aren't suggesting that Stu goes and works with the person who made him need to plead temporary insanity," another council member scoffed at the idea. "I think Stu would rather go to the mines and gain his first real calluses than work with this particular human."

Not seeming too worried about that, Snow shrugged and casually waved Joe off. "All he's doing now is sitting in a room, being forced to wear a muzzle anytime he comes out or is within earshot of another person. If you want to take responsibility for his conduct, I can have him brought to your workshop for... let's say six out of every twenty-four hours? I'll sweeten the pot by giving him double time toward his community service while working for you, as he'll be proving himself reformed. Also, just to be as absolutely, hmm, *smart* about this as possible, bring me the final diagrams you make with him before you activate any of them."

"You'll check them over?" That made Joe's ears perk up, and he smiled hopefully at the Grandmaster.

"If he messes with them, I'll assign him triple the doubled hours of his community service that he had removed," Snow grimly promised. "Feel free to inform him of this fact, at your leisure."

"You know…" Joe chuckled at the thought. "I think I might keep that to myself for the first one or two projects he works on. Thank you for the assistance, and… I'm looking forward to his help."

CHAPTER TEN

Shifting somewhat uncomfortably in his chair, Joe idly realized that he'd never considered how dark his workshop was until this moment. Darkvision was a boon from Tatum, and he'd gotten so used to casually and passively using the ability that he'd never really considered what it looked like to other people when they entered his space and saw him working in the dark.

It was likely that Joe would've taken a lot longer to realize this fact, but Master Stu pointed it out near-instantaneously upon having his leather gag removed.

Now the human and the Dwarf were sitting across from each other, staring each other down as each of them plotted how they would take control of the situation. Joe spoke first, his seeming nonchalance over the situation causing the scowl on Stu's face to deepen. "Welcome to day one of working with me, Master Stu. I hope that we can be professional with each other and work toward the betterment of Novusheim. No matter what else has occurred between you and me, I'm certain that you, in general, have the best interest of your people at heart. With that in mind, let me show you what I'm hoping to accomplish."

Joe figured that, by refusing to give the Dwarf a chance to speak, he could avoid the constant taunting and cutting remarks he was certain would be flying out of the Dwarf's main face hole. Scrolls, parchments, and papers began appearing on the table between them as Joe pulled them out of his storage space. Each of them depicted diagrams, symbols that those unfamiliar with rituals would consider cryptic, some of them partially charged with mana or created with aspects and therefore glowing in the dimly lit chamber they sat in.

Now showing some begrudging interest, Master Stu leaned forward and looked at what Joe was presenting to him. After only a few moments, the Dwarf shook his head and muttered under his breath, "Infernal Conflagration? More like 'only infernal idjits use this'. Where'd you even get such an archaic spell? I should *report* you; this spell is illegal in…"

Joe looked up at the Dwarf with an arched brow as the sarcastic Master trailed off. "Let me finish that for you. This spell is illegal on *Alfheim*. Yeah, something tells me it's *doubly* illegal, now that the Theocracy is in complete and total control. Seeing as it has extra effectiveness against magical defenses, this seems like something that should have been put in play against them. But we aren't here to discuss what should've happened. We're here to turn this into a ritual to get you familiar with making rituals. After that, I have other, more important work for us to do."

"I've got to admit," the Dwarf smirked at Joe as he contemptuously eyed the bald human. "You've got some cojones, *bald bro*. Calling me here to work with you on things that could backfire and blow up in your face? *Me*? I'm just wondering how you think this is a good idea."

"Whatever else you are, Stu, you know your stuff. Even if you're mocking your own people's vernacular." Joe shrugged as though he were completely unconcerned about whether or not the Dwarf would be helpful. "The better we can keep monsters out of the Town, the better off everyone here will be. Abyss, the more safe *you'll* be. I'm hoping that your desire for self-preservation is going to be stronger than your dislike of me personally, and especially my people."

"I guess we'll find out," Stu retorted lightly.

Joe nodded gently. "I guess we will."

"Why Infernal Conflagration? The damage you're going to do to the beasts makes the meat inedible. Are you going to take responsibility when the city can no longer feed itself?"

Joe glanced up from the notes he'd just started reading over, a hint of irritation showing on his face. "You should know by now that we have alternative food sources in the works. Plus, not every monster will be burned; there's a five and a half second cooldown on the spell. With how fast the monsters move, and how few of these rituals we'll have set up at a time, I estimate that less than half will take infernal damage. Half of thousands of monsters that weigh hundreds of pounds and are over a dozen feet tall? I don't think we're going to have any concerns with having plenty of fresh meat or not. I just need an effective, efficient way to beat the monsters back."

Stu grumbled softly as he crossed his arms. "Effective? Maybe. I guess you'll find out. I *still* don't see why I have to be involved in this nonsense. Community service as a punishment? Bah! I should just be able to pay a fine like every other Dwarf that's gotten in trouble over the centuries."

"Sure, go ahead and pay us one currency unit per hour of community service you have remaining." Joe chortled softly as the Dwarf across from him seethed. "Yeah, it's hard to pay a fine when we don't have a standardized currency, isn't it? Just do this with me, and all of your hours working here count double. But, if you just sit there and glare, I'll kick you out and find someone who *will* work with me, even if it'll be a less effective use of both of our time."

The Ritualist suppressed a sigh as Stu went silent, obviously considering Joe's words. Valuable insights lurked in Stu's anti-human depths… somewhere. Frankly, he didn't care *how* they were offered, as long as he was given the breakthroughs he needed to create better spells and rituals.

Ever-so-slowly, as the hours passed, the Dwarf got more involved in the work itself. Joe assumed that having some form of mental stimulation was the key here, as not only did the Master of Sarcasm get a chance to speak with someone, he wasn't being used as standard manual labor or as an energy source to empower building projects. He could only imagine that had been a massive blow to the ex-councilman's pride.

Putting the final touches on his new ritual, which was essentially the diagram for Infernal Conflagration inserted in place of the Wind Blade diagram in the Ritual of Proximity, Joe carefully double-checked his own work—triple-checking all areas Stu had made comments on. "Good. That should work perfectly for chucking out the spell as needed."

"Pff. Yeah, that'll do *exactly* what you told it to do." Stu snorted, practically turning up his nose at the ritual that had been created.

Eyebrow twitching, Joe glared at the Dwarf as he tried to figure out what he was getting at. "Now that we have this ritual completed, I should let you know that Grandmaster Snow will be checking it over. If you did something to negatively impact our work, she's going to add triple the hours onto your punishment."

Unexpectedly, Stu didn't have much of a reaction to that warning, simply nodding fractionally, as if that was only to be expected. "Yeah, yeah, throw out more threats at the prisoner. Work me to death if you want. I'm just saying, this is the most boring magical item I've ever had the misfortune of having to work on personally."

"What do you mean?" Joe glanced down at the beautiful, efficient, clean ritual he'd created. "This will do exactly what I want it to do. The spell will be cast, monsters will be killed, and—"

"That's right. It'll do *exactly* what you want it to do." Stu leaned forward, a glint in his eye and a snarky grin on his face. "How *boring* is that? You know what made the Dwarves a contender on the grand stage? Our golems. Did we create those to be *safe*? A machine that did what we told it to do? Or did we make a magical dynamo that had a wide range of functionality, and every once in a while exploded in our faces? Even then, we planned for the danger and used the detonating cores as a method of attack. This ritual you're forcing me to work on? It's bland. Tasteless. No room to express itself."

Remaining silent as he thought over what the Dwarf was saying, Joe looked at the excellent creation he had on the table in front of himself. His gut reaction was to ignore the Dwarf, assuming that it was an attempt to subvert punishment by claiming Joe had gone wild with his ritual, and that was why it backfired. But something the Dwarf was saying rang true. Ever so slowly, he wondered aloud, "I don't suppose rituals would be considered a form of enchanted object?"

"My guess is *yes*." Stu seemed absolutely delighted that Joe was catching on to what he was hinting at.

"All magical, enchanted objects are kind of alive. At high enough ranks, they're directly intelligent." Joe's eyes widened at that thought. "If I'm making high-level rituals boring, am I trapping a magical intellect in a state where they can never grow or improve?"

"Even Alchemical injectables need to be taken by a certain date, or the magical communities consider using them an affront to natural law. So these rituals?" Stu gave a light shrug. "It depends on how persistent they are, I suppose. But I'll also point out that I doubt you found any Master-ranked rituals or better that are single-use or consumable."

Joe had been attempting to find a pattern in rituals as to why some were ranked higher than others, even if they some-times had weaker effects than those of a lower tier. He decided to think on this more and put the issue to the side for the moment. "Let's say I want to listen to you. Go ahead and pretend for a minute that you were going to make this ritual exactly how you wanted to do it. What would that look like?"

"Joe, I've been a Master for hundreds of years." Stu scoffed at the insinuation that the human could wrangle secrets out of him without proper compensation. "I know exactly what I'd do, and how I'd do it. But that's not the job. What am I getting for teaching you how to pursue your own craft?"

Having expected something like this to come up, Joe had a ready answer. "You realize that, at some point, the bifrost will open? When that happens, I'm gone, Stu. The faster you help me make that happen, the sooner I'm out of your beard for good."

"Nice touch on the beard comment." Stu considered what Joe had said, eventually shrugging and leaning forward to tap the paper. "Fine, I'll walk you through how I'd do it. There's a whole bunch of things to keep in mind when creating a magical... anything, I suppose. The first and most important is the intent of the magic itself. This is an infernal spell. Backing up slightly, this is a *combat* spell."

"Meaning that the intent of the spell is to deal damage?" Joe hazarded a guess.

"*No.*" The smirk on the Dwarf's face grew. "I can see why you need so much help. The intent of this spell is to *kill*. If you wanted to eat the meat, you'd choose a spell that was meant to deal damage to specific areas. If you wanted more material, better cores, a way to keep the damage off of allies? Well, you'd use a spell that had a different intent. Infernal damage persists until it's cleansed. If you burn someone with this, they just die. It might take a while, but that's what'll happen. Real hard to cure infernal damage-over-time."

"Interesting." It was a strange way of thinking about things, but most importantly, it was a *different* way of thinking about things. Joe pulled out his notebook and started writing. Information like this was exactly why he'd wanted to work with the Master Dwarf in the first place.

CHAPTER ELEVEN

"You've been taking meticulous control and efficient resource consumption in the place of going out of your way to strategically *Thesaurize*." The session had devolved from working to a full-blown lecture, and Joe was listening raptly to everything Master Stu had to tell him. "The soul-searing flame of Infernal Conflagration engulfs a designated area in scorching, ethereal flames that burn hotter and fiercer than ordinary fire spells. Tell me, why is it that, when *you* cast the spell, the flames linger? Your spell description says nothing of the sort. I can also tell you that this ritual you created to mimic the spell won't have that effect."

"It won't?" The more the Dwarf spoke, the more annoyed Joe became with his current rituals. "Did that have something to do with the intent I had when using the spell for the first time? I needed the monsters behind me to burn... not just the one I was attacking, but any of them that were hot on my heels."

"You could easily recreate that effect in your ritual by placing your personal intent into the diagram." Stu tapped a symbol in the spell framework that had been left intentionally blank on its interior. "Right here? If you were to get in there and carefully inscribe *your* spell intent, not just *the* spell intent, you'd probably be able to recreate the persistent effect."

"But how do I do that?" Joe huffed in annoyance. "What am I supposed to do, copy over a paragraph of my diary in there?"

"Now *there's* a book I want access to." Stu chortled nastily. "No, that'd be too specific and ironclad. What you need to do is find a way to write something that's open to interpretation, in a format that somehow allows for prime number sequencing. That seems to be something important to these rituals... at least, the way you make them."

"Prime number sequencing in a ritual." Joe wrote that into his notes, then stared at the words that had appeared. "Like... a haiku? Is that why I kept finding those in–?"

"Five, seven, five," Stu interrupted, deep in thought over what Joe had mumbled. "Yes, a haiku would work perfectly in this situation."

Staring at the unempowered ritual, Joe allowed his thoughts to move in rhythmic beats as he tried to put his experience of casting Infernal Conflagration for the first time into words. After several iterations, he slowly wrote out the final product in the symbol Stu had indicated.

"Icy monsters prowl. Persistent flames claim their realm. Burning in their wake." As soon as the last letter was inscribed on the ritual, the symbol flashed a bright gold, and mana was *drained* out of the Ritualist; so fast that Joe slumped as his muscles went limp.

Skill(s) increased:
Words of Power (Written) (Student I).
Ritual Lore (Student IV).

"How?" Stu lunged forward, reaching across the table and wrapping his hand around Joe's throat. His eyes were bloodshot, and he was practically snarling the words as he started to squeeze. "How'd you manage to do that on the first try? That should have–"

Thunk.

The Dwarf toppled backward as a heart-shaped Ritual Orb zipped out of Joe's bandolier and smacked him between the eyes. The human sucked in a deep breath and glared at his stunned assailant. "Don't worry. If something like that ever happens again, Stu, I'll still work with you. But you'll be manacled to the *floor* the entire time. Explain what you thought was going to happen, or I'll find out what Grandmaster Snow thinks would happen."

Breathing heavily, teeth grinding, the Dwarf spat out an answer. "Altering your ritual like that should've sapped your vitality to *nothing*. Imbuing a powerful working like this with your meager understanding of spell intent? In a place like Jotunheim? No one would've blamed me for your death; no *respectable* Master has ever achieved that status without a deep knowledge of what they're doing. You wouldn't even have known what happened and should've died at least five more times before you figured it out."

Joe's hands were balled into tight fists as he barely refrained from physically attacking the Master. Taking a few deep breaths, he cursed himself for his naivete. He'd gone into this with the knowledge that the Dwarf loathed him and would be seeking any form of work around that would take the blame off of himself if Joe was sent to respawn. The Ritualist resolved to interface with another Master at the bare minimum before putting any new practices into play in the future.

"Happily for me, my Words of Power for written magic was already at the Student rank. It seems my lack of knowledge in one area can be offset by my firm foundation with my *dozens* of skills." Joe smiled coldly, pleasantly, at the Dwarf. "It seems that, even though I love my precision and efficiency, I've got a knack for circumlocution. How wonderful is that? Many thanks for helping me figure out what's been holding my growth back. But I think you and I are done for the day. At the *minimum*. I hope the next time we work together, you're more interested in bettering those around you instead of tearing them down."

Calling in the guards, Joe watched with no small pleasure as

Stu was gagged and frog-marched back to his house arrest. With newfound determination, the Ritualist set out to revise his rituals, to infuse them with a hint of ambiguity. Ever so slowly— after all, he was directly working against his personal preference —the diagrams became less rigid, the instructions more open to interpretation. It was unnerving to Joe, a direct departure from his usual methods, but the potential for unchecked growth was exciting.

When he thought back, every time he'd experimented with something new, there'd been only three possible outcomes. The most common was that nothing changed. Following closely on the heels of that probability was the shift leading to catastrophic failure. But every once in a while, in the rare moment of brilliance or breakthrough, the experimentation had led to something far greater than he had intended.

"I think I need to start experimenting more with alchemical and enchanted ritual circles." Joe stated aloud as he carefully redrew a diagram. "Adding Special aspects is great and all, but what am I missing by not seeking out the secrets of my class more intentionally?"

By the time he needed to stop for rest, the changes he'd made were individually minor, but they represented a complete reversal in how he would be working to create new rituals in the future. Joe decided to sleep on the floor, knowing that, when he awoke, he would be devoting himself to analyzing and revamping the Ritual of the Insomniac Stalker into something effective and not so dangerous for personal use.

Several hours later, his eyes popped open, and Joe hopped to his feet. He got straight to work, getting an injection of caffeine directly into his veins thanks to Automate knowing what was required of it at all times. Excitement filled the Ritualist at this moment, for a multitude of reasons.

Above all else stood the fact that he was expanding his magical knowledge and insights, and he hoped that would lead to ever greater innovations in the future. This was what drove him: an unwavering determination to better his craft. Second to this was his desire to help his friend, who was in a situation she didn't want to be in. He firmly told himself that was all there was to the situation, so much so that he even started to believe it.

A little bit.

In his dimly lit workshop, surrounded by scraps of paper, broken tiles, and chaotic atmosphere, Joe meticulously began studying the diagram of the Ritual of the Insomniac Stalker. It was a dark ritual, meant for war, perhaps for revenge or an untraceable assassination. Each line he drew out and perused made him thankful once more that he hadn't gone down the path of a War Ritualist. To be shoehorned into using magics like this, gaining the most experience only when he was inflicting suffering on others, was a shudder-inducing thought.

Keeping his hands steady, Joe ever-so-meticulously began stripping all of the additional fluff out of the diagram itself, a process that was akin to ripping out its potential for growth and change over time. When he was done and had separated out all the components, he wasn't left with a simple tracking ritual. No, what he was looking at was various fragments of a ritual that individually were useless, and even put together, they would create a subpar, broken version of what was once a powerful piece of magic.

"Here comes the fun part." Now, having figured out one of the basic steps that he'd been missing, Joe began to place his intent for the ritual on each individual subsection. The further he went into the alteration of the magic, the more exhilaration would surge through his veins. This was his version of trans-muting lead into gold, and Joe wanted to make sure that he did it perfectly, while also allowing himself to experience the thrill of experimentation and eventual success.

The *almost* evil nature of the ritual, originally fueled by far darker intentions, gradually transformed, thanks to Joe's skillful touch. His Master rank in Ritual Circles wasn't just for show, and now that he understood what he'd been missing, the process flowed like water off the side of a mountain. Each circle was remade as a standalone pattern, before he began to weave the sympathetic threads between them to make a single, unified whole.

As he came closer to completing the project, the symbols on the specially prepared parchments shimmered with renewed brilliance—as if his mana was responding to Joe's excitement. As he made the final connection, light spilled from the pages, shining through the room in a dazzling display. The ritual itself seemed to rejoice that it had been brought back from darkness.

Elation coursed through Joe, a wide smile on his face as he took in the final, cohesive creation he'd made. He could already tell that the transformation was a success, even before notifications started scrawling across his vision.

Then, out of nowhere, something *snapped* in Joe's brain, and he toppled over backward, head bouncing off the stone of the floor. He was saved from a concussion only thanks to his ever-present Exquisite Shell, and his eyes went wide as he sucked wind and tried to figure out what had just happened.

Congratulations! You have created a brand-new ritual at the Journeyman rank. By removing the spite and contempt of the original creator of an original ritual, you have managed to complete an impressive feat of magic.

Quest gained: Redeeming Rituals. You have started on the path of making the world a better place through the removal of dark or taboo rituals. Cleanse 5 rituals at the Journeyman rank or higher. Reward: Ritual of Cleansing (Expert). The Ritual of Cleansing can be set in any area to remove aspects of intent from ambient mana. There are many benefits to this process, including but not limited to a calmer, less chaotic atmosphere in the area.

Joe rubbed at his throbbing head, pleased for the new quest but still uncertain why he was in so much pain at the moment. It felt like he'd gotten his bell rung, but he had been preserved from physical damage. "Close notification. What's this next one?"

Congratulations! By continually bending your thoughts toward how to make the world a better place for, not only yourself, but the people around you, your Intelligence has undergone a categorical shift! Your Intelligence is now aligned to the light.

Light-aligned Intelligence: when attempting to create or alter something with the intention to improve the lives of those around you, there is a 20% chance to be inspired by the light.

Alert! Your Intelligence has drastically shifted from its original bound state. Either undo what you have done or rebind your Ritual Orb of Intelligence. Intelligence is at an effective -50% until this has been completed.

"Uuughh." Joe groaned wordlessly, unable to think of a better descriptor of the situation he'd just created for himself.

Perhaps because he'd just lost an effective ninety-five points of Intelligence, dropping himself below the third threshold.

CHAPTER TWELVE

"Well, *this* is an issue I need to fix…" What felt like several seconds later, Joe managed to say the remainder of his sentence: "…as soon as is humanly possible."

He needed several things in order to unbind and rebind his orb, which meant the Ritualist needed to leave his workshop and go over to the Pyramid of Panacea. Steeling himself for an unpleasant time, Joe threw open the door and walked out into the false sunlight of the area.

Scanning the area, he didn't see a single person. Brow furrowing, he commented to himself, "that doesn't seem right. There's tens of thousands of people here, and it's not like we have apartment complexes to retreat into. Where is everyone?"

Knowing he wasn't going to be getting answers without fixing his current issue, he hurried along to the pyramid, every moment feeling as though he were watching a slideshow instead of real life, watching the world at twenty frames per second. "What did this do to me?"

Having nothing better to do as he hurried along, the Ritualist pulled open his character sheet and nervously laughed at the information it contained.

Name: Joe 'Tatum's Chosen Legend' Class: Reductionist
Profession I: Arcanologist (Max)
Profession II: Ritualistic Alchemist (4/20)
Profession III: Grandmaster's Apprentice (14/25)
Profession IV: None
Character Level: 26 → 27 Exp: 379,972 Exp to next level: 26,028
Rituarchitect Level: 11 Exp: 65,950 Exp to next level: 50
Reductionist Level: 6 Exp: 27,891 Exp to next level: 109
Hit Points: 2,491/2,491
Mana: 3,769/5,163
Mana regen: 72.68/sec
Stamina:1,870/1,870
Stamina regen: 6.65/sec

Characteristic: Raw score

Strength (bound): 182 → 172
Dexterity: 184
Constitution (bound): 179
Light Intelligence (Binding broken): 190 → 95
Wisdom: 180
Dark Charisma: 142
Perception: 180
Luck: 116
Karmic Luck: 23 → 25

"No wonder I felt weaker; I thought it was just my mind." Joe shook his head, grimacing at the odd dissociation he felt between his brain and his body. "I totally forgot about the 'Mind Over Matter'... thing. Since my strength is being boosted by my Intelligence stat, to help bring them into balance, of course my Intelligence being cut down would also make me physically weaker."

Humm.

Joe's arms flailed as he tossed himself backward, away from the explosion of snow that had just erupted in front of him. He looked to see what had created the effect, but only saw snow hopping into the air like a wake from a passing ship. "Is this... my Perception is able to see where people have moved, but my Intelligence is just too low to process the information?"

The world was eerily silent, all but for the slow, constant howl of wind across the landscape. Carefully walking—ensuring he didn't fall into the temptation of Omnivaulting—Joe hoped he didn't slam into someone or get obliterated by a Dwarf who was simply strolling down the road. "I've never missed the 'basically a child' lane that was in the Dwarven capital as much as I do right now."

Thankfully, he was able to make it to the pyramid without further incident and knocked on the enormous doors. Just like always, it took a while for the doors to fly open, but this time, there was no one standing there waiting for him. Joe looked around curiously, wondering where Jake the Alchemist could possibly be, and decided to simply start cautiously walking into the building. An instant later, the world around him was flashing by, and he found himself sitting on a chair deep within the pyramid.

Moments later, Jake appeared in the chair across from him, sitting there as though he'd been comfortably waiting for quite a while. "Can you understand me, Joe?"

"Yes!" Joe practically shouted in excitement, having not realized how much this situation was throwing him off. "How are you doing that? Why couldn't I see anyone, wait, no, I think I figured that part out. My Intelligence binding broke, and I need to unbind and rebind my Ritual Orb."

Jake started talking practically as soon as the final word was out of Joe's mouth, obviously having had plenty of time to process and think about the information that the Ritualist was presenting. "I'm able to speak with you because I've had to have an enormous amount of practice speaking to people at such a low threshold. Basically, I plan out the conversation from the start and start speaking well in advance of your finishing, so that it feels like a normal conversation to you."

The Ritualist processed that for a long moment, wondering when he would need to start doing something similar to speak with regular people in the future. If he ever managed to get back to Midgard, would speaking to someone like his own mother feel this bizarre? Before he could ask any follow-up questions, Jake vanished again, and multiple alchemy stations began smoking and brewing compounds, as if by magic.

He didn't need to wait long. Within five minutes, Jake reappeared in front of him on the seat, gently setting several vials on the table between them. "I color-coded them for you because I know your Intelligence is broken right now. Red unbinds the Characteristic, green is the binding agent I believe you require. Obviously, in your current state, I'm not about to allow you to use my tools. Good luck, and goodbye."

The world spun around Joe once more, and he found himself standing outside of the pyramid with the door shutting behind him. Looking down at his hands, he found two stoppered beakers, one in each hand. Immediately, he stored those in his codpiece and looked at the open field between himself and his workshop. Swallowing his nervousness, he stepped out and began running as quickly as he could toward the building.

Almost immediately, he fell, bouncing off the ground dozens of times as he failed to properly control his extremely powerful body. Pulling himself out of the furrow he'd carved into the ground, Joe took a deep breath and focused on taking slow, careful steps. "Right... my other Characteristics are still two thresholds above Intelligence. Don't do the dumb, Joe."

He was certain there were numerous eyes on him, mocking conversations happening, and a bevy of other things he would have to deal with in the near future. But for the moment, he didn't need to worry about any of that. If anyone showed up and started insulting him, Joe was certain he wouldn't even notice. Their lips would move like hummingbird wings, and his brain would be unable to decode the information it was being sent.

A painful hour later, he had set up the Ritual of Unbinding

and managed to get his orb back to its original state. Holding the now spherical, silvery orb in his hands once more, he was faced with a challenge he hadn't been expecting. "Abyss, I don't know enough about my Intelligence's alignment to light. How could I turn that into the sympathetic connections I need?"

Pondering that issue while standing still, Joe found no easy answer. He could try to force a binding as it was, but it was unlikely to succeed, merely causing him intense pain and further damaging him if he did it wrong. Knowing that there was no escape from good, old-fashioned work, the Ritualist decided to follow the same steps that he'd taken the first time around.

Settling himself in a comfortable position, he started to meditate on his own mental state as deeply as possible. He tried this for a dozen minutes before giving up, deciding to cheat a little bit. Letting his finger brush against the orb containing Essence Cycle, Joe surveyed the workshop he was in, hoping he would find some remnant of the fickle energy that had suffused his Intelligence.

Unfortunately, due to the chaotic nature of Jotunheim, there was no hint of the change. Yet, simply watching the flows of power sweeping through the world was enough to allow Joe to sink deeper into his own mind, practically hypnotizing himself as he began to think deeply on the nature of the odd power and his own connection to it.

His eyes were closed, yet Joe stood at the precipice of his mental state as his damaged Intelligence weighed heavily on him. Just as with the world outside himself, internally, his brain was a dense cloud of fragmented chaos. The deeper he sank within himself, the more he started to pick out patterns.

There was no true imagery, only what his mind could conjure for him. Still, as it was his brain, Joe understood what was happening around him. Oscillating, strange images told him that his ears were hearing sounds, his body was feeling sensations, but they were stunted because his brain currently didn't have the strength to process what his Perception was feeding into it. If he understood what was happening correctly, part of the reason he was so confused at the moment was that an enormous amount of stimuli he'd grown used to was simply *gone* from the range of understanding... but still attempting to flood his brain.

Attempting to further remove himself from his senses, Joe tried to drop deeper into his meditation, setting aside all outside perceptions. Moment by moment, he became more practiced and successful at doing so. A mental image of himself appeared in the chaos, and for a moment, he felt a bright glimmer of hope. Realizing that he was still connected to his Ritual Orb and caught in the throes of his Essence Cycle skill, Joe understood that the light he was seeing was the very energy he'd hoped to witness in his workshop.

Vibrant hues were dancing and swirling through the air above his mental self like an aurora painting the sky above the polar ice caps. Watching the light, he was filled with the desire to bring positive change to the world, to allow everything around him to come into a harmonious whole.

As he stared at the lights, meditating upon their meaning, they gradually came into focus with more and more clarity. Each strand of the light soon represented a facet of the *intent* behind his Intelligence and coalesced into actual images that his mind generated to help him understand. They changed every second as the Ritualist strove to understand his own place in the energies, ever-so-slowly settling into the solid pictographs he desired.

Inside his murky thoughts, Joe slowly grew in understanding, metaphors coalescing into what the alignment with the light meant for *him*. As he understood it, they meant that he could bend his mind, what he considered his most powerful asset, into being a catalyst for positive change. Pursuing this further would allow him to become a wellspring of inspiration... or at least that's what his mind associated with his subconscious thoughts and desires.

As the lights settled into perfect, continuous patterns that he would be able to remember and replicate on his orb, Joe realized that, when taken together, they formed a small story. "What does being aligned with the light mean, other than offering order to a world sinking into entropy?"

This resonated with him on a profound level, and a sense of fulfillment washed over him. Joe already knew that, when he inscribed this short story onto his orb, the end result of the binding would be far more powerful than what he'd originally put in place.

With an unexpected confidence, Joe let himself surface from the depths of his mind, buoyed by a renewed sense of purpose and satisfaction.

CHAPTER THIRTEEN

Setting up his new Ritual of Binding was practically child's play at this point. The power linking to his Characteristics flowed so smoothly that he wouldn't have even noticed the intrusion of the magic, had it not been for the way his mind cleared up nigh-instantaneously. There was even a tiny bonus thrown in for his efforts to regain his full mental power.

Intelligence +2!

Skill increase: Ritualistic Alchemy (Apprentice II)

Joe wasn't entirely certain if he'd gained the points to Intelligence for being forced to deal with his altered mental state for a while, or if it was the fact that he'd been able to create a mind-scape of himself in order to fix the issue. "Then again, seeing as how I got two points, maybe it was one for each?"

Looking at the orb, Joe noticed another small change, compared to the previously bound weapon. Where his Orb of Intelligence had previously been an icicle-shaped, pointy orb, this one was sharper and had alternating bands of bright and dull metal. With a thought, he caused his weapon to start spinning, and it responded faster than ever before. The striation on the weapon created a mesmerizing display, something Joe was certain would mess with the depth perception of anyone trying to track its movement through the air.

Directing it around the room, Joe also found that the Ritual Orb of Intelligence responded to his mental input far more efficiently. It was faster, turned more easily, and he was certain it would penetrate deeper when striking a target. "Thank goodness. Hopefully, the next time I need to attack a Hoardling, this goes *through* its skull instead of glancing off and smashing my walls."

Walking over to the door of his workshop, the Ritualist flung it open and breathed a deep sigh of relief at the bustling Dwarves moving through the area. As far as the eye could see, hundreds, *thousands* of bodies were moving. The air was filled with noise as people shouted back and forth; Joe could process all of it. That didn't mean he wanted to hang around and watch people from his doorway like some kind of creeper, so he retreated back into the depths of his gloomy workshop and started preparing the final pieces he needed to start tracking Daniella.

Thanks to the unwitting, unwilling help of Master Stu, Joe finally had what he believed was a working version. He made a copy of it and sent it off to be checked by Grandmaster Snow, happy to wait on a reply as he got everything else up and running.

"I'm going to need dozens and *dozens* of Rituals of Bubble Travel." The bald man began working furiously as he waited on a reply from the exceptionally busy Grandmaster. "Who knows how far away she'll be, and I'm going to want to stop anytime I find something interesting. Not to mention whenever I'm at the maximum range the shrines can reach."

That made him realize he would need plenty of shrines as well, so he began alternating his creation of rituals. Two towers of potent magical effects began piling up in front of him, stacked casually, as if one of them breaking *wouldn't* create a chain reaction that would level his workshop. He'd made fairly decent progress when he got a return message from the Grandmaster, giving him the all-clear to attempt the activation of his new ritual.

Joe wasted no time at all, his heart beating with anticipation as he rushed into the empty vault-like room he would be activating all of his untested, dangerous rituals in. The Ritualist closed the door behind him, barring it from the inside, and began setting out his stabilization cubes. From there, he added in stabilization candles from his alchemical exploits then finally began drawing out the full ritual using his aspects. The brilliant lines of fire hung in the air wherever he placed the nib of his inscription tool, a beautiful effect that shifted the area from a completely dark space to a brightly lit, shimmering space.

"Kinda looks like the top of an oil spill in the ocean," Joe muttered to himself as he surveyed his circles, looking for any issues or blockages that would impact the power flow. "Or would, if someone threw a torch into it."

When the ritual was completed, Joe began placing out his Mana Batteries but stopped just before he would normally activate the ritual. His hand was hanging in the air, but with great frustration, he pulled back and looked at the ritual once more. "I've been wanting to expand on my skills, and even if it's something like this, I should be working to do better. How can I... what should I do to turn this into an *enchanted* ritual circle?"

Now that he'd drawn out every part that was required, there was very little concern that it would explode, at least until he actually activated it. In this in-between phase of being created but not yet working, it was as stable as properly stored dynamite. So long as there was no shock to the system, it should remain without breaking for a decently lengthy amount of time.

The Ritualist started thinking about what he was making and tried to look for drawbacks that he could mitigate. "Think, Joe, *think*! How could this be better? What does it do... okay, it sets two distinct targets. One is always able to find the other, no matter how far away they are. It'll tell me the direction to the target, and… and it'll be a perpetual effect. *Yeesh.* What if she's something like a *million* miles away? Will I always have her distance and heading at the forefront of my mind?"

That didn't sound pleasant. Conversely, it sounded like a great way to lose sleep. For a long moment, Joe wondered if this portion of the ritual was the one that caused the 'insomnia' portion of the Ritual of the Insomniac Stalker, but he shook that thought off and instead started casting about for a solution. "What do I know about enchantments? I've got plenty of lore, much less practical experience. First off, enchantments are always on a physical item. Unlike my rituals, which can just hang in mid-air, enchantments are designed to create or *hold* permanent effects. Okay, that's a good start…"

It just so happened that all of Joe's magical clothing had recently been destroyed, and the likelihood of getting a new set was close to zero while he was still on Jotunheim. Then, if he considered the issue further, he realized that his enchanted clothing dealer, Minya, had already warned him once about taking care of his gear. "I'm not going to be able to get new stuff even if I get off of this world. Abyss, I guess there's no time like the present to start learning how to dress myself."

His Lore skill wasn't just for show, granting him a firm foundation in the fundamentals of the craft that he was attempting to pursue. Seeing as the ritual he was trying to contain was a Journeyman-rank spell diagram, he had to—at the minimum—put his planned enchantment onto a Rare item. It'd be even better if he could get a Journeyman unenchanted item, but it was a well-established fact that materials could hold enchantments up to a single rarity above them. "Yeah. It's totally fine. It'll just break down twice as fast."

That was perfect for his plans, as he didn't really want to have an item that could seek out Daniella in perpetuity. He was fairly certain *she* wouldn't appreciate him creating something like that, either. Currently, he didn't have anything at the Rare rank that he would be comfortable enchanting, so Joe carefully locked the door behind him as he left his workshop. It was time to hunt down a Rare or better item from one of the shops he had equity in.

Thinking about what he was trying to do, Joe chuckled softly to himself. "I'm so glad I've always been super paranoid about people getting my blood. This curse of baldness was a blessing in disguise; at least it's really hard for someone to grab a fistful of my hair and run off."

After visiting a couple of shops, Joe had two options. The first was a monocle that he could wear on his face. That had been his first choice, for several reasons. The first was that it was a circle, and the sympathetic links to his ritual circles would be easier to ingrain in an item similarly shaped. The second was that he would feel like a character from an anime, able to see the distance and direction he needed to move as numbers that would pop up in a HUD-like format. "How many miles away is she? Over nine thousand!"

Joe chuckled to himself as he gently set down the glass eyewear. Unfortunately, his enchanting skills were simply not good enough to inscribe the enchantment onto the extremely thin ring of metal, or onto the glass of the monocle itself, without shattering it. That left him with his second choice, a plain white shirt made from the fur of a Hoardling. That would give him plenty of space to attempt his enchantments, and even if he needed to restart on a different part of the cloth, that wouldn't mean the destruction of the shirt.

Luckily, he didn't need to buy dyes or threads made from the same fur, as his Reductionist class allowed him to use aspects for any attempt at crafting. After a quick round of polite bartering, Joe returned to his workshop one shirt richer and an entire Hoardling corpse poorer.

Staring down at the shirt, Joe decided to begin practicing right above the lowest hem, which would hang a quarter inch above his rear if he was wearing the shirt. Placing his inscriber against the fabric, he started burning the pattern he had in mind into the fur.

Almost instantly, he needed to slap his hand down on the material as it lit on fire. "*Uuugh.* Sure, my Enchanting Lore is at the Student rank, but both my Enchanted Ritual Circles and my general Enchanting skills are in the Beginner ranks. I'm going to need some stabilization items, aren't I? What're they called for enchanting again? Foci?"

Joe looked down at the already-singed shirt, then to the inscriber in his hand, and he thought about what he wanted to generate. "I'm going to need to make a Rare enchantment on this garment to contain the Journeyman-ranked ritual. I'm going to need at least a double handful of Foci for the attempts… yeah, I might as well get back over there and buy a couple dozen shirts to practice with."

If he could get his Enchanted Ritual Circles skill up to the Apprentice rank, the Ritualist had a chance of making a Student-ranked enchantment, the crafting equivalent to 'Rare' on the general rarity chart. The chances were low, but he hoped that he could mitigate that by already having his Enchanting Lore in the mid-Student ranks.

Standing up and walking toward the door, Joe rubbed his smooth head in frustration at himself. "I just have to make everything more difficult, don't I?"

A chill wind blew around him while he hurried to secure all of the items he needed, and Joe slowly became more happy with his decision to be working on his skills. "You know, I think this is good, Mate."

Burble. The coffee elemental agreed with him without poking its tiny head out of its nice, warm, Ebonsteel home.

"No, I'm serious! Think about it like this: if I'm always doing the easy thing, I'll make my life hard in the long run. Since I'm doing difficult things when I don't need to do them, I'll be prepared for when I *do* need them. If I can just front-load the hard work like this every time, my life will be easy when I need it to be. Easy peasy lemon squeezy, instead of difficult, difficult, lemon difficult, right?"

Mate didn't look completely convinced, but before Joe tried to explain further, he shook his head and smiled. "Sorry, Mate, I just realized that I'm arguing philosophy with my coffee. You don't need to worry about that; you're perfect as-is."

Burble!

CHAPTER FOURTEEN

Joe stared down in disgust at the shirt that he'd once more failed to enchant. He was out of free space on the material, so he threw it to the side along with the other failed, rejected samples. The Ritualist tried not to think too hard about how quickly that pile was growing. At least there was a positive effect from all of the failing he was doing.

Skill Increase(s).

Enchanted Ritual Circles (Apprentice I)

Enchanting (General) (Apprentice 0)

"Somehow it seems appropriate that neither of my enchanting skills gave me a bonus when I got them up to the Apprentice rank." Joe rubbed his head, removing a slick of sweat. Cringing away from the filth on his hand, Joe reached over and used his recently rejected garment as a dew-rag. Since he was alone and working on extremely mana-intensive crafting, Joe had canceled every passive effect besides his ever-present Exquisite Shell. "Something about enchanting feels cold and calculating, even more so than any of the other crafts I work on."

Amending that thought, he shrugged and muttered,

"Except maybe, *maybe* low-rank rituals. But those feel much more personal to me, so maybe it's just my bias coming into play."

Even though he was consistently failing, repetition was the path to success. Either by accident or design, he would eventually succeed in making the Rare enchantment, so he took a few minutes to calculate the odds. "Let me see… Enchanted Ritual Circles is currently giving me a twenty-one percent bonus chance to use enchantments correctly in the creation of my ritual circles. Standard enchanting is giving me half a percent per level, so that equates to about a ten percent bonus. If I toss in my Enchanting Lore, at Student—hey! *Knowledge*: Enchanting Lore!"

Mana ripped through his body, condensing in his brain and resolving into knowledge on enchanting. Even through the odd enlightenment, Joe noticed something in the ambient energy of the air in his workshop. There were strange ripples of power bouncing back and forth, just on the edge of his ability to perceive them. Before he could put too much thought into that phenomenon, the notification on his skill increases appeared once more.

Skill increase(s)
Enchanting Lore (Student V)
Knowledge (Student III)

"Ah, abyss, I can use that skill on two Lore skills at a time now; why do I keep missing that?" With the skill back on cooldown, Joe resumed his train of thought. "Enchanting Lore doesn't actually give me any increased odds of creating the ritual successfully, simply reducing the overall cost of the components I use, as well as giving me the knowledge to fine tune the enchantments better. So, I think that comes out to something like a thirty-one percent boost, and the odds of creating an enchantment a rank higher than I should be able is something like five percent. All told, that should put me at a… six and a half percent chance. Wait, that's *it*?"

As soon as he realized how low the probability actually was,

Joe let out such a deep sigh that he sank into his chair and let his head rest on the table. "I really don't want to have to go and buy more shirts. They're going to look at me funny."

Deciding to simply bite the bullet and get to work, Joe grabbed his next shirt and made each design as miniaturized as he possibly could. The first attempt failed when he was halfway through, as did the second, third, and fourth. On the fifth try, the shirt lit on fire, and he needed to scramble to slap a blank ritual tile down on the material before the flames could spread too far. Sadly, he'd gotten so used to this that he had one on hand and completed the action nearly automatically.

By the twentieth attempt, he'd gained another level in his Enchanted Ritual Circles skill, and so had high hopes for the next attempt. "If I'm getting rewarded for using my skills, I have to be doing something correctly, right?"

There was only one area left non-charred on this shirt: directly on the chest, front and center. It was a large space, almost big enough for two attempts, but not quite. Joe gave himself a bit of extra room and began working in earnest, as carefully and meticulously as ever. To his surprise, and slight consternation, the enchantment snapped into place and *hummed* to his Magical Synesthesia senses.

He held the shirt up, smiling at the oval-shaped shimmering space that was outlined by what almost appeared to be circuitry that had been three-D printed onto the material itself. "Hello, beautiful! I suppose I should be glad this only took me twenty-one attempts, but all I can think is how badly I want a nap. Mate! Can you fix me up?"

Caffeine jolted directly into his veins, and the irises of Joe's eyes constricted slightly. He hopped to his feet, a manic smile on his face as he practically waltzed into his vaulted area. The door shut behind him, and Joe placed the enchanted shirt into the center of his ritual circles. From there, it was a simple matter of creating the sympathetic links with a combination of aspects and mana, and the ritual shrank down farther and farther, until it was all but sucked into the enchantment itself.

"The final component, and some mana to get the ball rolling." Joe laid the shirt flat, pouring the vial of Daniella's blood onto the open space. It hovered in the air for a few seconds, the ritual condensing one last time and altering its properties until the blood was gone, and a simple dye remained. From there, the ritual sucked in all of the mana that Joe was willing to give it, and the 'dye' sank into the large, oval space.

With a shimmering flash of light, the enchantment and the circle merged into a single, complete diagram. The altered blood then seeped over the open oval space until it was completely coated. Seeming to dry in an instant, the red coloration vanished, leaving behind a somewhat goofy, picture-perfect image of Daniella. Joe looked at the shirt, his face as still as stone. Then he reached down, grabbed the garment, and tossed it onto the pile of rejects.

"Yeah, we're going to have to put that in a place it isn't quite as noticeable." He glanced over at the shirt once more, realizing that each of the incomplete enchantments on the shirt had also been replaced with Daniella's face. "Such cringe. Very nope."

Unfortunately for him, he ran out of shirts before being able to recreate the enchantments again. That reminded him that he only had the single vial of blood, and no more was forthcoming. With a groan of frustration, he pulled his single, gaudy success out of the pile of garbage and contemplated what to do with the remainder of the shirts. There was far too much magical contamination on them to simply burn them to hide his shame, and he didn't have a convenient hollow mountain to drop them in.

Luckily for Joe, he had an alternative option that he was happy to take.

A single instance of his Field Array later, all evidence that he didn't perfectly create his items on the first try had been reduced to mere aspects. Holding the shirt out in front of him with two fingers, Joe contemplated it with a grimace. "I guess I'd better make sure it works?"

Sliding the garment over his head, his arms through the holes, Joe pulled the shirt down and tight. "Bleh. I look like a-"

His head snapped to the left as an overwhelming *under-standing* of where Daniella was appeared in his mind.

Bearing: one hundred and eighty-three degrees off assumed Jotunheim standard North. Distance: fluctuating, approximate range of ten thousand two hundred eighty-three miles.

With a force of will, Joe managed to completely remove the shirt and drop it on the table, and he stood there panting in exertion. After a few deep breaths, he realized that he *stank*, and so activated his Neutrality Aura. The stench that had been building up on him, and in his workshop, vanished over the next few seconds, allowing Joe to take additional gasping breaths without making himself nauseated. "I am… *so* glad I didn't activate that in my own head. No wonder the first target would hate the second in no time flat."

He took some time to go over his notifications, which had started appearing as soon as he'd completed the enchantment, only stopping after he had a complete, working tracking item.

Congratulations! You have created a Basic Hoardling Fur Enchanted (Blank) shirt (Rare). This item is specifically geared toward accepting a magical effect from an outside spell, but is less durable because of the partially empowered nature of its enchantment. Effects: Spell absorption and retention. - 50% durability.

You have activated the Ritual of the Unrequited Bloodhound! (Journeyman). Reductionist experience +400.

Congratulations! You have activated a Journeyman-rank ritual of your own design for the first time! Reductionist experience +500.

Your Reductionist class has gained a level! Reductionist 7 → 8!

You have created a new item: Shirt of 'I Stan Daniella'. This basic shirt has been Enchanted half with standard enchantment, half with a ritual, to allow its wearer to always find 'Daniella'. Upon donning the shirt, the wearer will have an intense understanding of their relative distance and direction from 'Daniella'. It has been nicely decorated with twenty-one images of her face, as well as a bright header over the main enchantment with the words 'I Stan'.

Joe was happy about the completed enchantment, but a little annoyed over the fact that the system was slandering him with slang that meant 'someone who is a very zealous fan', or a mix of 'stalker and fan'. Letting out a sigh, he stored the shirt in his codpiece, resolving to only wear it when he absolutely *needed* to decide which direction to go.

"Good thing I don't care if I have a stellar reputation." Joe got back to work, pausing a few seconds into creating another ritual of bubble travel. "But... maybe it'd be better if I made sure to burn this before she sees me."

CHAPTER FIFTEEN

"Ah, what a perfect day to leave the Town behind and go off in search of adventure, fun, and rare materials." Joe took a deep breath, leaning back with his hands on his hips as he surveyed the swirling cloud cover of Jotunheim. "Perhaps freeing a captive friend and filling the population of Novusheim with the residents of a few towns I destroy along the way so we can hit the minimum requirements for upgrade."

The skies above Novusheim were practically alive with the sounds of Dwarves, ritual towers, and monsters clashing in the killing corridors around the Town. A small part of him felt guilty over the fact that he was leaving everyone here to fend for themselves while he went off in search of a single person, but he'd done everything he could for the time being to improve their defenses.

Until they had another large boost in morale, it was going to be difficult for Joe to scoop up any more building slots, and creating Trash-tier towers that would just fall apart in a day was never worth the effort.

No, he'd waited long enough. Just as he would for any friend in trouble, Joe was determined to set out right that minute. Flippantly tossing out a ritual tile, swiftly followed by his stabilization cubes, Joe prepared to exit the Town from above. No one came to bother him, as he had managed to establish in their minds that being around him when a ritual was being set up was tantamount to volunteering to act as a power source.

Even so, the Ritualist triple-checked that no one was near him before he felt confident in quickly slipping on his new shirt, his brain immediately filling with the distance and direction he needed to travel in order to find the wayward Architect. Joe quickly input those variables into his ritual then took the shirt off as fast as he could without damaging it. It was created with a fifty percent reduction in durability, meaning that he, with his high level of strength, had a good chance of ripping it in half if he forced the issue.

Seeing as it was now a magical item, tearing it off would result in an explosion of the item wrapped around his torso. "Now *that* would be one not-so-magical hug."

In the next moment, he'd stored away the shirt and stepped into a bubble. An instant later, he was two hundred feet in the air and zipping along at a breezy eighty miles per hour. Joe had consulted his schematics, as well as sending a query to Tatum, and he found that the range of shrine-to-shrine teleportation was currently limited to roughly two hundred and fifty miles. If the Ritualist was willing to take the time to build a more impressive structure, a Grand Ritual Hall for example, that could be extended out to over a thousand miles.

"That would be a giant waste of resources," Joe murmured to himself as he settled into his studies. With three and a quarter hours until his bubble would land, he began going over his grimoire of dark rituals for a likely candidate for revamping.

If he was going to be stuck in a bubble for something like a hundred and twenty-five hours—not counting the amount of time it would take to build shrines and sleep—he needed to work on his class quests, create something interesting, or at least keep himself busy until he'd arrived at his destination. All of that aligned neatly with his new quest to take those darker, twisted rituals and cleanse them, turning them into something beneficial and... if not *nice*, at least not bent toward getting a bounty placed on his head.

A small part of his mind needed to remain on the terrain zipping by beneath him. When he'd explained his exploration plans to the council, Grandmaster Snow had only agreed to his journey so long as he marked down anywhere they might be able to find natural resources. According to her, this world had once been heavily traveled, if not highly populated by long-term residents.

Mostly, Jotunheim was a phenomenal place to go and get resources from monsters. Similar to a safari, it had also been the location for hunting trips, bachelor parties, and other extravagances of the super-rich or powerful. Seeing as the world had been locked down, and those same ultra-rich and powerful people were slain or captured, there was a high probability that this world was covered in loot buried beneath the snow.

Weapons, armor, and magics that had been lost to time? All of it was somewhere on this supermassive planet. Sure, it was likely that a good chunk of it had been crushed flat, degraded with time, or whatever else may have happened, but there was also likely a hoard hidden away under the snow that was protected from all but the most powerful creatures on the planet. Joe liked to imagine that he could find a cave of wonders somewhere that would open if he answered a few riddles, but he knew that was—to put it mildly—unlikely.

The farther he traveled, the more engrossed he became in his work. He'd started his attempt at cleansing additional rituals with the Ritual of Sacrificial Regeneration. This one was most likely the closest to 'positive vibes' of all of the darker rituals he'd been given, but given its rarity, it would still be extremely difficult to crack. "Choose up to four willing creatures, including the target. Whenever the creatures take damage, the target will heal for a portion of damage taken."

Joe closed the book as he pondered how he'd break that down further. Specifically, how he'd strip away all of the extras, then add in his own intention to power the growth of the Master-rank ritual. Taking a moment, he wrote down a symbol he had decoded on the Expert circle of the ritual, translated into a haiku so he could better conceptualize it. Since he'd been toying with so many of these recently, he decided to start there, even though he'd found seven different variations on symbology that could imbue intent into this ritual. "None of them were haikus! So, I'm totally justified in starting here."

Chuckling softly to himself in his otherwise empty bubble, Joe started pulling apart the mathematical formula that generated the words of the prime number descriptor. When he was finished, he read it out loud, wincing at how poorly the translation came across. "Pawn's pain feeds his self. Mage's power grows on each hurt. Healing bonds, life thrives."

"Well, that isn't very nice, is it?" Joe shook his head at the thought that someone would use this ritual, magic that everyone involved needed to agree to be a part of, and still consider them a pawn instead of a friend. "You know, I bet I could just replace 'pawn's' with 'friend's' and leave this one alone. At least, if I were trying to still gain Health when my friends are hit."

He had bigger, better plans for this ritual. Instead of letting his party sacrifice themselves or get hurt for him, Joe wanted to completely alter the targets of the ritual from people around him to creatures that were damaged. "If I can combine this targeting section with the Ritual of Mana Withering, I wonder if I could make a feedback loop that drains mana from anyone hit. If I could use that on my towers, they wouldn't even need a Mana Battery to function."

There was still an issue of combining this ritual with a secondary one which would do the actual attacking, but Joe had been doing well in setting up arrays of rituals. There was only one major issue with that plan, and it was a strong enough argument against it that Joe decided to abandon that train of thought entirely. "If I'm going to use a Master-rank ritual just to feed other rituals... that's just wasteful. Especially since I'm going to have Havoc creating a Mana Battery recharging station anyway."

Eventually, he landed on the idea of combining this ritual with an enchantment on a weapon to create a Master-ranked lifesteal enchantment. As the intent of the ritual wasn't actually to cause harm or kill other things or have them sacrifice themselves to empower the user, Joe figured the intent of the ritual would still be considered positive. "All this ritual wants to do is keep its user alive. I think that will be enough, so let's start creating some intent as we go through each of these circle diagrams."

Before he knew it, his bubble was landing, popping, and depositing him in the snow while he looked around in surprise, blinking owlishly. "What in the abyss? There's no way it's been three hours already! It's still bright out-! Oh. Right. Jotunheim."

Needless to say, a little over three hours was nowhere near enough time to strip down and rebuild a Master-ranked ritual, not if he wanted it to work and *not* explode in his face, that is. Joe hopped up, brushed some snow off the Exquisite Shell over his legs, and set up a Field Array. Moments later, he was ten feet below the surface of the snow and working on widening the area around him. "Monsters aren't going to come and stomp this flat if they can't see that it exists."

Joe hummed tunelessly to himself as he set up the ritual to create the shrine. No monsters interrupted him, and no strange sudden events transpired that he wasn't expecting. Instead, after a short while, he had a shrine growing in midair and was back in a bubble looking over his magical diagrams.

Twice more his bubble landed, and he got out to build a shrine before he was absolutely *sick* of sitting in an awkward position. "I think that's going to have to be it for the day. Jaxon may have had a point... this is pretty mind-numbing."

The Ritualist was approximately seven hundred and fifty miles away from Novusheim at this point, and he decided that now was the time to test out the fast travel system. Placing a hand atop the altar, he sent a cheeky wink up to Tatum in the sky. Fractions of a second later, he was down a few hundred points of mana and standing in the town square of Novusheim. Joe tossed his hands in the air, letting out a whoop and shouting, "It works! I didn't just waste a huge amount of time for no reason!"

His face fell slightly when he realized that meant that he got to sit in a bubble again for approximately another one hundred and sixteen hours. "*Ya~ay*. It works."

Still, he couldn't be too upset. The enforced alone time gave him plenty of opportunity to better his craft, and studying such a high-ranked ritual for so long was already giving him ideas on how to improve his other designs. The better he was at rituals, the better Joe would be able to kill monsters and keep this Town safe. Every incremental bit of growth was going to be necessary for when they attempted to push for a City, and he wasn't about to shirk his duties now.

CHAPTER SIXTEEN

Joe had never realized how popular his work had become until he started using large chunks of his day flying along in a bubble where no one could contact him for any reason. He'd expected to be able to spend a week or two floating along in his magical transportation, creating shrines without any interruptions. Instead, what actually happened was that he'd come back, appearing in front of the shrine, only to be met with half a dozen messengers that each demanded his attention for one reason or another.

He'd never seen his ritual towers need as much attention as when he was gone. At some point, someone had wandered into his workshop and messed up the sky by dumping a half pint of ale on the otherwise unsecured ritual. Another petitioner needed help, making it his problem by pointing out that he was an investor in their shop. They were threatening to go under because they simply couldn't gather enough raw materials—an issue Joe had an easy solution for. Still, between those and a dozen other tiny things that required his specific attention and couldn't be delegated, the Ritualist was *swamped*.

Beyond the concerns the people in the town had, there was

also the fact that Joe had finally created what he hoped would be a working version of the Ritual of Infernal Conflagration with the specific intention to create a lingering field of infernal flames. He needed to take nearly an entire work day to set up just *one* of them, as Socar simply wouldn't allow him to place that particular ritual almost anywhere. Apparently the 'heavy Yin influence' was liable to throw off the entirety of the delicate Formation they had been layering, resulting in subpar performance from all the other rituals.

That was obviously a concern that the Ritualist couldn't simply ignore, so he had to not only set up the tower, but move a half dozen of the other ones to preserve the integrity of the powerup. As a silver lining, this had led to another breakthrough. Joe got so annoyed with manually ripping down and putting up the towers that he realized he had a perfectly good Ritual of the Traveling Civilization lounging around Town doing not much at all.

From then on, all of the towers were marked by that ritual, and he was able to move the towers as needed. The new method of tower management sparked additional work, as Joe could now create a huge number of the towers and keep them in reserve at the edge of Town, not active nor impacting the formation. Those backups could be used to replace any of the currently active towers, and all too soon, some lazy but effective employee realized that it would be faster to swap out the towers than to simply swap out the Mana Batteries at their source.

This led to a complete overhaul of how the towers were built, shifted, placed, charged, and repaired. A new tower would be built, swapped out with one that *wasn't* currently blasting monsters, and the old one would be recharged and repaired in a nice, safe, warm environment.

For everyone else, this was a *spectacular* upgrade. But all it meant for Joe was that he not only needed to build dozens of additional towers, he also needed to generate the rituals that would be put into play on those towers. That meant additional stabilization cubes as well, and he found himself working alongside Dwarves, pounding on aspects even as the Dwarves reshaped his failed attempts into workable items.

Two weeks passed in a flash of incredibly intense work followed by long stretches of sitting and studying in a cramped environment before Joe finally found something in his flight path.

He'd flown over so many monsters at this point that it had stopped being a notable experience, but he'd never seen them moving like this from the air before. Hundreds of them were gathering, streaming toward a location in the distance, and the Ritualist realized immediately that he was seeing a Beast Wave that was just getting underway. Straining his eyes, he could see some flickering light that indicated a fire of some sort in the distance, and he tried to decide on a good spot to burst his bubble.

"Yeah, that's one of the major downsides of flying in a ritual-made bubble." Joe grumped to himself as he pulled a dagger out of his codpiece. "The ritual itself stays wherever I place it, and I just have to hope I get a good landing spot. Or, make my own."

With that, he shanked the air next to him and fell toward the ground at breakneck speed. "Abyss! Too high! I knew I should've taken some time to make the Ritual of Featherfall-!"

Luckily, Joe slammed face-first into dozens of feet of powdery snow, arresting his momentum and allowing him to pop back to his feet without having taken even a single point of damage to his Exquisite Shell. His rapid descent had a secondary benefit, it hadn't given either monsters or people living in the area the chance to see him arrive.

Taking advantage of this fact, the Ritualist kept low to the ground as he moved closer to what must've been a Hamlet. Currently, the population center lay in ruins, its streets bustling with people. However, where Novusheim was boiling with activity as people created things and pursued objectives, this place was mired in combat. Screams, growls, shouts, and bright sprays of arterial blood were common sights.

Eyes scanning the devastation, Joe assessed and tried to determine what would be the best way to take advantage of the situation. The monsters were still active, and every once in a while, he caught a glimpse of a pointy-eared Elf as they cast bolts of sizzling light magic through the ranks of Penguins and Hoardlings that were swarming through their base. "Okay... I have multiple thoughts on how this should go. I need to save the humans, kill the Elves off, and it wouldn't hurt to progress the quest with Havoc by being the one to destroy the Town Hall."

All Joe could do was shake his head as he watched the Elves band together, back to back as they fought off the unending swarm of monsters. It wasn't difficult to notice the fact that there weren't any humans within their ranks, no doubt a byproduct of their theocratic hierarchy. "If I can get rid of the Elven overlords and make sure they can't respawn anywhere nearby, maybe I could even persuade this population to come back to Novusheim with me."

Slowly, the Ritualist nodded at that idea. In order to reach the status of a City, their population needed to be far higher than it was currently. There were no other groups on the planet that were already aligned with the Dwarves, but if he could take these people back willingly, recruiting from villages in the future would be far easier. He'd be able to prove that they had good treatment and weren't being harassed due to their choices from the previous planet. "Which means I have to make sure to convince the Dwarves not to treat them badly."

That thought made him wince, but he figured he could perhaps do something about it. Even as he watched dozens of people and monsters being torn apart, he was also plotting out how to build a smaller settlement somewhere in the walls that surrounded Novusheim. "Maybe I can bill it as a first line of defense for the city, giving all of the people here a chance to prove themselves before eventually earning the right to live in the city itself?"

All too soon, the time to act had arrived. Joe exploded out of the snow bank with Omnivault, racing toward the already badly damaged Town Hall. When he'd closed half the distance, all of his ritual orbs swarmed into the air around him like wasps flying out of their hive to attack a random innocent passerby. The heart, icicle, barbell, or simple spherical-shaped weapons flew forward; barely staying ahead of him as he pushed them with his mind while compelling his body with might and magic.

The Town Hall, unsurprisingly, was modeled after the Elven versions of the previous world. It was beautiful, spacious, with perfectly fitted windows, carvings, and embellishments. If this Hamlet would have been able to progress all the way to City rank, it was likely that a building like this would be a beacon of hope to anyone aligned with these people. To Joe, all the flowery artistry meant was that the structure itself was extra flimsy.

His weapons barely arrived before a squawking Penguin, knocking out the final support structure and reducing the final durability of the building to zero. The tilting remnants of the structure collapsed in a cloud of dust and snow, and a dark surge of accomplishment-fueled adrenaline rushed through Joe's mind. He pumped his fist in the air, smirking over the fact that he'd secured the last hit, claiming the victory for himself and advancing his questline.

Quest updated: This planet isn't big enough for both of us. 1/3 Elven settlements destroyed.

His exuberant dancing came to a swift end as beautiful voices cried out in alarm and fury at his interference. Joe immediately threw himself to the side, avoiding a particularly nasty spell that went on to hit another damaged building, bringing it down as well. "Time to switch over to guerrilla tactics!"

Seeing a likely escape route, Joe dove into a snowbank and began pushing through it with his enhanced physique. He burst out of the other side, keeping low as spells flitted through the snowbank behind him, melting it rapidly but giving him enough time to break out of the Elven line-of-sight.

The Ritualist called over his ritual orb of Constitution, the heart-shaped metal coming to a rest in front of him. With a fleeting thought, several of the other orbs unspooled, and Joe activated the bound ritual and spell, Planar Shift, summoning Morsum into the world around his orb in no time flat. "Hey there, my creepy friend! Want to chomp on an Elf or two?"

The cold, dead eyes of the Pseudo-Lich were already lit up with ghastly, ghostly green fire, but that didn't mean they couldn't *shine*. The head couldn't move itself, so Joe controlled the orb to make the summon nod vigorously. Then it rocketed into the air, twenty feet above Joe's shining, bald brow. Preparations complete, the Ritualist peeked around the corner of the rubble he was hiding behind, immediately locking eyes with an Elf who was obviously on the hunt for him.

The Elf was caught off guard by his sudden appearance, having apparently assumed he would need to root Joe out, then he'd be an easy target. As magic began to collect around his beautiful hands, Joe sent Morsum down from above. In the same instant, the Ritualist attacked with his prepared Dark Lightning Strike.

Gold-tinged lasers blasted out of the Elf's hand, the spell moving even faster than Joe's. It struck Joe directly in the face, as he hadn't even had an instant of time to dodge. His Exquisite Shell dispersed a good amount of it, the tiny facets of the spell causing him to shine like a disco ball as a chunk of the damage was mitigated before being absorbed.

Exquisite Shell: 10,859/12,002.

The light show cut off almost as soon as it hit Joe, his own dark-aligned lightning sizzling into the Elf and causing him to freeze for a moment.

That was all the time Morsum needed to latch onto the flailing opponent's neck like a vampire, its terrifying fangs piercing through the magical defenses surrounding the caster with ease. As Joe's current nemesis let out a gurgle of horror—somehow managing to still be melodious—the human forced himself back into the fight, shaking off the lingering realization that the attack he'd just been hit with was meant to be a channeled spell.

If he hadn't already had a duo of attacks on the way, he was near certain that the Elf would've pumped his entire mana pool into the attack, eventually melting Joe's head like it was a tempered chocolate dome over a decadent dessert.

Belatedly, Retaliation of Shadows came into effect, slapping the Elf across the face even as it attempted to pull the Lich skull off its throat. That was when Joe realized he was finally starting to truly participate in high-level combat: the spells and attacks were moving so quickly that even his automatic defenses were slower than the exchanges. Not wanting to give his adversary any help, but also unable to stop himself from taunting the shining being that had nearly destroyed him, Joe called over, "What're you even doing? If you actually manage to yank him off, all that does is rip your throat wide open!"

That earned him a pained glare, and the combatant Mage began struggling to cast additional magics. For a fraction of a second, Joe was confused as to why he hadn't already been hit by two or three more spells, but then realized that the fangs clamped onto the foe's neck likely were acting as a form of a spell silencer. If the Elf was trying to cast anything that required vocalizations, the spell would fail or rebound onto the caster. As he realized that he couldn't have planned this better if he tried, Joe let a ghost of a smile appear on his face and whirled a hand, the motion copied by his ritual orbs.

The remainder of his weapons began to orbit the Ritualist, and he sent them forward one-by-one to attack his target. The ritual orb of Intelligence was the swiftest, flashing through the air and driving into the Elf's inner thigh, where it was held back by the magical barrier the Elf was coated in. Sparks began flying as the drill pressed forward, attempting to sink into the flesh only fractions of an inch away.

Two more orbs had already been sent at that point, but seeing the sparks flying, Joe changed the target of his next one. It was a standard sphere of metal, having not yet been bound to a Characteristic, yet it worked perfectly as a hammer on the back wedge-shaped portion of the sharp one. As the orb slammed into the Intelligence-bound version, it provided enough force to shove the barrier out of the way. Golden-tinged blood flew as the spike drove into skin, then flesh, and a sharp whine announced it had found a bone and was attempting to move through that as well.

Joe activated Cone of Cold with a thought, the spell erupting from the tip of the spike and directly into his foe. Without giving his opponent a single opportunity to recover, the Ritualist beat him down with a barrage of magic, weapons, and the ever-increasing life drain from Morsum.

You have slain an Elf!

"No experience?" Joe waited a long moment, recalling his orbs to his bandolier, all except Morsum, who went back to hovering in the air. "You know what? I'm okay with that. I'm not a huge fan of incentivizing the murder of intelligent, sentient beings. Or... humanoids, I suppose. Kind of hard to forget that the highest-level monsters on Jotunheim are going to end up being at least as intelligent as we are."

He'd been surprised that their fight hadn't been interrupted, but as he began running down the street, Joe immediately understood why that had been the case. The final group of Elves had been overrun by monsters, likely when they'd sent one of their few remaining Mages to hunt down an intruder instead of focusing on self-preservation.

"Excellent! Now all I need to do is clear out the monsters and establish a connection with any survivors. I'm sure we'll have a great rapport after I helped destroy the last little bit of their town and leaders. This is going to go great."

CHAPTER SEVENTEEN

Luckily, he had plenty of experience fighting off monsters. Joe spent the next forty minutes or so finishing off the last of the Penguins and Hoardings, the only monsters that had come out during the current Beast Wave. The defenders had done a spectacular job with holding back the tide of bodies until the very end. He chuckled quietly to himself as he kept a wary eye out for any Elven survivors. "They just weren't good enough to stop *me*."

Eventually, the final monster was slain by a combination of Joe hunting it and barely more than one hundred human survivors working together. As the dust settled, the surviving Hamlet folk turned their eyes on him, though they put away their weapons before cautiously approaching him.

Joe tried to assess them as fairly as possible, but no matter how he looked at them, he could tell that almost all of the humans were likely here under duress. It wasn't just their poorly maintained weapons and armor, the way that they shivered in the constant debuffing wind of Jotunheim, or the fact that they looked absolutely exhausted. No, it was the fact that they were looking at him with a mixture of excitement and suspicion, which slowly shifted to glimmers of hope.

Taking a deep breath, the Ritualist put a smile on his face and began working to swiftly gain their trust. "Hello, everyone! I'm here to let you know about a Town that's been secured and would be happy to take you in!"

Immediately, their faces fell, and people began looking at him with more intense scrutiny. Joe internally cursed himself lightly, then let his own smile fall. "Okay, fair enough. Let me be as honest as possible. I came here with almost the entirety of the Dwarven nation, and if you were to come with me, you'd have to fight for every scrap of respect and opportunity. But! I'm now a member of the council, and I'm able to represent humanity directly to the leaders of the Town."

People began speaking to each other quietly, clearly debating still on whether to just attack him or listen to him further. Joe glared around at them, and it could have been the cold, the fact that they just suffered a huge loss, or perhaps he was actually more intimidating than he felt, but nobody made a move. "I can give you a safe respawn point, a chance to get out of this world, and a way to build your skills and combat ability. Yeah, you're going to have to fight for everything you earn. But if you're not okay with fighting, why would you want to stay out here, where there aren't even any walls to slow down the monsters?"

The Ritualist let out a sigh of relief as he saw his Dark Charisma starting to sway them. He'd realized that he had been appealing to the incorrect emotions to leverage his capabilities to their fullest, which is why he'd switched away from his planned speech. A brown-haired man stepped forward, his eyes intense as he marched up to Joe, stopping less than a foot away from him as though his close proximity would allow him to discern any lies. "Three questions for you. Can you guarantee us what you just said… or are we going to follow you straight into a prison cell if we listen?"

"I promise that we'll get there." Joe nodded slightly.

"There's a good chance that, as soon as we get back, you'll be surrounded by troops and held until I'm able to get an area set up for you. You're going to be the first group I bring back, because you're the first that I found. That means we'll have to make an entirely new plan for what to do with you."

The man looked back over his shoulder, getting a few nods from the other assembled men. Then he got back into his strong position, towering over Joe. "Second question, then: you said you're going to give us a chance to get out of here. You mean this area or Jotunheim as a whole?"

"My goal is to have the bifrost in our city as soon as possible. We've already been able to secure our settlement as a Town, and we're building up toward City rank as we speak." Joe gestured around at the group that was growing larger by the second. "That's one of the reasons I'm out recruiting at the moment. One of the requirements for a city is a population of a hundred thousand. So I need you, just not as much as you need me."

"Glad to see where we stand in negotiations." The spokesperson for the destroyed Hamlet muttered with great annoyance. "Last question then, is your Town all male, all female, or mixed?"

"Uh. *What?*" Joe scanned the people in the crowd around him again, this time with a specific thought in mind. He started to laugh quietly as he realized what was going on here. "You mean to tell me that the Elves sent you through as groups of men or women, but not *both*?"

"It's supposed to help us temper our minds. We were told that, after a few years of advancing in the theocracy, we might be trusted to live within a few miles of each other. So long as we had *chaperones,* due to being under seventy-five years old." There was a collective grunt of dissatisfaction from the entire group, which made Joe break down laughing.

"I've never been so happy that I joined the Dwarves!" Joe collected himself quickly, the glares from the people surrounding him helping with that greatly. "Yeah, not something I've really spent a lot of time thinking about, but we have tens of thousands of humans. No one's been splitting us up, so... mixed?"

Not a single person chose to stay behind.

The entire group marched out of the destroyed settlement, following Joe as he tried to retrace his steps to where he'd fallen out of the sky. It took a while to find the exact spot he had landed, as he'd come in from the top and burrowed through the snow for a while before poking out. As soon as the location was found, Joe dug out a large space and immediately built a shrine.

There were dozens of exclamations of surprise as the building appeared out of nothing but what seemed to be floating fire and mana. Joe was glad that there were no debuffs impacting his ability to work on this at the moment, and he was able to maintain an air of mystery and power. He wanted to offer the survivors a means of escape, a new home where they could begin to rebuild their lives without the strange, stringent rules forced on them by near-immortal beings. The Ritualist muttered to himself as he worked, shaking his head in confusion. "Say what you will about the Dwarves, they don't particularly care what you do... so long as you can afford it."

With the shrine complete, Joe activated the fast travel system, then turned to address the raggedy survivors. "Give me ten minutes to talk to the people over there, then choose your destination as 'Novusheim'. All you need to do is touch the altar and pay the mana cost."

An instant later, Joe was standing in a town square over a thousand miles away. A quick glance around the area showed that none of the new settlers had ignored his request for ten minutes, but a dozen messengers had noticed his arrival and were sprinting toward him. Barely managing to stay ahead of them, Joe Omnivaulted toward the council chambers and burst past the receptionist.

Upon flinging open the door of the room and gathering a half-dozen startled glances, Joe realized something was amiss.

Grandmaster Snow raised an eyebrow at him archly, "You're *late*. Did you not get the memo?"

"I didn't." Joe opened his mouth to apologize then shook his head sharply and refocused. "I just got back from finishing off an Elven settlement, and I have a couple hundred refugees that want to come to Novusheim."

"*Elves?*" One of the councilmen thundered darkly, the air in the room immediately turning dense and stale as his aura erupted into the environment around him.

"No, of course not." Joe waved away that question, and the sudden tension ramping up in the room quieted and swirled into confusion. "It was an Elven town, but they're all dead. All I have are the human survivors who want a fresh start and a chance at earning for themselves again."

"There's no *way* we can allow—"

The blustering councilman was cut off by another, this one nearly as pale as Grandmaster Snow. He was by far the oldest Dwarf that Joe had yet met, and he was petting at his beard as he spoke. "But we *must* take them in. I can already tell the arguments that our fellow councilman is going to make. If we are to attain the status of a City, we're going to need to either rely on humans that bypass Alfheim entirely or work on rehabilitating the humans that come here with the Elven theocracy yoked to their shoulders."

Grandmaster Snow frowned, and her next words were ones of dissent. "I'm not certain we're ready to begin receiving outsiders. How are we supposed to trust them? Trade with them? How will we know if they're selling our secrets to their Elven allies?"

"We could read their mail." Joe suggested brightly and sarcastically, as he had no intention to do anything of the sort. Seeing her wince, he knew his point had been made. "Look, we're going to have to let them earn their place in our eventual City. I was thinking we should make a small suburb within the walls that monsters will pass through to come here. That way, even if there are still Elven sympathizers among them, they'll need to fight off monsters—even if it's just to stay alive."

"Doc? How would you go about this rehabilitation that Joe is proposing?" Snow turned to the ancient Dwarf, who'd been silently considering them as they spoke.

"What a fun day to come in person instead of sending a proxy!" The old Dwarf chuckled ruefully, then gestured at the table. The stone top shifted as thousands of tiny stone sutures erupted across the entirety of it. In a moment, it had turned into a strange, tiny, to-scale replica of the entire Town of Novusheim. There were a few additions to the walls, which the Dwarf pointed out to begin explaining his thoughts.

"Instead of a single, small suburb within our walls, I propose *four* of them." He tapped the outermost small circular section of wall, nearest the entrance to the labyrinth. "All of the converts to our cause will start here. Many of them will die. Many, *many* times. We can issue a quest for them to defeat monsters and protect our interests in the area. Councilman Joe, your shrines act as a respawn point for your people, do they not?"

"They *can* be used that way." Joe confirmed with a hint of confusion in his voice.

"Perfection. In that case, each of these four areas will have a shrine that the humans are bound to. When they're slain, they'll return to this same small suburb. Once they've completed the first of what will no doubt be a lengthy series of quests, they'll be allowed to move up to the second section. There they'll have greater luxury, freedom, and ability to work on skills outside of their fighting prowess. At this point, we'll allow them to retain a portion of the materials they collect from monsters."

"You want them to have *crafting* stations?" The Dwarf at the table who spoke with a dissenting voice was nearly shaking in anger, and Joe looked at him with great confusion. He'd never seen this Dwarf before, but seeing as how Doc had sent a proxy, perhaps this furious person was here as one as well. "What're we going to do, *trade* with them? Trust that their goods won't be booby-trapped?"

"Yes. We will trade with them," Doc calmly stated, reaching into his front pocket and pulling out a pair of perfectly round spectacles. Joe winced at that, hoping that this wasn't a sign that the Dwarf was a member of the Scholars Guild. As far as he knew, there was still a bounty on his head from them. "The further out they are from being full members of our fine *City*, the less they'll get in exchange. By the time they're admitted into full membership, they'll be so accustomed to working with us, trading with us, finally earning full price and discounts, that there's no way they'd ever go back. At that stage, all we can do is consider their rehabilitation complete and hope for the best."

"I *insist* that we make them wear an identifying name tag that's bound to each of them." The angry Dwarf could see that he was on the losing side of this argument, and tried to throw in conditions. "If they venture outside of their assigned area, closer to the Town, the towers must attack them. Otherwise, I won't agree to this and will fight against it every step of the way."

"Ugh... Master Frenzy, I understand that you're new to the council." Grandmaster Snow took a calming breath before continuing, "but you are quickly following the path of your predecessor, Master Wrath. Perhaps we could—"

"I can only take that as a compliment." Frenzy spoke with obvious passion about the subject. "Master Wrath abdicated his position in an attempt to focus on the final stages before he achieves the rank of Grandmaster. Knowing I'm walking a similar path—"

Joe interrupted the argument as it began to spiral. "I like the idea, actually. Even when I was in the army back on contemporary Earth, we were made to wear badges with embedded RFID chips. Without them, our own people would've fired on us, and our automated defenses would've brought us down. This is no different in my mind, and I absolutely agree with the motion Master Frenzy has proposed."

That stopped the argument cold, and even the fiery new councilmember seemed taken aback. "You'd willingly put limitations on your own people? This proves my point. How terrible are humans that you have so little faith in them?"

"On the record, or off the record?" Joe queried the Master, trying to make a joke. When the expressions around the table turned grave, he rolled his eyes and gave a proper answer. "Just like with anyone else, we have a bell curve. Most people are perfectly fine. Some are paragons of light, virtue, and justice, while others are… not. Trust, but verify. I'm all for it."

The door to the chamber slammed open, and a Master Sergeant of the Legion roared out, "We've captured enemy combatants in the middle of Town!"

All of the commotion was halted as threads of mana wove around the entire area and stopped anyone from doing anything rash, Grandmaster Snow had finally decided to take control of the situation. "Let's get this handled. Joe, if you're going to bring lost sheep back to the fold, it is incumbent upon *you* to provide them with a stable."

"Yeah, *yeah*. I'll go get the bubbles."

CHAPTER EIGHTEEN

After making temporary housing for each of the people who had rejoined what Joe considered the most civilized, polite society on the planet, he set out to make sure they had food and some comfort, at the bare minimum. He explained the rules of their stay, and to his surprise, got over a hundred notifications that people had accepted a quest he'd given them. After getting past his initial shock, Joe realized that he was considered a leader of this Town, and it only made sense that he'd be able to offer quests to people for the betterment of the Town as a whole.

Even so, when he got back to the Town Hall, he was quite annoyed to see that the overall morale of the Town had taken a nosedive. Not only were the new additions considered extremely negative, but there'd been very few Dwarves happy to see a new group of humans formerly aligned with their racial enemy being escorted to the edge of Town to help defend them. "I guess I'm going to have to introduce new people pretty slowly if I'm going to... no, wait, I can just have them appear at the outer shrine in the future. That'll make *everyone* involved quite a bit more comfortable."

With all of the fires put out, all of the tasks he needed to complete done for the moment, Joe stepped across the world, using his system of shrines, and stood in the snow once more. Squawking, snarling, and growling echoed over to him, so he cautiously slunk his way through the precipitation and peeked toward where the settlement had once stood. The Ritualist needed to hold himself back from letting out a low whistle.

Thousands upon thousands of monsters were milling about the area, clearly the result of several more Beast Waves that had arrived while Joe had been working back in his own Town. "That's right, just because the Town Hall is destroyed doesn't mean the rest of the monsters don't show up. I wonder... is there a way I can exploit that?"

Joe spent a few minutes fantasizing about creating a ritual that would be strong enough to wipe out this enormous throng of beasts in a single fell swoop. Since he wouldn't have to worry about any collateral damage, loss of life or levels, it was at the very least *possible*. He muttered quietly to himself as he slid on his belly back toward the shrine, "I think the mantle of this planet is too deep to make a volcano a viable option... maybe I should figure out a way to convince Havoc to drop meteors on a location like he was hinting at being able to do."

Then he remembered that he'd need a firm foundation in earth and fire magics, and decided to give up that plan for the moment. At least unless he could convince his mentor to part with a spell diagram that he could convert into a ritual. Joe let his power fantasies play out in his head as he worked on his next bubble, but he didn't fully relax until he was once more in the air and speeding along. "Let's put a little extra mana here and warm this up... *there* we go."

He massaged his half-frozen fingers, pulled out his notes and grimoire, then got into a proper wizardly mindset. Eyes flicking back and forth as he scanned the words on his paper, Joe reminded himself exactly where he'd been in his thought process.

Hours passed in this way, as his bubble hurtled along at a

consistent speed and heading. To his excitement, as well as a hint of consternation, as his transportation was reaching its maximum range, the chaotic, magical currents of Jotunheim began to whisper to him.

It took Joe a few moments to realize that it wasn't some creepy extra-planar being. It was his Hidden Sense skill screaming to him, tinged with his Magical Synesthesia as an afterthought. As soon as he made the realization, Joe's eyes went wide, he scooped his materials into his storage, then he began examining the area he was flying over in greater detail. "There's something out there... something significant. Powerful and important enough to call out to me through the obscuring environment. Down we go!"

Lashing out with his knife, Joe once more had the unpleasant experience of dropping out of the sky. This time, he attempted to land feet-first but ended up stuck in a pencil dive pose nearly ten feet below the surface of the top layer of snow. Joe tried to think of the positives of the situation and decided that the fluffy drifts managing to collect to this height was a sign that nearly nothing came through these parts, willingly or otherwise.

Rather than struggling to free himself in an undignified manner, he simply set up a Field Array and converted all of the snow above him into Trash-tier aspects. Then it was simply a matter of closing his eyes and following his extra senses as the feelings became louder and louder.

Eventually, no matter which way he walked, the sensations began to get softer. Since there was obviously nothing on the surface, Joe started digging. Enormous chunks of snow vanished one after another until he hit the hard surface of the planet itself. Even then, he needed to go deeper. Chunk after chunk of stone and earth was destroyed as he sought out what his mind swore was there.

Then, in a very unexpected twist, one of the chunks refused to fully dissolve, leaving behind a strange spire of dull metal. Walking over to it, Joe tapped on its surface and gasped in pain as a huge chunk of his mana was sucked out of him, as well as having the odd effect decimate his magical protections.

Exquisite Shell: 1,200/12,002

At the same time as he pulled his hand back, the surface that he'd just brushed against shifted from a dull metal to a slightly-glowing enchanted metal. "Sure didn't like that."

Joe still had no idea what he was looking at, and he decided that it would be in his best interest to dig out the entirety of whatever he'd found. Dozens of Field Arrays later, he still hadn't uncovered it, but he'd at least determined that it was a *structure*. Specifically, a building of some kind. There were all kinds of reasons that was an exciting prospect to him, but the glow that had started near the tip of this enormous obelisk had covered the entirety of the surface he'd unearthed; and there was no way he was going to risk touching it again, let alone trying to break in.

It took nearly an hour of digging around the metallic structure before he found something that could be a door, but as he approached it, his senses began to scream that this was a bad idea. Joe paused, took a deep, annoyed breath, and walked away. "Time to get some outside assistance."

He was pleased that he'd at least gotten most of the distance he needed out of this trip, so he didn't mind putting down the next node in the shrine network he was building.

Within an hour of returning and explaining the situation, a full expedition had been declared. Dozens of Dwarves, as well as hundreds of humans, were swarming around the strange structure deep under the snowy surface of Jotunheim. The bizarre building was exuding an aura of mystery and power, somehow completely untouched by time. It was also giving off quite a bit more light than Joe wanted, seeing as nearly every single person that had come along had found some way to poke the building and lose a huge chunk of their mana to it.

No matter how many warnings they gave out, every single human had touched it at least once, some more than that. Most of the Dwarves had also done so, but they'd at least tried to be subtle about it. Joe could only roll his eyes at how predictable everyone was.

Still, he couldn't blame them. His magical skills were still tingling, filling him with anticipation. Anyone who had any kinds of treasure-seeking skills was having a similar reaction, but the Dwarves were treating this with a strange academic detachment. As the person who had found the building, as well as dug it out, Joe had total say over who got to do what with it, which meant he got first access to any information. It worked out well for him, but he hadn't been able to make a decision on it until a scholarly Dwarf strode toward him with gleaming eyes.

Her mustache was bouncing in place as she tried to hold her smile back, failing when she got within a few feet of Joe. "Excellent, I get to be the one to tell you all about this. I do hope you'll remember my contribution when we unseal the vault."

Even if he hadn't been interested, that phrase would've caught all of Joe's attention. "A *vault*, you say?"

"Ohh, yeah," she breathed out, practically hissing in excitement. "As far as we can tell, going by the intricate enchantments and markings on this building, we believe that this was a vault for the elite hunting groups of Vanaheim. We'll need to break it open to be certain... still, there's a good shot that it's full. It's going to be difficult to make this happen, but the potential rewards are too enticing to ignore. It could be a cache of powerful weapons, legendary armors, preserved trade goods, or perhaps relics from the distant past that could explain the history of this world."

Any of those options would be amazing, and it took Joe a few moments before he could trust himself to speak. "How long do you think before we can get in?"

"Not soon," was all she could answer, though that statement was *firm*. "There are other, more pressing concerns as well. The presence of living people, as well as the glow coming off of this, is going to get pretty noticeable to the denizens of this planet. We need to think about setting up defenses, and figure out what we're going to do when attacked. I'd recommend putting out an official quest for anyone who wants to help protect this, but the rewards are going to have to be pretty good."

Joe's face fell. "I don't know what I can offer people. I kind of doubt they'd take soap, and we just don't know what's in there. If it's not something easily divided up, I don't know if we can offer a percentage or—"

"So long as you offer a part of the profit to the Town, I think you can use your position as a councilman to make a fairly open-ended quest reward." She shrugged at his plight, earning herself a light glare from Joe.

"That's a pretty cavalier attitude to have when spending someone else's money." His words indicated his annoyance well enough that he didn't feel the need to say anything more.

All that earned him was a raised eyebrow as she gestured at the enormous structure. "Joe, I know a bit about your class. Even if there's nothing in there worth having, you get to take this building with you. Or, at least you'd be able to build your own version of it, if we manage to remove those magical protections. I'm pretty sure you're the one who stands to gain the most profit from this place, no matter what happens."

He couldn't fault her logic, so he discussed with her exactly what the phrasing of the quest should be, then brought that to a few other people to see if they could see any loopholes that would cause him annoyance in the future.

Getting the go-ahead from several of his trusted sources let Joe feel at least *better* about the idea. Still, he was somewhat uncomfortable with the idea of being the source of quests. He had seen what could happen when you didn't pay up promptly and had no interest in that terrible punishment landing squarely on his shoulders. Unfortunately, there was no great alternative, so Joe spoke the words that offered a general quest to anyone from Novusheim who was in good standing.

"I need people to defend researchers as they attempt to crack into a building we found in the wastes of Jotunheim. We need warriors, mages, and people of all types to attempt this. The quest reward will be based on contribution, as well as the value of what's found within the protected building. To accept the quest, simply go to a shrine and set your destination as 'mysterious vault'."

He tried to control his breathing as he had over a hundred people accept the quest within five seconds, and the number began rapidly counting upward as more and more people appeared in the area.

"Great... yeah..." Joe fought against the tide of arrivals, moving around until he found an empty area. "I guess this is taken care of for now, so I'm gonna keep going."

Amidst the hubbub of the suddenly chaotic area, only one researcher watched as a shimmering bubble filled with an anxious bald guy shot into the sky and flew away.

CHAPTER NINETEEN

Several days of traveling in the air and planting his shrines felt nearly anticlimactic after the duo of back-to-back successes. Joe was itching to destroy another village or find a hidden gem like the strange obelisk from the elites of Vanaheim. Abyss, at this point he'd even take finding a field of snow flowers he could use to start growing local flora in his greenhouse.

But, instead, Joe was merely traveling over a vast, empty world, as per usual. He couldn't be too upset about the forced alone time, as he was making great progress on altering rituals. As it turned out, figuring out how to cleanse the Ritual of Sacrificial Regeneration had been far too complex with its Master-level quotients and variables, so Joe had set it aside in favor of doing a few less intense versions as practice. Currently, he was trying to figure out a way to combine several of his other rituals into a single one with a unified purpose.

"Gravedigger's Requiem, Ritual of Proximity, Ritual of Structural Repair." Joe had found multiple points of similarity between the three magical diagrams, and he was looking for a way to get ahead of the power curve of the upcoming Beast Waves. They hadn't had to deal with any kind of underground attack yet, as they'd set up their mines outside of Novusheim. But somehow, Joe had the feeling that, when they upgraded to a City, they'd be tested in an entirely new way—not just with new monsters.

"If I can set this up to go off when it senses something burrowing, maybe I can collapse the tunnels those creatures are making, taking out any beasts following along behind them." Joe was still stuck on the 'intent' phase of his project and was trying to determine exactly what should happen as the end result. "If I can work in the Ritual of Structural Repair at the same time, I can keep the walls up on the surface from collapsing as the underground tunnels are destroyed."

Joe made a few more notes, and slowly his vision began to come to life. "What if, instead of collapsing the tunnels, we filled them in with surrounding materials? Then, all I'd need to do is set up the ritual to pull loose dirt and stone from the surroundings from the entirety of a single layer of the ground. Eventually, that would make everything in Town sink a few inches. If it happened enough, perhaps the city would someday be entirely underground."

Something told him the Dwarves wouldn't mind that too much, so long as there were limits to how deep it got. Still, there were plenty of issues to work out, but Joe felt that he was starting to get a proper setup going. He continued working on that for a while, and when his brain started to feel like it was going to melt, he switched over to simply continuing his work on creating a functioning Ritual of Featherfall.

That was easier mentally, because he simply had to generate something that already existed, instead of designing it from scratch. Still, it was slow going, due to the sheer amount of math he had to account for. Depending on the height he began to fall from, he needed different equations. If he was falling from a height below where he would reach terminal velocity, the ritual needed to expend much more power in a short amount of time; whereas if he was falling from a *greater* height, he needed to create some form of altimeter. That would let the ritual ping the ground and wait to activate the main portions of the ritual until Joe was within a certain range of hitting an object.

There weren't many things that made him happy to do high-order math, but falling out of the sky twice within the same number of days was one of them.

Originally, he'd intended to just create the ritual as it was, but he'd been spending more time with Master Stu, and the Dwarf seemed especially extremely eager for him to rely on this ritual, for some reason. That made him cautious, and he eventually found the issue: the magical diagram was optimized for a different planet with a different mana density, as well as slightly different gravitational pull. There was a good shot that, if he'd used this, and it was set for Midgard or even Alfheim, he would've hit the ground at full speed before it even started to slow him down.

Eventually, his bubble landed. Joe created a shrine and popped back to Novusheim, ready to get a good night's sleep and do it all again the next day. Mana drained out of him, and the Ritualist appeared thousands of miles away from his previous location.

It was the smoke that told him that something had gone terribly wrong while he was off gallivanting around. With great concern, his eyes swept over the scene, expecting to be met with chaos and destruction. Luckily, although it was evident that a brutal Beast Wave had occurred, there was no sign of damage to the civilian sectors.

Still, it seems like a section of the killing corridors was on fire, he could see cracks in the innermost walls, and hundreds of corpses were being pulled in for processing. "Well, at least the water towers are going to be refilled today. We're all going to need a shower after this is fixed up."

Mentally rolling up his sleeves, Joe ran to the nearest cluster of workers who were milling about so that he could figure out where he was most needed. "I just got back into Town, can someone fill me in on what happened?"

Eyes that were blank with shock slowly gained a bit of life as they registered the presence of the member of the council in their midst. Yet, it was a human who walked over, happy to have someone to speak with. The Dwarves sank back into their uncharacteristic moroseness, and Joe tried to memorize their faces so he could find information on them later. For an extremely warlike society, to have people this unused to the effects of combat seemed… odd.

"It was one abyss of a Beast Wave, partner!" The man spoke with a clearly Texan accent, going from empty-handed to holding up a bowl of jambalaya for Joe to chow down on while they spoke. "Looks like we still get bosses coming every once in a while, even if we don't have a Town upgrade going on. That was one mighty fearsome creature that was particularly unhappy we were in its path. A bunch of humans died right away. For some reason, they were practically sitting ducks at the entrance to the walls. No one's heard much from them yet, since almost all of them are still waiting on respawn. But to hear the Dwarves talk about it…"

Here his face gained a slightly pained expression as he quickly glanced around to see if he was in earshot of any Dwarves. "They almost seem glad? Don't suppose you'd know why that is, do ya? Seems strange that they'd want their allies to suffer."

As thanks for the soup and the information, Joe filled in the chatty man about the situation with the humans and the requirement that the Dwarves had made for their rehabilitation. Even as he spoke, Joe found himself deeply dissatisfied with the callous treatment of his fellow man, and he resolved to do something about it.

He'd been holding off on creating one type of tower that Socar had offered to him: a bunker-like structure that would allow people to enter it and attack with relative impunity. But if he was going to force people to stand and fight, he was at least going to give them a chance at living through it. Otherwise, this wasn't going to end with people happy that they were joining Dwarven society; it was going to turn into hundreds of people ready to burn down the city as soon as they got access to it.

After mopping up the last vestiges of his meal, Joe wasted no further time in moving out to the walls to assess the damage and organize the necessary repairs. Creating a Ritual of Structural Repair was very straightforward for the Ritualist at this point—especially as he'd been spending lots of time in his bubbles recently studying it and trying to break down each individual part. That made finding a stone or other object that could contain the ritual the most difficult portion of creating it, keeping in mind that it was best to use something that wouldn't break down too quickly under the effects of Jotunheim's environment.

Making a half-dozen of the rituals, he passed the objects off to work crews that had been assigned to him, sending them off to fix the damage that had been done to the walls. After a quick survey of the stonework, Joe grimaced as he realized how desperately they needed to find a way to enchant the high-tier stone against cold and extreme impacts. "It's going to take so long to repair each individual section... still, there should be plenty of time before the next Beast Wave hits."

Repairing the walls was one of the easiest tasks that needed to be done, even if it would be extremely time-consuming. Far more frustrating was the fact that Joe needed to replace multiple fallen towers. That was going to require aspects, time, and mana. Most of the towers that had fallen had been fully destroyed upon impact with the ground, rendering the Ritual of Structural Repair useless on them. There was a strong likelihood that the ritual that had been assigned to them had been destroyed as well, which would in turn shatter any of the stabilization cubes that had been set into the claw-like edifices.

"Four fixes because one little section of wall went down. Bleh. Looks like I have my work cut out for me." Joe had never been afraid of hard work, but at the same time, he didn't want to get trapped in a repetitive loop of his talents creating something then being forced to *maintain* them forever. Not at the cost of being unable to further pursue his craft. "It's a prison sentence if I need to keep doing work without meaning. Honestly, I don't know what I'd do if I couldn't delegate most of this off."

He let out a sigh of relief at his forethought, turning his attention to the task he'd set for himself of creating Rare-ranked bunkers. When he went to the area where the humans had been setting up camp, he found a group of hopeless, despondent people who were trapped between two options: stay, fight, and die; or leave and try to survive in the frozen wasteland surrounding them.

Joe didn't offer them an alternative fighting area immediately. First, he replaced the bubble rituals that had been destroyed by the rampaging beast, resupplying the humans with shelter. Then, he made sure that a hot meal and drinks were brought out for them and had them relax as he and his temporary workers began creating defensive encampments.

The bunker was very straightforward to make. Essentially, it was a large single room covered on all sides with a layer of dense Rare-ranked metal. When the first of them had been completed, he stepped back to admire his handiwork and realized that, when the back door was shut, it would look almost exactly like the shell of a box turtle. The main differences were that there was an open area where weapons could poke out. "Plus, it's a building—not a turtle. Heh. Why is Jaxon living in my head today?"

For some reason, that inane thought made Joe laugh, and he started planning out the placement of the next bunker. They were large enough that he couldn't just drop a bunch at a time, but small enough that monsters should go around them in an effort to get to the Town Hall instead of attacking the building directly. "Pretty sure I'm just making traffic circles for monsters. But, if it works, and it keeps people safe, it's worth doing!"

He waved over the nearest group of relocated people, who were looking at him with great admiration in their eyes. Before Joe could say anything, the tall spokesman that he'd interacted with in the past marched right over to him, thrust out a hand, and gave Joe a firm handshake. "We thought you lied to us, and this was just going to be another form of torture. Thanks for not making us want you dead anymore."

"I can see why they chose you to speak for them. You're... articulate." Joe could understand their feelings, so he didn't press the issue further. Instead, he brought everyone over to the new 'tower' and showed them how to use it properly. The openings for weapons and spells to exit didn't appear unless the large metal ramp was pulled up and secured to the side of the safe haven. This was to ensure that enemies surrounding the building couldn't prepare a nasty surprise for anyone who was running to get into it.

After he was done with the bunker, Joe took a bit more time to see what other issues the people were suffering from. Unsurprisingly, it was mostly the same issues that they originally had in the center of Town. For one, the false sky didn't extend out this far, leaving them with two weeks of day or night depending on where they were in the cycle. Joe promised to remedy this, as well as setting up a ritual to give them clean water whenever they needed it.

With their basic needs met—or at least having a plan in place to fix them—Joe felt confident in taking a deep breath and turning to the next task on his list. He looked up at the entrance to the walls, where there was a conspicuous lack of defensive ritual towers.

"It's almost like the person in charge of moving the towers out here wanted to see some Elven sympathizers suffer." He rolled his shoulders, pulling out the blueprint for his most updated and upgraded ritual tower of Infernal Conflagration. Socar had already agreed to Joe's plan, though he did so with a pained expression and muttered calculations as the Ritualist took the agreement at face value and ran off. "Let's go ahead and make sure this Town is safe for anyone who needs it. Kinda weird that I'm going to protect people with blasts of unholy fire, but whatever it takes."

CHAPTER TWENTY

Bang!

Joe had been standing before the ritual tower, his notes open in front of him as he worked to duplicate his newest version of the spell diagram for the Ritual of Infernal Conflagration. It was a complex spell diagram, designed to unleash a devastating infernal inferno on the packed ranks of enemies that would be swarming below, and with his changes, it should work well to create lingering flames that would devastate enormous swathes of the enemy.

But, as soon as he started channeling his mana, carefully tracing the intricate circles of his ritual, things went wrong an instant before it reached the final stages. The nearly complete ritual detonated in a cascade of fire, unleashed energies sparking off stone and rebounding from his magical defenses as the ritual tower crumbled into rubble from the blast.

Joe was given exactly three and a half seconds to reassess his life choices as he zipped through the air like an arrow shot downward, impacting the packed snow and dirt of the ground with enough force to knock the wind out of him, even through his Exquisite Shell.

He bounced and rolled across the ground for a few dozen feet before coming to a painful stop. Dust settling around him, Joe slowly pushed himself up to his feet, wincing at the bruises and cuts that had appeared on his body from the sheer force of his own protections slapping against his flesh. He blankly surveyed the destruction around him, even as stones continued to rain down. Disappointment in himself flashed through his mind, but he gritted his teeth and stood tall. "So... that one is too unstable for practical use, it seems. Back to the drawing board."

Grumbling under his breath, the Ritualist realized that he would now need to spend even *more* time refining and perfecting his spell diagrams before attempting to ensconce it in the towers. "Abyss, I really thought I had it that time. Where'd it go wrong? I bet it was probably somewhere in the pigeon-holing problem set on the fourth circle..."

With a sigh, Joe shook his head and started back toward the center of Town. He'd need to move a different, *functional* tower out into that space until he could get a handle on this one. It was frustrating that the continued safety of Novusheim, and especially its newest residents, felt like it had been plopped directly on his shoulders as though a seagull had passed overhead and–

"No, don't think of your responsibilities as a metaphor for bird poop," he chastised himself gently, working to put the failed attempt behind him. There was far too much at stake to get sucked down that rabbit hole at the moment, and he would work on revamping the spell diagram when he was once more traveling via bubble.

For a moment, he considered joining the workers in clearing away the debris and salvaging what materials they could from the destroyed tower, but just as he was about to offer, he noticed that luxury goods were exchanging hands at a rapid pace, nearly half of the people wearing smug grins while the others seemed sullen. When he realized that there were active bets on whether he would succeed or not, Joe decided they could handle the cleanup by themselves.

With that thought in mind, he hurried back to the enormous metal block imbued with his Master-rank Ritual of the Traveling Civilization. Seeing it used so casually by the townspeople to simply move the towers back and forth like a mana-intensive shell game was a bit frustrating, but that was just his inner craftsman being insulted about how his current masterwork was being used. "We need a couple acid bubble towers at the entrance to the killing corridors. Also, if I find that our new residents are suffering in that space without magical support, I'll fire everyone that's on shift that day."

Seeing as there were very few paying jobs in the town at the moment, Joe's words were taken with deadly seriousness. Instead of any backtalk, or snarking like he had originally expected from the Dwarves, they simply nodded at him with grave expressions. The annoyance on their faces reminded Joe that he had a scheduled meeting coming up with Master Stu, and he let out his own disgruntled sigh as he hurried over to his workshop.

The Dwarf was already sitting inside, and the guard raised an eyebrow at Joe before pulling the muzzle away and walking out the door. Stu spat on the floor and glared at the human. "Just because you aren't here doesn't mean I'm not doing my time."

By now, Joe's Neutrality Aura had fixed up his minor scrapes and bruises while ensuring that he was clean and presentable. Unfortunately, it didn't impact his mood. Already, he was glaring at the Dwarf, and when he slapped his notes on the table and shoved them over to the Master, the ex-councilman started to grin. "Hard day, usurper?"

"I just had one of my rituals explode in my face," Joe calmly announced, frustrated that he needed to say it aloud. "Your task today is to look at the highlighted areas and tell me why my alteration of intent on these circles caused it to short-circuit and detonate."

Then he did his utmost to ignore the Master of Sarcasm, who eventually realized he wasn't being listened to and started inspecting the work. Both of them did their own tasks diligently, although if Joe had been holding a physical quill instead of his aspect inscriber, it would've snapped in his hand at least three times as he worked on a few backup ritual diagrams for use on new towers. Eventually, the Dwarf started chuckling, and Joe leaned back in his chair and stared at the ceiling. "*What*, Stu?"

"Oh, not much. I'm just impressed by how you managed to butcher this section so badly. Seriously, your talent in rituals is greatly surpassed by your apparent affinity for butchery. I think you should be out cleaning carcasses, not—"

"Tell me or get out and forfeit your time," Joe demanded impatiently, snatching the document out of the Dwarf's hand. He looked over the section Stu had been indicating, seeing nothing wrong with the variables or immutable objects he'd set. Eventually, he slapped it down on the table and raised a brow at the Dwarf to show his impatience.

"Not even a casual attempt to better yourself by solving your own issues." The Dwarf shook his head in mock sadness. "That's fine, I not only understand, I *expected* it. Look here, you wanted *this* to create a lingering wall of flames so badly the main focus of the diagram shifted. You tried to give this two competing main functions. The *wrong one* is for it to leave a wall of infernal fire for enemies to flash fry in. Unfortunately for you, the purpose of this spell is to create an explosive burst of fire. When a spell is told to detonate *and* told to linger, it won't do either. It'll just hurt itself in its confusion."

"I truly dislike how competent you are." Joe let out a sigh as he confirmed what the Dwarf had been pointing out. "I feel like it'd be easier for both of us if your skills were as bad as your attitude."

The Ritualist stuck with the rest of the session, glad at least that he had a starting point for his next attempts. When he was done supervising Stu's community service for the day, he hurried over to his shrine and took a step that landed him thousands of miles away.

"I'd literally rather sit in a tiny enclosed space doing my homework for the next nine hours than anything else." Joe had slightly shifted how he traveled. As the bubble appeared around him, he pulled a passable attempt at a bean bag chair made of monster hide and filled with shaved Hoardling hair out of his storage device. He settled in with a sigh, and a small lap desk also appeared. Now traveling in comfort, Joe began attempting to fix his errors with the Ritual of Infernal Conflagration.

Hours passed in this manner, until a shift in light caught Joe's eye. This far off the ground, he could see night approaching like a curtain being drawn slowly across the surface of the world. He was heading directly into it and would likely enter it within the next day or two.

Just as he was about to turn back to his diagram and put the finishing touches in, Joe saw something else extremely strange, especially in Jotunheim's environment. "Is that... *smoke*? If there's smoke, that means fire. If there's fire, that means people! It makes me wonder... why am I finding so many towns as I move in this direction?"

A single strike from his dagger later, the Ritualist was falling through the air in a manner he'd gotten far too accustomed with. Before he reached the ground, Joe snapped his fingers as he realized the most likely culprit. "This must've been the path the bifrost took when moving away from our Town! It probably moves in a straight line for a set amount of distance before turning or moving into a different direction. That means I'll likely find all of the towns that I need for my quests just by chasing down Daniella."

After landing and working to pull himself out of the snow, Joe couldn't help but feel a small amount of gratitude toward the person he was attempting to rescue. If she wasn't in trouble and in need of his help, there's no way he would've been able to secure the opportunities that he was finding. "I should do something nice for her. Besides… rescuing her. Maybe I can get her an expedited path to citizenship?"

He raced through the snow as fast as he could, somewhat annoyed at sinking into it up to his knees with each step. In a moment of inspiration, Joe focused on his Exquisite Shell and directed it to 'protect' an area approximately three inches around each of his feet. It was an unnatural task for his spell, but he was able to make it work by reducing the amount of protection he gained for the rest of his body. After half a minute of wrestling with control of the mana, it stayed in place, and Joe was able to run across the powdery surface as though he were wearing snowshoes.

"Yes!" Speed doubling in an instant, Joe rocketed across the frozen wasteland, the column of smoke reaching toward the cloud layer growing closer with each passing moment. Thanks to the frozen nature of the air and the fact that he was running directly into the wind, he could already hear that the settlement was bustling with activity.

There were shouts, clanging, hammers driving nails into planks, all of the cacophony of life that happened as people went about their daily tasks. Soon the air was filled with the scent of productivity and too many people packed into one area, to the point that Joe double-checked to ensure that his Neutrality Aura was running at maximum power. He was getting very close to the settlement at this point and realized that what he was running on was no longer just snow. No, only the top layer was snow.

"Oh look, my first time here, and I already found an open sewer!" Joe grunted in annoyance as he sprinted along, doing his very best not to look down. "Why is it that I always seem to find the worst places? At the very least, I need to promise myself that I won't set up a workshop in this cesspit. I'm finally better than that."

He had a smirk on his face as he got close to the walls and started to slow down, well past the dump area. Quickly scanning the walls, he took note of the casual guard that had been set and timed his entrance to make sure he would be going over the flimsy protection against monsters.

A single Omnivault took him over the wall, and he landed in a quiet section, ready to blend in with the locals. Cracking his neck, he calmly walked forward, pulling a bag of herb-scented soaps out of his codpiece. In his other hand, he lifted his coffee mug and had Mate fill it with a steaming medium-roast blend.

"There we go... no one looks twice at someone walking around with coffee and smiling."

CHAPTER TWENTY-ONE

"You there! Why are you *smiling?*" An Elf came practically sprinting toward Joe as he walked down the street, his eyes scanning the area carefully for the Town Hall. "Is a lowly one such as you attempting to show dominance? Pah! Here is a penance sheet; you will do these tasks, or your life coach will *scourge* you on my behalf!"

Joe took the sheet with numb hands, blinking in surprise at the sudden shift in the tone of the town around him. No one met his eyes, or even seemed to realize that he existed. The Elf turned and began walking away, then stopped and looked over his shoulder sharply. The human felt power attempting to drill into him and quickly set his title as 'Immovable Object'.

"*Hmph!* For a moment, I thought that perhaps you were an Excommunicated serf that had wandered into town instead of completing a daily task. I suppose all of you humans look alike though, don't you?"

Not trusting himself to speak, Joe simply bowed forward fractionally, the motion unnoticed as the Elven overlord vanished into the distance. Keeping his chuckle internal, Joe stood upright and began following the trail the Elf had made in the snow. "I can't believe I was planning on establishing trade or something to that effect. Here I was, planning to barter monster corpses for luxury goods or other services. Silly me."

The Ritualist wasn't entirely sure why he'd expected the Town Hall to be anywhere except the center of town, where it was the most protected with their current setup. As soon as he laid eyes on it, Joe began wandering around town looking for anyone who didn't seem to be happy to be here. That turned out to be a harder task than he expected, as all humans were apparently expected to keep a serene, stone-like expression on their face at all times.

Eventually, Joe found a group of people sitting and meditating out in the cold, and they even seemed to be doing so willingly. He sat in line with them and pretended to join in, though his selected location afforded him a decent view of the surroundings. As time passed, he expected that people would get up and leave, but instead they seemed to be in some sort of competition with each other. A few people were even removing their outer sets of clothing to expose themselves to the frigid environment.

They wouldn't be gaining any kind of resistance to the deadly cold of Jotunheim; Novusheim had a population of tens of thousands, and no one had figured out a way to gain resistance to the bitter chill. Still, he was able to use the act for its intended purpose. A few hours after he'd settled into position, a group of humans wearing still-bloody pelts of monsters walked into town. Some of them carried monster corpses, some were holding shovels and pickaxes, and *all* of them looked frustrated.

"Hmm, these must be the Excommunicated 'serfs' the Elf mentioned." Joe watched them with a glint in his eye as they marched over to drop off their collections, then tracked them as they were directed over into one of the shoddiest buildings he'd ever seen. Slowly turning his head, Joe recognized he wasn't the only person watching them go. A good number of their fellow humans in this area were watching with either sadness or sneering at the misfortune of their fellows.

Joe waited another forty minutes before getting to his feet and walking serenely across the area. The Trash-tier building was near a gate, far away from the other, more respectable buildings. While he didn't want to draw attention to himself, it wasn't like he could wait until nightfall to make contact.

Pretending he was going toward the gate, he casually bent down as though he were going to tie his shoe and leaned to the side of the wall of the house until he fell over, hopefully vanishing from the view of anyone watching him walk away. There were no doors or windows on the back of the building, but it was put together so poorly that he was able to pull on an oversized plank and slip through the opening he'd created.

On his hands and knees, Joe looked up to see half a dozen pickaxes hoisted into the air above him, ready to come down and chip away at his health. One of the men had a decidedly unfriendly smile on his face as he went down to one knee and leaned toward the crawling Ritualist. "Hello there, *friend*. Come to mess with us? You don't think your babysitters out there are doing enough to torment us or something? Boys, I think we should send this one to respawn. As long as we're out working when he gets back, no one can pin anything on us."

A general rumble of malevolence filled the air as the other people started to press closer, but Joe held up his hands to show they were empty in a universal sign of surrender. "Hold! Wait! I'm here to rescue you!"

A moment of silence was followed by mocking laughter as the others began shaking their heads. "Great, we have a bleeding heart on our hands! You're here to rescue us? To *where*, Baldy? This entire planet is a prison, and your golden friends out there aren't exactly going to be happy if you try to walk off with their prisoners of war and set up a rival settlement nearby."

"I have just a couple questions before I tell you guys anything." Joe's serious tone caused a flash of anger across the other men's faces, but they held off as their curiosity ignited. "Are all of you Excommunicated? Do you want to get out of here and leave all of these Elves behind? If I could offer you a safe path to making that happen, would you take it?"

Once more, he was met with silence as the men scowled at him. "Of course we'd take it! You think we're here by choice? We're not like you, we didn't get the—"

"Good." The floor began to shine as Joe's Field Array spread out and down. "Make sure you block anyone who tries to leave. If they do, they're probably spies."

In the next instant, the floor was gone, and the group dropped nearly ten feet straight down. Joe set up another, smaller Field Array, cutting into the ground and forming a large chamber that was enclosed on all but one side by rock and dirt. "Be careful; the ceiling isn't exactly stable. I don't usually set stuff like this up underground, since I don't know how to properly protect against collapses, but I'm not going to chance the Elves seeing the light show."

At this point, everyone was silent, merely watching him with calculating, cold eyes. The hair on the Ritualist's neck began to rise as their killing intent increased. Joe fully understood that if, at this point, he was unable to perform the miracle he'd promised them, they would likely hunt him down for destroying their floor, on top of giving them false hope. Happily, there didn't seem to be anything blocking him from using his magic, and after he set out his stabilization cubes, he activated the ritual to create a shrine.

Over the next few moments, aspects and mana flowed out of him and into the previously dark dirt and stone room. As soon as the shrine was fully constructed, Joe walked over and activated the fast travel portion of its magics, then he turned to the captives. "When you touch this, set your destination as 'Novusheim Wall Camp One'. Don't forget to set the shrine you exit at as your bind-point, or you'll be thrown back here if you die."

Ever so slowly, with confusion written large on his face, one of the captives walked over and touched the shrine. His eyes went wide, and he turned to flash a smile at the group standing in the pit. "It's real!"

A moment later, he was gone.

Joe was nearly crushed as the others rushed to use the shrine as well, and in moments, he was alone in the room. Sitting up from his new position on the ground, Joe brushed off some imagined dirt and shook his head. "Probably should've told them I needed them to stick around until I've set the Ritual of Raze up. Ah well… guess I'll just have to wing it."

He climbed out of the pit of his own creation then out the back of the building once more. Part of him was expecting a contingent of troops to be surrounding him as soon as he exposed his face, but nobody particularly seemed to care about what the prisoners of war were doing in their space. Trying to keep his nerves steady, Joe walked over to the rear of the Town Hall, sitting with his back almost against it while scanning it with his senses.

"Nothing hidden, nothing magical, as far as I can tell." He continued pretending to be meditating, his light garments helping him fit in with the group he had walked away from a while ago. After sitting for half an hour, he was fairly certain no one was going to interrupt him or see anything strange about what he was doing. Joe leaned back, pulling out a ritual tile and pressing it against the building. He had put some water on the edges, and the tile quickly froze against the wall without any issue.

He stood up and looked around before walking toward the gate as if he were going to be leaving. That was *ri~ight* about when things started to go bad.

"You there! The *smiler*! Why are you not working on the tasks I gave you?" A voice he was already sick of called out to him, and Joe continued walking as though he hadn't heard. The sound of running feet accompanied the Elf snarling a little more intently. "Are you already *done* with a full week's worth of penance? This one would be *delighted* to inspect your work!"

The back of Joe's head was gripped by a hand, and he was

flung downward, his face impacting the packed snow in the same motion. A crisp *smack* rang out, and a collective gasp from the onlookers informed Joe that he probably should've deactivated Retaliation of Shadows before coming into the Hamlet if he had wanted to continue flying under the radar.

His stealth option gone, Joe pushed himself into an Omni-vault from his prone position. He rocketed forward, mere feet off the ground. A shriek of outrage rang out as the Elf realized what had happened, and Joe chanced a glance backward while he flipped in the air—just to see the Elf cupping his cheek as though he had received a mortal wound. This time, he didn't attempt to mock his aggressor, maintaining his focus on escape.

It wasn't meant to be, as an Elven voice raised in pain was a more effective alarm than any bell ringing. Guards and warriors of all sorts flooded the area, many of them coming out of buildings ahead of Joe. He launched himself up and over, noting that the guards on the walls were now looking in, and magical shields were starting to spark to life above the flimsy barriers. "Ah... *that's* how they've survived until this point."

The next time he touched the ground, Joe slightly shifted his angle. Instead of trying to get over the wall, as was his original intent, he shot straight at the slightly open doorway of the shack the Excommunicated serfs had been living in. Spells and arrows began slamming into the flimsy walls in front of him, the best-aimed of them glancing off of his Exquisite Shell, but he had momentum and surprise on his side.

Before anyone took in his objective, he had soared into the building. Unlike the people coming after him, Joe knew the floor had been replaced by a giant hole. As soon as he was inside, he tucked and rolled. It was still a hard landing, but the magic that had been following him blasted through the walls and over his head.

Letting out a sigh of relief, he pounced onto the shrine, even as the building above him started to collapse. He touched its surface, traveling back home as tons of stone, dirt, and rubble fell and buried all evidence of his actions.

CHAPTER TWENTY-TWO

Joe stood before not only the members of the council, but also a large number of assembled residents of Novusheim. He had called for an urgent meeting to address the matter of accepting the recently rescued prisoners of war. Even though they'd obviously been on the Dwarves' side in the previous world, this was going to be a delicate situation.

"They deserve a chance to get their lives going again without having to cycle through the camps around Town. Haven't they suffered enough under the Elven Theocracy? They risked their lives and were captured by the enemy. They should be welcomed as heroes with open arms!"

"You know the real problem, Joe," someone called out. The press of people was so thick that Joe couldn't quite see who was speaking, but going by the voice, he knew it was someone on the council. "They were prisoners, but they were also under the thumb of the Elves for who *knows* how long! There's no way to tell just by looking at them if they'll betray us. Put 'em in the walls!"

There was a resounding cheer of agreement at this, and it seemed that Joe was on the verge of losing his argument. The meeting had been raging for over an hour already, and he needed to find a new way to attack this issue. Going silent for a moment, he tried to think of how he'd want to be treated… his head snapped up and a smile bloomed on his face. "Fine! I *will* let this go… so long as we codify it into law that *anyone* who's captured by enemy forces for any reason will need to undergo the trials to prove their allegiance once more! That would be the only fair way to do this."

At first, people seemed to be on board with his words, but the excitement stopped after what he was saying sunk in. That was an extremely broad statement, and no one present wanted to be forced to linger in the cold, monster-infested area outside of the safety of Town just because they may have been seen with someone unsavory. Soon, the air was filled with murmurs of uncertainty and skepticism, and Joe knew that he had won.

Luckily, the trials that they'd set up were fairly new, not some form of long-standing tradition for newcomers. After the initial surge of fear had passed, creating two paths for admittance to the Town would be easy: one for Elven sympathizers and one for their wayward prisoners of war. All Joe needed to do was get people on board with that plan, and he'd be able to step back and let them hash out the details.

Driving his point home, he continued, "These people have suffered by demonstrating their loyalty to the Dwarven cause. They fought alongside us but were unlucky enough to be captured. By accepting them back without subjecting them to trials, we are sending a message to the Elves, to our people, and to each other, that we will stand united and not abandon our own."

Even as the words left his mouth, he knew it had been the wrong thing to say—at least with the alignment of his Charisma. Quickly, Joe amended his words. "Besides! Now we have the opportunity to tap into their skills and learn from them! They survived in the worst conditions on Jotunheim and have a first-person understanding of what the Elves are doing out there! If we can get great information on them, we can take the fight to those pointy-eared whiners and drive them off of this planet for good!"

That earned him a round of cheering and much more consideration from the Town as a whole. He let out a sigh of relief that he'd remembered to phrase things in such a way that his Dark Charisma came into play on his behalf. Eventually, the area quieted down once more as the council debated with soft, thoughtful words.

Finally, Grandmaster Snow stood up and spoke, her voice filled with authority. "You've earned our trust, Joe, proving yourself time and again. Please don't think we don't understand the importance of unity, and let it be known that we'll accept these lost brothers directly into the Town without trials... but still under the guidance of mentors who will help them adjust to the area, the Town, as well as keeping an eye on them to ensure the Theocracy hasn't planted spies among us."

It was already more than Joe had hoped for, so he merely nodded and took a seat as other issues were brought up. Relief flooded him now that the decision was made: finally he could stop worrying about individuals and start thinking about the things he needed to do to protect the entire community. As the impromptu meeting wrapped up, he barely noticed people congratulating him and spreading out to return to their typical tasks.

When about half of the area had cleared out, Joe wandered toward his workshop and spent a short time finishing the newest iteration of the Ritual of Infernal Conflagration. He had spent dozens of hours refining the spell diagrams, making them more stable, cohesive, and—he hoped—powerful. When he was finished, he sought out Master Stu and had the Dwarf look it over just so he would then have an excuse to take the final product to Grandmaster Snow and have her scan it for issues.

It took her a bit longer to confirm that his changes should be effective, and Joe went over to the tower creation work yard with a smile on his face. "Now I just need to make sure the tower can withstand the energy these will be throwing out. I don't have to worry so much about the kick of the spell, like I would with a rifle, since it's created and launched in midair. Still, since it's going to be a ritual of a higher rarity rank than the tower itself, I need to make sure it won't degrade the materials it's placed on."

The first step was completing the ritual itself, so Joe had a blank tower sent out to the entrance of the walls, then he went out to draw out the ritual well away from the population center. Aspects and mana mingled as one, and he was able to complete the Expert-ranked ritual without issue—specifically, without it exploding in his face and taking out a chunk of the tower or the wall.

"Good…" Joe muttered to himself as he pulled out Mana Batteries and fiddled with the placement of every part of his setup. Triple-checking the whitelist of the ritual to ensure he wasn't going to blast himself or his people, Joe activated the ritual and held his breath as it spun up.

The colorful circles made of aspects were consumed, replaced by activated mana as the ritual stabilized. That was the first hurdle they had to pass, and Joe let himself relax fractionally as everything else clicked into place without giving him any further cause for concern. Finally, the ritual tower was armed with the potent magic, ready to unleash unholy fire on his foes.

"Al-*right!*" He still needed to set up the clone of this ritual on the tower across the gap between walls, but in his mind, that was practically a done deal. He was already envisioning his next task—adjusting and implementing a new version of the Ritual of the Crawling Storm.

Whenever he couldn't bear to work on Infernal Conflagration, he had switched over to the next in line and researched it extensively, making detailed plans and fiddling with every portion of the ritual that would impact its final state. "I'm definitely ready to finish that one up as well."

Just as he was finishing the second ritual for the entrance towers—almost as if answering his dedication and desire to test the efficiency of the magic in battle—a Beast Wave descended upon Novusheim. Shouts of alarm went up, and Joe could see the people trapped in the outermost camp rushing to their defensive bunker. He was so caught up in watching how everyone was reacting that he barely managed to throw himself out of the path of an infernal fireball as it was generated in the air and launched toward the leading ranks of camouflaged monsters.

He got back to his feet, laughing from the sheer adrenaline of it, and watched as the fireball hit a pack of Salamanders and exploded across their ranks. It wasn't often that he got to hear lizards screech in agony, but at the moment, it wasn't an unwelcome sound.

For the next several seconds, the entrance to the walls around Town shifted into a blazing inferno as the ritual towers alternated in attacking with their unique style of magic. The lingering flames lasted a shorter length of time than Joe would've liked, but they managed to wash over dozens of the creatures at a time. The Ritualist observed in satisfaction as his magic worked with apparent glee, spewing flames and consuming enemies a handful at a time.

"Next time I rework this, I need to do it with a higher rank in the spell, so I can get more damage output." As per usual, he was already planning out how he could make these rituals better and more effective over time. Still, he had plenty of other things to do. Slightly unwillingly, he turned away from the battle and headed toward Town once more, with only a minor pause to make sure that the people at ground level had all been able to find safety. "Everything's looking good... it's bubble time."

When he got to the shrine, Joe had a small, unexpected, but pleasant surprise waiting for him. The shrine that he had created and left behind in the enemy occupied Hamlet was still there. It was still devoted to Tatum, so it hadn't been found and converted, but it was unavailable as a destination for teleportation. All of this added up to a single conclusion: "The shrine got completely buried, and nobody bothered to clean out the Trash-rank building and search through the wreckage. At least, that's the most likely thing that happened... if I ever see it available to teleport to, I'll know that they found it and have a trap prepared for me."

He lost some of the ground he'd covered in his previous travels, meaning he'd have to add another three hours to his time traveling through the sky. That was acceptable to him, and the Ritualist was surprised that he hadn't had more of his slowly growing network found and destroyed by the denizens of this world already.

Joe transported himself, hopped in his bubble, and took off. "I'm more than halfway to you, Daniella. Hold on, help is coming!"

CHAPTER TWENTY-THREE

Once more speeding through the sky, separated from it only by a thin plane of force and water, Joe stared intently at the landscape below as he came to the point where he had been forced to flee, and his shrine in the hostile settlement remained buried.

From his vantage point, he could see the signs of a large Beast Wave unfolding in the distance. The attackers' ranks were nowhere near as orderly and linear as the ones Novusheim dealt with, due to the walls surrounding the upcoming Hamlet on all sides. "I love that no one except us figured that out so far."

The light outside was growing ever more dim, which was no impediment to Joe's ability to see, thanks to his class. Instead, the world becoming shrouded in darkness was only a benefit to him and his ability to move unnoticed through the sky. Conversely, each time the Hamlet's walls were struck, the sky above them flashed with strobing light as their wards and magical protections flared brightly.

"Oh, *dear*! It seems they're under attack! If only there was something I could do to help." Without hesitation, Joe lifted his Ritual of Remote Activation, pointing it at the Town Hall of the enemy settlement. It wasn't necessary, as it worked off of sympathetic connections, not direct line of sight, but it made him feel better. "Let's see what—*wait*... ohh, that was a close one!"

Joe quickly set out his stabilization cubes, barely managing to fit them all in proper placement in the cramped space. From there, he felt confident injecting a touch of mana into the tiny ritual in his hand, which resulted in a blaze of light from the center of the Hamlet in the distance. He could just *barely* make out one of the edges of the Ritual of Raze hanging in the air above town, but that was enough for him. He was certain that the building was done for.

"There you go, monsters! Those mean Elves were attacking you, but this should help out." Glancing side to side at the bubble he was in, his smile grew wider, and he settled into his bean bag chair. "I'm practically the good witch Glinda to those Penguins right now. A regular, bald, fairy godfather."

Since the Town Hall was such a low rank, it stood no chance against his magical force. It crumbled in approximately thirty seconds, and he only knew this thanks to the notification he gained about progressing his quest with Havoc once again. Even so, it brought a grim satisfaction to the Ritualist. It was always nice to know that he was causing enormous setbacks to his adversaries while making his own position stronger. "They're going to have to re-fight all those Beast Waves, then do it again before they get back to this settlement rank."

He tried not to think too much about the humans who would be caught in the crossfire as the walls collapsed around them, but he was extremely pleased that the Elves would most likely be wiped out over the next few days. Since there was no major settlement around them able to revive the Elves, they would likely be thrown all the way back to Alfheim for their respawn. Given the complexity of the time dilation effect between the worlds, Joe was certain he wouldn't be seeing them again.

Only ten minutes later, he was touching down, his maximum range to connect to his shrine network already stretched to its limit. "I suppose I could consider that shrine in the soon-to-be destroyed Hamlet as a relay point, but there's a good chance that the monsters eventually destroy it. Better to be prepared for that."

He went about his usual preparations, sinking a large hole into the ground before creating the next shrine. Once it was up, running, and as camouflaged as he could make the shrine with how casually he was dropping these, Joe decided to get his bearings on Daniella before continuing. He pulled his newly magical shirt out of his inventory, wincing slightly as the pattern of her grinning face across the entirety of the shirt seemed to mock him slightly.

He pulled it on and was infused with the knowledge of her location. His head snapped to the side as he stared into the distance, a wide smile on his face as he saw that she was under a thousand miles away. "That's less than two days of travel, if I only go for my normal amount of time!"

It felt slightly surreal to be excited that someone was a thousand miles away, to be relieved by that as a *close* proximity. Chuckling to himself at how strange things could become in a magical environment, he began changing out of his shirt. As the material came up over his eyes, his arms held above him pulling the shirt, Joe found himself face-to-face with a skeletal creature that was draped in tattered, frost-covered robes shimmering slightly as it came out of stealth.

Its grinning, skeletal features were sharp and menacing, its eyes burning with icy-blue flame. It moved with an eerie grace, gliding across the intervening distance without leaving a trace atop the snow. Joe was too surprised by how close it had come to him before he had noticed it, and he failed to avoid the icy projectiles that shot from its outstretched hands.

A half-dozen icicles launched toward him, smaller than spears, larger than arrows. Besides the simple frozen water, they were propelled by powerful gusts of wind that battered him around with intense turbulence, even as the frozen projectiles smashed into his Exquisite Shell. Joe only stumbled back a few feet, managing to maintain his stance only thanks to his Immovable Object title.

Exquisite Shell: 8,378/12,002 (3,624 piercing freeze damage taken!)

As he attempted to fight back, the Ritualist found that he was still tangled in his shirt, and the material had stiffened under the freezing effect of the creature and its magic. Flailing about slightly, he heard an ominous *snap* and found that his arm was free. He twisted to the side, pulling the shirt off of himself and leaving his torso exposed to the elements. The magical item was glowing and flashing as mana was pulled in from the environment around it. "*Abyss!*"

Realizing the imminent danger, Joe twisted and flung the partially-frozen item like a frisbee at the skeletal creature. He hadn't noticed how close it had come during his moment of distraction, and the fabric settled around its outstretched arm— freezing in place as the frost effect emanating from the creature hardened it further.

Joe Omnivaulted backward, up and out of the hole he had dug, just in time to escape the shirt going supernova. Flames and arcing energy erupted as the garment disintegrated and released all of its stored power. The hole contained the blast fairly well, and a wash of heat rolled over the Ritualist as the fire consumed the very air around it for fuel.

He sank to his knees, breathing heavily only due to the surge of adrenaline. "Great... she's a thousand miles away, and now I have no way to track her. What *was* that thing?"

Only when he realized *he still didn't know* did Joe recognize that combat was ongoing. A flash of panic suffused him, and he Omnivaulted straight up, staring down at where he had stood just in time to see a bony arm lash through the air where he had been standing as the creature broke stealth. "Dark Lightning Strike!"

Black lightning struck the creature, and the skeleton released a hiss of fury as its eyes locked onto him. Its single remaining hand, which had been glowing an ominous blue-green, had its color fade away as whatever spell it had attempted to use on him failed.

Joe was just as upset as the creature. "Why aren't you dead yet?"

The skeletal apparition clacked its teeth, and Joe realized that it couldn't answer him, even if it wanted to. As he began descending toward the ground once more, the creature glided across the ground to be in a good position to catch him when he fell. It lifted its arm straight up, and its hand once more erupted in the strange frozen flame effect.

"No, *no!*" Joe's mind whirled as he cast about for a solution, surprising himself with actually finding an answer. The enormous explosion of heat had converted a large amount of snow directly into steam, and even though it was rapidly cooling and dropping to the ground, there were still wisps of it in the air. "Omnivault!"

Pushing off of the water vapor, Joe changed his trajectory and shot in a horizontal arch away from his assailant. Ritual orbs launched away from him like an aircraft releasing chaff, turning and being guided through the air to *thunk* into the creature's body. Even that wasn't enough to take it down, and Joe cursed at the mountainous durability and Constitution that every creature on Jotunheim seemed to possess.

"Cone of Cold is out, so—*Acid Spray!*" A hiss of either pain or fury escaped the grinning face of the speedy creature as his spell, clearly super-effective, began destroying its exposed bones. Even being rapidly frozen didn't seem to slow the damage, and in only a few moments its head fell off of its body. Even then, Joe didn't get a notification that the creature was dead, so he spent a few moments having his orbs pound the skull until it had shattered into ossified chunks.

You have defeated an Undying Ice Wraith! Experience gained: 1,120!

After falling apart, the skull revealed a core shining in the eye socket of the twice-deceased wraith, and Joe went over and scooped it up without any hesitation whatsoever. At this point, he was more than familiar with looting his enemies after their death. He had lost all squeamishness on that front, for sure. In fact, he was happy he didn't have to dig through messy, gooey remains, only snapping a few chunks of bone growth off of the shining gem.

Item Gained: Core (Unique). You are able to convert this core into 8,900 experience if you'd like! Wanna go for it? Yes / No.

Joe looked at his message with slightly pursed lips. "Did my prompt writer change or something? I hope I didn't get my assigned mod fired... either way, no."

He stuffed the core into his codpiece then returned to the shrine to inspect it for damage. There was slight charring and a few chunks broken off, but it was nothing that would inhibit its ability to function. The Ritualist could only shrug, set up his Ritual of Bubble Travel with his new coordinates, and hope for the best.

"Going by the previous settlements, there might be two or even three places Daniella might reside in on my path. I'll just have to make sure to take the next couple of days very carefully, and... maybe it's almost time to bring the others along. They did say they'd come with me if there was a good chance that there'd be something interesting happening, and I'm no scout."

Then he realized he had been able to walk through the previous Hamlet unhindered because he didn't have an Excommunicated title. That thought led him to the realization that, if he was going to infiltrate the town, perhaps Jaxon was *not* the best person for a stealth mission.

"Maybe I'll just bring Heartpiercer." The Ritualist nodded gravely to himself at that thought. "At least until we know it's time to go in, T-rex head hands a-blazin'."

CHAPTER TWENTY-FOUR

He continued flying on his normal route, leaving himself less than a day's travel away from where his ritual had indicated Daniella could be found. His gut was churning with anticipation mixed with apprehension. The rescue of his friend was within reach, but he was still unable to shake the odd nervousness that came with the thought of seeing her again.

She'd double-crossed them by working with the Elves, then triple-crossed the Elves by creating an opportunity for Joe and Jaxon to escape. Frankly, Joe didn't know if his mind could handle a quadruple-cross. If it seemed that she was about to betray them... he wasn't sure if he would be able to stop himself from cursing her with the darkest rituals he had available. The Ritualist didn't want to get to that point, but he knew he would—as his first option.

That was one of the things holding him back from being too excited: the knowledge of how violently he would lash out if this was all some elaborate trick to waste his time and weaken his settlement.

As he completed his final shrine for the day, Joe took a deep breath to calm his churning emotions, then sent himself back to Novusheim. The loss of mana at the sheer distance traveled hit him in the gut like a punch from a cyclops, and he bent over wheezing as a full eight thousand mana was yanked out of him. Sucking wind, he quickly calculated how far he'd just traveled in an instant for almost the entirety of his non-reserved mana pool.

"That was… something like nine thousand miles in a second." He heaved for breath as his mana regeneration kicked in, filling his depleted pool with nearly seventy-three at mana each second. "Still… less than a point of mana per mile. Efficient. Thanks… Tatum."

He dry heaved for a moment, managing to keep everything in his stomach as he settled into his box-breathing pattern. "I'm good. I'm okay. Whew. Sorry, big guy, no 'donations' for you today."

Joe chuckled as he walked away from the shrine, remembering the prank he'd played on Tatum in the past to clean up after a bunch of people who'd gotten sick all over an altar. Now with a smile on his face, he began searching for his group. As per usual, with the immense density of the population in a relatively small area, it was much more efficient to hire a few people to seek out who he needed than to try and find them with his own two eyes.

Compared to the last time he'd done this, the price had skyrocketed; Joe found himself grudgingly agreeing to an entire Salamander corpse per message sent, though it made him *itchy* to give up so many raw materials for such a seemingly simple task. "I guess if I ever needed a push to work on my 'Message' spell, this is it."

His eyes lit up as he remembered that he had a Ritual of Communication, and he rushed back to his workshop to make the low-ranking magical diagram immediately. "Where is it, where is—here! Yes! I was right. Ritual of Communication, has a range of fifty miles centered on the ritual. Well, that's more than enough to start chatting in Novusheim. It gives twelve hours of communication, but that's toggleable. If it's not on, it's not using the time up. Good…"

Joe checked outside, not finding his teammates anywhere in the vicinity. "I have time to make one of these for each of us, right? I totally do."

This was an extremely basic ritual, and luckily it was considered as 'active' only when linking two of the rituals together. Otherwise, Joe would need to figure out how to connect it to a series of stabilization cubes, which would bring the ritual from a nice, small tablet-sized chunk of tile all the way up to an unwieldy item someone would need to lug around.

In a very short amount of time, Joe was able to create a total of eight of the rituals, linking each pair together and keeping four of them for himself. As Jaxon, Heartpiercer, and Socar showed up, he cheerfully handed each of them one of the devices and demonstrated how to use them. Each of them understood how to use a phone, and this ritual was barely more intricate than pressing a 'call' button. After familiarizing them with its usage, Joe got to the meat of the meeting.

"I believe that I'm only a single day's travel away from Daniella at this point, and I wanted everyone to be ready to swoop in and haul her out of there." Joe went over the information he'd gathered, the settlements that he'd stumbled across, and what he was hoping for with the next plan of action. As he drew to a close, the Ritualist solemnly met each of their eyes. "Thank you all for being willing to help me with this; it's a personal matter, and I'm not sure how it'll go. For the first stage, I was hoping to only bring Heartpiercer with me to help scout out the situation."

"Wow, that was quite the adventure you've been having with your face pressed against a bubble!" Jaxon excitedly clapped his hands and cracked his neck back and forth. "I'm *so* ready to go in there. My fingers really have a taste for Elf flesh at this point. Yes, that is somewhat strange, I know. But my research is pointing at the fact that dinosaurs used to be the main predator of Elves, but then they started figuring out magic and managed to fight back."

"You're able to research this?" Socar interjected with a frown. "How? Where?"

Jaxon pulled a book out of his pack and dropped it on the table as if it were a priceless artifact. "You see, the Dwarves have a deep and abiding understanding of their enemy, and they packaged it in this easy-to-read manual!"

Joe read the title of the book, 'Dinos vs Elves', which was splayed across the cover of what was clearly a children's book depicting an Elf being bitten in half by a pterodactyl. Deciding against saying anything, he instead looked over at the Archer to see if she was willing to tag along with him on the last leg of his journey. It was clear that she didn't particularly care to do so, but nodded along with an eyeroll and a sigh.

"Yeah, I'll go. You've made me pretty disgustingly rich, thanks to those ritual towers. I suppose I owe you one." Her words came out in a warmer tone than expected, earning her a grin from the Ritualist.

"Thanks, I'll take all the help I can get." Just as he was about to clap and announce the end of the meeting, Socar cocked his head and blinked a few times in confusion.

"Thanks for telling us all about this, but I truly thought you were calling us here to go to those mysterious ruins that you made a quest for. Last I heard, the excavation teams over there are right on the verge of getting the doors open. Did you *not* want to be there for that?"

Needless to say, Joe wasn't certain how to respond to that information other than running out the door with the others following him as soon as they realized where he was going. No one wanted to miss out on this discovery, and certainly not on the rewards that it could potentially provide. The Ritualist himself was half-terrified that the excavation team would manage to breach the doors before he got there—mainly because the people who had gone out to secure the area all seemed to have one common trait.

In their minds, gear adrift was a gift. If Joe wasn't there to take an accounting of whatever could be found inside, it was likely he'd be left with a building completely emptied out of anything of value.

Together, they raced through the Town toward the shrine, anticipation and excitement building with each step. Something about the physical motion helped soothe Joe's anxieties, and soon enough he and his team each had their hands pressed upon the shrine. Fractions of a second later, the shining metal obelisk stood before them, a grand vault practically begging them to uncover its secrets.

Chattering filled the air as the excited teams gathered around the entrance, scholarly looking Dwarves and humans fiddling with strands of mana and arguing back and forth as to the right way to finish the unlocking sequence of the doors. Joe and his companions hurried forward, pushing through the crowd until they were at the very front of the groups.

"I hear you've made great progress!" His bald head and gentle smile earned him double-takes from the scholarly Dwarves, though the humans didn't seem to find anything about his appearance out of the ordinary. Then came the customary wince as the Dwarves realized that Joe had no hair—facial or on his head—and they tried to collect themselves. At this point, he wasn't even annoyed by their habits; it only made him chuckle at how uncomfortable his visage made them, for reasons he couldn't really understand. Cultural norms had never been his forte.

Offering a salute, the mustachioed Dwarf that Joe had previously met with about this project took on the role of speaking for the group. "Councilman Joe! You have... *suspiciously* fortuitous timing. We believe that there's only a single tumbler remaining before the vault doors are opened, but we're faced with a choice. We need to complete one of these runes, but our assumption is that, if we fail, the consequences are going to be more dire than simply having to restart."

Rune magic was something Joe wasn't particularly good at;

the practice was somewhere between enchanting and invoking. For a moment, he missed his old teammate: Bard the Skald, who could've likely solved this in an instant. But the man was two worlds away, and someone would be making an attempt on this in the next several minutes. The Ritualist took a deep breath. "Can you walk me through what brought you this far and give me your reasons for why you think it should be one or the other?"

"Certainly." The Dwarf cleared her throat and intoned the various instructions they'd been able to work out. "The first stage of passing this threshold was to stand before the door, gazing upon its intricate design and feeling the weight of its power. It is a majestic building that guards hidden knowledge or ancient treasures."

Just before he opened his mouth to sarcastically ask if that was truly necessary, Joe realized that this building was heavily enchanted and had been here for untold millennia. There was a good chance that it was somewhat sentient at the *bare* minimum, and there was certainly no harm in trying to butter it up a little bit.

"Next, we needed to concentrate our will and attune ourselves to the interstice of the essence of these enchanted walls and the weight of Jotunheim attempting to scatter it. The first lock is in that fractional aperture, and only then were we allowed access to the mechanical mechanisms." Her eyes were sparkling behind her glasses; clearly she'd gained some insight into her own abilities by managing this feat. "From there, it was a matter of aligning the internal locks and pushing them back with our combined force of will, as this building is far too powerful for any one person to do it alone."

For a moment, Joe felt a feeling of *'pleased'* emanating from the structure behind her, and by the way his magical senses were tingling, it wasn't just his imagination. He thought over every word he'd just been told, taking each one of them far more seriously. "Now, all that remains is aligning the rune?"

"As far as we know, yes." She then waved at the odd scribbles of power that were shining along the seam of the door. Joe could tell that a single point of mana would be enough to bridge the gap in dozens of locations, but for some reason, they had narrowed them down to only two. "We've been working on a translation of the runes, and we have a rough estimate of what they all say. Most of them are actually instructions when taken literally, while only the last two could finish the incantation portion of the rune."

She lifted her finger and traced along the lines as she spoke, obviously reading the translated version for his benefit. "In the realm of spells, the physical is but an illusion. Let your mind's eye perceive the depths of the lock's inner workings. Manipulate the ethereal threads of magic, feel the resistance as the door relinquishes its grip on the world. Unravel this riddle; let your intuition guide you."

"*Runes.*" Joe sighed in slight annoyance as he shook his head. "I much prefer the clean, cold lines of enchantments and rituals myself. But I suppose shamanistic magics such as this are equally impressive in their own way. Unfortunately, I'm stumped by this one."

Surprisingly, it was Jaxon who reached out and gripped Joe's shoulder, pulling him close and whispering in his ear. "Wait, I have an idea."

The Ritualist pulled himself out of his friend's grip and wiped his ear. "That's great. Can you share it with the *whole* class, instead of licking my ear when you speak?"

Jaxon made a slurping sound at him and chuckled. "Tastes like a lit candle, your ear does. Listen, I think this is actually being literal when it is talking about your mind's eye. Unlike the rest of us, you have an *actual* magical eye in the middle of your forehead. Yeah, it's a tattoo, but it is a gift from a royal. Maybe this vault is secured so that only people with royal blessings are able to get into it?"

With everyone looking at him with great anticipation, Joe could only shrug and half-heartedly smile. "I guess it's worth a shot?"

CHAPTER TWENTY-FIVE

There were several options that Joe could pursue at this moment, but he was going to go with what Jaxon had mentioned, which made the most sense: taking the message as literally as possible, using Essence Cycle to see the flows of power and where they had broken. From the *very* little amount of information that Joe had been able to gather about Vanaheim, it was a wizarding caste system where those with the most power had the most influence.

If that ended up being accurate, it would make sense that they would be interested in the additional senses that could be given by royals and leave it as a backup in case they locked themselves out of their own vaults. With that in mind, and going off of the context clues in the wording, Joe closed his eyes to block out his physical sight.

To his surprise, with his extra senses fully active and trained on the door in front of him, the words still seemed to be burning on the back of his eyelids. He couldn't read the script directly, but two of the sections seemed dull and gray, instead of mimicking the shimmering opalescence of the others.

"It's... not enough." It took him a while to make that realization, but simply seeing it didn't reveal what he needed. Joe activated his Magical Synesthesia—another sense given by a ruler—and attempted to listen to the magic of the building itself echoing out into the world around it. He manipulated a single strand of mana from the tip of his finger, bringing it closer to one of the two spaces. Something began letting out a high, clear note, and Joe paused, uncertain whether it was a warning tone or excitement over being whole once more.

He pulled his mana back, dropping it down to the secondary space, which also let out a note, but of a different tone. Joe watched as both tried to reach out and grasp the final circuit they would need in order to open, and frowned. "The coloration. It's... *wrong*."

At first, the Ritualist had ascribed the strangeness of the words to being broken, not their completed versions. But, as he read over them again, an ability he hadn't been able to put much use into was practically shouting at him. "Both of them are wrong. This is a trap. The *actual* Runes are somewhere else."

Usually his ability from Tatum to see if written words were 'true' or not didn't work with magical enchantments or the like, but this seemed to be an exception, since the instructions were actual *words* instead of magical formulae. Keeping his eyes closed, Joe fumbled around the vault, seeking answers as his head began to pound with terrible pain from keeping all of his extra senses activated at the same time. He could feel steam boiling off his skin as body heated up, and his mind began overloading with sensory information.

But he was able to look *deeper*. Reading over the ancient words, he attempted to see the magical cores of the Runes instead of what was written on the surface. "The physical is but an illusion. Let your mind's eye perceive the depths of the lock's inner workings. Feel the resistance as the door relinquishes its grip on the world."

Over and over, he repeated the words as his headache built. Finally, he noticed a discrepancy. Looking closer, he found a word that was actually acting as a lock, instead of being a part of the instructions as it was pretending to be. Using the mana he'd extended on his finger, Joe scratched out the single word that had been translated as 'the resistance'. With that gone, the instructions read as, 'feel as the door relinquishes its grip on the world'.

There was a burst of static electricity as the Rune fizzled out, followed by shouts of anger and confusion, which cut off as the door let out a grinding *clack*. Having clearly been closed for untold millennia, it loudly protested as gears began shifting, mechanisms became moving, and the enormous entryway began unfolding. Joe released his orb as well as his other skills, gasping for breath as he massaged his throbbing temples.

Perception +3!

Luck + 2!

Socar led him away to sit as the doors continued to shudder and grind. "Are you going to be okay, buddy?"

"Yeah. Just need a moment. Gained a couple Characteristic points. Perception makes sense; I pushed it to my limit, but why so much Luck?" Joe was already feeling better, but took all the time he needed until he felt perfect. He hopped to his feet, rubbing his arms with his hands to try and get the blood flowing. "Is it just me, or is it getting colder?"

"Colder for sure." Heartpiercer pointed at Jaxon, who had stopped moving entirely, his eyes open and lightly frosted over. "Are you *sure* he's not part snake? Whenever he's left alone too long, he tries to hibernate."

"Snap out of it, Jaxon!" Joe called at his friend, who began wiggling back and forth once again.

Right about then, the doors began opening enough to see inside. One of the Dwarves even had his face pressed up against the gap as it widened, and everyone was clamoring to do the same. Then that Dwarf went stiff and let out a strangled gasp as a wrist-thick icicle slammed through his face and out the back of his head.

For a mere instant, there was total silence as the Dwarf fell back, caught by the press of bodies behind him. A blast of frigid air pushed out of the doors, flinging them wide and sending dozens of gathered people flying. Joe's heart seemed to fall into his stomach as the open doorway revealed a dimly lit antechamber filled with an eerie aura.

Instead of treasures or artifacts, a chilling sight awaited them. Dozens of Undying Ice Wraiths were standing there, those in the front showing signs of moving, while the ones directly behind them seemed to still be coming out of a coma-like state.

Congratulations! You have opened the Vault of Winter's Life! A new enemy type will be added to future Beast Waves for any settlement you are a part of on Jotunheim!

Quest update: A vault you issued a quest for has been opened! Make sure to accurately assess the value of its contents.

Going by the cursing and shuffling, Joe was certain he wasn't the only person who had gotten the first message.

The area erupted into chaos as wraiths unleashed their icy powers, some of them vanishing entirely as they entered stealth and closed in on the intruders. The already frigid air gained a frostbite aura that slowed the reactions of the warm-blooded people, sapping their energy. The very essence of decision-making seemed to freeze in their minds, leaving them vulnerable to the sudden and vicious attack.

Around the entirety of the area, a blizzard sprang up, engulfing the area in a whirlwind of snow and ice. The raging storm cut off any chance of escape, creating an arena where visibility was reduced to mere feet. It also had the unfortunate effect of making the stealthed wraiths even more effective, allowing the creatures to strike from unexpected angles and sowing further chaos among the ranks. Joe finally got to witness what happened when one of them managed to grip someone with the blueish-green touch spell: the affected limb turned black nearly instantly, succumbing to a devastating frostbite that left the area looking necrotic, like it needed to be amputated immediately.

The Dwarves were seasoned warriors, and thanks to their

centuries of experience, they were able to swiftly adapt to the situation and form ranks. Their disciplined movements allowed them to push back after only a few moments of vulnerability. Weapons lashed out, axes biting deeply into outstretched boney limbs as hammers swung with deadly precision, beating skulls into powder—even if doing so required a half-dozen strikes.

At the same time, the back ranks of fighters were struggling to find their targets. Arrows were deflected off the dense bones of the wraiths, unable to find a fleshy area to penetrate or sink into. Frustration mounted as the archers shouted back and forth at each other, their already seemingly futile attacks often blown off-course by the howling wind to strike allies. Mages were having an issue similar to the archers, as any type of area-of-effect spell was going to damage their own side as well, and many single-target spells would be ineffective or downright dangerous to use in these conditions.

Still, a few skilled marksmen among them adjusted their tactics and infused their arrows with skills in an attempt to bypass the hardened defenses. Heartpiercer lived up to her name, arrows finding their mark one after another, striking true on their chests and leaving shattered bone debuffs ready for the melee fighters to take advantage of.

Long moments of the clash passed, and they were clearly becoming overwhelmed by the numbers and devastating attacks of the wraiths. It was nearly impossible to regroup or communicate effectively, and Joe made a snap decision to attempt a retreat. "Everyone, get out of here! Fall back, fall back!"

He tried to lead the way, but the combination of the blizzard immediately isolating him and the fact that two glowing hands reached out of thin air and tried to clamp on his face—which he barely avoided—convinced Joe that escape was likely not in the cards at the moment. A sense of desperation began to set in as the casualties mounted, but the surviving fighters struggled intensely to hold their ground.

Now back in the mix, Joe once again attempted to direct his team, as he had already faced one of these creatures in combat and had a better sense of how they would attempt their attacks. The tide ever-so-slowly began to turn in their favor, the approximately eighty defenders whittling down the number of wraiths as time passed.

The more wraiths that fell, the weaker the blizzard around them became, until a high-ranking Dwarf was finally able to be seen and heard above the storm and managed to rally the remaining people and coordinate their movements. The battle raged on with a heavy focus on brutal attacks to batter through resistances, each clash of metal against bone echoing through the howling wind and inspiring everyone to fight harder.

Suddenly, the air was its usual level of calm, with only a constant, single direction of wind blowing through the area. Joe took a step toward the open vault door, unknowingly moving out of his defended position in the formation. Two stealthed wraiths lunged forward, and Joe jumped back with a yelp, causing the first to miss, but allowing the second to latch onto his ankle.

His Exquisite Shell flared brightly where the hand was clamped, and Joe tried to shove the creature off of him, failing to do so and only managing to give the wraith another leg to grab. Intense cold literally *burned* at him, and he watched in real-time as the strength of his shell plummeted.

Exquisite Shell: 7,991/12,002 (Caution! Damage is continuing to accumulate!)

Exquisite Shell: 6,040/12,002

Jaxon slid into view next to Joe, his fingers jamming down into the hollow eye sockets of the wraith. With a grunt and a twist, he popped the head off of the body of the monster, and its grip went slack. "No, you numbskull! *Bad!* Things like this are why you get a terrible reputation, stop it! *Bone* voyage!"

He pulled a leg back as though he were going to drop kick the skull, but Joe's shouted warning reached him in time. "You need to destroy the head! Otherwise, it won't count as defeating it."

"Ah, what a shame." Jaxon *tsked* at the information and

began pummeling the vulnerable skull against the icy ground. The other creature had already been slain by this point, and Joe pulled himself to his feet. He felt shaky, like he would never be warm again.

"Did we get all of them?" Looking around the battlefield, the Ritualist's eyes went blank as he took in the devastation. "What...?"

The area was strewn with fallen warriors and shattered bones, showcasing their victory and the price that had been paid for it. Then he remembered that he could do something about it. "Everyone! Gather the bodies of the slain; clear out the skulls. Move fast! I'm a Cleric, and I can mass revive everyone!"

The lamentation and fury that had been building vanished as soon as people were able to process his words, their thoughts still muddled by the chilling debuff they'd been subjected to. Once the message was clear, everyone moved as quickly as their bodies allowed, pulling each of their fallen comrades into line next to each other.

Even with the tension that was rapidly mounting, Joe refused to activate his spell until the last of the skulls had been gathered and accounted for, then moved out of range of his magic. Taking a deep breath, Joe prepared to activate his new, upgraded spell for the first time. "It's going to suck not having any magic for a whole day, but if ever there's been a time when it's worth it... *Mass Resurrection Aura!*"

Anything he was going to say in the next few moments was cut off as he choked, his mana completely vacating his body and *dumping* into the surroundings. As it passed the outer membrane of his skin, it shifted into a dark energy that was clearly of a higher order than what his body produced naturally. There was no mistaking the fact that this was a Deity-channeled spell, instead of something that Joe had managed to learn and make functional on his own.

Tendrils of darkness reached out for every body on the ground around him, and if they were too far away, Joe ensured that he got close enough for the spell to touch them over the few seconds it was active. "If I could only combine this with Omni-vault, I can't *imagine* how many people I'd be able to bring back in a warzone."

As the spell ended, Joe collapsed to his knees, his connection to his mana pool severed. He couldn't remember the last time he'd felt so weak, so powerless, but just before his eyes rolled up into his head, he saw the bodies on the ground around him begin to stir.

"Worth…" was all he managed before darkness took him.

CHAPTER TWENTY-SIX

Time until mana is available to you once more: 20:32:52.

Skill increase(s):

Mass Resurrection Aura (Apprentice VI).

Artisan Body (Apprentice II)

Battle Meditation (Student VII)

Hidden Sense (Student III)

Magical Synesthesia (Beginner IX)

Congratulations! Through the use of three skills that have a similar effect though a different method of achieving the same goal, you have found that these skills have supreme resonance:

Essence Cycle

Hidden Sense

Magical Synesthesia

Would you like to combine these skills in the Soul Forge? Note: You will need to unbind Essence Cycle from your ritual orb first. Yes / No.

This was far too much information for Joe to process right as he woke up, so he dismissed everything and automatically selected 'no' on the combination. Even in his bleary, sick-feeling state, he remembered the warning that Queen Marie had given him when he'd first earned sensory magic. He smacked his lips and pulled a face as he went over the words she had said, "I'm not supposed to combine that under any circumstances. Also, *bleh*... why does everything taste terrible?"

His hands were sticky, so Joe clenched and unclenched them a few times before pulling them up to see what was on him. His eyes focused on the crimson ice that was stuck there; realizing in that moment what it meant to be without his spells for a whole day. Joe was covered in blood, he didn't even *own* a toothbrush at this point, and everything was incredibly dusty.

That last realization made him perk up, and he looked around to see that he was inside of the building they'd been attempting to crack. Joe pulled himself to his feet, wondering why he was alone and unguarded... until he realized that there were dozens of Dwarves and humans likely ransacking the vault at that very moment. "Great. I'm filthy, I stink, I'm likely being robbed blind at this very moment, and I can't even scare the thieves away with some lightning."

Grumbling like an ancient wizard being shaken out of his research to help find a broom for the janitor, Joe hobbled deeper into the building. Without his magic flowing through him, and his auras keeping him comfortable, the Ritualist felt weaker, and everything in the world around him felt *itchy*. All of this combined to make him a powerless, grumpy, weak, shell of a wizard. "Whose idea was it to put me in a cloak made out of hair? What was I thinking? How does anyone else do laundry? Lastly, who tossed me behind the door so I'd be *out of the way!*"

The last of his thoughts were shouted at the Dwarves bustling about in the extremely large building. The interior was far more spacious than expected, indicating that there was some spatial magic trickery at play here. No one replied to his raspy, accusatory shout, so he had to content himself with grumbling and moving forward to see what had everyone so... casual.

The structure had been sealed off for untold thousands of years, and he could only imagine what sort of treasures and knowledge had awaited him if he'd been awake enough to actually get them. His frustrations quickly turned to excitement as he realized that everything had already been gathered, accounted for, and laid out in a central area. He could see the shine of lights off of the edge of still-sharp weapons, could hear the murmuring of appreciation as certain pieces were looked over, and his hopes began to rise.

"Joe! You're awake!" The scholarly Dwarf in charge of the expedition rushed over, grabbed his arm, and pulled him to the pile of goods. "We've been cataloging this for the last few hours; you really dodged an arrow on that one."

Her words caused Joe to realize that perhaps he'd been focused on the wrong things since he had woken up, alone, cold, on a hard stone floor. Taking a breath to center himself, he turned his eyes on the mustachioed Dwarf and solemnly asked her the question that *should've* been his first thought. "Did I manage to bring everyone back?"

She went silent for a moment, shaking her head and biting her lip. "Unfortunately, we missed a few people in our mad dash to get everyone together."

Joe grunted as a hard weight solidified in his gut, as though he'd just had a knife embedded there. As he'd had that experience first-hand, the comparison was quite accurate. When he didn't manage to respond to her, the Dwarf continued speaking quietly. "Of the thirty-eight people who were slain by the wraiths, there were four people who had been completely covered by snow, and we didn't notice them. I'm not sure how long we're going to have to wait for them to come back before we can give them their rewards."

"What?" Joe perked up at that, his eyes widening. "We only missed humans? We got all the Dwarves back, though?"

"Yes. I'm sorry for the losses that your people took because of it." She did truly seem ashamed at the moment, but a bright smile was blooming on Joe's face. "We should've expected some kind of trap or fight would be coming–"

"We didn't lose any *Dwarves!*" Joe shouted into the air, pumping his fist. His good-natured bellow was taken up by everyone in the surroundings, especially those who had gaping wounds in their armor and bright scars that showed they had been recently revived. After a moment, the Ritualist calmed down enough to hold his conversation again, but he felt as though he were walking on air at the moment. "I don't want to downplay the sacrifice of my human friends, but a death here and there is only *annoying* to us. The rest of you? You're irreplaceable."

There were a few people in the crowd who made mocking noises at him, but he knew it was all good-natured fun.

"Awww!"

"I didn't know he cared so much!"

"Look at that sweetie. He's not so bad, even if he *is* bald."

He waved the crowd off, and they laughed and refocused on their own tasks and goals. "Sorry, I haven't meant to be so terribly rude, but I haven't caught your name yet."

"Eh, I go by Ryu." She flashed a grin at him as she held up a notebook and quill. "Because I write as fast as lightning."

Joe rolled his eyes but decided against calling her out on it. "If you already have all the information on these items…"

As he trailed off, Ryu grimaced slightly and shook her head. "Prepare for disappointment, and make it double. Once upon a time, these were all probably powerfully enchanted weapons, excellent spell books, potentially even formidable Artifact-quality items. But time… has not been kind to them. After having been steeped in the chaotic energies of Jotunheim for so long, locked away and the stasis spells never refreshed, most if not all of their power has been lost."

The Ritualist managed to contain his disappointment, and he patiently looked over the items one by one as Ryu described their properties.

"These blades are still sharp, even if they could use a touch-up. Everything was well preserved and will be a useful base for re-enchantment if we can ensure that there's no residue or imbued resentments in them that would mess up new inscriptions." From there, she moved over to the books, which were what Joe was the most excited about in the first place. "Unfortunately, as soon as anyone tries to turn the cover, the paper interior falls to dust. They must've been freeze-dried for an unholy length of time to be in this state."

"Weapons that are mundane but useful, books that were magical that are destroyed." Joe let out a sigh, rubbing his bald head and having his hand come away slick with sweat. His left eye twitched at the feeling as he wiped his hand on his hairy cloak. The Ritualist muttered to himself before turning back to his Dwarven companion. "Just gotta keep telling myself I'm glad I revived everyone. Ryu, this can't be all there is, right? The amount of work that went into opening this, the fact that we now have to fight these in future Beast Waves?"

She could only shrug and gesture around the otherwise empty room. "There's still layers of frost and such on the ground, walls, and ceiling. We're going to need to get this place completely cleaned up before we can start inspecting it for anything that might be hidden."

Perking up at that, Joe looked at his skills and tried to determine if his Hidden Sense required the use of mana. As far as he could tell, it didn't. Before he said anything to the Dwarf, he looked at his status sheet and winced at what he saw.

Name: Joe 'Tatum's Chosen Legend' Class: Reductionist
Profession I: Arcanologist (Max)
Profession II: Ritualistic Alchemist (5/20)
Profession III: Grandmaster's Apprentice (15/25)
Profession IV: None
Character Level: 27 Exp: 392,972 Exp to next level: 13,028
Rituarchitect Level: 12 Exp: 76,950 Exp to next level: 1,050
Reductionist Level: 8 Exp: 39391 Exp to next level: 5,609
Hit Points: 2,496/2,496
Mana: 0/8,393
Mana regen: 0/sec
Stamina:1,870/1,870
Stamina regen: 6.65/sec

Characteristic: Raw score

Strength (bound): 182
Dexterity: 184
Constitution (bound): 179
Light Intelligence (Bound): 192
Wisdom: 180
Dark Charisma: 142
Perception: 183
Luck: 118
Karmic Luck: 20

He'd made significant progress in his level thanks to the constant, if low, experience from his ritual towers fighting on his behalf. Joe was slightly confused to see that both of his Specializations had increased in level without him noticing. After a moment of consideration, it made sense, thanks to having been so close to attaining them—and that was even *before* he'd spent a ton of time building ritual towers. Not to mention outfitting them with new spells so that they could be swapped out in the event of a tower being destroyed. "Kinda odd that I didn't see them, but all that really means is that I didn't gain any reward for increasing them. Also... what did I do to lose so much Karmic Luck?"

Checking his notifications just to double check for any discrepancies, Joe confirmed everything *should* be correct, so tried to move on. "No mana whatsoever, but I think my magical senses still work. I guess we'll find out?"

He began walking around the open area, moving very slowly just in case his powers took a moment to kick in. The downside to this was that it was quite boring to stare at the floor —or the walls—with nothing else to do, and no idea if he was missing something. Joe began fidgeting with his ritual orbs, having them pull out of his bandolier and twirl around his fingers, as he usually did to practice with them. Only after he had been doing this for a few minutes did he realize that he was able to use his weapons without magic. "Oh! Good! I'm not totally defenseless! Right, using these takes an 'exotic' skill, some kind of psychic energy. No mana required."

Somehow, simply having that option made his current state much more palatable, and he continued strolling around the room with a smile. After he had marched across the perimeter, Joe went to the next most likely spot.

Instead of slowly making his way across the floors, he simply went straight to the center of the open space and sat down, trying to get a feel for the area. Immediately, something began tickling the back of his mind, and a near-feral grin slithered across his face.

"Jackpot."

CHAPTER TWENTY-SEVEN

Half a dozen people worked on clearing the floor, starting by taking off the top layer of sleet from the slowly melting ice that had covered nearly every surface. As fast as they could manage, they scraped away enough buildup to find seams in the floor, eventually resolving into a large square. Once the larger tools had been put away, out came buckets, mops, and various other scrubbing implements so they could push through the millennia of dust and gunk that had accumulated.

When the final cleaner stepped away—a process Joe *knew* would've been much faster if he had access to his Neutrality Aura—there was a four-hundred-square-foot area of the floor that was shining with a near-mirror polish. A vast magical diagram was contained within the space, which Joe and everyone else that could push into the area began examining. Excitement surged through the bald man as he recognized the intricate magic that had been laid out on the floor. He had only seen something like this once before, but it was unmistakable.

"This is a ritual key. Just like the one at the Grand Ritual Hall that the Dwarves had hidden away." Joe's words were breathed in a whisper, reverence for the literal masterwork of magic causing him subconsciously to be as quiet as possible. His eyes roved the space, taking in all of the swooping swirls, whirling formulas, and various sigils in another language that likely described the intent of the ritual itself.

Filled with determination and an eagerness to learn more, Joe whipped out a notebook and began working to start deciphering the weathered, inactive sections of the ritual. This design had clearly suffered the effects of time and neglect, but he was nearly certain that he'd be able to draw out the essence of these circles and reactivate it in the near future.

It helped that he didn't have to decode the entire design, although he most *certainly* would need to meticulously restore each of the missing elements piece-by-piece. "Before I reactivate it, I have to scrub the ownership and put in my own. Otherwise, all I'm going to do is lock myself out until the ritual itself fails again, and who knows how long it took the first time?"

Ever so slowly, the gathered crowd began to realize that the next part of this puzzle was going to involve a mountain of research and fiddling. People left in droves, knowing they'd be able to eventually collect their quest reward in the future. Some people stayed on to offer protection until the work was finally completed, hoping to increase their share when all was said and done.

Yet, Joe knew this wasn't likely to be a quick process. After copying down each of the sections he needed to work on, he closed his notes and stood up. "I guess we might as well head back to Novusheim, huh? Maybe we leave a small guard just to make sure nothing takes up residence in here while we're gone, but otherwise I think there isn't much point in sticking around."

With this final confirmation, most of the people scrambled toward the shrine to exit the area. Only a few staunch guards sneered at those trying to avoid work and settled in at the doorway to defend against outside threats.

Joe eventually got in line, nearly the last person who would be able to leave. When it was his turn, he placed his hand on the shrine, selected Novusheim as his destination, and stood there for a half dozen seconds waiting to be teleported. Then he closed his eyes, took a deep breath, and let it out slowly. "Right. It costs *mana* to teleport."

Dramatically, he threw his head back and marched back to the entrance of the huge building like a child being sent to their room. Walking past the guards, who gave him a confused glance, only convinced Joe to not explain what had just happened. He was perfectly fine with them thinking that he wanted to stay and keep working, instead of having forgotten that he couldn't leave. "Nothing to do but keep decoding this, I suppose."

The Ritualist sat in the center of the intricate design, his eyes focused and his mind concentrated. "At this level of ritual, every single detail is going to be important to the final effect. Let's think this through... it's etched directly onto the surface. First of all, at this rank, the circles have to spin when they're active. That means this entire section is likely a gyroscope when it's going; in other words, don't be sitting where I'm sitting when it's started."

That thought made him chuckle: he could do all of the work, fix up the ritual, *own* it, then still turn himself into mince-meat by accident when he tried to get it going. Joe let his fingers trace along the etched symbology, noting each point where the carving was deep or light compared to its standard etch depth. Before he knew it, he was tracing out the entire ritual circle into his notes, something that he'd decided against doing originally.

Dozens of sections were labeled with depth, positioning, and questions on how it would relate to the constellations and movement of the planet and moons. Joe was still learning how the movement of celestial bodies would affect his magics, and he thought it would be important to do additional research into it while he was looking at a masterwork like this.

Slowly he traced the intricate lines, memorized patterns, and began deciphering the cryptic symbols while attempting to discern the meaning of the archaic words. Joe hoped that the language used wasn't absolutely imperative to preserve, as he liked to understand what he was doing before he followed through on it. Still, every intersection of lines was a piece of the puzzle that would eventually unlock the ritual and whatever it was protecting.

"This is… *old.*" Joe suddenly became acutely aware of the dense mathematical sequences that had been put into play on this design. None of the 'newer' concepts in mathematics had been used, such as a sine or cosine wave that would allow for rapid transitions between directionality of the design. Instead, every angle shift had a corresponding numerical value that would give directions on how the curve should move, and for how far, in sequence. "No wonder this is a Master-rank ritual. I can't *imagine* how much time went into the creation of this."

Idly, he went over a section in his notes and made his own annotations with a far simpler and more elegant equation to handle the shifts that were shown. When he'd finished, Joe realized that this entire ritual could likely be minimized into a mid-level Expert ritual, instead of a mid-level Master ritual. The design made him wince, even as his respect for whoever had created this in the first place was rapidly raised. Even with as meticulous as he was, Joe would've probably lost his mind trying to manage all of the finicky details required. Twice.

"Then again… I suppose if I actually am able to achieve immortality, spending a few months or even years on a single circle for a ritual wouldn't be all that big of a deal." With that thought bringing him hope, Joe kept at his translations. As he continued to parse the diagram, he could practically feel a connection between himself, the ritual, and its original designer. It was unlikely that the person who'd made this was still around, but if they could be found someday, Joe promised himself that he'd seek them out and exchange pointers.

Then, out of nowhere, a line of golden light flashed between himself, the ritual, then at an oblique angle that shot into the sky. It was gone so quickly that it could've been his imagination, but some deep part of him that had been opened up when he'd gained his Karmic King trait whispered that he would indeed have some fate with the designer of this ritual. Whether it was the original person or their successors, Joe didn't know for sure.

He half-expected a quest to appear, but... there was nothing. The Ritualist felt slightly shaken, and it took him nearly half an hour to return to the flow state that he'd been working in previously. Time seemed to lose meaning for him as he slowly immersed himself in the magics that he could see, adjust, but not touch with his current restriction. Even so, with study came wisdom, and his mind worked to absorb, expand upon, and adjust the knowledge to make it his own as well as improving upon it.

His unwavering focus wasn't enough to solve the issue at hand in a single fell swoop, but it brought him further than he'd expected by the time he finally had to close his eyes and step away from the intricate patterns. He wasn't tired, exactly, thanks to his Constitution, but he still needed a solid mental break. Casting around for something to take his mind off of this for the moment, he saw the off-duty guards dealing out a hand of cards, and he hurried over to join them.

If nothing else, he could bet his luxury soaps to eventually boost his Luck, while he waited for his mana to be accessible once more. He had a feeling he was going to need as much of the fickle fortune as he could get.

The remainder of his timer seemed to tick by with a near-insulting slowness, but as it reached its end, his eyes were on the clock as the countdown finally reached ten seconds, nine...

Mana Unlocked!

Joe heaved in a breath of air as his power bloomed in his chest like a lotus blossom emerging from a muddy pool. The power began to trickle through him, and he started to relax into it as the familiar feeling filled him once more. Then his eyes went wide, and he realized that he had a rare opportunity to push his mana to a more condensed state at the moment.

Usually, he had so much infusing every part of his body that attempting to condense it was futile. But now?

He folded his cards and stepped away, dropping into a seated position and focused on constricting the power that was already starting to rampage through him. Joe didn't exactly want to keep it contained to one single area, as his traits wouldn't allow for that. Instead, he wanted each strand of power to be more cohesive, stronger, thinner, so more of them could exist in the same area at once.

Perhaps it was the state he was in, perhaps it was the fact that he'd been using so much of his mana recently, but the skill level came easily.

Skill Increase: Coalescence (Journeyman II).

With hopeful eyes, he checked on his Mana Manipulation skill, which almost always seemed to gain a level alongside Coalescence. He wasn't *too* disappointed to see that it hadn't increased, though he was *slightly* frustrated at how slow the progress was for such common-seeming skills. Putting that aside, he returned to the task he had been working on for nearly a full day.

"I've got two sections completed, and the third one is going much faster than they did." Joe gritted his teeth, trying to decide if he should finish here, return to Novusheim to make sure everything was moving smoothly, or collect his team and get back in his bubble. Daniella needed help... but would another day or two really matter?

Ever-so-slowly, his eyes turned back to the ritual diagram, and Joe sank to the floor. His quill came out and began moving faster and faster as his eyes lit up with the simple joy of the magic he was getting to work with.

"I'm sure whatever is in here will help with all of the other situations. There. Perfect. I justified my choice to myself."

CHAPTER TWENTY-EIGHT

However flimsy his excuses were to focus on his one true love—magic—the results spoke for themselves. In a mere four days, Joe was able to completely repair the ritual to his satisfaction.

Staring down at the floor, it was clear to see where he'd added his own work. The previously weathered sections had been replaced with simplified, elegant lines of light from his aspect inscriber. The entire room was filled with a low level of ever-escalating energy, as if the world itself was taking notice of what he was doing.

Joe could only hope it approved of his actions.

When he had first completed the ritual, he'd cheerfully gone to activate it, panicking momentarily when he realized that this was a Master-rank ritual, but he didn't have a matching Artifact core to activate it. Then he realized he was being ridiculous: thanks to the difference his changes had made to the original ritual, a Unique Core would more than suffice to get it up and running.

Still, he'd learned his lesson by now, and he had gone all-out in ensuring his work was protected. Not only did he carefully go over each of his lines, he had dozens of people formed up around the area that this ritual *should* open up, just to make sure there were no surprises with monsters popping out of the wood-work once again.

Reasonably certain that they would be able to handle any nasty surprises, Joe started pumping mana into the diagram and hoped for the best. A passing thought crossed his mind, and he sharply sucked in some air. "I hope opening this doesn't give us yet another monster type to have to deal with."

Even speaking quietly, enough people heard him that they shuffled in place uncomfortably. Still, disquieted or not, Joe wasn't about to stop after having put in this much effort. Mana surged through the inner circle of the ritual, expanding out until it was coursing through the entire diagram. Ancient mech-anisms creaked and rumbled as the design of the ritual revealed itself by lifting up from the floor on one side and sinking in on the other. "Gyroscope. Called it."

Mana from the ritual drained down into the square of the floor, and bolts were drawn back from deeper and deeper recesses, sliding into place with a groaning creak and a clink of blessed finality. Finally, the ritual stopped in place, completely perpendicular to the ground, and the ground started to shift.

The entire square area lifted slowly out of the ground, revealing an enormous metal box, finally resolving into a smaller version of the immense vault they were in. When it had fully emerged from the ground, the wall facing the outer door of the building split in the center, a seam going from top to bottom slowly pushing apart straight out to either side. Everyone who could see it leaned forward, weapons raised and spells prepared.

They needn't have worried. As the door opened fully, a light flicked on, and their breath was taken away. This inner vault was filled with thousands upon thousands of stacked, gleaming ingots of a type of metal Joe didn't recognize. As far as he could tell, there was only that and a small folder that sat atop it within the innermost sanctum.

"Okay." Joe took a deep breath, trying not to be disappointed that they'd gained... crafting materials. He was certain it would be extremely useful to everyone else. "This has to be pretty valuable, why else would they go to such lengths to protect it, even going so far as to have a secondary vault with a Master lock on it?"

A Dwarf Joe had seen working in the forge on many occasions stepped forward, raising his hand halfway up toward Joe, though his eyes were locked on the metal in the vault. "Mind if I take a whack at identifying it?"

The Ritualist motioned him forward, but the Dwarf had already started moving. Joe watched as the bearded individual lifted an ingot, letting out a grunt of approval at its weight. Then things got... somewhat strange. Hefting the metal was only the start: the Dwarf tried to bend it, examined it very closely with what looked like a jeweler's examination tool, licked it, and even tried nibbling on its edges. Finally, he turned and whipped it at a wall, where it bounced without leaving any visible damage on either surface.

"Was that necessary?" Joe inquired with a bit of bite in his voice.

"Kinda yes, kinda no." There was a smirk nearly hidden by the bushy beard as the Dwarf motioned for someone to pick up the ingot. "I only needed to do it if it turns out that I was right."

"*Yeowch!*" The person who had picked up the bar of metal dropped it, shaking their hand and quickly dropping it to the freezing cold floor. "How's it that *hot?*"

"Yes!" The apparent metal-identifying expert hurried over and grabbed the ingot with a pair of tongs, before bringing it back and setting it atop the stack. Soon thereafter, a gust of warm air blew Joe's hairy cloak out around him, offering him a moment to appreciate the warmth and how clean his clothing was. As far as he could tell, the rest of the metal had absorbed and somehow *increased* the amount of heat that the first bar was giving off. "It's *gotta* be Jotunheim Alloy."

Only a few people seem to know what that meant, and by their hushed excitement, Joe took it that they thought of it as a nearly legendary metal. The Dwarf turned and swept a hand at the pile. "It's a superconductor of energy, whether that is heat, concussive force, or all manner of things like that. It's extremely useful in weapons because, even without enchantment, you can get a lengthy fire buff just by swinging the metal through a fire before heading out to fight. That's just the most common usage of it; I'm sure there's all manner of things we can do with it."

By the end of the impromptu lecture, Joe was practically salivating over the significance of this discovery. This was an alloy with the inherent ability to create intense heat, and it would most certainly be an effective, formidable tool against the frozen monsters that roamed this world. But, the most exciting thing to him was how many ideas were popping into his head of what he could use this for.

Almost immediately, he started muttering as he stepped forward to look over the pallets of ingots. "Cut them into small chunks, and we have instant hand warmers. Pull them out into wire, and I bet we could figure out how to fix the water tower issue we've been having with it freezing after being left alone for too many hours. Ooh… what if we installed this in our roads as we build them, so they constantly stay toasty and melt the snow and ice that lands on them?"

The metallurgist Dwarf seemed nervous at what he was hearing, "Look, lad, there's quite a bit of this, but not enough for *roads*! You'd be hard-pressed to make… let's say, a thousand weapons out of this? Maybe two?"

But Joe wasn't listening. Instead, his eyes were on the small folder, which had a few wisps of smoke rising from it where it was resting on the pile of ingots. He snatched it off, patting out the tiny sparks that were trying to catch hold of the ancient, dry document. He opened it and found himself reading a manual detailing the process of creating this particular alloy. "Ahhh… so that's what it is. The entire vault system, all of the contingencies, even the monsters that must've been herded into here? It wasn't to protect the stacks of alloy. All of this was put here to keep this recipe safe."

"Ye' found the *recipe* for it?" The Dwarf nearly stumbled over his words as he rushed over to try and grab the document from Joe's hands, but the folder vanished into the human's codpiece before the hairy fellow had taken his second step.

Joe put a bright smile on his face as he looked around at all of the people staring at him with hunger in their gazes. "I don't know about the rest of you, but I think we can call this quest *complete!*"

Even as he reveled in their find, and the Dwarves murmured amongst themselves, a low rumbling began to fill the air. At first, everyone moved back into formed lines, ready to defend against the threat, but then a section of the ceiling fell to the ground. Joe wasn't sure who it was, but a mad dash for the exit ensued over the next few seconds when someone screamed, "The whole place is collapsing! It's a contingency trap!"

Joe didn't stick around to try and play a hero, or make sure that everyone else got out first. A single Omnivault let him exit the doors along with the stampede of Dwarves, their immense speed ensuring that everyone escaped into the open before the structure began crumbling to the ground, tipping over as it did so. Finally, the huge obelisk fell into the walls of snow around it with a calamitous **boom** as though it were the largest bell in Eternium.

"If *that* doesn't draw monsters in, I'd pay double." Joe growled at the interruption, casting worried glances at the building and hoping that they'd be able to claim the rest of their prize before they had to flee. Surprisingly, the collapse of the building had been arrested, thanks to the snow and ice around it propping it up. Making a snap decision, he threw himself back inside, rushing over to the inner vault.

The Ritualist wasn't able to store the thousands of ingots into his codpiece, but luckily, he wasn't the only person motivated by greed at the moment. A dozen people stood around him, accepting armloads of the extremely heavy metal and rushing out of the doors, some of them even coming back for a second load after tossing the ingots to other waiting arms. As the last of it went out, Joe started for the door once more, only to notice that the inner vault section had remained in its position when the rest of the structure had partially sunk around it.

"The ritual has it!" Joe sprinted back to the now-floating cube, Omnivaulting to the top of it and grabbing hold of the swirling gyroscope. He was familiar enough with the design at this point that he was able to slightly shift one of the rings, and immediately the box started floating toward the door. "Of course, a super advanced society wouldn't want to carry all of this by hand. Flying elevator, let's go~o!"

Riding the floating vault out of the falling vault, Joe had a wicked smile on his face as he hovered over the Dwarves and pretended he was about to lose control. That worked only the first three times, then he started getting people tossing him rude gestures instead of throwing themselves out of the path. He laughed out loud, only to be nearly knocked unconscious as a chunk of the larger building fell to the side, smacking him and the cube out of the air like a fly swatter hitting a gnat.

Even as he tumbled across the surface of the snow, Joe only tried to regain control to see what had happened to his metal box. When he laid eyes on it, pure nervousness filled him.

A small section of the top of the box had been sheared away, and mana was beginning to spill into the air around it. Joe thrust a finger at it, shouting at the top of his lungs, "Master rank magic going critical! Evacuate *immediately*!"

Throwing himself forward, Joe latched onto the ritual and tried to figure out a way to cancel it without allowing the magic to detonate. After only one full second of study, he was able to decide without a shadow of a doubt that he had a better chance of finding a warm, sunny beach on Jotunheim than fixing this before it went *boom*.

Just before he abandoned it and started running for the shrine like everyone else had done, something caught Joe's detail-oriented eyes. Where the ceiling of the metal cube had been damaged, retractable bolts were holding onto the walls. Hoping that he wasn't sentencing himself to another death, he got *inside* it and cast around for anything that looked like… "There! An emergency release lever!"

He yanked on the lever, and the ritual-inscribed ceiling launched into the sky, while the rest of the walls fell off of the container and clattered to the ground. There were still a few stragglers near him, so they and Joe grabbed the walls and floor, moving as quickly as they could toward the shrine. "I hope this works!"

The Dwarves were laughing maniacally. "Can we *hold* stuff while we teleport?"

"I've never shown up naked before, so I've got a good feeling about it!"

"Just go one hop over," Joe instructed them quickly, "otherwise the amount of mana it's going to take is—"

Then he couldn't hear his own words. The sky was shuddering with such intense turbulence that it was chopping up what he was saying. A glance upward told Joe that it was *definitely* time to go; he was fairly certain the clouds had melted, and the entire horizon was falling toward them even as he watched.

Activating the fast travel, Joe whooped as the adrenaline from evading the consequences of his greed hit his system.

CHAPTER TWENTY-NINE

Standing at the door of his workshop, Joe looked between the normal-size door, comparing it to the enormous sheets of metal that had, until recently, been part of a vault. "Yeah, no way I'm getting these through there without putting them in storage and taking them out inside. Even then, I think they're going to be a little too long for the ceiling."

Pondering his options, Joe walked around and decided that the best option was actually going to be to demolish a section of his workshop, place the sheets of metal to create a better-secured area, then rebuild the walls around them. "There's no way I'm giving up these super-cool sliding doors. That *has* to be added to something I'm gonna keep."

That raised a fairly significant issue he needed to take into consideration. If he wanted to change the underlying structure of his building, he needed to find an Architect that could draw up the plans; then have them actually built by construction workers. Joe was unable to work directly with this material by himself, though once the design was completed, he could scan the building and make as many copies of it as he wanted.

Socar was an Architect, but his specialty was in abnormal

styles of buildings. Joe needed something functional, sturdy, that didn't impact the ambient flows of energy in the world. In other words: he needed to get Daniella. That put a wry grin on his face. "The reasons to rescue you just keep stacking up, don't they?"

Certainly, he could try and get in the queue for a Dwarven Architect, but as a part of the council, he knew exactly how long that line was.

After going to the warehouse and convincing Maximus to let him put his walls into a secured corner, Joe walked toward the shrine to finally finish his self-set goal of rescuing his friend. He was *slightly* nervous about the functionality of his fast travel system; his recent journey to the mysterious ruins had been calamitous to that area.

Initial reports indicated that nearly a hundred feet of snow had accumulated atop the area they had been working, in a radius of over two miles. Hundreds of monsters were already assaulting the area, slowly stomping the fallen snow flat.

He was hoping the mountain of precipitation that had been dumped on his shrine wouldn't impact his ability to use it in his travel network. It hadn't been an issue in the small Hamlet that he'd managed to get destroyed, but that was a handful of dirt in comparison.

"It makes me wonder if those clouds are really just floating mountains of snow up there..." He looked up, only to meet with the false sky that he had created, which showed a bright, cheery, sunny morning. "I doubt it, but maybe when an explosion like that sucks them closer to the planet, all of the condensation falls as snow?"

Not having anywhere to go with that line of thinking, his mind skipped over to the quest he had issued. Frankly, Joe was relieved at how well everything had worked out there. The Council of Novusheim had agreed to hold all of the Jotunheim Alloy and was distributing it as the quest reward to the people who had participated. The overall contribution of most of the

Dwarves was fairly high, thanks to the monsters they'd needed to fight against.

Even so, Joe himself had been considered as a thirty-percent contributor all by himself, thanks to being the one to crack the final layers of the outer vault as well as the inner vault. He'd seen the chance to earn some brownie points with the Town as a whole, so the Ritualist only claimed the broken walls that he was going to use in his workshop. Even the recipe for the alloy was going to be handed over as soon as he managed to create his own aspect-based recipe. So really, he wasn't even taking that as a reward, he was just exercising his right as a councilman to examine it.

That had left a substantial amount of the upper Expert-ranked material for the Town's usage, and even the most human-leery councilman had given him a bright smile and pat on the back as he walked out without requesting any further reward for donating his portion.

Joe had earned a major favor with his actions, and he already knew how he was going to spend it. "Get Daniella back here, convince the council to let her work for me, and put her on the same community service track Master Stu is on. Unless she somehow gained a whole bunch of combat ability, the usual path toward citizenship is going to be a massive hardship. Solid plan. Let's go!"

Moments later, his mana pool was near empty, and he was over nine thousand miles away. Joe shivered as he set up his bubble once again, ready to brave the skies of Jotunheim. By the time he was done with his initial setup, his mana pool had recovered well enough that he was able to easily power the ritual.

Flying through the air, lounging in his bean-bag chair and wrapped in warm blankets as he drank his coffee, Joe watched the ground level of the planet as the night deepened. "It's a tough quest, but I'll finish it soon."

Slurp.

"Mmm. Good choice on the brew today, Mate. Is that Kona

coffee? If not, it's close," the Ritualist idly commented while pulling out his notebook and going over a few changes he wanted to make to his routine when he was done with this project. "How can I harness the odd qualities of Jotunheim's energy fields to my advantage? The magic in the air is dense, but far too chaotic for standard usage, unless I'm able to alter it from its violent state. I wonder what the gravity is like here... it feels like Earth normal for me, but so did Alfheim, after I figured out how to push through. I bet if I go to Midgard, I could practically fly by thinking really hard at this point."

He began writing his ideas out, centering them around how to harness the chaotic mana in the air and find a way to utilize what he assumed was greatly increased gravity for various training purposes. "Maybe I could lighten the gravity across a large area by creating a ritual to focus it in a single building? If I did it well, I could create a training zone to push even the strongest individuals to their limits. That would allow them to adapt and grow stronger even faster."

The idea was fascinating to him, but it was nothing new. People had been trying to figure out ways to get stronger since the dawn of time, so this went on the low priority list. Still, there was one aspect of the plan where his mind kept returning.

"I need to destroy one more Elven settlement to get Havoc to finish creating the plans for a Mana Battery recharging station. With how dense the power in the air is, I don't think it'll be any issue to put the stations almost anywhere and have them work without any additional input. Part of me thinks that'll have an effect on the rampant power in the area, at least if I make strong enough versions of the enchantment. What do you think, Mate?"

The elemental declined to answer, instead quietly filling up Joe's coffee mug and unsummoning itself. Joe bobbed his head. "Totally agree, nothing more to be said on that subject for now."

With plenty of other work to do, Joe didn't slack while he was traveling, making what he deemed as acceptable progress on his rituals. He landed once, and on the second bubble flight, he prepared himself to return to Novusheim and get Heartpiercer to join him.

After creating the second shrine of the day, he placed his hands on its surface and attempted to teleport back to Novusheim. When he didn't move, Joe initially panicked, thinking that one of his shrines must have been destroyed along the route. It was only when he saw the message appear in his vision that he was able to take a deep breath.

Mana cost for transportation is too high for your current mana pool!

"Maybe I should upgrade the shrine in town to something more... impressive. Maybe that would help mitigate some of the travel cost." Quickly deactivating Retaliation of Shadows and Neutrality Aura allowed him to pay the necessary cost, and in only a few minutes, he was activating his Ritual of Communication to get Heartpiercer's attention.

As they'd discussed this plan ahead of time, the Archer came running over, dressed and equipped for the bitter cold of Jotunheim. "I'm ready if you are; which shrine are we going to?"

"That depends on how much mana you have." Joe offered a weak smile at her questioning look. "Reaching the end of the road just yoinked eighty-five hundred mana out of my mana pool. If you have less than that, you might want to break up the trip a bit."

"Abyss, Joe." Heartpiercer seemed to be rethinking her agreement for this mission. "Whatever, just give me the coordinates I need to bounce to first."

Both of them put their hands on the fast travel shrine, and Joe set up the path she should take. "If you go to shrine twenty-three, 'aurora six', 'not avalanche three', then to 'one hop out', I'll meet you there."

"Please tell me these names were automatically assigned, and you didn't name... never mind, of course you named them. How else would you be able to figure out the pathing this easily?" She rolled her eyes at Joe's stricken expression, concentrating for a moment before vanishing, hopefully along the path that the Ritualist had set out for her.

"It's not my fault that I need to name things in a memorable way." Joe grumped slightly at the situation, allowing his mana pool to top off before teleporting all the way back to the end of the line.

Nearly fifteen minutes later, Heartpiercer finally arrived, heaving for breath as her mana once again nearly bottomed out. "That sucks, and I'm not doing that more than one more time. You better hope she's where you think she is."

"I'm… let's say eighty percent certain that she's within three hours of travel from here." Joe was still lamenting the fact that his enchanted shirt had been torn, but so long as the settlement that Daniella had been imprisoned in wasn't destroyed yet… he cut off that line of thinking, knowing that he had no other options for attempting to track her down if she wasn't in the area.

It was a tight squeeze to get into the bubble, at least compared to how Joe was used to traveling at this point. His teammate declined the use of his bean-bag chair, which made him uncomfortable with bringing it out and taking up the majority of the space. Then, when he tried to get some work done, she glared at him and thrust a finger directly at his face.

"If *you* think *I'm* going to sit here for hours on end and be ignored, you have another thing coming. I will pop this bubble *so* fast."

CHAPTER THIRTY

The duo of the Ritualist and the haughty Archer cautiously approached the outskirts of a small, brightly lit Elven Village. Joe had destroyed enough settlements that he could tell that this was of a higher quality by far. Even if his eyes hadn't been so discerning, the clearly enchanted walls, vigilant guards, and half-dozen buildings of at least Uncommon quality that were peeking over the walls would've given it away.

It was obvious that this Village was well protected, but Joe could only hope they were only guarding from the outside threat of monsters and hadn't yet set up any way to detect intruders from opposing alliances. Certainly, he wasn't going to bet his life on that, but that was why he'd brought Heartpiercer in the first place.

"Are you seeing anything I can use to get through? Something tells me hopping over the wall isn't going to be as easy here as it was in the last settlement I had to wreck." Joe was agitated, so he spun his ritual orbs above his hands nearly unconsciously, having practiced with them so much that finesse with three of the orbs didn't require much attention.

Long moments of contemplation went by as they circled the Village twice. Eventually, his companion shook her head and gave her verdict on the situation. "Joe, you're not getting in there without them knowing you're going in. Wait, let me rephrase that, you might be able to get *in*, but you'll most certainly never get out. The guards are active, rotating, and each is within eye and earshot of the next. I'm going to have to recommend we leave and come back with a full war party."

"I was really hoping you weren't going to say that." Joe pressed his hands together and took a deep breath. "Okay, here's what we're going to do. I'm going to walk right through the front gate, pretend to be a merchant, and get as much information as I can before they catch on."

"Oh, so you've chosen death." Heartpiercer snorted at him derisively. "Great plan. Should I go hang out by the shrine for the next couple of days while I wait for you to respawn?"

When his eyes lit up at that idea, the Archer shook her head and opened her mouth to talk him out of whatever inane plan he was concocting. Joe cut her off by waving both hands and motioning for them to retreat away from the Village. One of the Elves, likely a supervisor of the guards, had paused in his usual walk around the top of the walls. That was more than enough for the Ritualist to decide it was time for them to go.

After they had retreated to what he hoped was a safe distance, they began making their way back to the shrine. "I think that I have enough favor with Tatum that I can request a boon that would be helpful here. Let's go and see what he has to offer me, and if it doesn't work out... I guess we can only hope we can convince a couple thousand people to come and destroy this Village with us. The problem is, there's a good shot that no one living there survives, then the whole mission plan is scrapped."

"Yeah... I do agree that our short, hairy friends are... *thorough*." Heartpiercer at least didn't seem actively opposed to Joe's plan at this point, so they hurried back through the darkness of the frozen wasteland as quickly as they could.

When they were finally standing next to the altar, the Ritualist walked over and whispered his thoughts. "Hey, big guy! This is going to be a tough nut to crack, and getting in there and back out is going to require some finesse and subtlety that I don't naturally possess."

Here he rubbed his hand over his bald head, which reflected any light that landed on it twice as brightly as it hit him. "*Yea~ah*. Anything that you can provide would be super helpful here."

When he touched the shrine, a notification popped up immediately. Reading over it made Joe smile, and he cracked his neck in anticipation.

You have received a temporary Boon of Neutrality! The deity of neutrality, Occultatum, has bestowed upon you a shroud that will mask your presence, conceal your affiliations, and deceive skills and spells designed to discern truthful statements. This shroud will be effective on all skills and spells up to and including the Expert rank. Time remaining: 23:59:58.

"Now that's what I'm talking about. Thanks, Tatum!" He didn't receive a reply, but the boon was more than enough. After sharing the details of his temporary abilities with his companion, Joe walked back to the Village in a roundabout manner, eventually approaching the front gate with newfound confidence. Before he came within clear eye shot of the guards, he pulled a large traveling pack out of his spatial codpiece, filling it with luxury goods and samples of the wares he had access to from Novusheim.

Then, he walked directly up to the gate, waving his hands and calling for attention. Thanks to his Darkvision ability, he was able to see *exactly* how many arrows and spells were being pointed at him, but as a standard human, he shouldn't have been able to pierce the veil of darkness. He tried not to react, as though he were as blind as the arrogant Elven Guard Captain would expect him to currently be.

"Who goes there, and more importantly… *why?*" The voice that reached his ears was as titillating and melodious as Joe expected, and his loss of the Dwarven Superiority title allowed him to fully appreciate it.

"Why... *hello* there." Joe tried to act the part of an overly Charismatic merchant, sweeping into a bow as he pretended not to be able to see exactly who was speaking to him. "I am a humble merchant who's been moving between settlements and bringing the finest luxury goods around so everyone can enjoy a few moments of decadence each day. I was ever so pleased to see the lights of your fine town, as I have been wondering in the outer darkness for... let's just say, too long."

"I suppose the next thing you are going to tell me is that you didn't bring your own light source because you didn't want to attract monsters?" The harsh tone of the questions had softened into merely exasperation, which Joe felt was a good step forward. "Merchants... fools, the lot of you. If there hadn't been a general decree to allow your kind to continue your work for the betterment of the Theocracy, I would strip you of all of your merchandise and have you completing penances for at least a month. Where are your guards?"

Joe let a smug smirk appear on his lips. "They are at home, *not* eating into my profit margins."

"Twice a fool. Your Luck must be your highest stat." A few shouted orders later, and the gate opened just enough to allow him entry. He stepped through, only to be met with the Elf he'd been speaking to, along with a small squadron of humans. "You will be chaperoned the entire time you are within our walls. If you decide to join our settlement, you will be given favorable rates for trades, though your taxes will increase by three and a half percent."

"Your magnanimity shows no bounds! Please allow this humble merchant to offer you this small gift as thanks for your beneficence." Joe reached into his pack and pulled out a small gift basket of soap, socks, mittens, and a matching hat.

As he handed over the small selection, he wistfully stared at the Hoardling-hair beanie, wishing he could wear something to help his head to stay warm. He knew better than that, as his curse was still in effect. The effects of his curse of baldness had been made a part of him, and putting something like that on was just *begging* to have the hat and the top of his head catch on fire.

Yet it seemed that his stare was misinterpreted, and the gift was received with glee at his discomfort at giving it away. The Elf let out a *'humph'* as she accepted the small bribe, though she took out the warm gear and put it on immediately. "It seems the old adage holds true even in this world. Parting a merchant and their profits still causes them physical pain. Before you go any further, *Sense Truth.* Are you who you say you are? Are you affiliated with the Elven Theocracy? Do you have any designs against our town or our people?"

"Yes, yes, and no in that order." Joe responded immediately, confident that his deception wouldn't be noticed. The Elf looked at him for a moment longer, nodded, and whisked away to return to her duties atop the wall. The Ritualist smiled at the humans, who were looking at him with great curiosity, and clapped his hands together. "Going by the smell, I think everyone here will be *overjoyed* to know that I am selling soap! I can bring it in bulk, or I can sell for inflated prices to allow only the best among you to stand out with your sweet scents. Which would you prefer?"

The group looked at each other then back to him with wide smiles. Joe already knew what their answer would be. In an incredibly competitive and contentious society such as the Elven Theocracy, any small advantage was worth its weight in... he panicked for a moment, as he realized he had no idea what he should be charging for his goods. Luckily, his internal panicking wasn't picked up on, and one of his minders sidled up and threw an arm around Joe's shoulders. "I'd absolutely love to know what sort of exclusive deal you could offer me!"

"Offer *us*, Trevor. If you try to make a deal and cut us out, I'll put you down right here and make sure you don't get a *whiff* of what he's offering." The tip of the speaker's staff was glowing, pointed directly at Trevor's head. Joe was deeply uncomfortable with this fact, especially when he was gently pushed to stand in front of the slightly-nervous chaperone.

"Plenty to go around!" Joe nervously chuckled as he tried to extract himself from Trevor's grip. "Is there anywhere I can set up shop?"

The tense silence from the group didn't abate until Joe finally decided he had enough and started walking away from them. Then, to do their duty, the squad had to fall in around him to make sure he wasn't up to anything nefarious. Their attitude had suggested they'd be at each other's throats the entire time, this group had clearly been working together for a long time with how easily their argument was put behind them.

"So... what's up with me needing babysitters?" he playfully questioned the people around him.

"Yeah, sorry-not-sorry about this," Trevor spoke up, his eyes gleaming as he looked from Joe's face to the large pack on his back. "A few days back, we had some random respawns in our Village Hall. Apparently, someone snuck into a Hamlet and sabotaged their settlement during a Beast Wave. Everyone died, and we got saddled with nearly a quarter more people. If there weren't a couple of nearby Villages to send them to, we'd have people sleeping in the roads even now."

"A *couple* nearby Villages?" Joe grit his teeth at that, hoping he wouldn't need to replicate his subterfuge. Something told him this was going to be the easiest settlement to enter. "Where'd all of this happen? How worried should I be?"

The Mage who had threatened Trevor shook her head and muttered something under her breath, before looking over at him with a droll stare. "Yeah, it was a continent's distance away, as far as we can tell. Couple thousand miles at least. But as soon as there's *one* saboteur, the rest of us have to pay for it."

"They were probably just looking for a reason to use that prison they built." Trevor grumbled under his breath. Still, it wasn't quite enough, and a few of the squad hissed in alarm and smacked the man on the back of the head almost simultaneously. "What—ah, abyss, please don't report me. I wasn't *trying* to disparage our life coaches."

"Ah, don't worry about it." Joe waved off the squad's concern easily, and each of them relaxed minutely. "Traveling around as much as I do, you learn to let things go. Just out of curiosity… where'd you say they built that prison?"

CHAPTER THIRTY-ONE

It was strange to attempt to draw attention in an enemy controlled area, or at least a *hostile* zone. The Ritualist truly didn't want to consider his fellow humans as enemies, nor did he have any long-term plans to go after Elves. Frankly, if they wouldn't attack him as soon as they knew who he was, Joe would *actually* work to set up proper trade routes and exchange of goods and services between them. But, as it was, he was careful not to reveal his true intentions, purpose, or affiliations.

Initially, the villagers were cautious about a newcomer. The rumors that had been spread, combined with the harsh circumstances made everyone a bit more on edge than they otherwise would've been. Still, as Joe brought forth item after item, they gradually warmed to his presence. His exotic merchandise and the stories about the fearsome creatures roaming the land around them brought in dozens of people who were more than happy for the diversion from their normal routines.

Joe made sure to downplay his role in any of his stories, making sure that his part had always been seeing the monster from a distance and hiding until it was gone. Eventually, even his chaperones felt relaxed around him and began walking with their hands *off* of their weapons when he moved around. It was a small thing, but it brought great relief to the Ritualist when he noticed.

As the hours passed, he subtly steered conversation away from himself and onto more local gossip. Very intentionally, he didn't ask any questions about what they spoke on, merely encouraging people to speak so he could 'rest his voice'. At first, the topics were very light, as those around him carefully gauged his reactions to the less-than-perfect living conditions that the Elves were the cause of.

But eventually, the conversation shifted into hushed tones as one person who seemed less fearful of punishment spoke out, his anger at the situation palpable. "Three Villages within an hour's travel at a dead sprint, less than eight thousand people all together, and the Middle Village feels the need to spend their Rare building slot on a prison? If that doesn't tell you what they think of the rest of us, I don't know what to tell ya."

"Are you *inebriated?*" To Joe's surprise, it was Trevor who hissed in the man's ear, "They hear you talking like that, half a month of penance is going to be the least of your concerns. If you want to see the inside of that prison you seem to dislike so much, keep it up."

For the first time, Joe decided to hazard a question about the situation. Leaning in toward Trevor and the now wide-eyed man, he whispered, "Why would the Elves need to build a prison? It just doesn't make sense, does it? Worst comes to worst, wouldn't exile be more fitting in a place like this?"

Trevor relaxed his grip on the terrified man's arm, turning to Joe and letting out a sigh. "There's no harm in letting you *know* about this; it's common knowledge. Fungus here was just saying it in a way that made a certain group sound bad, which *all* of us know wasn't his intention."

"Absolutely," Joe agreed easily.

"You see, the Middle Village is entirely *human* run. One single guild. Our Elven friends let them set up their own place as a test, but they made sure all of the original residents are the most *zealous* among us," Trevor quietly stated as he gently shooed away Fungus. "Everyone there is working very diligently to prove they're driven with an unyielding devotion to the cause of the Theocracy. They're *very good* people, and very *excited and enthusiastic* about helping everyone get on their level."

"I see." Joe completely understood the message that Trevor was trying to get across and stopped pressing immediately. Already, he was worried that he'd gone too far, as several of the squad of chaperones were giving him considering looks. The fact was, this was supposed to be common knowledge. If he didn't know it, that meant he was from outside the area. After making a couple more sales—happily, they were using cores for bartering—the Ritualist handed each of his minders a small gift and bowed to them in the style of a high-ranking Elven authority.

He'd fought and been captured by enough of them that he could mimic their movements fairly easily at this point. When everyone went still, eyes wide, Joe merely kept a gentle smile on his face and nodded at them. "Thank you all for your purchases; I think I should be on my way. With how crowded the town is, I would not want to burden you with my presence any longer."

Trevor stammered a few times, trying to rectify what he was seeing with the mannerisms that had been drilled into him. Then Joe's words registered, and they began escorting him out of the Village. When they arrived at the gate, Joe once more thanked them for their assistance and having him in their care, ensuring that his gratitude appeared sincere. Frankly, he *was* extremely thankful to them—the information he'd gained was vital to his success.

After having Trevor point out the most direct route to the Middle Village, Joe walked away with determined steps. He waited until he was three times as far away as he thought he needed to be, then doubled back and around to the shrine, ensuring that no one had followed him.

Heartpiercer was waiting for him. "Glad to see you made it back. How was it?"

"That was probably one of the most terrifying experiences I've had in Eternium," Joe admitted, finally able to relax enough that he started shaking slightly. "That was definitely an extrovert-level infiltration, not something I think I can do twice."

"Did you figure out where she is?"

Joe was already nodding his head by the time the Archer finished her question. "Yeah, apparently there's an impressive prison in a Village about an hour's sprint that way."

"Are you going to try this again?" Heartpiercer fell silent as Joe shook his head. Then a smile cracked her face, turning malicious in only a moment. "Do we get to go get Jaxon?"

"Yeah. I think that'd be a good idea." Joe hesitated momentarily, then recanted his statement. "Actually, perhaps we should go check out the place we're going to be busting into ahead of time. Jaxon doesn't exactly have the stealthy gene, so if we don't have our plan of attack ready before we get there, we won't get the chance to make one."

"Fair." They shared a chuckle that softened into a sigh as they thought about their friend. He was always fun to be around, but it was a well-known fact that he was slightly… off.

They began their trek across the frozen tundra, their path illuminated only by the intermittent light of enchanted walls being tested by monsters in the distance. The cold, crisp snow reflected and refracted the light at a great distance, almost like lightning on the horizon. Joe had a general idea of which way to go, thanks to the information he'd gained in the Village. But, as the night deepened, he hoped that the Middle Village would be at least as well-lit.

"It's supposed to be an hour-long sprint to get there, so let's take it easy and keep an eye out for any issues. For anything that we can use against them, too, I suppose." The last part was said doubtfully, as the landscaping in this area was equally as flat as the terrain around Novusheim.

The wind was beginning to pick up, and Joe's Neutrality Aura was having a hard time pushing back against the intense debuff that was trying to stack on them. Even if they weren't sprinting at top speed, they were still running as quickly as they safely could, which had the unfortunate side effect of stripping their body heat just as quickly as they generated it. Joe took the lead so he could take the brunt of the wind, providing a small lee against the wind for Heartpiercer to shelter in.

Their footprints left imprints on the frozen ground, but far less than expected. For Joe's part, he had extended his Exquisite Shell around his feet to be able to run as if he were wearing snowshoes. As far as he could tell, Heartpiercer had some ability to stay atop the snow as well, which he attributed to her skills as an archer and scout.

Joe felt like all of his senses were in overdrive, a mixture between excitement and adrenaline at nearly being done with this portion of his quest, and fear of the unknown around them. The only sounds in the completely still night were the crunching of snow under their feet and their heavy breathing as they maintained their rapid pace. He bit his tongue before saying anything about it, as it was clear that he was even louder than she was. The Ritualist tried to control his breathing more carefully, to run along lightly on the balls of his feet instead of simply barreling forward.

The tundra stretched out before them, a vast expanse of stark whiteness, punctuated by strange, broken silhouettes. As they pressed forward, Joe realized that the silhouettes were moving. He held up a hand to alert Heartpiercer, slowing down in the next moment as the darker shadows in the night resolved into a flock of Penguins moving in the same direction they were.

"Don't worry," Heartpiercer whispered into his ear. "They're larger and much louder than we are. I can hear them squawking from here, there's no way they're going to pick up our noise at this distance. Just keep going."

Not trusting himself to speak, Joe simply nodded and picked up the pace once more. He'd never seen the creatures running *away* from him and was surprised to find that the feathers along their backs shimmered in various hues in the darkness. Pointing that out to his companion only earned him a blank look and a shake of the head, so Joe assumed his ability to perceive the oddity was thanks to his Darkvision.

As they pressed forward, there were a few dicey moments. At one point, they sprinted past a large snow bank, only for a dozen Penguins to suddenly stand up, shaking off the snow that had been covering them. They were facing in the wrong direction to see the humans who broke into a dead sprint, but some noise must have alerted them to their presence; they began squawking and looking around for whatever had caught their attention.

Luckily, it seemed that their night vision was nowhere near as good as Joe's, and they waddled off to join what must have been the start of a full-on Beast Wave. He breathed out a sigh of relief, knowing that the comical appearance of the enormous Penguins was deceiving. They were fast, with sharp beaks and a weighty body that could easily send the two of them to respawn if they were caught.

They moved more carefully along the treacherous landscape after that, slowing down significantly to ensure they could move cautiously around any snow drifts or pillars of ice that could be hiding a foe that would alert the larger swarm. Joe was on edge, his eyes constantly scanning the area around them for any signs of danger. He wasn't certain how well Heartpiercer could see, and took on the responsibility of watching for threats on both of their behalf.

He was somewhat surprised at how strangely beautiful the frozen night was. The sky was filled with swirling clouds, as usual, but as magical defenses in the distance were tested, and other various crackling energies lit up the sky, they filled with a breathtaking aurora. Ribbons of green, blue, and purple, swirled within the unending clouds, casting an extremely dim, otherworldly glow that Joe was able to perceive only thanks to the gifts Tatum had given to him. Times like this reminded him of the magical nature of this universe, and he swelled with pride at the knowledge that he'd someday be able to effect it with his own strength.

The flashes of light they were drawing closer to seemed to be acting as a dinner bell for the monsters, and soon they needed to evade more and more of the gathered beasts. What should have taken a single hour of sprinting stretched into what felt like an eternity, but eventually the walls of the Middle Village were visible in the distance.

Just like all Elven-based architecture, the enclave seemed to be a cunning combination of styles that embodied both the natural environment and the artistry of its residents. Despite what he'd been told, somehow Joe doubted there were *only* humans within those walls. He'd never known the Theocracy to not maintain a presence in an area they owned, and the unmistakable Elven craftsmanship whispered to him that there was more to the story.

Joe and Heartpiercer circled around the Village, inspecting every inch of it for weaknesses, writing down the patterns of the guards, and as the Beast Wave began, they were even able to see how effective the defenses were. The Ritualist even allowed his finger to brush over his ritual orb containing Essence Cycle, and he inspected the flows of power around the town. What he saw left him deeply frustrated.

"This is no random Beast Wave… the structures are shifting and transforming. I can see their city center elongating and pulling in power from the world around it. This Village is on the verge of upgrading into a Town."

CHAPTER THIRTY-TWO

The defenders of the Village were prepared for the attack, *eager* for it, going by the zeal that they put into each blow against the massive creatures coming for them. Arrows whistled through the air, so many that Joe wouldn't feel safe being anywhere in range while hiding. Clearly trained by their 'betters', the Archers rarely missed, their projectiles finding their mark with impressive accuracy.

A half-dozen of the Penguins were brought down every couple of seconds, the metal-tipped shafts of the arrows piercing through the birds' thick, feathery armor. When Joe compared the ranged attacks of this Village with his own, all of which were almost entirely his own devising, the scales in his mind didn't balance. Novusheim might be lacking in that department. "Take it easy... there's no way they're going to be able to match us in our close-combat efficiency, so we've got that going for us."

A few seconds later, enough of the creatures had approached the walls that the spellcasters took their turn. It was clear they'd been standing at the ready, because the tops of the walls lit up in scores of areas near-simultaneously. Incantations echoed through the strangely-still night air, bolts of arcane energy crackling and detonating amidst the swarm. Fireballs erupted, engulfing the creatures in flames, beams of light sliced entire creatures in half over fractions of a second, and enormous boulders rained from the sky as if they'd been thrown by trebuchet.

"I guess we know how they've been able to progress so quickly," Heartpiercer whispered into Joe's ear. "Their efficiency with each kill is off the charts. I don't know if we should try our luck here... it's clear to me that the entire population of this town is *elite*."

Joe didn't say anything for a few moments, watching as the attacking creatures were pushed back in a symphony of martial prowess and magical might. With each arrow sent flying, every spell cast, the ranks of the onslaught were brought to a standstill. Even when larger creatures began to show up, managing to get close enough to try their luck at the barrier in their path, they were met with the unyielding magical resistance that had been imbued into the walls themselves.

He turned to his companion, his expression grave. "I totally understand where you're coming from. This is going to be a crazy risk, and... you don't have to take it with me."

"We need to plan out a *pace*," she returned without hesitation, earning a blank look from the Ritualist. "A primary, alternate, contingency, and emergency plan. Pace. From the look of this place, I think you should try to replicate your merchant act. That was pretty abyssal successful, and it'll let us get the lay of the land. We have no vantage point; we can't look down from above and plan our route. This is going to have to be a snatch and grab, where we get Daniella and high-tail it outta here."

"Yeah, I can get behind that." Joe pondered her words for a long few moments, then motioned for her to follow him. They retreated approximately a quarter mile from the walls, and he dug a slanted tunnel down through the frozen ground. Then the Ritualist created a large room with the use of his Field Array, having to relocate only once due to the top of it collapsing immediately. "I'm going to build a shrine here, so we have an escape route built in. It's pretty close to the other one, so there shouldn't be much mana cost. If we only do a single hop, we can come in here practically empty and still get away."

"Good. What's our alternate?"

"Plan B is smashing our way in-"

Heartpiercer shook her head sharply, cutting him off before Joe could finish his thought. "That is contingency at the earliest, more likely *emergency*. I don't think you're going to like this, but I think that, if you can't get in as a merchant, you should be thrown in as a prisoner."

"You're right, I *don't* like that." Joe's lip curled in a sneer as he thought about allowing himself to be trussed up like a turkey and tossed into a cell with the minimum space available for him to survive.

"Rig yourself to be sent to respawn." As the Archer continued talking over him, Joe made a few sounds and held a hand up to his ears.

"La, laa. Strange, I can hear *myself*, can no one else hear me?"

Heartpiercer lifted an eyebrow in annoyance. "If you think we can get this done with no risk whatsoever, you're dreaming. Are you seriously going to tell me that you would go into an Elite area like that as a fake merchant, with no backup plan in case you're captured? I know you can set conditions on your rituals, so make one of them blast you into a crater and take a chunk of the town with you if you need to do it. Otherwise, you'll be in a cell *without* an escape plan."

"Gotcha." Joe let out a deep sigh of frustration, knowing that she was right about this. "If I hate it, but if it works, it's still worth doing. Can we at least make the contingency something that doesn't involve me offering myself up like a present to the theocracy?"

"*You* can. I've used up all my ideas for this project." The Archer sat against the side of the shrine and pulled out a small jar, then began oiling her bow to keep it in top form.

"Fair enough." Joe winced as he realized he'd been taking his frustration at the situation out on her. "Look, I'm sorry, I've just been working on this for weeks now, and I'm so *close* to being done. Then this enormous, seemingly insurmountable obstacle jumps in the way? I somehow have to get into a prison, inside of a fortress, then get back out while making sure Daniella—who has very few combat or survival skills—doesn't get sent to respawn as easily as those Penguins just did."

He needed to sit down as the seriousness of the situation crashed over him, and he took a few deep, calming breaths before trying to speak again. "Contingency. I think I might be able to set up a few Rituals of Raze to take down the walls during a Beast Wave. I'd want more than one going, just in case they're able to quickly find one of them, or there's some interference or backlash from the enchantments. Hopefully, that'd cause enough mayhem that I'd be able to slip in and raid the prison while they're fighting off the creatures."

The Archer paused in what she was doing, still not looking over at him. "Emergency?"

"Blast it to rubble, send every single person to a new spawn point after this place is completely leveled." Joe's eyes hardened, and he stood straight while pulling his coat tight around him. "Then I'll just need to hope that Daniella goes to one of the nearby towns when she respawns and can find someone sympathetic enough to help her get away. I will... need to figure out some new way to find her, but with enough time, anything is possible. Good enough for me. Action time."

"Are you going now?" Heartpiercer looked at him quizzically as he started crawling up the air shaft he'd created. "*During* a Beast Wave? Are you looking to get filled with arrows?"

"You know me. New experiences are always my target, and I think this one might really hit the mark. Depending on how this goes, I'll either be quivering with excitement... or just a-quiver." His humor sailed over her head, but Joe ignored the droll stare and finished ascending to the surface.

What he wasn't telling her was that, if he wanted to be able to get to his contingency plan in time, he'd need to activate the Rituals of Raze when the Boss monster approached. At this point, Joe was absolutely certain that requirement was the only one holding the Village back from moving to the next settlement rank. If all else failed, he *needed* to have that contingency in place. "Still, gotta admit, she has some great ideas."

"Also incredibly sensitive ears." The comments and a chuckle floated up out of the hole in the ground, and Joe blushed slightly at the knowledge that his inner thoughts had been overheard. Doing his best to ignore that, he kept low to the ground and crept toward the walls in the distance.

He hoped that a combination of keeping a low profile, having a much smaller size than the monsters, and not moving quickly enough to cause concern would be enough to keep him from being noticed. More specifically, to keep him from being attacked.

Crouching was never his favorite thing to do, but his inflated Characteristics allowed him to function without any pain in his joints as he moved along. As he went, the Ritualist mentally flipped through all of the different options he had available to himself for mutually assured destruction, in case his ruse was seen through. By the time he was approaching the firing line, he'd decided on a combination of keeping a few of his stronger rituals, such as the Ritual of Infernal Conflagration, primed to a certain phrase.

The changes needed were easy to make: all Joe needed to do was remove humans from the 'safe' list, and he would be the first target. Between that and planning to completely remove his Exquisite Shell before entering the town, the Ritualist knew he'd be able to get back to Novusheim, even if the worst outcome came to pass.

During his movement from the very edge of the range of the Archers until he managed to get to the wall, Joe had been stepped on no less than eight times. Happily, the fact that he was crawling along the ground at this point, the attackers were drawing the aggro, and the compulsion of the Town Hall forcing the monsters to focus on the destruction of objects instead of people all worked together to keep him from being targeted for more direct attacks.

All in all, it was an only slightly painful, if surreal, experience.

Finally, he was pressed against the wall and out of visual range for any of the defenders. Pulling out a Ritual of Raze, he placed the tile against the wall and resumed his crawling. "Let's do three more of these, then see if I can charm my way inside when the wave ends."

For some inexplicable reason, the thought of playing pretend with the people inside the walls made his stomach churn. "Why's that worse than inch worming through a monster assault with arrows and spells whizzing overhead? Oh, right. It's because the beasts at least don't pretend to be something they aren't. They won't invite you in and stab you in the back."

As he placed the second tile he planned to use to backstab the people who would invite him in, Joe amended his ironic doomsayer thoughts. "Then again, who knows? They might be perfectly pleasant, reasonable people. Then I can be as well. Here's hoping."

CHAPTER THIRTY-THREE

Knowing that he would need to sell his act in the near future, Joe stripped away his Exquisite Shell, Neutrality Aura, and Retaliation of Shadows while pulling out and putting on his oversized pack. Almost immediately, he began to accumulate filth and small injuries as monsters bumped into him in their enthusiastic attempts to smash through the wall.

Dozens of arrows slammed into the most recent creature to knock him to the ground, and a voice shouted out from above, "Someone fell over!"

Over the next few seconds, the intensity of the attacks raining down around Joe increased precipitously, but each of them missed him—even if only by a hair's breadth. He was gasping from pain, even while chuckling to himself at their zeal in rescuing him. "I suppose that's *one* way to get inside."

A rope came flying over the wall, frayed and basic to ensure nothing with the incredible weight of the monsters could use it as a way to either damage the walls or get over them. Joe grabbed the literal lifeline and hauled himself up, managing to kick himself to the side as a Penguin slammed into where he had been only a moment previously. The Ritualist shot up the rope as though he were a competitive athlete, getting no assistance from the people attacking the monsters above.

Seeing as they were keeping his legs from getting chewed on or beaked, Joe was completely fine with that fact. When he pulled himself over the wall, he was shoved to the side, and another defender stepped forward to begin launching arrows immediately. Not wanting to be trampled by the people around him this soon after surviving being squished by monsters, Joe rolled to his feet right away. As soon as he was upright, he sank down slightly and didn't bother hiding his absolute exhaustion, nor his visible injuries that were still pumping blood into his clothes.

Wiping off his forehead and leaving a trail of the bright red fluid on his shirt put a grimace on his face. "Great, I probably just gave myself a dozen infections."

"You'll survive. Or you won't, but then you'll be back after that." An iron grip clutched Joe's shoulder, and a quick glance showed a grim-faced soldier who began leading him away from the lines of battle. "You aren't one of ours, so ya better start talking immediately, or we're going to throw you back to the birds."

Luckily for Joe, thanks to removing his magical protections, he'd allowed all of the subtle signs of his recent 'hardships' to show. They were able to further enhance the authenticity of his disguise as he explained that he was a merchant moving between the three Villages. The fact that he'd come from one the same day and was able to list off the names of the people he had been with was enough for the guard to accept that he'd just come to the Village at the wrong time.

"You either have an amazing Luck stat or a terrible one." The soldier shook his head and pushed Joe toward a ladder. For a moment, the Ritualist thought he had gotten away and was completely in the clear, but then the man shouted down, "We've got a merchant! The son of a gun managed to survive by wedging himself in at the base of the walls. You should've seen the Penguins trying to lean forward far enough to peck him!"

Laughter floated up but died out as Joe descended the ladder and looked around at the people waiting for him. They were hard-faced individuals, but each of them studied him with bright, inquisitive eyes. Joe struggled to slap a smile on his face, then gave a proper Theocracy-style bow of someone of a lower station greeting a superior. "This humble merchant thanks Middle Village for offering refuge in a time of turmoil! To show my gratitude, I would greatly appreciate being brought to a life coach or leader who is able to accept a donation showing exactly how *much* I appreciate the safety."

He wasn't certain why the Elves were going by the title of 'life coach' instead of High Cleric or some other malarkey, but he assumed it had something to do with needing to interact with hundreds of thousands of humans who didn't appreciate being pushed onto a single path. His smile grew wider as he realized that this was proof that even a rigid society such as the Elves had been forced to make concessions because his people were so wild and untamable. "I love humans."

"What was that?"

Joe hadn't even realized he'd mumbled the last part out loud, but was able to easily cover for himself. "I said, I love you man! That was a really dangerous situation, and I thought I was going to be stuck in limbo for at least a week."

"Mmm." Joe's escorts in this Village were even less verbose than in the previous one, and he could feel at least three sets of eyes boring into him at all times. Something told him not to bother trying to offer gift baskets to gain their affection. These people were... strange. It was only after realizing that nearly everyone they passed had the same odd intensity that the Ritualist realized exactly what was going on.

There had been an offhand comment that this entire place was run by a single guild. That meant these people were hard-core role-players and wouldn't break character for *any reason* when they were out and interacting. Strangely enough, that thought settled some of the churning fear that he'd been feeling. There was a difference between someone who was a fanatic for *the* cause and someone who was a diehard for *their* cause. If nothing else, he could get behind deciding to go all-in on them making this world their entire focus.

The farther they went, the more comfortable he was with the silence. It was normal for him, and he subconsciously found himself walking with them in the same marching pattern. Left foot, right, left… it was practically hypnotic how easy it was to fall into some of his oldest habits. They were able to quickly traverse the streets, which were nearly completely empty. As far as Joe could tell, not a single person was avoiding combat on the walls, unless they had a very good reason to do so.

He took note of the elaborate architecture in the surroundings, something that had become more and more important to him as he progressed as a Rituarchitect. Each of the buildings flowed into the next, even if there was a large gap between their placements. They were a symphony of graceful curves, intricate carvings, and the vibrant colors of fresh life. Joe stared hungrily at the greenery growing from the living structures, a color he hadn't seen much of since arriving on this world. He promised himself he'd go spend some time in the greenhouse when he got back, to make sure he wasn't this desperate in the future.

"I've always loved how our structures blend seamlessly with nature. It's like living in a town that the world itself grew and gifted to us." Joe let out a deep sigh of longing, speaking quietly as though he were talking to himself, but knowing he was loud enough to be heard. "I hope that, someday, Jotunheim will be able to sustain proper forests."

There was no verbal reaction from his escort, but it seemed he was moving in the right direction with his thoughts. Joe was perceptive enough to pick up the fact that his musings were calming them down slightly, and he was seen as less of an outsider by the moment. As they got closer to the center of the town, the cozy buildings gave way to ornate archways decorated with delicate floral motifs. Magical light fixtures bathed the path they were walking along in a soft, warm glow, allowing Joe to see that every path connected back to this one space.

The Town Hall was a small building at the moment, but it was connected to a grand structure that was still under construction directly adjacent to it. Unless Joe missed his mark, this Village was in the process of creating a colossal temple. He'd already seized the benefits of being the first to build shrines and the like, but it was clear to see that they had their own plans and designs on benefits from the deities. Hiding the smirk on his face, Joe made a mental note to create a proper Grand Temple overnight when he got back to Novusheim. It would be a cathartic experience to snatch first place and any additional rewards right out from under their noses.

Under the watchful eye of his babysitters, Joe pulled a large basket out of his pack, stuffed to the brim with soaps, other small luxuries, and no less than a dozen cores. He handed it to one of his escorts, bowing once more and smiling. "It is a small offering, but I hope it is useful."

"Decadent," the guard stated as he looked at the basket distastefully. "Not to mention, not a single one of the plants you have woven this basket with survived your journey."

Joe tried not to panic: of course the Elves used *living* plants in their baskets. It was too bad for him that there wasn't a Dwarf alive who bothered with that practice, and each of his gifts had come from one of their shops. He paled slightly, wondering if any of them had added personalized notes or some symbol that indicated it had come from Novusheim. "Ah… the bitter cold is so difficult to account for. Please forgive any offense this one has caused."

Speaking in this manner made him want to grimace in disgust; it was far too subservient. Still, it was either putting up with the indignity of his playacting, just as they were, or dealing with the blades that would no doubt sheath themselves in his body if his true origins were found.

Nothing else was said on the matter, and Joe was led back to the edge of town, where he was informed that he could set up a makeshift stall to showcase any of his goods that he wanted to part with. Then, Joe was alone. Or, at least, it *seemed* that way.

His Hidden Sense was screaming at him that he was being watched by someone just out of view, and he knew better than to ignore the warning.

So, Joe did exactly what any other seasoned merchant would do. He set out samples of his goods, surreptitiously checking each of them for anything that would give him away, then prepared to call out to anyone passing through the area. "They want to act like hardcore reenactors at a Renaissance festival? Two can play that game."

It wasn't very long before the Beast Wave was coming to an end, and soon weary warriors flooded the streets as they hurried to complete their usual tasks before the next attack took place. Joe stood the entire time, waving his arms and calling out loudly to the surprisingly stoic residents of the town. He began hawking his wares, coming up with fantastic descriptions of his preserved monster parts, shaved ice, and other trade goods and trinkets that had managed to survive the trip from 'Alfheim'.

Surprising even himself, he managed to pique the curiosity of dozens of people, and before he knew what was happening, Joe was practically sold out. In exchange, he had gathered several baskets worth of Uncommon cores, which… were practically useless to him. His sales had flourished too well, and now he was out of good and had no reason to stay in the Village, let alone explore it. He stared at the baskets, not entirely certain what he should do next. Then, unable to stop himself, he snapped his fingers and reached down to lift both of them.

As soon as he started marching toward the center of town, guards appeared around him once more, wearily looking him over but not stopping him. "Where are you going? You were assigned a sales area. Is that not enough for you? Do you have somewhere *better* to be?"

"Ah!" Joe tried to make the sound come out somewhere between excitement and surprise. "I am flattered that you'd take such an interest in such a humble merchant. To my great delight, the fine people of this town had great interest in what I had to sell. If I had known that they would find so much value in what I had to offer, I would have funded a caravan to bring much more."

They waited in silence, and Joe realized he hadn't actually answered their question. Lifting the baskets in a shrugging motion to call attention to them, he cleared his throat and nodded toward the center of the Village. "I felt that my original gift was somewhat lacking, as this was the last stop in my journey. But since I made such a profit and completely sold out in record time, I thought it would be appropriate to leave these for the Village as an additional gift."

"You're not attempting to bribe our settlement, are you? While I'm certain these will be well-received, our laws clearly indicate that we can give no favorable rates to anyone." The guard carefully explained, "if that's something you're after, perhaps you would be better served by holding on to them for yourself?"

Joe pretended to think about it for a few moments, then shook his head and offered the baskets to the guard directly. "No, no. I stand by what I said. Please, let me offer these as a gift to the Town, as respect for the impending success of your upgrade."

Just as he thought his plan was succeeding, a wave of magic washed over Joe, causing him to stumble from surprise at the unexpected spell. He looked around in confusion, and his eyes landed on a clearly high-ranking Elven Theologian. Even as Joe recovered, he felt the Shroud of Neutrality get fully stripped from him.

"How strange… now why would you need to wear a spell like that shroud?" Joe gulped as the piercing gaze of the Elf drilled into him, seeming to cut through his carefully constructed facade with ease. "Well? I expect an answer *immediately*."

CHAPTER THIRTY-FOUR

Joe didn't know what to say, so even as his mouth worked, no sound came out. The Elf clasped his hands behind his back, leaning forward and looking the Ritualist up and down. "Hmm... nothing to say, merchant? I sense no titles explaining a negative reasoning for your presence, nor is there a negative balance in your reputation with my people. Very strange... even more odd is the fact that you seem bland, like a bowl of plain white rice that sat in too much water and cooked for too long."

Taking a few deep breaths, Joe's mind spun into action as he perused the data that he'd been offered. First, and most important, his extreme animosity with the Elves was either still hidden, or the balance had been wiped clean because they were on a different world. He was too nervous to take the time to open his stat sheet at the moment, so he had to assume that there was still some trickery in the mix, courtesy of Tatum.

Second, it seemed that he was considered at true neutral for all purposes, at the moment. The most important thing was going to be edging that upward, at least for the moment. "It's... I sell things."

"Mmm*yes*, that's what merchants *tend* to do." The Elf

agreed with him, voice dripping with patronization. "What I am interested in learning is why you had such a powerful aura hiding your true intentions from us. Are you here... as a *saboteur*?"

Even though the question was stated in a light tone, Joe could practically taste copper-tinged blood in his mouth from weapons being readied to skewer him in the next few moments. In an effort to avoid that bad outcome, he skirted the direct question and let out a sigh, as if he knew that he'd been caught doing something bad, but not to the extent that the Elf was accusing him. "It's, you see, if someone cannot tell if you are giving them the real price, they don't argue as much when you ask them to pay. We sell things."

"I *see*." The Elf looked down at the baskets Joe had been trying to push on to his guard. "You journeyed across Jotunheim, risking freezing to death a countless number of times. Practically offering yourself to the monsters as a mere morsel. Getting caught outside of our walls, then brought to safety. All so you could war profiteer? How practically *Dwarven* of you."

Joe had the presence of mind to recoil in shock as everyone around him sucked in a breath. "That's not it!"

To his utter shock, his chaperone stepped forward and offered a deep bow. "Your excellency, we kept track of every transaction he made. Every barter that he made resulted in him gaining another monster core. Each of those made it into these baskets, and none into his pockets. When he had sold out, his first thought was to donate all of it to the town in the name of the Theocracy. In fact, he demanded it and even pushed it further when we told him not to do so, as a test of character. If nothing else, perhaps during his fire sale, the merchant saw the error of his ways."

Silently regarding the man who was speaking, the Elf drummed his fingers on his leg in thought. Then he turned to Joe, his eyes narrowed and his voice level. "Is this all true? Every sale that you made, you were donating the full price without leaving room for your own expenses?"

"Yes, Your Excellency." Joe was proud that he managed to make even the direct answer he gave become ambiguous by only responding to the second question.

"Then, in light of your intentional penance, you are to spend two standard days in prison among the worst of our criminals. There you will see what path your life *almost* took. After that, you will complete one Jotunheim day of hard labor in service to the Town." Joe felt like he'd been punched in the gut as the Elf casually sentenced him. For a long few moments, he considered activating his last resort and hoping that it would be enough to catch the Elf off guard. "Well…?"

"Oh. Um. My… thanks? For your benevolence?" Joe took a deep breath and managed to finish his statement. "Your Excellency."

"Barely adequate." The Elf shook his head sadly and turned, strolling off at a walking pace, yet covering distance incredibly quickly and efficiently. Joe blinked as he realized that he wasn't the only one letting out a sigh of relief as the Elf left. It made him look at the 'fanatics' around him with hope, but none of them were willing to meet his eye.

"Hope you didn't have any plans for the next few days." One of them grunted as the Ritualist was frog-marched to a nondescript building Joe had assumed was an apartment building. "You should be *real* happy to be given such a light sentence. Can't believe that turkey-brain stuck his neck out for you like that. He was practically begging to be tossed in there right next to you."

"What was his name?" Joe's eyes tracked the man who had put himself at risk for him as the man walked away stiffly before vanishing into the crowd. "I'd like to be able to thank him someday."

"Quiet, you! Prisoners lose all rights, and that includes speaking to those in good standing." The demand was coupled with a cuff to the back of Joe's head that nearly sent him tumbling across the snow. Only the fact that he was an Immovable Object and well-balanced stat-wise kept him on his feet and moving toward the prison at a rapid pace.

Still, he got the message and kept his mouth shut. As they walked into the Rare-rank building, Joe felt his mind constantly picking out contradictions. The exterior could have been any apartment complex, but the interior clearly had only a single purpose. Despite the planned use for this place, it was clear that someone had built this structure with elegance in mind, devoting an inordinate amount of time pouring the maximum amount of craftsmanship into this facility.

The wood that made up the walls was somehow marbled then adorned with delicate vine motifs that created a soothing atmosphere which seemed terribly out of place. As he was being led to his cell, Joe couldn't help but notice that, even though it was small, it was impeccably designed. At least at the surface level, there was nothing put in place that was below Rare rank. Even the bars separating prisoners from each other and the rest of the world were spun out of a strange natural material that swayed slightly like a vine, but they had the durability of spirit oak.

It was obvious that, even though the Elves and their minions controlling this Guild wanted to take no chance with ensuring their prisoners stayed contained, they also wanted anyone who had to stay here to leave having had a still-positive experience. Joe had kept his eyes open as he was frog-marched through the halls, studying every face he could see through the bars. Unfortunately, all he found was a smattering of bored political prisoners and annoyed humans who were clearly counting the seconds until they left this place, but no Daniella.

On the plus side, everyone was either sitting in comfortable chairs, laying on comfortable beds, or pacing around without any sense of urgency or fear in their step. Joe let out a soft breath as he realized that he wasn't going to be facing pain or humiliation, other than merely sitting and thinking quietly for a few days. "Abyss, all we need to do is sit and think? That just sounds like a normal Tuesday."

"Quiet!" Once again, the command was followed with a swift punch to the back of his skull. As he recovered, Joe worked to display an air of refinement and dignity, heavily colored with fear. It seemed to work, because no further words or blows were sent his way.

Finally, they arrived in front of an empty room, and the bars of the cell swayed to the side with a single motion of the guard's hand. Joe was pushed inside, and the odd branches settled back into their original position. Even as he turned to look at the people who had put him in here, Joe saw that the branches were growing leaves which covered most of the viewing area. The guard looked through a hole at head height that remained, roughly a two-by-two square.

"You're basically here for a slap on the wrist, so you get to keep your privacy. Here's a list of penances you can do while you wait for release. Each one of these that you complete gives you ten reputation. I know that's a fraction of what you can get with your normal actions, but at least you're able to focus on those in here." With that, a paper made of dried leaves was shoved into the space, and the guard marched away.

Joe scoffed at the idea of doing any of the tasks for a long moment, but he perked up when he realized that he could potentially use a list like this to train up his townspeople. If they managed to achieve neutral status or better with the Elves, they could walk into an Elven settlement and start an attack from within. He took the dry paper and put it in his codpiece, a smile on his face. "Don't mind if I do."

After waiting a few minutes to ensure that the guards weren't coming back, the Ritualist moved to the hole that had been left in his cell and spoke out into the hallway. "Are we allowed to talk to each other?"

There was no reply at first, so he kept speaking into the open air. "Hello, anyone who is listening! I'm a traveling merchant who got chucked in here for turning a profit. Going to be direct here, I'm not coming back unless I've a good reason to do it. I sell soap and luxury goods. Pretty hard to find those on Jotunheim, and being jailed for making a profit is a surefire way to drive off any business in the future."

"I miss showers." The voice that responded didn't even seem to be speaking to Joe directly, more like being someone lost in their own thoughts.

"I've been given a bounty." Joe finally decided to just go all-in. "There was a lady at a town I used to sell goods at who got accused of being a traitor, and I have a few people looking for her. If I can verify the information, I can at least make up the losses that I took here, then I can guarantee I'll come back in the future. So, if anyone wants a discount, or even just to be able to buy nice things, let me know if that story sounds familiar at all."

It was quiet after that, long enough that he was certain no one was going to bother answering him. Just as he let out a small sigh, a cautious voice spoke out.

"You're not talking about *Daniella*, are you?"

CHAPTER THIRTY-FIVE

Just like that, he knew he'd come to the right place. Joe tried to keep his voice level as he asked question after question, but his heartbeat was thundering in his ears so hard that he could barely make out the answers.

Bit by bit, a story started to be pieced together. From what Joe could tell, Daniella had arrived in this town after the settlement she'd been in most recently had been fully destroyed, and she had been hurtled across the world. Apparently, she'd been far too sanguine about the fact that her settlement of residence had been destroyed time and again. Eventually, someone had decided that, perhaps, instead of just living through the destruction of her town, she had been—at least in some small way—a part of it.

From there, Joe was able to make his own guesses about how things went down. This was a far more militant, focused Village than any of the other lesser settlements that she'd been put into. They were *far* more proactive, and had started intercepting her mail when she tried to send it out. While the Ritualist wasn't sure if they could go through old messages, he was certain that the things that she'd sent to him would be enough to get her placed in solitary confinement or whatever the equivalent was here.

"She just *had* to make jokes about destroying her Hamlet to find a better place to live." He clicked his tongue against the top of his mouth and shook his head. Frankly, the only good news that'd come out of this situation was the knowledge that she was still somewhere nearby, most likely deeper in the prison. "Let's see what they do when every one of their captives is released at the same time."

Joe slipped a Ritual of Raze out of his codpiece, sticking it directly on the wall of his cell. Before he activated it, the Ritualist took a few deep breaths and pondered the ramifications of activating the ritual at this moment. By doing so, he was going to oust himself as an enemy, and if he ever needed to come back… it was going to be as a hostile invader.

Two things spurred him forward. The first was that getting deeper into the prison was going to necessitate doing something that got him placed there, which meant he would be searched, and his prepared rituals would be unavailable to him. That made escape likely impossible, which meant a complete failure of rescuing his friend.

The second was… he was tired. He'd spent far too much time searching at this point, and all desire for finesse and subtlety was *gone*. Without allowing himself to put more thought into it, Joe activated the ritual with a surge of mana and a rush of excitement.

As the magic spun up and took hold, the wall of the building and the ritual tile had been placed on was rapidly torn away. His moment of triumph was short-lived as the defenses placed on the prison roared to life, interfering with and negating a good chunk of his ritual. Instead of the material of the building peeling away as reusable chunks, the wooden exterior was *shredded* as though it had been tossed into a wood chipper, small, finger-sized chunks at a time. "Um. That's not supposed to happen."

Then the ritual sputtered and fully failed, a sudden scent of ozone and the raising of the hairs on Joe's arm giving him only a moment to throw himself away from the wall as the enchantments that had just been interrupted backlashed and caused the spinning ritual to explode with a sound like too-close thunder. Wood chips and unstructured magic lanced through the room, miraculously *mostly* missing Joe.

Damage taken: 560 combination damage.

Health: 1,936/2,496

"*Abyss*! Whatever that Elf hit me with must've taken off more than my Shroud of Neutrality." The Ritualist was bleeding from dozens of tiny punctures that had gone directly through his fur cloak, and before he did anything else, Joe made sure to fully activate his Exquisite Shell. From there, a quick casting of Mend closed up most of his wounds, then a recasting of it brought him to full... then more than full.

Health: 2,630/2,496

"Ah. Right. The 'maximum Mend' bonus. Let's get Exquisite Shell back in place before we run." Shaking off the aftereffects of the massive concussive blast while his mana was shaped into a scintillating personal barrier, Joe turned to inspect the damage that he'd managed to inflict on the building itself. As far as he could see, only a large portion of the wall the ritual had been placed on had been stripped away. Annoyingly, the detonation of the ritual and backlash of its protections had done nearly as much as his magic had. "Gonna need to make this ritual stronger or hardened against counterspells."

The Ritualist looked at the ground and realized that he had two options at the moment. Try and use the confusion this magical mayhem would cause to force himself deeper into the prison, hoping that somehow he'd be able to make it out in one piece... or run for it. His breath started to come to him in a ragged manner, and even as he watched, some of the damage to the building began to repair itself. "What is that? Plant magic?"

For the first time in a long time, Joe felt effectively countered. Clearly, someone had set this building up with an expectation that magic would be used to try and destroy it. Even if they weren't planning against him directly, it made sense to assume that most of the people affiliated with Elves would be heavily magic-reliant. Building a prison specifically to contain them made good sense, but... Joe leaned forward and looked out of the hole in the wall, seeing dozens of people rapidly approaching the building.

What he didn't see was anyone *leaving* it. That could only mean that most of the people here knew better than to try and escape their punishments. There would be no blending into the crowd of escapees; he'd be showing his true colors with no way to avoid being noticed. "Even if nothing else in this town is resistant, the prison itself could keep me trapped. I don't know where Daniella is, and the enemy is closing in. What should I..."

He made his choice.

Joe leaned out farther, pushing off the edge of the jagged tear in the wall with Omnivault just before he would fully fall out of the opening. He *blasted* across the open air, flying farther in a straight line than any object had a right to move. Before he had even touched down a single time, three arrows were in the air, zipping toward his face. Joe tucked and rolled, barely managing to get out of the way of the projectiles, which slammed into the roof of the building he'd targeted and tore out enormous swathes of shingles.

"Would you look at that?" Joe knew he wouldn't be able to hide again, so took the time to taunt them even as his heart pounded in his chest. "Looks like I've got myself a following! Don't you all have anything better to do than keep people locked up? Can't you let little ol' me go?"

The only response to his taunts was a barrage of arrows and the smell of burned air and superheated stone as spells began impacting around him. The best-aimed of them were dissipated by his Exquisite Shell, but as far as Joe could tell, the strongest members of the Village were going to be on the walls. At first, he was relieved by that fact, but his mouth set in a grim line and dread filled him as Joe realized he needed to escape *over* the defenses.

Joe weaved and dodged through the air, lavishly relying on his Omnivault to push him ever farther in front of his pursuers. "How many times have I had to run for my life like this? Am I getting better at it?"

An arrow bounced off the base of his skull, perfectly aimed to strike him as he dodged. "I guess that answers that. *Not* getting better, I'm just getting more predictable."

With that thought in mind, Joe decided to stop trying to be fancy and tricky, and he relied on the sheer explosive speed his Omnivault granted him. His lightning-fast speed allowed him to stay one step ahead of the well-aimed attacks, narrowly avoiding death each time he needed to land and push off one more time.

Curses, shouting, and warnings were sent his way. Most were directed at him, though some were mere attention grabbers for the defenders on the walls. As he got closer, Joe realized that he had timed his escape extremely well: it seemed a Beast Wave had come early.

Delighted that the people in front of him were going to be distracted, Joe looked back over his shoulder and bellowed in a voice laced with bravado as he did a flip to narrowly avoid a crescent of energy that melted the snow it passed over. "Okay, that one was close, but *c'mon*! You can do better than that! Are you just going to let a prisoner escape? Where's your pride?"

Letting out a final bark of laughter, Joe tucked into a spinning somersault as he shot over the wall like a cannonball.

The defenders on the wall shouted in a combination of concern and anger, drawing the attention of the monsters swarming on the tundra below. As dozens of bows turned toward the falling man and away from the beasts below, the creatures took the chance to surge forward and begin beating on the barricade in front of them. Attempting to use the chaos to his advantage, Joe declined to use his jumping skill again, instead dropping to the ground and sprinting through the approaching monsters.

With every enormous paw dodged, each claw that caused his Exquisite Shell to spark in protest as it got a little too close, Joe felt his odds of escape growing. Every second allowed him to put more distance between himself and the wall, all but guaranteeing his–

The ground in front of him erupted as an artillery-like spell landed directly in his path, blasting a huge geyser of dirt and snow into the air and causing the Ritualist to stumble and misstep. He hit the ground and rolled—momentum completely gone. Joe forced himself to his feet, his breathing ragged and body burning with pulled muscles. Sparing a glance behind him, he saw exactly what he was afraid would be there.

Unless he missed his guess, the silhouettes flashing through the ranks of monsters who were going to be the strongest members of the Guild closing in, their determination unwavering, eyes locked on him. "Look how close you are! Abyss, this must really suck for you. But that's not going to be enough to catch me. *Buh*-bye!"

His escape and salvation was within reach, but his pursuers wouldn't know that until he was already gone. Still, Joe couldn't allow his guard to go down. The taunts that had followed him inside the Village itself were nowhere to be found. No, the people hunting him now were silent, efficient, the only sounds coming from them being whatever invocation they needed to create and cast their next spell.

Joe had already used up his tricks, so he kept pouring everything he had into speed. Sprinting and Omnivaulting directly at his shrine wasn't how he'd *wanted* the day to go, but the only way he was going back to that prison was at the head of an invasion force. "Just a little bit farther, oh *abyss*, I hope Mcshootypants sees us coming."

Launching himself forward one more time, Joe angled his head *down* instead of trying to land on his feet like each time before. As he hit the ground, he slid directly down the angled tunnel he'd dug through the surface of Jotunheim like a Defeatist Fluttering Penguin going in for the kill. As he reached level ground, his speed and sudden appearance caused him to tangle up in his Archer's legs and tackle her to the ground.

Together, they tumbled toward the shrine, coming to a painful stop right at its base. "Ow! Joe, what the *abyss*? You almost made me shred this map I've been making, why are you-"

"Heartpiercer." Before she could say anything more, Joe met her gaze and let her see exactly how exhausted and furious he was at the moment. "Contingency plan. Time to rally the troops."

CHAPTER THIRTY-SIX

"It's gone." Joe let out a quiet sigh of frustration, his eyes closed as if that would help him ignore the fact that the shrine by Middle Village had already either been destroyed or converted. "That means a much longer walk than I wanted to have to deal with."

Even as frustrating as it might've been, Joe would have no trouble getting plenty of volunteers to walk that short distance and attack the Elven encampment. Abyss, the hardest part of it might be convincing them to go around the first one in favor of the stronger second target.

He turned away from his shrine, headed for his workshop with a swift stride. "First thing I'm going to do is figure out how to burn that prison down to the ground. Second thing I'm doing is convincing people that my plan will work. Then–"

A warning cry went up moments before a heavy detonation of mana swirled into the air from somewhere in the distance. Joe went completely still as he felt one of the tiny tethers to his spirit break, indicating that one of his more permanent rituals had just failed. The sound of rubble bouncing off stone reached his ears a moment later, indicating that a tower had just collapsed.

He joined in the tide of warriors headed for the walls, prepared to make a stand against the invading monsters. As he ran, Joe's mind buzzed and whispered to him that it was important to note the fact that the Village he'd just left behind was also under attack. "Hmm. Is there a single, overarching hive mind that controls the frequency of attacks? Do they all happen at approximately the same time worldwide? Maybe that's why some of ours are early or late? To facilitate multiple attacks happening at the same time?"

Unfortunately, he had no one to confirm his answers one way or another. Still, by the time he'd arrived at the walls, the all-clear had gone out, and he was able to slow his pace. He could still hear the sounds of his ritual towers firing in the distance, but apparently whatever had caused the collapse had been dealt with. Joe was still determined to figure out what had caused one of his structures to be destroyed, and so continued deeper into the labyrinthian walls. "Seriously, you leave for just a *few* days, and people start letting things break."

A quick inspection showed him that most things were working well, but the closer he got to the end of the maze, the more he saw signs of weathering, chipped walls, and chunks torn out of towers. What he *didn't* see were any maintenance crews, nor anyone else that he'd paid to keep his towers functional and whole. Finally arriving at the end of the maze, Joe found his rage bubbling to the surface, and he tried to let it escape with deep breaths instead of going and finding whoever had been neglecting their job.

The people who had been brought in from Elven Villages were only now beginning to come out of the defensive bunker that he'd put here, but not because they were slow. No, it was because the bunker itself was so badly damaged that getting the mechanism of the door to work correctly had taken them as long as rushing through to the entrance had taken Joe. The weight of his skipped responsibilities started to bear down heavily on Joe's shoulders as he stood at the very edge of his Town's area, and he felt torn between things that needed to be done.

On one hand, Daniella was stuck in a prison, in danger of being lost to him forever. A huge part of his mind was urging Joe to rush back to that area, magic blazing, burning anyone who got in his way to ash. The other part of him was feeding him guilty reminders that he was the one that was supposed to be in charge of the health and safety of *all* of the people out in the suburbs of his Town. Joe had done more than the bare minimum to ensure that they were comfortable, being able to guarantee water, food, and shelter.

What he *hadn't* done was expand the range of his other quality-of-life rituals. It was dark here, and very little light filtered into this area from any source. Without personal skills or spells, the people that were living here had been left in total darkness while he'd been gone. His ritual to take spilled blood and convert it into water had also failed to reach out this far from the Town, leaving the area looking and smelling like a charnel house.

Rubbing at his bald head in consternation, Joe murmured to himself. "I thought this was all taken care of? The core of the Town has the best resources and protection that I've been able to make... why wouldn't they extend that same courtesy and resources to the people out here that want to be part of them? Why did I assume that they would? Abyss, this is totally on me. Why would anyone else take responsibility when they can just ignore the issue?"

He'd been trying so hard to fix up all of the areas in his life that needed help. Working on his rituals, expanding his network of shrines to eventually find Daniella, even managing to make his employees' jobs easier by allowing them to use his rituals to transport towers in and out of the Town as needed for repairs and re-energizing. That brought his eyes up to the entrance of the area, where a ritual tower that had been containing an Infernal Conflagration had detonated. "Making things easier for them has been working out *perfectly*, hasn't it?"

Letting out a growl, Joe decided to finally stop ignoring the pangs of guilt that were ramping up. The fact of the matter was that, by letting himself be stretched in too many directions, important things were beginning to slip through the cracks. These people deserved better, especially as they'd been captives of the Elves and not sympathizers. He wanted to rescue Daniella, but even if his heart ached with the realization... she wasn't his *responsibility*.

These people freezing to death in a labyrinth of his making? They *very much* were.

"I have to stay here and fix this. They might move Daniella, hide her, turn her against us..." Joe's voice was barely audible, even to himself. "But I just can't abandon these people. My people. They need me."

His shoulders sagged as the words left his lips, a heavy sense of resignation settling over him. Joe still had a chance to fix the issues at hand, mending the physical damage and soothing any righteous anger the people gathered here had toward people living in comfort in the center of Town, and he was determined to start immediately.

Joe walked over to the large group of gathered people, offering a sympathetic ear while assuring them that he was going to hang around for a few days and make sure they were getting the amenities they required. Frankly, the Ritualist was amazed at how quickly their grievances had accumulated. Most of what they brought to his attention was fairly straightforward to fix, but Joe started with getting them access to a Ritual of Repair that they could use without having to wait on anyone else.

Apparently, not every repair crew was sympathetic to their plight, and every once in a while, repairs on the bunker that kept them alive during Beast Waves was... 'missed'.

Next, he personally walked the *entire* group of people to the second suburb section of the labyrinth. Many of them were

concerned because they were uncertain if they had done everything they needed in order to fulfill their side of the quest, but
Joe was having none of it. "The Town, at least *someone* in it that
has influence, has been allowing you to be treated poorly. In my
mind, you've all moved on to the second part of this quest, and
if anyone has something to say about it, they can come directly
to me. I'd *love* to talk it over with whoever has been doing this
behind my back."

For dozens of hours, the Ritualist worked tirelessly to fix
literally any problems he saw. Walls were smooth out, towers
were replaced, and the suburban assimilators were amazed as
they saw the sky above the Town expand, the light it offered
finally being granted to them. Thanks to his efforts, the time
between when a grievance was aired to the time it was fixed
rapidly began to shrink. As necessary as all of it was, this
burned through minutes and hours, enough that Joe despaired
of ever completing his self-set mission.

Still, with each passing moment, the mood shifted. When he
went to the Town Hall, he could directly see the benefits his
efforts had to morale. Anger and frustration that had been
simmering unchecked beneath the surface started to give way to
a sense of hope. Even with his annoyance over the disparities in
treatment, he'd poured his time and resources into the repairs
and upgrades, working carefully to ensure that the entirety of
the Town was protected as much as possible.

By the time Joe was finished with his work in the killing
corridors, each part of the walls and towers had been inspected
for damage and repaired as needed. The outer settlements were
flourishing with newfound camaraderie, realization that they
may actually someday be accepted in the Town, and a fresh
sense of purpose. Seeing that they were nervous—desperate—
to ensure their safety, Joe had expanded their access to his rituals, and now more than half a dozen people out in the suburbs
had their own Ritual of Repair. They walked along the walls,
fixing them up as needed, repairing towers between the defensive structures being rotated in and out of use.

There was a second, more unfortunate reason for his seeming altruism. When he'd first started with fixing what his and the Town's employees *should* have been taking care of, Joe had gone back to the center of Novusheim in a rage. It was only when he arrived at the usual meeting spaces that he had been bluntly informed as to why the walls and towers were failing in the tiny amount of time that he'd been gone.

The answer was short and bitter: all of his employees had quit.

Joe had been furious at first, thinking that someone else had swooped in and hired them out from under his employ. When he realized the truth, he could only shake his head and try not to scream in frustration. As it turned out, people hadn't left because he'd been absent, or because the work was difficult. Frankly, many people had been working with him because they wanted to remain safe, and felt that having their personal touch in the defenses would improve their odds. No, for the first time, everyone had walked off the job for a simple, understandable, annoyingly timed change.

The council had finally settled on a new currency to standardize payment, and Joe hadn't been using it.

CHAPTER THIRTY-SEVEN

"One hour of unskilled work is worth a quarter gram, skilled is a half!" A town crier was shouting into a milling crowd of people looking for work. "Expert and above is paid upon negotiations; we're looking for up to a dozen people willing to—"

Joe ignored the rest of what was being shouted, his face twisted in disgruntlement as he walked toward the forge. "Of course, *I* was the one that gave the council enough metal to start using Jotunheim Alloy to hire all of my workers out from under me. It doesn't even matter, I think I'll need... what? An hour? Two hours, tops, before I can offer people a higher salary than anyone else. Gonna get all new people, though—no way am I bringing back anyone who walked away."

To his annoyance, the Ritualist was going to need to wait to actually make Jotunheim Alloy until he'd reached the Expert ranks in Ritualistic Forging, so he wasn't going to be able to flood the budding kingdom's currency with a massive influx all by himself. Yet.

Still, he did have something any smith worth their salt was going to want: Ebonsteel. He couldn't make the metal directly into ingots that he'd be able to trade, but it would be extremely easy to create dozens or even hundreds of the mugs, then have them melted down into a usable form. Even when he failed, thanks to the building having a forty percent chance of a completed item reverting into its base materials, he would be getting exactly what he wanted: the basic metal.

Joe went to a workstation and began working immediately, eventually paying a nearby Dwarf to pound everything into ingots after removing the gems that were automatically added to its makeup.

"Why don't you stop skipping steps and just make them directly into ingots?" the Dwarf grumpily inquired as he heated up a forge.

"Because then I won't be able to pay you for your services!" Joe chipperly evaded the question while batting his eyes.

The Dwarf's gaze shot up to the top of Joe's head, as he seemed to have mistaken the playfulness for flirting, and winced at the light reflecting off that bald surface. Then he looked for any traces of beard or mustache and saw none. He shuddered —gagging slightly—and got back to work, not asking any further questions.

Joe was fine with this reaction, as it allowed him to forgo explaining how his powers worked: the real answer was that he didn't have a pattern or recipe to make Ebonsteel ingots; he could *only* make coffee mugs.

When he had a decent supply, he set up shop at the door, offering to trade one ingot per two ounces of Jotunheim Alloy. Before long, he'd exchanged all of his material, and everyone involved in the trading was pleased with the outcome. "Ah, capitalism strikes again, leaving everyone involved happier and wealthier. Love it."

Now that he had what he hoped was enough of the newfangled currency in hand to fund an expedition, Joe immediately went to the Town Hall to issue a quest for as many warriors as his money could hire. He was still working out the details in his head when he set foot in the building proper, and a message appeared. "I got mail? I never see mail anymore, thanks to the wonky time dilation. Who would…"

He went silent as he saw the sender's name: somehow Daniella had managed to get a letter out to him.

Subject: Just stop.

Joe, you were here and made everything worse for me. I Appreciate what You were trying to do, but Please don't ever Come Back, For both our sakes. i'll try to live with my choices here, and if i do well, they'll send Me to the first village eventually. I just Need To Get the proper mindset, stay Away.

-Daniella.

Eventually, someone else needed to use the door, and Joe was finally forced to move out of the entryway. His mind was whirling with confusion and frustration, but most of all, he was angry that Daniella had given up when he was so *close* to being able to rescue her. "Come get me, don't come get me. Which is it?"

A thick cloud of smoke washed over him, and Joe turned to look at his mentor. Havoc was lounging in a chair next to him, looking at his Apprentice with an annoying smirk on his face. "Lady troubles, Baldy? I can't say I'm shocked. Your good looks are only matched by your sparkling personality."

"It's Daniella," Joe grumbled with great annoyance. "First time she's sent me a letter in weeks, and all it says is to go away and stay away. I can't even tell you how much time I've invested in trying to figure this out, and now–"

"Yeah, I got you. Trying to understand her is probably like trying to solve a jigsaw puzzle with missing pieces while riding a unicycle on a tightrope." Havoc interrupted rudely. "Now, combine that with her jailer being able to read her mail and feeding her what to say to you…"

As the Dwarf trailed off, Joe's eyes went wide. "Abyss, no *wonder*! What was I even thinking?"

"Yup. If you're busy looking a gift horse in the mouth, you might just end up hearing the truth there." Another cloud of smoke drifted toward the first, punching it out of the air after settling into an indistinct fist shape. "Only way you're going to hear the facts is by getting her out of there and to a safe place before asking the question."

"Strangely helpful. Thanks, Havoc." With the thought in mind that he might need to look at the message more closely, the Ritualist opened it and tried to read the *intent* behind what Daniella had been saying. As he perused through it a third time, his eyes went wide as he realized that there were words capitalized that shouldn't have been, in order to be grammatically correct. He mumbled them as his eyes trailed over the text. "Joe, I appreciate you. Please come back for me. I need to get away."

"Celestial *feces!*" Joe turned and ran from the building, only to try to skid to a stop, slip on the snow, and tumble across the slick surface. Then he ran back in, generated his quest, and left again while trying to keep the snow from melting into his clothes. The entire time, he was cursing himself as a fool. "I can't believe I almost *missed* that."

Hurrying to his workshop, Joe started pounding out rituals that he thought would be useful against the defenders of Middle Village. "Ritual of the Crawling Storm, that's an absolute yes. Is my Thesaurized version ready for a test run? Let's… try it out on a few monsters before activating it indoors. You know what? Let's *never* activate it indoors. At least not here."

For the next half of a day, Joe put together Rituals of Infernal Conflagration, Acid Bubbles, Dark Lightning Strikes, and anything else he thought would be useful during a siege against the distant Village. Finally, he determined that enough time had passed, so Joe went back to the Town Hall to gather everyone who'd signed up for his quest. If he hadn't been able to store all of his newly created weaponry in his codpiece, Joe definitely would've been walking gingerly. While it was *unlikely* that shaking one of his rituals would set them off, with the magical arsenal stacked on top of each other, he wouldn't want to chance it.

Throwing open the door, he strode up to the surly receptionist with a bright smile on his face. "Hey there, ya ball of sunshine! I'm here to get the names of everyone who signed up for my quest to attack some Elven settlements?"

The receptionist raised an eyebrow then reached into his desk and pulled out a sheet of paper. Joe knew something was wrong as soon as he saw that the bearded Dwarf actually had a twinkle in his eye while he did his job. "Here's the list."

"This is a blank sheet of paper." Joe announced after a long moment of staring at the cream-colored page. "No one signed up for a chance to go on the attack?"

A shrug was Joe's only response, so he sat still and stared at the Dwarf until the hairy individual let out a grunt and explained a little better. "No Dwarf is going out there to die, and no human wants to go on a ten-thousand-mile march across a hostile world."

"We don't have to march! I set up a fast travel system!" Joe slapped the paper back on the table then narrowed his eyes suspiciously at the receptionist. "You didn't include that in the quest offer, did you?"

"You didn't specify that I should."

Even before the Dwarf had finished speaking, Joe had turned and was walking out of the building. "I'm definitely calling this one malicious compliance. Let's see if we can find someone else who'll do the job. Consider yourself fired."

"You don't have the *authority*–" Before he could hear any more of the drivel, Joe slammed the door and marched off, fuming. The only way he could update the quest was by offering a larger reward. Until the time to join had run out, Joe wasn't able to take it down and repost it with better information.

"Great. Now I'm gonna need to go to people, hat in hand, and hope for the best." If he was going to be able to convince anyone, Joe would need to have a meticulous plan laid out. As annoying as the receptionist had been, his malfeasance had shed some light on the key requirement areas that Joe was miss-ing. At face value, the quest absolutely seemed like a one-way trip with not much of a reward. Even as he dug a little deeper into his thoughts on the matter, the Ritualist realized that a frontal assault was likely going to end the same way.

Still, he was determined to see this through. Abyss, even if he needed to make the attack on his *own*, he was going to figure out a way to get the job done. As he entered his workshop, Joe began to meticulously organize all of the data that he'd accrued about the Village. "I have thirty-six rituals ready to go; I can use that to distract the defenders while I... wait a second, I didn't put together any utility rituals or escape plans. Let's start there; if I guarantee a way to safely retreat if needed, that's probably going to be more enticing than saying I can provide us with cover fire. Good, what else?"

The Ritualist started putting together a large-scale assault plan, silently thanking the fact that Heartpiercer hadn't been idle while he was in the town playing at being a merchant. She'd drawn a decent map of the area, detailing the walls, defenses, and any of the minor variations in altitude around the Village. It was only a matter of a few feet, but seeing as she was an expert in fields of overlapping fire, those minor details had the potential to be an enormous boon for the attack.

Knowing he couldn't afford to overlook any details and fully understanding that he would lose his only chance at rescuing his friend if he didn't take the time to properly prepare, the Ritualist tried to envision every possible scenario. When he had eventually run out of steam, unable to think of a single thing he could've missed, Joe turned his mind's eye to envisioning Daniella's circumstances. "Highly likely that she's wearing basic gear that offers no resistance to the cold, protection against spells, or armor value. Doesn't have much going for her in the way of attacks, but she's a smart lady. I'm sure she's making her own plan to navigate through this."

Even though he had plenty of faith that she could turn the situation to her advantage if given the chance, Joe's best option was still going to be shoving her in a high-speed travel bubble and getting her out of the settlement as quickly as possible.

"Wait, what if she has some kind of tracking on her, or another spell that keeps her bound to the area? Hmm…"

Nothing he had would allow him to dispel other people's magic, so Joe made a note to seek outside assistance with this problem. With the planning portion out of the way, he began packing essential supplies into his spatial devices, such as additional fur coats to protect against the bitter chill of Jotunheim and even swords and other weapons that he couldn't use—just in case he found sympathizers trapped amongst the Elven-aligned people.

In addition to the more mundane survival gear, he prepared several utility rituals, focusing on the emergency Bubble Travel rituals. As much as he wanted it to be, his plan wasn't to have to fight and defeat every person living in the town just to get to his friend. No, the more he thought about it, the more Joe realized that this needed to be a mission focused to the utmost on stealth. If at all possible, he wanted to be able to break into the Village and fly away with the target of his plans with no one the wiser.

Despite all of his preparations, Joe couldn't shake the feeling that all of this was simply inadequate for the task at hand. "I need more people, or to be more powerful, have more time to prepare…"

He thought over the message that Daniella had sent. It was unlikely that she was going to be sent away from Middle Village anytime in the near future, going by how she'd said that she needed the 'correct mindset' before they would send her to another nearby settlement. Joe tried to think of any additional parallels between her current location and his own, remembering that, when he'd come back to his Town, a Beast Wave had been ongoing. "Unless I'm completely missing my mark, the attacks are synchronized."

A quick chat with a guard outside of his building revealed that there'd been a 'Boss Monster Watch' put in effect for his local area four days from now. It wasn't a guarantee, but going by the sparse historical data that they'd been able to accumulate so far, an incoming super-monster was likely.

Now Joe had a proper deadline.

"I need to improve as much as I can in the next few days and figure out who're going to be the most effective teammates." The Ritualist took a deep breath, trying to suppress the nausea welling up within him. Steeling his resolve, he activated his Rituals of Communication in sequence, reaching out to his friends in the hopes that they'd join him.

He was going to need all the help he could get.

CHAPTER THIRTY-EIGHT

"I have no idea how Jaxon figured out how to set up an automated voicemail for that ritual." Joe grumbled as he pounded on glowing aspects in the forge. "I can't tell if I'm more annoyed that he knows how to do it and I don't, or that not a single one of them answered the call. I *really* hope they're just out of range on a mission or something."

The alternative was that they were ignoring him, and that made Joe somewhat nervous. He'd been asking for their help quite frequently recently, and he wouldn't be terribly surprised if they were getting annoyed at his constant requests. But, he was trying not to think about it too much, and simply planned to try again later. In the meantime, he'd figured out that one of the most rapid and efficient ways to increase his personal power and gain access to things he didn't currently have was to complete his class quests.

They'd been stagnating practically since he'd arrived on Jotunheim, and some of them were so abyssally easy that he had put them off for when he needed a quick win. "That time is now."

Joe pulled the glowing stabilization cube off of the anvil he was working on, holding it in the air as the ambient temperature rapidly cooled it. "There, now I have five Student-ranked cubes."

Setting the items on the ground, Joe made a Field Array around them that perfectly encompassed the cubes. With a tiny burst of mana, they were converted back into aspects and sucked into his codpiece.

Quest complete: Apprentice Reductionist II. Reduce 5 items you have created that are at least Apprentice ranked back into aspects. Reward: Access to Apprentice Reductionist III and a permanent 10% boost to the speed of reducing items!

Quest gained: Apprentice Reductionist III. You have had practice reducing items of quality aspects, now it is time to focus on quantity! Reduce 10 tons' worth of Rare-ranked materials to aspects. Reward: A Spatial Ring that can hold up to five tons of any item ranked Rare or lower, enchanted with the ability to reduce the weight of its contents by 50%. Access to Apprentice Reductionist IV.

Joe looked at the quest and its reward with an unamused flat look. "But I already have an awesome storage device. Look at all of those qualifiers... it can only hold Rare-ranked or below items? Only a fifty percent reduction in weight? Am I spoiled?"

He thought about that for a moment, firmly nodding in agreement that yes, he *was* spoiled, and he wanted to stay that way. Still, at least it was a progression in his quest line. Joe wasn't entirely certain if the ten percent increase in speed of reduction was going to be noticeable, but percentages eventually added up to extremely large numbers—and he *did* like being efficient with his time.

With that quest complete, there was only one other that would be manageable within the time frame he'd been given. Even as he read over the information, he walked out of the forge and began searching for a suitable location. "Apprentice Rituarchitect three. I only need to build one more meaningful monument to get the reward, and I hope this counts."

He pulled the blueprint for the ziggurat out of his storage, hoping that, because he basically ran the infrastructure of the entire Town by way of rituals, this would be extremely 'meaningful'. Joe had never had the privilege of seeing this structure in person, having gained the blueprint thanks to completing his Novice Rituarchitect class quest. "No time like the present to see what this can accomplish."

It took him longer than he expected to find a space he felt comfortable setting the monument up. Joe originally wanted it to be as central as possible in order to impact as many of his rituals as it could, but he eventually realized that most of them were currently stored in his workshop, so the placement should have literally no bearing on its effectiveness. "That would've been pretty silly of me… choosing an artistic location would have been like upgrading the monitor on a computer and expecting that it'd increase the performance of my computer."

Having finally settled on the best location, Joe set out his stabilization cubes, primed the ritual, and made sure no passersby were in the space the structure would be erected. He was greatly surprised by how easily the building started to grow, smoothly and without a hint of the odd turbulence Jotunheim often inflicted on his rituals as they spun up.

It almost seemed like the long, pointy building shot up out of the surface of the planet as if it was just happy to be seen. Fully in place, the four-sided obsidian monument was fifteen feet tall and steepled at the top with the perfectly smooth sides coming together as an isometric pyramid. Unlike the other projects Joe worked on, as soon as the structure was complete, the blueprint blazed with fire and crumbled into ash in an instant. "Ah… it seems I only get one of these?"

Please apply four rituals to the surfaces of the ziggurat.

Joe waited to see if his quest would complete, but it seemed that there were still a few steps to take before then. As he decided which rituals would be the most meaningful ones to expand on for the Town, small slots opened up on the surface of the monument, perfectly sized for his ritual tiles to be placed on. "Huh. I guess I'm not the first person to ever make those.

Good to know. Now, what's going to be the most useful thing for the Town?"

Thinking over what had been the most useful for the people on the outskirts, Joe came to the conclusion that what was good for one group was good for *all* of them. Going to his workshop, he selected three tiles. The first contained the ritual that adjusted the false sky in Town. After that, he decided on the ritual that collected blood and converted it to water. Finally, with great hesitation, he picked out an unactivated ritual that would create a bubble shelter when used.

He decided to put these in and hold off on the fourth to see if he could change out his options after they'd been selected. The ritual tiles went into the slots as if they had been custom fitted, and the obelisk pulled them silently to its interior.

Three rituals have been selected. Would you like to add another at this time? Inserted rituals can be adjusted, added, or removed once per 48 hours. Yes / No.

"Great, that answered a couple of my questions right away. No, this is plenty for now." As soon as he made his choice, three of the four glossy black surfaces of the ziggurat lit up. Joe could see the rituals right under the surface, larger than they actually appeared on the tile, as though sections of them were being zoomed in on.

Ritual selection 1 summary: Active daylight, night-time light adjustment. Range expanded 33%, active light shifting added based on preference of the creator of the ritual. Automatic combat detection guarantees daylight conditions for all hostile encounters.

Ritual selection 2 summary: Bodily fluid collection. Speed of collection increased by 31%. Range of collection expanded 50%. Separation speed increased by 25%.

Ritual selection 3 summary: Temporary housing solution. All matching rituals within one kilometer are 20% more permeable and resistant to destruction. Heat generation efficiency increased by 21%.

Ritual selection 4 summary: Not available.

As far as Joe could tell, everything that had been added was having a great impact on the Town already. Looking into the sky, he could see that the lit up area was rippling out as it expanded, as though he was looking at water that had been poured on a glass table. There was also a subtle shift in that light, and he realized that the two modes he'd created, full day or instant night, had been blended. If he had to guess what the sky was showing him at the moment, Joe would've sworn that he was looking at a sunrise. "Oh… that's *definitely* going to help morale."

When he looked at the second summary, Joe grimaced slightly. "Yeah, I hadn't really intended for that ritual to collect 'bodily fluids', just blood. I might need to tweak that one if we start getting… flavorful water. Taking a sip out of a cup and knowing that it's really a mouthful of sweat doesn't exactly sound pleasant to me."

Yet, it was the third ritual that he truly thought would have the most impact on the Town. His lips curled up into a huge smile as he saw that people would be able to get in and out of their temporary homes faster, without risking having to reactivate the ritual, and they'd be able to spend a fifth less mana to stay as warm as they were used to. As the changes took effect, Joe could practically hear a satisfying **click** in his head right before a notification appeared.

Quest complete: Apprentice Rituarchitect III. Create three meaningful monuments in your settlement: 3/3. Reward: access to Apprentice Rituarchitect IV.

Quest gained: Apprentice Rituarchitect IV. Greetings, esteemed Rituarchitect! You have been granted a challenge worthy of your skill as an Apprentice. In order to showcase your skill, as well as to plan for the future, you must create a marvel that will allow you to study celestial movements. You have been granted a blueprint for a Rare-ranked observatory. Create it. Observatory built: 0/1.

This project may take years to complete, in order to accumulate the Rare-ranked materials, finicky components, as well as securing enough space to build it. With this structure, you'll be able to witness the night sky no matter the hour and gaze upon the dance of celestial bodies up to a month ahead of their actual movement. Caution! While rare, it is possible that the celestial events can become unpredictable. There is never any guarantee that the predictions will be perfectly accurate.

Item gained: Celestial Sightseer Observatory Blueprint.

"I see that this quest doesn't have a reward listed. I promised myself I was going to ignore that kind of quest, but…" Joe stared at the swarm of flavor text that had crowded his vision, dismissing all of it and letting out a deep sigh. He turned and started walking, arriving at a mostly empty field near the walls, far from the Town center. Setting up his ritual, stabilization cubes, and Mana Batteries, he erected the Celestial Sightseer Observatory in under fifteen minutes.

Quest complete: Apprentice Rituarchitect IV! Astounding! You have completed this quest faster than any other person who has ever received it. The new time to beat for all future attempts is: 23 minutes, 13 seconds. That's a high bar to set!

Reward: having an observatory is its own reward! The applications for its usage are massive for all Rituarchitects as well as Ritualist-base classes.

Record-breaker reward: Ritual of Remote Activation (Expert).

Quest gained: Student Rituarchitect I. Create 10 Rare-ranked buildings. Reward: Ritual of Mass Repair (Student). Access to Student Rituarchitect II.

When he saw the reward for completing this quest, Joe's eyes lit up. "*Now* we're getting somewhere. Good, I'll just take a quick peek in the observatory, then go knock this one out, too."

CHAPTER THIRTY-NINE

Joe stepped into the magical observatory and was taken aback by the odd sensations that washed over him in the next few moments. Similar to the Grand Ritual Hall back on Midgard, stepping into the open area felt like walking into space itself. Yet, the air was thick with a strange mix of scents that the nearly sterile environment of the Grand Ritual Hall wasn't subjected to.

Even though the building itself was brand new, Joe could practically *soak* in the sensations of age-old books, scrolls made of parchments and papyrus, hints of incense hanging in the air, and a subtle song coming from each of the celestial bodies hovering far above the ground. Joe looked around in wonder at the reflective dome above him that seemed to stretch into infinity, "This must be the difference between a highly focused build and a more general-use structure... I wonder if this is actually an accurate representation of what space looks like in Eternium."

As a Ritualist, specifically as one who had reached the Master ranks in ritual magic, Joe was highly attuned to the ebbs and flows of energies that would impact his spell diagrams.

He'd been given hints before, sometimes even having the knowledge blatantly shoved in his face, but never before had he truly *felt* how the arcane currents of the celestial objects resonated with his class.

The only time he'd ever felt this connected to his craft was in the Legendary Grand Ritual Hall in Alfheim, but... this was a *Rare*-ranked building. It shouldn't have this kind of impact on him. He felt strangely hesitant to move deeper into the area, but Joe pushed past the oddities and approached a series of brass knobs and dials mounted on a shard of pure ebony.

He almost didn't notice the dais that everything was settled on, barely keeping himself from stumbling as he tripped over its edge. His hands moved forward almost of their own accord, hovering over the intricate controls before finally reaching down and adjusting one of them after noting its original position. Joe sucked in a breath as the night sky above him swirled, moving not just across the sky as he would view from the surface of the planet, but at a distinct tilt to show how much the planet itself was moving and on what axis.

"So *that's* how it's going to show what the sky will look like up to a month out." Joe pondered the ramifications of this knowledge as he studied the constellations above. He'd seen these before, whenever he looked up at the night sky, so it was no surprise to notice that the alignment was completely different from what he'd grown up with on Earth. Abyss, he'd even practically gotten a close-up view of them each time he was flung between worlds on the bifrost.

"How can I better plot out my rituals by using this? Mythology through the ages states specific dates and times, as well as positions of the sun, stars, and moon as being a focus of power for magics like mine. How true is that, I wonder?" Deciding that a practical application would be for the best, he adjusted the dials back to their original position and lifted a hand into the air. Then, Joe hesitated as he tried to decide where to go from here.

With his digits still outstretched, he studied the night sky for what could've been minutes or hours. His Constitution would allow him to maintain a non-strenuous position like this for *days*, if he so desired. Joe had actually found that fact to be the detrimental source of his inability to feel or think about time passing. "Heh. I can tell people I got caught up in the ballet of the celestial bodies, and it's not even going to be too pretentious. It'll just make me sound even *more* like a high-powered wizard."

Finally, his eyes caught on a series of stars that were slightly brighter than the others around them. Utilizing Somatic Ritual Casting, he followed them with mana flowing from his fingertips and almost didn't even realize as he drew out a Ritual of Glimmering.

"This circle encompasses all of those stars, and the seven sigils contained in the diagram match up to the stars themselves. Even the activation portion of the ritual lands directly in the center of the constellation." With the barest *touch* of mana, the ritual activated and blazed brightly enough that he had to shield his eyes. "*What!* It's so much brighter... it's *stable!*"

He hadn't even thought about setting out his stabilization cubes, having been so caught up in the moment, and he watched in awe as the light that he'd set up washed out all of the stars above him just like having the sun in the center of the sky would. "Great. Now I get to try to find enough time to sit in here and match up my rituals to constellations. Oh! Even better, now I get to look at the sky a month ahead of time and hope for the best. Looking at millions and millions of stars and finding matching patterns sounds just *lovely*."

Skill increase: Ritual Lore (Student VII → Student IX).

"Stopping all complaints immediately! Haa... this is even more worthwhile than I'd expected." Joe chuckled ruefully as he considered the absolute *monster* amount of time investment that was going to be required to make the best use of this knowledge. "You know what? Unless my previous students show up in the near future, I'm just going to go ahead and start a new coven here. They'll be focused on mapping out stars and matching them to my rituals for me. I'll call it the apprentice fee."

An ominous premonition crossed his mind at that moment. "I wonder what I'm going to have to pay for what Havoc is doing for me as his apprentice… or is the torment he's inflicting on me counting against it?"

Shaking that thought off, Joe reluctantly started to leave the building, looking up at the stars a few more times until the false daylight that his rituals created drowned out his view. "You know, I should gift this building to Socar. I bet there's also some synergy between formations and constellations. Ooh, maybe I can use it as a bribe, if he'll help me with this Daniella issue."

He'd been training for a while now but still had time before he *had* to make his move against Middle Village. Unfortunately, all of the low-hanging fruit from his quests had been grabbed, and Joe still didn't feel anywhere *near* prepared enough for the undertaking that was approaching. "Let's check my status."

Name: Joe 'Tatum's Chosen Legend' Class: Reductionist
Profession I: Arcanologist (Max)
Profession II: Ritualistic Alchemist (5/20)
Profession III: Grandmaster's Apprentice (15/25)
Profession IV: None
Character Level: 27 Exp: 400,727 Exp to next level: 5,273
Rituarchitect Level: 12 Exp: 77,850 Exp to next level: 150
Reductionist Level: 8 Exp: 43400 Exp to next level: 1,600
Hit Points: 2,496/2,496
Mana: 6,127/8,393
Mana regen: 73.35/sec
Stamina:1,925/1,925
Stamina regen: 6.68/sec

He skipped reading over his basic stats, clearly being able to see that nothing had changed besides his overall experience. "That's strange, I feel like I should've been getting more experience than that. The last time I checked was… a while ago.

How'd I get less than eight thousand, when *last* time I jumped by more than ten thousand in even less time?"

When no answer came from the system, Joe phrased it in the form of a query to Tatum and quickly received his answer.

Experience gain not allocated when out of range.

"Because of course it's not." Joe let out a half-hearted chuckle then remembered just then that he'd been given a new ritual as a quest reward. The Ritualist pulled out the shimmering booklet that had been deposited directly into his codpiece and looked it over. "Ritual of Remote Activation. I already have you, which begs the question: what's so different about the Expert version?"

As Joe perused the *insanely* more complex ritual, he was slowly able to put together an answer to his question. "Interesting... if I had to make a comparison, I'd say the basic version is a switch. It either turns the ritual on or off. But this? If I'm reading it right, it's comparable to a remote desktop application. If I had this going on a ritual somewhere, I could activate it, adjust its settings, and directly view everything about it from a distance. That's *way* better. Wow, okay. Solid reward, system."

The first thing he wanted to do was run back to his workshop and create this ritual, but it didn't offer the instant boost to power he was hoping for. Instead, Joe walked over to the Town Hall and checked on the Town's morale modifier, as well as any available building slots that were open. To his surprise, *dozens* of slots at Rare and lower had opened, as well as two Unique and even one Artifact—which they wouldn't be filling anytime soon.

"What in the-?" The only thing Joe could think was that perhaps his ziggurat had more of an impact on how comfortable people were than even *he* had expected. The logical part of him was muttering that it likely had more to do with having not lost a single person in a countless number of Beast Waves, but Joe decided to allow his ego to win this fight. "Abyss, I'm *awesome!*"

He practically skipped out of the structure, barely managing to stay ahead of the door as the receptionist swung it closed at him in an 'innocent' attempt to keep the cold air outside. Joe didn't mind; in his opinion the Dwarf was already working on borrowed time at this point. "What's another ten Rare buildings I can get away with setting up? Let's not be wasteful, so... towers it is!"

After collecting a baker's dozen of people, Joe led them to a large, open area and got everyone in position. Since he didn't know exactly how much of the council's money he'd promised them for their help—seeing as he hadn't explored the value of Jotunheim Alloy—the Ritualist was able to maintain the bright smile on his face even as their beaming expressions tried to drown his out. He clapped his hands gently in front of himself to draw their attention, then activated his rituals, one after another.

With only a few hours' worth of work, Joe was able to create all ten of the towers, set the stabilization cubes, and even place several of the rituals that he had set aside for town defense. With two of them, he was extra cautious as he inserted the ritual tile, still uncertain if his Thesaurized variation on the Ritual of the Crawling Storm would be a viable spell diagram. Still, he could only shrug and hope for the best. "No way to know for sure until I start running mana through the circuits."

As he walked over to the enormous Ritual of the Traveling Civilization to get ritual markers for the new towers, Joe's eyes lit up as a great idea struck him. "Ooh! I should set up the Ritual of Remote Activation in conjunction with this! Then I can put this block of metal somewhere *way* more secure and still be able to swap out the towers and such no matter where I am on the planet. I wonder if I can figure out a way to have it alert me if one of the towers is badly damaged or destroyed? I suppose I could just rely on someone having a Ritual of Communication for that, but what if I'm out of range?"

Joe cheerfully mused on these ideas as he continued his preparations, eventually heading back to his workshop and beginning work on his brand new ritual. Until he had more people gathered and ready, he was already as prepared as he could get for his upcoming attack on the Elven Village.

But being idle made Joe *itchy*, and the thought of being able to adjust his towers on the fly from a comfortable chair, or maybe in a hot tub, all while sipping coffee and gaining experience the entire time? "Now *that* I like the sound of."

CHAPTER FORTY

The Ritualist squinted at the half-drawn spell diagram that was floating in midair. He wanted to familiarize himself with the first circles of the creation of Expert-ranked Ritual of Remote Activation, both to increase his capabilities with Somatic Ritual Casting, as well as to be able to recognize enough of the components that he could recreate them at an instant or notice mistakes when stabilization issues began to arise.

At this level of complexity, it was a headache and a half to not only complete, but just maintain as he continued building and expanding outward. Not only did each new section need to be completed with the mentally taxing combination of aspects and mana, they needed to be maintained as each new portion was written out. "When I finally switch back to just writing this on a tile, it's going to feel *so* easy."

Theoretically, as Joe had been able to push his Somatic Ritual Casting skill up to the Journeyman rank, he should be able to maintain five full circles without needing to give in to the temptation of making it easier on himself. In *reality*, the situation was far different. He'd only just achieved that rank and was only able to hold up to the third circle in place without becoming so mentally fatigued that the energies deviated and caused the circles to detonate. Still, the only way to progress was to push himself to his limits.

He couldn't count how many attempts he'd made, but as he finally locked the fourth circle in place, Joe let out a sigh of relief and dismissed the crackling power. He safely untangled the woven energies, sucking the aspects back through a Field Array and into his codpiece. "Good enough. That's enough practice for now; let's make the real thing happen."

Just as he was about to begin, Joe realized that, even though he wasn't going to be designing these circles to be free-floating, that didn't mean he couldn't practice his skills. Using only his mana, he conjured a perfect replica of the Novice-rank circle and used it as a guide for his aspect inscriber. Tracing the lines allowed him to be slightly more free with his motions, and he was able to get the time of completion for the Novice-rank circle down to under half a minute.

"Am I using a powerful skill and burning through mana, just so I can create what's essentially a stencil?" The Ritualist chuckled ruefully as he continued his work, resigned to the fact that sometimes even the most potent capabilities were mere stepping stones for even *more* power. His lips curled into a self-satisfied smile as he continued his work.

Hours later, he managed to fully build out the ritual and—with a final, deliberate flourish—connected the last of the sympathetic connections between the circles and the glowing sigils. Then Joe took as much time as he deemed appropriate to inspect the incandescent internal mechanisms he'd designed. When activated, the surface of the ritual should turn flat and glossy, not reflecting the world, but a ritual it had been assigned to. "Pretty sure I just made a very specific, single-purpose computer. Crazy to think that I can do this with an Expert-ranked ritual… kinda makes me want to tackle a Grandmaster one sooner than I should."

But his experience working even Master-ranked rituals was enough to convince him to hold off until he was actually ready to push through that bottleneck. Joe stood and left his workshop, on a mission to activate this ritual for the first time in conjunction with the Ritual of the Traveling Civilization. No one got in his way, and Joe's adrenaline surge promised him it was because he looked too impressive at the moment to be bothered with trivial things.

By the time he approached the enormous metal block, he was practically strutting. He looked between the two rituals and had a thought that made him deflate slightly. "Wait a second… if this is a computer, and I'm connecting it to another ritual, does that just make me a magical network engineer? Wait, no… is this basically magical I.T. work?"

Letting out a small, self-deprecating laugh, Joe realized that perhaps he was getting back to his roots after all. Still, he was skipping a few steps, as he hadn't yet activated the ritual— meaning it still needed a massive mana injection. As an Expert rank, it was *absolutely* going to be far too draining for him to power by himself. Not for the first time, Joe grumbled at the fact that his coven hadn't yet graduated to Jotunheim, and he seriously considered simply starting a new one on this world.

"I think Dawnesha mentioned that she'd be pretty gung-ho about learning from me. If it's good enough for a princess, it should be good enough for… well, pretty much everyone else." It went on the to-do list, with a little star next to it to show that it was an important task he should look into sooner rather than later.

Over the next quarter hour, Joe was able to convince enough people to join in on powering the ritual that he met the minimum requirement he felt would be needed. As much as additional people and power would be nice, making for a less draining experience, everyone now wanted to be *paid*. They didn't want to barter, they didn't want I.O.U.s, they wanted cold, hard alloy. While he was rich in material goods, that *specific* resource hadn't had much time to build up. What little he did have practically flew out of his pockets.

"Minimum requirements is at least the *minimum*," Joe told

himself over and over as he tried to psych himself up for the process. "We've got this. Ready everyone?"

Without waiting for an answer, he activated the ritual. Immediately, the tile flew up from its central position as the ritual circles expanded to encompass every person that was actively participating. Mana drained out of them, and only the least of Joe's concerns came to fruition. A few people lost their lunch through the first few moments of shaky stability, but the fact that the ritual was focused *inward* instead of creating an outward effect seemed to help it firm up quickly as the outrush of power was collected into a small space.

When the ritual completed, and before he could test out its efficacy, Joe poured one-ounce ingots of metal out of his storage device and into the hands of the people who had helped him out. A few of them had some fresh stains on their clothes, and the Ritualist winced as he noticed those fluids lift off of the clothes and fly through the air into the distance. Keeping his voice down, he shivered lightly and tried not to feel sick to his stomach. "Looks like I'm going to have to watch out for vomit-water. Great. Need to adjust that ritual *asap*. Urg, no, it's sterile, it *separates!*"

With the difficult part of the activation over, Joe carefully connected his pseudo-tablet to the enormous metal block, generating a link of mana between the two of them that pulsed like two separate, erratic heartbeats. As the powerful spell diagrams came into synchronization, the energy smoothed out and eventually became a single, solid line to his magical senses. Then, even *that* winked out and shifted over to what appeared to be a quantum-linked resonance.

Joe stared at the small connection point of his ritual, wishing he had a dozen scientists with him at the moment to examine a feat of engineering theoretical science that had eluded humanity for the entirety of their history. He let his fingers trail over the glassy surface, wondering when it would be possible for him to share his discoveries with people who could use them on a wider scale. "I wonder what humanity as a whole is going to look like in a hundred years, if this is how much we've changed in only a few?"

Shaking off the odd feeling that should have only been triumph, Joe decided to give the ritual a test run. Tapping on the 'screen', he was able to select one of the ritual towers connected to the Ritual of the Traveling Civilization. With another tap and a mental command, an abundance of mana flowed out of Joe and into the Ritual of Remote Activation, continuing on into the Master-ranked ritual, and from there adjusting the movement of the tower. The Ritualist sucked in a harsh breath at the cost, which was nearly seventy-five percent higher with the remote activation then it was with just using the main metal block by itself.

"Looks like this is going to be something only *I'm* using in the near future." Despite the high requirements, he watched in excitement as the spell diagram went to work. A tower that had been kept in reserve seemed to disintegrate not even fifty feet away from him, only to reappear—or at least he hoped it did— in the correct positioning atop the walls surrounding Novusheim. After it vanished, he watched its position shift on the topographic map provided by the Master ritual. Joe could only shrug and hope everything had gone according to plan.

Seeing as he wasn't going to be attaching a half-dozen Mana Batteries to the tablet so a new hire could use it once or twice, Joe instead slipped it into his codpiece and moved on with his work. "Looks like that's working exactly as planned, so… Rare buildings! Let's make sure we don't run out of towers anytime soon."

The nice thing about creating the defensive structures was that he was able to pay all of the people he needed to help him out of the coffers of the Town Council. One after another, the oddly-shaped edifices came into being. Even though Joe heard a message informing him that his quest was complete, he waited to check it until there were a round dozen of them, then he dismissed the helpers with a smile and his thanks, finally allowing himself to check his notifications.

Since he wasn't expecting anything of this magnitude, the absolute *wall* of text nearly paralyzed him.

Quest complete: Student Rituarchitect I. Congratulations! You are now considered a true Student of this discipline! As expected of a proud caffeine addict who meticulously crafts their morning brew, you've poured your expertise into creating 10 Rare-ranked buildings as rapidly as possible without letting the jitters create errors. Reward: Ritual of Mass Repair (Student). Access to Student Rituarchitect II.

Item gained: Ritual of Mass Repair (Spell Diagram). With this ritual, you can think of yourself as the equivalent of a magical structural engineer! Perform the maintenance equivalent of foundation repair, patching, wall replacement, roofing, plumbing, and so much more for up to five buildings that have at least 1 section within 100 feet centered on the ritual. All structures that will be repaired by this ritual must be designated at the time of its creation. Upgrading a building will cause the ritual to no longer be effective.

Quest gained: Student Rituarchitect II. Just like the satisfaction of finishing one cup of espress-joe—ha!—only to start another, your journey as a Rituarchitect is just beginning. Create Rare-ranked buildings with the following conditions:

Alchemical artistry: create two buildings using a Ritualistic Alchemical treatment. Think of this like trying to balance the ratio of sugar and cream in your standard drink. 0/2.

Forging finesse: create two buildings with a Ritualistic Forging treatment. Like with a proper espresso, heat and pressure can mold anything into something incredible. 0/2.

Matrice Masterpiece: two buildings should be designed with a keen eye for their best position within the Town. You wouldn't just slap your coffee mug on a walnut desk; you need a proper coaster. 0/2.

Mathematical Perfection: that's right, two mathematically perfect buildings. That's right, think Fibonacci sequences, pi, and differential equations! The details matter, which is why balancing the altitude they are grown, sugar crystal content, and water drainage of your coffee beans allows for the best breakfast brew! 0/2.

Freestyle: we are not monsters, the final two buildings are up to you!

Build them however you would like, just like adding syrups to your latte because you like to be wrong. I mean, adventurous. 0/2

Rituarchitect has reached level 13!

Reductionist has reached level 9!

Normally, you wouldn't gain a reward for either of these attaining a level, but we like the simultaneous increase. It's impressive, so have an attaboy!

Item gained: Large plate of chocolate chip cookies. (24)

Joe stared down at his hands, where a large platter containing two dozen steaming cookies had suddenly appeared. Completely nonplussed, he picked one up and bit into it. "Oh. Fresh baked. That's *good*. Maybe a coffee to go with it, Mate?"

Burble.

"Yeah, good call. Espresso's on my mind, for some reason."

CHAPTER FORTY-ONE

The Ritualist took a look at the sky, smiling gently as he noted that the ziggurat had integrated so well with the ritual controlling the day and night cycle that he couldn't even see the edges of its magical influence. Logically, he knew that it was full dark now and was just before midnight ten thousand miles away at Middle Village. "What perfect timing... when the clock strikes midnight for them, we're going to be making our move. It's almost poetic."

If anyone had been looking at Joe as he walked away from his backup tower area, they would've seen a strong, calm councilman with a backdrop of defensive ritual towers shimmering with the telltale glow of structured magic. Between his personal preparations and the strength of the Legion, Joe was certain that the imminent Boss wave would be dealt with easily. "I don't need to be here; magic and might will hold the line, even if I'm busy. If I say that enough, maybe it'll stay true."

Taking only one last glance back at the mesmerizing vista that his power had generated, Joe fully turned his mind to his current task. Jaxon had reached out, the last of his impromptu team who needed to return to Town before he was comfortable making his move. Heartpiercer and Socar had already sent word that they were waiting for him at his workshop, so somehow Joe had ended up being late to his own event.

Oftentimes, waiting and planning was the most difficult part of a mission. Sure, there was often more strenuous activity and pain involved with carrying out the tasks, but to get the rest of his team on board with the attack, Joe knew exactly what was going to be required. He entered the workshop and exchanged a few pleasantries before pushing forward and showcasing his plan for the attack.

"Thank you all for coming." A thick stack of documents landed on the table a moment later. "You know why you're here, now please allow me to convince you that it's a good idea. At the least, I'll be able to show you that I've thought this through as much as possible. Before we begin, Socar; do you have a way to cancel magical effects on someone? I'm sure that Daniella is going to be booby trapped, tracked, or have some other active effect on her. My plan was created with the assumption that we'd be able to get rid of that."

After exchanging a glance with his feline familiar, Socar gave a sharp nod. "Yes, that's something I can manage. I'm a mid-range fighter, leaning toward long range for sure. Can I get a guarantee that *I* don't need to go into the Village? I don't mind coming along, but... I'm not going to put myself or Nimue at risk. Not even for you, Joe. Well, maybe for you, but not for this random person you want to save."

"Who has already betrayed us before!" Jaxon declared with a double thumbs-up. "I'm excited to give her a chance at redemption! This is normal for me and not uncharacteristic at all."

"Glad to hear it." Joe smiled at the Chiropractor, who looked back at him with a quizzical expression on his face. "First off, I'm going to do my utmost to keep *all* of us out of the line of fire. This is going to be a stealth mission. Our objective is to infiltrate Middle Village, extract Daniella, then get out of there and never see any of those people again. We need to be fast and stealthy. Clear?"

"Squeaky clean, like a giant penguin! You got it, boss." Jaxon slapped the table, unable to contain his enthusiasm.

Joe let out an internal sigh, fully uncertain how much of his instructions were getting through. "Close enough. Heartpiercer, you'll be happy to know that I took your advice and put together a proper pace plan. I would love all of us to look it over and try to figure out anything I missed. Right now... I'm not going to lie, this feels a bit like a safety net made out of spider silk. Thin, fragile, but hopefully enough to keep us from falling into disaster."

"Your primary plan is to sneak in and get her out without anyone the wiser?" Heartpiercer clarified with a snort, shaking her head and mumbling, "so we're *actually* starting with the alternative, aren't we?"

"Rude, but I suppose I deserve that." Just like the Archer, Joe had very little faith that they'd be able to be undetected in a town that was not only hostile but aware that Joe had unknown methods of finding and getting to them. "The alternative plan... again, all of this is designed to keep you guys as safe as possible. I'm certainly not going to ask you to do something that I wouldn't do, so that means I go in alone."

The other three people looked uncomfortable at his words, but no one countered his statement, so he pressed on. "The alternative. If the alarm goes up, I want the three of you to attack the town directly, being as flashy as possible to try and draw their attention. That way, even though they'll know there's something happening, hopefully they'll be too busy dealing with the monsters—as well as what I hope they'll think is a full-fledged invasion—to chase me down."

"Hmm." Socar half raised his hand, shaking his head slightly. "So you're predicating this with the assumption that they're going to care more about defending their walls than recapturing a prisoner who has been broken out of jail? Are you *certain* that'll be their reaction?"

"I'm-" Joe paused as he thought about the hardcore role players they were going up against. "Frankly, no. It could be that they will drop everything, sacrifice their entire town if needed, to make sure they aren't shaken out of their delusion. Perhaps they think that, if one person can escape the 'game' they have going in their heads, it'll start making other people want to stop playing."

"The whole point of making a full-fledged plan is to assume some part of it is going to fail." Surprisingly, it was Heartpiercer who was offering the olive branch in the conversation. "Alternative fails, what happens?"

"Scorched earth." Joe started dropping stacks of ritual tiles on the table with meticulous care. "All of these are set to attack anyone in range, except for me. Of course, *this* pile is set to hit me as well, as an emergency backup."

With that, he set a stack of tiles on the table that was twice as large as the other. Jaxon looked at him sidelong, and Joe could only shrug. "I'm not going to risk being stuck in that prison. Respawn is preferable to stagnation and indoctrination."

"That is *your* emergency, what about ours?" Socar nervously questioned. "I'd much prefer not having to go to respawn, nor being captured."

"Emergency bubble travel." Joe handed each of them a small tile which was glowing a bright blue, showing that it was active and ready to be used. "Put a drop of blood on the center of your tiles, and if you take health damage that drops you below twenty percent, it'll automatically encapsulate you in a bubble and send you to the altar we're going to travel to. As a word of caution, the acceleration won't be... pleasant. You might take a bit more damage, so don't get hit too hard. Maybe even poke yourself if you think you're going to be surrounded or something."

Over the next few hours, every detail of the plan was scrutinized, every angle they could come up with was covered. No one was perfectly happy with the plan, but they were experienced fighters, crafters, and powerhouses in their own right.

They knew that this had been eating away at Joe, distracting him, and would continue to do so until everything was taken care of. Eventually, there was only one final detail that every member of the team insisted Joe agree to before they would accompany him.

"As a final, emergency requirement..." Heartpiercer stared directly into Joe's eyes, and he squirmed internally at the steel in that gaze. "If all else fails, you need to leave. Then you need to put this behind you. If you can't get her out of there, even with all of this preparation, you won't be able to for a *long* time. If we miss our chance, even while a boss is attacking... you're done with this. Swear this to me, and I'm in."

Joe looked around at the others, his eyes widening as each of them nodded along with her statement. The Ritualist's first thought was to refuse, but he swallowed his words and agreed, even though the thought of leaving Daniella behind to her fate tasted bitter on his tongue. Unfortunately, logic told him that his team was right. Sometimes, a small sacrifice for the greater good of a much larger population needed to be made. There were too many people relying on his abilities at the moment to devote his life to a prison break.

"Oh..." Joe swallowed the building nausea, forcing the words out of his mouth. "Okay. If this fails, and we come back here, I'll give up on this until you all agree that it's time to try again. I swear it."

You have been bound by an oath! Jotunheim is a harsh world, and your word means more here than in the forgiving places you have traveled. Breaking an oath will result in a mandatory Warlock title, blocking of all Cleric skills until you complete a task for your Deity, as well as any other punishments you have agreed upon!

He closed his eyes as the message appeared in front of him. Joe had been worried something like this would occur and had always been *very* careful not to take oaths or verbally swear to do something. Apparently, each of his teammates understood exactly what he was going through, because their rigid stances relaxed somewhat as soon as his notification appeared. That made Joe realize that they had also likely received a confirmation message on their end.

They stood to leave, and Joe felt a slight, exceedingly subtle *click* in his head. He knew that feeling; one of his spells had just come off of cooldown. "Oh...? Oh! Nice, normally I'm too engrossed in what I'm doing to notice. *Knowledge*: Enchanting Lore, Calculus and Number Theory."

As he cast the deity-gifted spell, Joe expanded his Exquisite Shell out around his body as far as he could, leaving a space for air against his skin in an attempt to try and control the echoes 'slapping' off the ambient mana that this spell caused. It made him vibrate in a *very* unpleasant manner—his eardrums especially buzzed sharply—but from what he could tell, the ripples were expanding out far less than usual. Progress.

Joe took a deep breath as his eyes unfocused, and the information on two completely separate topics was inserted into his brain and categorized. He was pleased with his progress; after all, he'd been using this spell as often as possible—showcased by most of his Lore abilities closing in on the Journeyman rank. As his mana settled and started regenerating his mana pool, he looked at his Lore skills and allowed himself a moment of excitement at how much each of them had grown over his time on Jotunheim.

Lore Skills
Alchemical Lore (Student V)
Architectural Lore (Student VII)
Enchanting Lore (Student VIII → Student IX)
Knowledge (Student VIII)
Ritual Lore (Student IX)
Smithing Lore (Student III)
Calculus and Number Theory (Apprentice VIII → Apprentice IX)

Apparently, his efforts at containing his effect on the environment weren't as effective as he'd hoped they'd be. Halfway to the shrine, an eruption of snow shot from the ground in front of them. As the ever-present wind blew the flakes away, Grandmaster Havoc was revealed, watching them with sunken, sullen eyes. The corner of his mouth opened slightly, allowing a cloud of cigar smoke to escape and swirl around him in a display the breeze couldn't interrupt.

Joe might even have been impressed by the dramatic entrance, if he hadn't flung himself to the side in preparation of whatever had just detonated on the ground. Before he could start complaining about boundaries and moving at speeds that they could see, the Dwarf shook his head slowly. "Now's *not* the time, lad. You're needed here. The council needs to show a unified front, Boss waves make people twitchy. Makes them want to abandon ship even before it starts sinking. Don't abandon your responsibility."

The Ritualist was taken aback by the gravitas Havoc was imbuing into his words. Instead of his normal flippant tones, his mentor was deadly serious, his voice sounding like stones being ground down into arrowheads. For a long few moments, the rest of the world seemed to fade away, leaving only Joe and Havoc staring at each other. The human's heart was thundering in his chest, and his eyes darted over to his team. All eyes were on him, and he knew that they'd follow whatever decision he made.

Joe was no fool. He knew that his team didn't particularly want to undertake this mission, that they'd agreed only because it meant so much to him. The Ritualist fully understood that he had a responsibility to Novusheim, to be the bridge between Dwarves and humans as their representative.

Seeing no easy answer, he swallowed hard, his gaze shifting between the ground in front of him, his deadly serious mentor, and the distant horizon... where even now he knew that monsters were converging on the town holding Daniella prisoner. His voice came out as a whisper as he made his choice. "I can't... I *won't* miss this chance. Most likely, I won't get another one."

Meeting the eyes of his mentor, Joe firmly stated, "I'm sorry, Havoc. But I have a friend to save."

CHAPTER FORTY-TWO

The group of four, plus one cat, appeared near-simultaneously over ten thousand miles away from Novusheim. To accommodate everyone's varying mana levels, they'd broken the trip up, remaining together for maximum security. Their arrival was greeted by the distant echoes of monstrous roars, the flash of enchantments and spells being tested and utilized, and even the wind carried the scent of burnt flesh and hair.

"The dead of night! A perfect cloak for our daring escapades!" Jaxon dramatically placed one hand against his forehead and threw the other back. "How will our intrepid heroes fare with the might of an entire Village arrayed against them? Find out in the next novel by the inspiring scholar D. Kota!"

Joe wasn't certain how to respond to that, but Socar rescued him from his confusion by explaining that an impromptu theater group had sprung up out of sheer boredom due to the conditions in Novusheim. Apparently, Jaxon had been going to every single one of the shows, no matter how repetitive it ended up being, and had been trying out for a position in the troupe. The Mage motioned for Joe to come closer, whispering in his ear, "It's made him a bit of a diva, if I'm being honest."

More than anything else, the information made Joe feel like a bad friend. The fact that he had no idea what else was going on in his friend's lives at the moment made him resolve to spend more time pursuing their interests—instead of only his own—when he saw them in the near future. But for now, they were on a mission. The Ritualist felt his focus sharpen as the biting wind blasted particles of ice into him, and he began their march to Middle Village.

They moved quickly, Joe knowing what to avoid, how to navigate around monsters lying dormant in the snow, and having intimate knowledge of where he needed to take them. Their journey across the frozen expanse was nearly silent, only the pounding of their feet and their heavy breathing punctuating their movements.

To Joe, the trip passed in a flash, and he only allowed himself to slow down when enchanted walls appeared in the distance. Exactly as they'd hoped, the settlement was under attack. The scene was utter chaos: rampaging Hoardlings threw themselves against the wall and pounded on the flaring magic keeping the defenses intact. Penguins bounced off other monsters, throwing themselves ever higher in the air as they attempted to simply evade the barrier, only to bounce off the invisible extended protection that the wards created. Salamanders caused sections to flicker and flare with their aura of a deadly cold—the Ritualist intently noted that the lizards were targeted with ruthless abandon.

"Likely weak to elemental interference. Good to know." Joe began to limber up, his eyes on the far distant walls. "I'm sensing a window of opportunity here, so I guess this is where we part ways. Keep a Ritual of Communication open at all times, would you? I'd rather not send up a flare if I need to get your attention."

"Can-do, bald daddy-o." Jaxon threw out a mock salute, and Joe tried not to vomit in his mouth.

"Please… never say that again." Joe continued his preparations, even as his teammates looked at him as though he'd lost his mind.

"Are you really going to try and run in there in the middle of an attack? You're definitely going to catch your death out there." Socar gently admonished the Ritualist. "You only have one chance at this. Don't you have a better option?"

"I could make it," Joe scoffed defensively, holding up a hand to wave off the negative vibes. "I'm not going to try that, though. Even though I absolutely *could* just hop over the wall, we can see that the enchantments extend up to protect it. Don't worry about it; I'm betting on the fact that the magic only extends a certain distance. Since nothing in this world can fly, at least nothing that we've found, I'm hoping that they aren't so paranoid that they're already protecting from above. Wish me luck."

Eyeballing the distance, Joe pulled out a ritual tile and made a small alteration before activating it and being captured within a bubble. Any complaints or gasps of surprise were lost in the wind as his bubble shot into the air, accelerating to nearly two hundred miles per hour in only two and a half seconds. A basic human would have been crushed by the rapid G-Force changes, but Joe merely felt slightly uncomfortable being pressed against the distorting surface.

"Here comes the difficult part." The Ritualist braced himself as the bubble reached its maximum altitude and rapidly slowed. He was thrown to the top, flattening himself as much as possible to minimize the chances of popping the thin surface. It traveled in a straight line from there, moving until it was almost directly over the center of the Village before rapidly accelerating once more, this time toward the ground like a meteor falling from space.

If his calculations had been correct, Joe would land directly atop the prison. Unfortunately, he'd slightly misjudged, and the roof of the Town Hall rapidly came into view, growing from the size of a postage stamp to filling the entirety of his field of vision in an instant. The bubble slowed, and Joe was thrown to the bottom of it, and this time he was unable to assist the bubble in staying intact. He burst directly through it, his momentum only slightly arrested.

He barely managed to catch himself in time, stabilizing his fall and landing on his feet with a shockwave that rippled out across the top of the building. Enchantments on the structures around him flared to life, whining and sparking as their power rapidly drained, thanks to the terrain damage his Superhero Landing title inflicted. The wards held out, barely. "Well, I'm betting *that* set off an alarm or two. Time to not be here any longer."

Rushing to the side of the Town Hall, Joe prepared to Omnivault off, only to slide to a stop and shake in indecision. Before he could completely freeze thanks to choice paralysis, the Ritualist slapped a ritual tile containing the Ritual of Raze into the rain gutter. "There! A contingency to my backup, just in case I need a little extra *oomph* in my distractions."

His heart was pounding as he threw himself off the roof of the building, never more aware than he was right now about the fact that his shiny head was basically a beacon in the night. Joe could only hope that, as had been the case the last time he was here, every able-bodied person was on the walls fighting for their lives. There would be at least a few guards below, but hopefully they would be focused on the Town Hall, especially with the warnings that had likely just gone out.

"Just keep your attention outward, not inside your walls," Joe murmured almost as a mantra as he beelined toward the prison. He'd timed things right, he'd prepared meticulously, and now he just needed a little luck. That and a whole lot of hope that Daniella was where he expected her to be.

His first thought was to try and blend in with the shadows cast by the mana lamps lining the streets, but then he realized that it would be just as suspicious to be wandering the empty sidewalks as it would be to continue on as he was. Omnivault after Omnivault brought him closer then finally halfway up the wall of the prison. Joe reached out and gripped a windowsill, pulling himself up and looking inside.

For once, the Elven, open-concept design of the structure was working out in his favor. No glass barred his path, no bars, for that matter—a real concern at a prison. He was able to pull himself in, finding that he was dangling nearly fifteen feet off the floor. It was a great vantage point, and his gaze roved the prison, alighting momentarily on each person within. There were two prison guards, both of them appearing as bored as he expected them to be.

No one really tried to escape from here; at least if they weren't actually a Dwarven spy like he was. The post must have been extremely easy, to the point that it was practically unnecessary. As much as he sneered at the methods the Elves used to discipline the people who had chosen to willingly work with them... he had to admit that their totalitarian tactics worked wonders for maintaining control. Finally working up the nerve to start moving slowly, he slunk into the prison, easily avoiding the guards and their practically robotic patrolling patterns.

While the Ritualist had no skills relating to stealth, his Characteristics were high enough that he was able to remain silent as he passed through the hallway, descending deeper into the prison. "There's fewer staff here than at a coffee shop on a slow day... ugh. Why do I do this to myself? Now I want a mug."

Even though the place was built to contain powerful people, it was still only a Rare-ranked building. There were only a total of two additional floors under the ground level, and the deepest was where the solitary confinement area could be found.

Unfortunately, unlike the previous floors, the guard here was attentive and alert, scanning the environment for any changes, regularly moving to check on the only room that actually had a prisoner.

Joe had a glint in his eye as he watched that, knowing that there was only one person who could cause this much disruption: someone they believed to be a traitor and saboteur. "Found ya."

CHAPTER FORTY-THREE

Now the issue became how to eliminate the guard or subvert him without causing a commotion. Joe had very few options for silent kills, and anyone who'd survived through two worlds and been on Jotunheim for any length of time was certain to be strong, and—more annoyingly—durable.

Wincing slightly at the fact that he'd have to sneak attack another human in as brutal a fashion as possible to minimize his own chances at being noticed, Joe lifted his ritual orbs out of their bandoliers and arranged them carefully. The orb of Intelligence went at the front, and he hoped that its armor penetrating properties would allow him to earn a coup de gras when he followed through on his imminent attack.

He held the orb of Strength in his right hand, gripping the bar in the center of the dumbbell-shaped weapon, then set the heart-shaped orb of Constitution back behind his elbow. With a thought, the other, standard, ball-bearing shaped ritual orbs were pressed along his arm to provide him stability for his next action.

As the guard stepped forward to peer in the small window one more time, the Ritualist lunged out of hiding with a Omnivault-powered movement. In a fraction of a second, he was in position directly behind the completely oblivious man. Joe swung his hand forward as though to punch his target in the back of his head, spinning up his orb of Intelligence up to give it maximum penetration.

Then, just before his blow would have landed, Joe slammed the ritual orb of Constitution into his elbow as hard as possible where the standard orbs were placed.

The intense force of the strike moved through each of the orbs in turn, finally arriving at the ritual orb of Strength and sending it forward with more than three times the force that Joe's body and will could generate individually. His fist shot out, the metal of his clenched weapon slamming into the spinning spike and driving the metal icicle deep into the guard's brainstem.

Just to be extra sure, Joe sent a Cone of Cold out of the orb, locking the corpse in place as a block of solid ice. The man never knew what hit him.

Critical! Damage doubled! Sneak attack! Damage doubled! Coup de gras, instant kill to prevent suffering.

Ritual Orb Alpha Strike registered: Newton's Deadly Cradle.

Newton's Deadly Cradle: align your ritual orbs with your mind, might, and magic, dealing (Intelligence+(sum of durability))*5 damage. All orbs take 30% durability damage based on the orb with the highest durability.

Caution! 5/6 of your Ritual Orbs have 40% durability remaining!

Joe let the information flow over him, deciding that he would save his extreme excitement for another time. Alpha Strikes were incredibly powerful single attacks, and someone had once told him that they were ranked by how frequently they could be used—more specifically, by how long it would take to reset them. He promised himself that he'd look into it further in the near future then set about searching for a method of opening the door in front of him.

Eventually, he was forced to settle on dousing the plant matter with acid, figuring that no one else was around to hear the sizzle of the caustic fluid nor smell the sharp tang as it ate through the organic material. After several tense minutes, his path was clear.

Joe rushed in, silently in an attempt to wake Daniella up as quietly as possible. He knew he'd gotten in fairly easily, but with two people, leaving without being noticed would be much more difficult.

"*Daniella!*" he hissed excitedly, reaching out and gently gripping her shoulder. "It's time to get out of here!"

She rolled toward him, confusion in her eyes for only a moment until her sleepy eyes focused on his face. Her blond hair was pooled around her nearly artfully, and her golden eyes kept getting wider as she saw that he was real.

He was almost able to let the discrepancies go, but... blonde hair? Golden eyes? Before he could pull back, the illusion vanished like a soap bubble popping, and Joe locked eyes with the scholarly elf who had chased him out of town not nearly long enough ago.

Mwah. The Elf made a kissy-face at him, sent along a wink, then released a spell that he must have been holding for *hours* at the least.

Joe screamed in fury as a pillar of light blasted him up, through the ceiling, then through the next one, where he finally came to a stop embedded in the now-smoking wood.

Exquisite Shell: 0/12,002

Health: 1,847/2,496

As Joe started to fall, blood spurting from the hole punched through his gut, the Elf launched out of the opening that the human's body had drilled for him—an orb of glowing light on his outstretched hand.

"You should already be dead. Oh? It didn't count as a sneak attack? Hmph. Doesn't matter in the long run. Tell me: why are humans *so* predictable?"

For a long moment—almost too long—after he had been hit, Joe was understandably confused, likely concussed. His Exquisite Shell was shattered, his head had bounced into or through three different ceilings. The Ritualist saw the shimmering ball of light on the graceful, delicate hands coming toward him, and his only thought was, "When did disco come back into style?"

The fraction of a second that Retaliation of Shadows required to activate passed, and the Elf was slapped *just* hard enough to slow his ascent, allowing time for Joe's Characteristics to kick in. The Ritualist forced his body forward, placing his feet on the ceiling and shoving off at an oblique angle. He twisted in the air—barely succeeding in avoiding the spell-coated hand lashing out at him—and landed against a wall thirty feet from where the Elf came to rest.

Joe dug his fingers into the wood, tearing through its surface just enough to allow himself to hang in place like a frog. All he needed to do was stall for time, both to get his Exquisite Shell back in place, as well as to figure out how to turn this situation around. The Elf came flying at him once more, the wood he was pushing off exploding into splinters as he lunged. But aerial combat was where Joe excelled, likely having more experience with this type of fighting than any currently living human.

As the Mage approached in an *almost* impossible-to-track motion, Joe pushed away and bounded off the walls, keeping himself airborne for significant stretches of time and distance. The magical onslaught continued, and just as Joe began to wonder why the Elf wasn't using longer-ranged spells, his own mana pool finished refilling fully.

He began the process of generating his magical barrier, which took *far* longer to complete than he wanted. With his concentration split between protecting himself as well as evading, he had no time for witty banter, taunts, or demands. A glowing palm was approaching? Duck and shove. That same palm was extended? Flip, dodge, leap, repeat. From the moment he'd pushed off the ceiling for the first time until his Exquisite Shell snapped back into place, nearly twenty-three seconds of pure adrenaline-fueled acrobatics had passed.

Joe was confident he could evade or survive anything the Elf threw at him at the moment, so he took a moment to catch his breath and throw out his first, then second question. "Where's Daniella? What's wrong with all of you that you're so insistent on keeping someone that clearly doesn't want to be here?"

The brilliant smile on the smug Elf face made Joe want to start blasting, but the words that reached his ears a moment later gave him pause.

"Daniella? We don't want her, *Joe*. We don't care about her, *Joe*. We want *you*, Joe. As far as we can tell, there's not much that we can do to entice you to willingly walk into a trap. So, when you let us know about something, some*one* you'd do anything for? How could we just let her… walk away?"

With a sinking sensation, Joe realized that the reason that his friend was stuck here wasn't because of anything *she* had done. It wasn't due to her communications with him, nor her actions that might've been viewed as treasonous. Daniella had been in a bad position just because she was his friend. Their already-strained relationship was seen as the best way to get to him, and a moment of introspection made Joe wonder why he had so few personal connections that they went after this one.

It almost would've been funny, if it wasn't so sad.

"Welp, goodbye forever!" Joe went head-first out of the window, tucking and rolling as he hit the ground, then bounding upward and launching high enough to land on the roof of the next building over.

"That's right, *run!*" the Elf taunted as he half-dangled out of the window Joe had escaped through. Heat was radiating from the hand gripping the window frame, causing the wood to smolder and warp. The voice was laden with an unsettling mirth, and he seemed to be savoring each word.

"As you make your escape, a minor detail for you to mull over. Your dear, sweet friend? She's here, safe and sound. Furthermore, I swear that she *will* be found here, in the Town Hall, for a mere thirty days. But her tenure will be fleeting. After that time elapses, she'll be joining a caravan, her position ever shifting, ever elusive, constantly on the move until *we* grow weary of this game."

Joe paused, and the Elf took several deep, shuddering breaths as he laughed at the human. "Or you could consider a generous offer that I have been allowed to make. A simple trade. Her... for you. I think an agreement could save us all a lot of time and effort, don't you agree?"

With that, the Elf raised a hand and launched a sphere of light into the air that exploded like a firework. As soon as it was noticed, a shout went up across the walls, and a quarter of the defenders poured back into the town, rushing toward the Town Hall to cut off any attempt Joe might make to get to Daniella. "No? How sad for her. Go on then, scatter to the wind! I know you'll return for her, but *to* me. The scoreboard is one to one. You landed a sneak attack on us, and we reciprocated. Next time, both of us shall be ready. I'm practically *tingling* with anticipation."

Cursing at the Elf and his own miserable luck, Joe slapped a ritual of Bubble Travel and shot into the air, up and away from his most recent failure.

As it adjusted course and sent him toward the shrine in the far distance, Joe suddenly lashed out in fury and popped the bubble, falling through the air like a majestic brick. When he hit the ground, his entire body and view was obstructed by the snow that was kicked up.

The Ritualist was seething; he stood and walked away from where he had landed with fists and jaw clenched.

If he stayed, he'd be a captive in no time flat. If he went back, his oath to his friends would kick in, and Joe would be forced to give up on freeing Daniella for... well, likely forever. There was only one other option he could take, so Joe walked into the blowing snow, alone, hoping to find answers before he froze to death.

CHAPTER FORTY-FOUR

The Ritualist stomped along the frozen surface of Jotunheim, his Hoardling-hair cloak offering him meager protection in the form of camouflage from any of the monsters that called this area home. Part of him knew that he was being absolutely foolish right now and was taking a risk with practically no chance of reward. Still, he couldn't stop himself from taking out his frustrations on the ground with every heavy stomp.

Soon enough, he was moving along in an almost trance-like state, his thoughts grinding at a glacial speed. "Maybe it's *because* I'm stomping that I'm not having any problems. Maybe the monsters think I'm actually just one of them passing through."

Time wounds all heels, and heals all wounds.

Eventually, he was simply unable to focus on his anger any longer. The cold was gnawing at him with its icy teeth, and Joe completely understood that he was deep in the stacks of a 'chilled' debuff. He welcomed it. All of his thoughts slowly faded away, taking his anger, frustration, and self-doubt with them. Still, even as he approached severe frostbite and worse, his mind wouldn't allow him to accept being sent to respawn in this manner.

Practically unconsciously, he refreshed his Neutrality Aura whenever it became overpowered and fizzled out due to the debuffs. That allowed him to maintain his comfortably numb state while never allowing it to go too far. Each time the spell reactivated, it was accompanied by a sudden ramping up of his thoughts. "How did I not see that coming? Am I so narcissistic that I never expected that they'd try and ambush me? Why have I never tried to figure out any skills that allow me to detect danger or deception? Everyone else seems to be able to do it. Did I miss a day in class where they went over that?"

Even his parkour to freedom had been more luck than skill, certainly at the start, and it left a bitter taste in his mouth when he had enough presence of mind to think about it. An odd *crackle* coming from his belt drew his startled attention for a moment, but it was just the last of his Ritual of Communication tiles failing ahead of schedule, thanks to the cold eating away at it.

During his trudging, his teammates had attempted on numerous occasions to contact him, but he simply couldn't muster up the energy to respond. They'd activated the tiles hours apart from each other to give him the maximum possible time for responses, and now he couldn't reach out to them, even if he wanted to.

His teammates didn't deserve this treatment. They probably thought he was slain or captured, and he felt like an absolute brat about it. Still, there was nothing to do at the moment except resign himself to needing to make amends in the near future. "Yeah… probably not going to last too much longer out here."

It was just after midnight on Jotunheim, and the howling wind was stripping away his body heat, applying debuffs quicker than his Neutrality Aura could remove them. Joe, in his current state, had simply taken too long to notice the trend, and now what felt like an electric shock tingled through Joe's mind, and his head shifted to the side to glance in the direction that he'd been pulled. "Was… that… Hidden Sense?"

It felt like his words took a minute apiece to leave his mostly-frozen lips, but he'd altered his direction immediately. There was something out here, something hidden, and he could only hope that it was shelter. Of course, a simple scan of the landscape informed him that there was most certainly *not* protection from the elements out here. Most likely, he was about to find a few coins that someone had stuffed under a snowball or something.

His cold, cynical thoughts were replaced by a belated sense of surprise as the ground around him gave way, the icy landscape being replaced by darkness as he fell through a crevasse that had only a thin layer of ice coating it. By the time he blinked twice, he was dozens of feet underground and still accelerating. His Neutrality Aura seemed to be working overtime now that he was out of the intense wind and the strange magic that froze anything on the surface. As his speed increased, the debuffs affecting his mind and body were rapidly peeled away.

With a start, the Ritualist finally understood exactly what was happening and began working to save himself from going *splat*. He was spinning through the air, so the first thing that he did was push his body into a slightly unnatural position, catching the wind and stabilizing himself in his fall. If he'd have been aware at the start, he would've been able to catch at the sides of the hole and pull himself back to the surface, but at this point, the crevasse had widened out far enough to make that no longer an option.

Mind now working in overdrive, Joe reached into his codpiece and pulled out a ritual he hadn't had a chance to test yet. It should be ready, and if it wasn't... "I either die by hitting the ground or the ritual exploding in my face. If neither of those happens, it worked."

Pumping mana into the Feather Fall ritual, Joe gritted his teeth as a mounting sense of dread promised him that he was approaching the ground. He was right, but luckily, he didn't learn that with his face. Instead, he was jerked to a rough stop in midair, then resumed his fall at a normal pace. A quick glance at the ritual showed that it was beginning to overload. He could feel it shaking and vibrating in his hand, and the glow of the pre-detonation allowed him to see that the stone floor was barely a man's height below him. Joe threw the tile away like a frisbee, as hard and fast as he could.

Even before he managed to touch down, the concussive blast of the ritual detonating sent him tumbling, bouncing, and scraping along the bottom of the crevasse as curses boiled from his mouth. Finally, his motion was interrupted ignobly as he was flattened against the icy wall. The lack of friction on its surface meant that he slid to the ground immediately, where he remained for a few long moments, groaning and trying to get his spinning head aligned with the rest of his body. "Don't puke, *don't* puke…"

The feeling passed a few moments later, and Joe managed to get his breathing under control. He was in complete darkness at the moment, so much so that his Darkvision had absolutely no light to work with at all. Still laying on his back, Joe lifted his hand above him with a grunt, pulling out his aspect inscriber and etching a Ritual of Glimmering in the air, intentionally using the constellations' alignment as his guide.

Between his Journeyman rank in Somatic Ritual Casting and the confusing—yet impressive—stabilization provided by properly aligning his magic to the stars, the ritual was rock-solid and activated with nary a hint of dissonance. Purple light filled the area, more than enough for Joe to be able to see every detail for hundreds of feet in each direction. "I fell into a cave system? Is this… abyss, is this where the monsters come from for the Beast Waves?"

Deciding that discretion was the better part of valor in this instance, he kept his breathing light as he studied the cavern he'd fallen into. As his eyes trailed around the area, what he found made the cold and frustration he had experienced feel like a mere inconvenience.

Only a short distance away from him was a cave carved by

hand into the bedrock of the world. The entrance, sealed by a thick, translucent ice, yawned before him and gave Joe only the barest hints of what was on the other side. But even that was enough to create an eerie spectacle that would make *Havoc* shudder. Though it was partially obscured by the foggy ice, rows and rows of perfectly preserved corpses stood mere feet behind the entrance, their frigid power offset by a light in their eyes that was slowly growing brighter as if in response to Joe's own incandescent ritual.

"Ice wraiths. That's so *many* ice wraiths." Currently they were dormant, frozen behind the icy barrier, but at least one of those statements was changing by the moment. "Time to leave. No way can I fight that many wraiths. I barely took down *two* of them at the… the *vault*."

Ever so slowly, as his greed pummeled his self-preservation into submission, Joe turned back to examine the wraiths in closer detail. Step by step, he got closer to the barrier of ice that he felt was not *nearly* thick enough, his eyes sweeping the area around the wraiths in hopes of finding whatever treasure, lost knowledge, or hint at what place of power these monstrous entities were guarding. "How do I get in there and keep you from getting out here and chasing me no matter how far I run?"

Joe fell silent as he realized exactly what he had just vocalized. He almost burst into manic laughter as his mind tantalized him with an idea so audacious that it was almost enough for *him* to cast it aside entirely. "*Ea~asy* there, Joe, figure out an escape route first."

Cautiously turning his back on the frozen barrier, he walked the length and breadth of the crevasse, finding neither entrance nor exit. With a deep sigh, he mentally rolled up his sleeves and got to work. "I guess I'm going to have to do this the hard way. Shocker. *Field Array!*"

His plan was a simple one, even if it was going to be time-consuming. Joe set his Field Array at an upward angle, and over the next few hours carved an enormous, sloping tunnel up and out of the crevasse until he met with the surface.

As the fresh air blew snow around his face, Joe needed to convince himself to go back down after deciding which direction the Middle Village was in. It was harder than he expected to force himself underground, especially knowing that, at any time during his upward tunneling, the wraiths may have escaped their cage and might be waiting for him even now.

With the immense talent they had at remaining invisible in the snow, he would never know until it was too late. Still, for his new plan to work, Joe needed to risk it. Grabbing a large chunk of ice, he shaped it into a sled using his Field Array then hopped on and slid down the nearly mile-long ramp he'd made.

"Even if this doesn't work… I'm glad I'm trying and having fun while doing it!" Joe whooped in excitement as he hit a bump, getting sent flying into the air as his ice sled shattered into a thousand pieces. He landed on his stomach and found out that his Exquisite Shell worked perfectly as a replacement.

"Yes! This is even *faster*!"

CHAPTER FORTY-FIVE

The Ritualist stood before the dense ice wall, his mind screaming that he should find at *least* one more thing to put as a barricade between himself and the deadly monsters on the other side. After inspecting the slick surface for damage, Joe let out a sigh of relief and turned away. "I still have time."

Backing away from the ice while keeping a close eye on it, Joe eased himself across the open space until he was on the other side of the crevasse. From there, he hollowed out a large room in the stone and set up a ritual to build a shrine for him. His thoughts on this project were fairly simplistic: he didn't want to lose this location and whatever reward was waiting for him. There was a good chance the wraiths would ignore the tiny structure in favor of attacking him, and even if they didn't, it wasn't much of a loss. Joe had a great sense of direction, even if his ability to keep track of time was questionable at best.

Muttering a few pleasantries to Tatum, half-hoping to get a buff but not disappointed when he didn't, Joe turned back to the frozen-over cave and prepared himself. "Time to let the genie out of the bottle."

He walked over to the ice and set up a Field Array that

encompassed almost the entirety of the open space. The Ritualist was almost positive he'd extended the array a few inches beyond the ice on the other side, which meant that every bit of protection he had against the monsters was about to vanish. "As soon as the reduction is complete, just turn and run. Don't try to see if I got any neat aspects, and *don't* look back: they're definitely following me. Even if I can't see them—scratch that, *especially* if I can't see them."

He pumped mana into the Field Array, and the dense frozen obstacle vanished without a hint that it had ever existed. Joe turned and tried to run, only to slip on the ice and fall flat on his face. "*Wahh!*"

Luckily, it seemed that the wraiths were either still coming out of hibernation or were as shocked at his flub as he was. No cold, desiccated hands latched on to his ankles, no rotten, fetid air washed over his neck. If nothing else, he had enough time to regain his footing and start building up speed. The Ritualist ran directly at the mouth of his homemade tunnel, hitting the slope and letting his excitement show on his face.

Joe's eyes were burning; his smile was beaming. This was what he lived for: the chance to do wondrous, amazing things. His magic had brought him this far, getting him in and letting him create a path to escape. Even though he was now running for his life, all he could think about was how excited he was.

Dozens of hisses of fury filled the air behind him, creating a spectral chill that raised every hair on Joe's body and even some on his cloak. His incredible smile dimmed slightly, but his resolve hardened further. The frozen tunnel stretched far, far into the distance—a mile-long uphill race that he *needed* to win. "Personal trainers *wish* they could motivate people like this!"

For the next handful of seconds, he had a commanding lead. But the environment was heavily in favor of the wraiths, and all too soon a light appeared, the glow of it casting Joe's shadow so far ahead of him that he knew the source of the illumination was practically *touching* him. He'd been waiting for this moment and had the perfect skill for this icy escapade. "Omnivault!"

His mana flowed into his feet, and Joe launched forward and up, regaining his lead once more. As his feet pounded against the ground, he realized he needed to lift them higher; already, the uphill climb was causing his muscles to burn in exertion. He would've fared much better if he'd taken any time to sleep in the last four days or have a proper meal in the last two. Constitution and Stamina could only take him so far before his body began to fail, and it was a painful lesson he was hoping to be able to put off until another, less lethal time.

As the minutes passed, his escape turned into a deadly game of cat and mouse where he needed to win every single time, and the wraiths only needed to win once. With as much dexterity and grace as he could put into his movements, Joe bounded off the frozen walls, defied gravity by keeping his body only inches above the slick surface of the ramp, and catapulted himself dozens of feet forward each time he activated his skill.

Each launch was a thrill, as he only allowed himself to use his skill when his senses were screaming that the monsters almost had him. Even so, his panic-laughter began to echo along the entirety of the tunnel walls, the thrill of barely staying ahead of his death giving him a rush he'd been missing for far too long. There was no politics involved, no nasty threats or putting other people at risk. Only staying alive or falling prey to the wraiths.

Then his foot slipped out from under him, the wind pushing into the tunnel having slicked down a section of the stone where he hadn't been expecting. As he landed heavily, sliding forward before completely losing his momentum and beginning to drop back down the tunnel, the wraiths swirled closer, releasing haunting calls of glee as frigid claws lit up, reaching for his face, his eyes. As their extended digits brushed against his cloak, an instant away from enveloping him in an icy embrace, Joe swung his legs forward and Omnivaulted *backward*, down the tunnel.

He knew he had confused the deadly things by the way they

went completely silent and invisible once more. Joe could only hope he wasn't about to tackle one of them as he flipped in midair. Getting his feet behind him, the Ritualist used the flat surface that his boxy carving with Field Array created on the ceiling of the tunnel as a jump pad, pushing forward and propelling himself up and over his previous location like an arrow.

As far as he could tell, he'd managed to thread the needle directly through the pack of beasts. But, he couldn't be completely certain. As the exhilarating and terrifying game of evasion continued once more, he could only hope as much as possible that one of the monsters hadn't managed to get ahead of him.

Joe was so focused on his effort that he almost didn't notice when he burst out of the tunnel and into open air. He overestimated his landing and had to tuck and roll as he came down on the powdery surface of Jotunheim. Even though he'd promised himself he wouldn't, the Ritualist chanced a look backward. The only hint that the monsters were still coming after him was fractional indents in the surface of the snow that rapidly approached him. "*Nope*! Noping *right* on outta here."

He turned the momentum of his fall into the motion he needed in order to regain his footing, wincing as a frost-fire coated hand sparked against his Exquisite Shell. "Too close!"

After a few feet and only one Omnivault, he was starting to hit his stride. Huffing and puffing, Joe sprinted toward the horizon, his eyes locked on the glow in the clouds created by the lights of Middle Village.

He was coming for them, and he was bringing friends.

As more and more ice wraiths poured out of the tunnel, their collective presence caused the wind to start to howl, and in no time flat, an enormous blizzard was racing after Joe: a natural disaster on a mission.

Not only was the Ritualist perfectly fine with this... it was exactly what he'd been hoping for. If a distraction wasn't enough to give him an advantage on a stealth mission, he could only hope that completely blocking out all visibility would afford him enough time to go in *loud*. As he ran, Joe toyed with a few of the ritual tiles he'd brought with him. "I think I know *exactly* where I'm going to shove these."

His fatigue began to increase as he continued running and as debuffs continued to accumulate. Even so, he was going to make it just fine. Joe had wandered through the tundra aimlessly for hours and hours; a straight-line sprint was practically guaranteed to bring him back to the town in one piece.

Every half minute or so, he was forced to Omnivault forward to escape the grasping hands of the furious monsters. They were faster than him, though not by much. If Joe had wanted, he could've made a clean escape by launching himself away as frequently as possible, but his goal was to lead the monsters, not to lose them. With so much going on, time seemed to fly past, and soon the walls of Middle Village were looming large in the distance.

Joe inspected the shifting light in the distance and cursed softly under his breath. "I guess I shouldn't be calling it Middle Village anymore; looks like it's officially Middle *Town*. Abyss, I hope this doesn't complicate things."

As he got closer, dragging the blizzard behind him, Joe tried to work out where he should turn and run alongside the walls to hit on the other side of the Town. His hope was that the monsters would be influenced by the proximity of the Town and fall under the compulsion to attack the Town Hall instead of him. He began zigzagging slightly, and when the raging storm finally continued on in a straight line, Joe didn't.

Omnivault after Omnivault allowed him to gain distance from the storm, and he kicked up snow as his arms and legs pumped furiously. When he got into position, Joe prepared to charge at the walls and go over them like a pole vaulter, hoping to evade the wards and detection thanks to the snow and ice that was now kicking up.

Pushing as hard as he could, he leaned forward and ran

with maximum effort. He gauged the distance, and prepared to jump in three seconds, two…

Oof!

Joe bounced half a dozen times as arms wrapped around his waist and tackled him to the rock-hard ice. A harsh voice growled in his ear, "Gotcha! I *knew* you'd be back; we were waiting for you."

CHAPTER FORTY-SIX

Joe looked up with shaking eyes into Jaxon's intense glare, worried for a moment that the hand clamped over his mouth and nose to keep him silent would squeeze tighter and cut off his air flow. Two silhouettes emerged from the howling snow, and only when they got within a foot and a half of him could Joe recognize the familiar forms: his friends, his team.

The people he had left twisting in the wind while he ran away.

Even with the fury etched onto their faces, a sight that felt like a punch in the gut to the Ritualist, seeing them here almost brought tears of joy to his eyes. He hadn't expected them to still be in the area, not after he'd gone incommunicado and practically thrown himself into the wilderness to die. Even as gratitude filled him, and he opened his mouth to try and make an excuse, or perhaps apologize for his actions, Jaxon's hand clamped down tighter.

It was exactly what Joe had been worried about; he closed his eyes in acceptance and tried to ignore his tunneling vision. Then he noticed that he was being dragged away, and the Chiropractor whispered in his ear, "Don't make a noise. Don't even make a smell. I can't impress on you exactly how high of an alert they are operating on right now."

Once they had reached what was apparently deemed a suitable distance, each of them took a turn tearing into him. Heartpiercer's words struck him in the heart, targeted to deal as much damage as she could inflict. Socar's confusion and disappointment blasted him all over, like an area of effect spell gone bad. Even Jaxon took a turn chastising him—though much more gently than the others.

But it was Jaxon's final words that adjusted his perspective on the issue at hand, "-and if we had let you go in there, you wouldn't be coming back out. Socar's familiar recently returned from infiltrating the Town, looking for *you*, I might add. Apparently, every single Mage who can twist a spell has spent the last handful of hours weaving a web of... I suppose 'magical trip wires' are the only way to describe it."

"It's bad, Joe." Socar took over with a solemn tone. "They laced every surface of the Town, and it's all ready to spring at the lightest touch. This isn't a Town anymore; it's a Town-sized trap designed to catch one very specific rat. You. The bait is in place, and they think that all they need to do now is wait."

Joe let out such a deep sigh that it felt like his chest was collapsing to his spine. "They're probably right. I'll be as straightforward with you guys as I can. All of my anger and frustration at the situation has really cooled down during my walkabout. I'm going in there, but I'm not going to be dumb about it."

There was a long silence as the other three members of the team exchanged a series of exasperation-laden glances. Finally, the Chiropractor shrugged. "I told you. He's not going to listen to reason. Plan B it is. Fine, Joe. You want to go in there? Then I'm coming with you."

"Jaxon, no, I can get myself—"

"I think you're both going to get yourselves killed." Heartpiercer informed them with a sharp shake of the head. "Or worse, captured. What do you think that would look like, Joe?

Because I think it would look like you being fed resources and forced to expand the Town up to a City as rapidly as possible. You know, completely edging out the Dwarves and giving them no bargaining power whatsoever on this planet, too? Well, I'll tell you this. *I'm* not going in there."

"Are you sure you just can't…" Socar let out a sigh at the mulish look in Joe's eyes. "I'm not going to go in there with you. But, I can work with you to try and get everything set up. You say scorched earth. What does that mean to you?"

Joe's hard stare melted slightly as his calculated strategy brought a wicked glint to his eyes. The three of them leaned closer together, and the Ritualist sketched out his plan on the ground, using the powdery snow as a canvas. "Here's the Town. Right now, they have practically no visibility, and I'm pretty sure there are ice wraiths pounding on their walls. I'd noted earlier that the wards etched into the walls seemed to be particularly weak against elemental effects, and unless I miss my guess, they haven't been able to fix that issue yet."

As the others waited to hear his plan, Joe pulled out his ritual tile and tapped on the Expert-ranked Ritual of Remote Activation. "Since the walls are already taking a beating, and we have some cover thanks to the blizzard, I'm going to yank a bunch of the ritual towers out of Novusheim and surround this place. I'll disable all of the safety mechanisms and set them all to start attacking any structure, person, or monster in range."

"You're taking a *lot* of risk, Joe," Heartpiercer stated warningly. "You have no idea what's happening back in town; are you sure you want to yank all of these away and leave them defenseless?"

That gave Joe pause, but he pushed past it. "When you put it like that, anything would sound bad. As a warrior society, they aren't defenseless. They'll be fine. Now, if I have all of you helping me, I think I can minimize my risk here."

"The Town is too big." Jaxon shook his head as he tried to follow Joe's logic. "Your rituals, even given a height boost thanks to the towers, don't have the kind of range you're going to need."

"Good thing I have an expert in Formations, as well as an expert in fields of overlapping fire." Joe sent a solicitous wink at his friend, who completely ignored it. "As I run, I'll be activating the rituals I'm carrying with me and throwing them into any group of people I see. Between that and boosting the range of the siege towers to their maximum potential, I think we could set up the bombardment in such a way that our Archer extraordinaire can make a path for me to follow and close it off behind me. I think this has a good shot at success."

"That just sounds like falling on your sword, but with extra steps." Heartpiercer muttered ruthlessly, though a lot of the fire had gone out of her words. "Socar?"

The Mage looked pained and stayed silent as he did some calculations in his head. Just before Joe would've gone crazy and asked him to spit out whatever he was thinking, Socar winced and put his left hand on the back of his neck. "*Yea~ahh*. Yeah, I can do it... but you're going to have to sacrifice all of your ritual towers and the rituals on them. There's a Formation I know that'll be able to channel the yin energy of the Formation to its maximum, but as soon as the attacks stop, they'll consume themselves."

Joe didn't even flinch, simply nodding in acceptance. "I already wrote off anything I brought, gear wise. I can rebuild the towers, and I can even make them better next time. That way, no one gets too upset when they notice that I took all of these. I can just say I was swapping them out with an upgraded version."

"Yeah, so long as you don't die and vanish for the next five days waiting to respawn," the Archer grumbled with great annoyance. "I've got the Town mapped out, thanks entirely to Nimue and not at all to you. Let's get this job done before we lose what little chance we have to make it work."

That was enough for all of them to buckle down and start working. Socar had a Formation already in mind and merely needed to adjust its specifications based on the number of towers that Joe would be able to pull over, and the terrain that they were going to be placed upon. Yet, the most time-consuming portion of that was the finicky positioning of the various scoops and dangly bits and bobs that interfaced with the ambient energy and amplified only certain portions of it.

After Socar slapped Joe's hands away from the tablet for the third time—insisting he had all the mana he needed to run the ritual—the Ritualist simply had to agree to let the Mage use the Ritual of Remote Activation to set the destination or they would've been there for hours as Joe tried to fiddle with it to get it just right. Surprisingly, that was a relief to the Ritualist. If Socar was the one adjusting the towers, Joe could be ready to scale them and make the necessary alterations.

After the final design was decided upon, and the increases in range and area of effect had been calculated, they handed the map back to Heartpiercer. She started working out the route that Joe would need to move along to avoid getting himself lit on fire from a blast of Infernal Conflagration, trapped in an acid bubble, or fried by a Ritual of the Crawling Storm targeting him because he was a Mage.

The entire time that they were furiously working, scribbling notes, and having rapid-fire exchanges, Jaxon relaxed and watched them while limbering himself up. Eventually, the man went silent. A few minutes later, Joe looked over to see him covered in a thin layer of ice. Instead of commenting, he simply shook his head and muttered to himself, "Jaxon isn't turning into a snake. He *can't* hibernate; he's just messing with me. Why? No idea. The real question is, why is it *working?*"

Finally, it was time to bring in the first of the towers. With bated breath, the three of them watched as a tower located thousands of miles away was pulled from Novusheim and plopped down in front of them, approximately fifteen meters away from the wall. They had decided on that spot because visibility for them was less than five meters, and they hoped someone with a high perception would have at maximum a visibility of ten. Joe had to admit that Socar handled the movement of the towers with the precision of a surgeon; internally, he accepted that he could learn a thing or two about planning placement so perfectly.

When no alarms went up, and no attacks fell on the transferred structure, Socar moved to put the next in position while Joe climbed up and started making alterations. The Ritualist built in a thirty-minute delay, after which time the ritual would start attacking, whether they were ready or not.

With the clock ticking, Joe finished his requirements then threw himself off of the tower, trusting that the next one would already be in place. He couldn't see it for certain, which was the entire point of using the blizzard as cover, but the last few hours had shown him that he needed to have a lot more trust in his team.

As he slammed into the side of the tower and immediately started climbing, Joe let himself realize that his new faith in them was justified and let himself face the fact that they had his best interest in mind. Abyss, they'd followed him here, into the lion's den, putting themselves at risk just to try and help him through this difficult mission.

He would sacrifice his towers, his rituals that he'd meticulously crafted with dozens of hours of work, and hundreds of hours of research. The price was irrelevant to him. Towers could be recreated with enough time and aspects. Rituals could be rewritten. Celestials, Joe had invested *weeks* of time floating along uncomfortably, just so he could get close enough to find a friend whose trustworthiness was still in doubt.

He could only hope that his character was blatantly on display for the friends he had around him. If Joe would do this for someone who'd once betrayed him—even though she tried to make up for it—he would go to *far* greater lengths than this for those who had only ever been there for him.

CHAPTER FORTY-SEVEN

"Time's up." Joe needed to shout over the wind to be heard, and even then, it was only thanks to their Characteristics that his teammates were able to hear him. The towers were in place, and the rituals had been altered to attack anyone and *anything* they could.

There was exactly one place where Joe and Jaxon could enter the Town to evade the increased range and firepower of the towers, designed specifically to be where one of Joe's Rituals of Raze had been set against the wall.

Even as the Ritualist finished speaking, a stream of shouts managed to reach their ears. Checking on his time, Joe realized he'd already missed the first wave of projectiles that had been launched from his ritual towers. There was likely a large group of humans atop the wall who were melting from the first acid-filled bubble that had splashed on them. Joe paused, shook his head, and amended that thought, "No, their enchantments would keep it off of them. Hopefully it's messing up the wall, though."

After giving the remainder of his rituals a chance to initiate their deadly attacks, Joe activated the four rituals he'd placed against the walls directly. Thanks to their proximity, the group could hear a resonating hum fill the air as the enchantments on the walls began to fray, fighting to continue existing as the Ritual of Raze began tearing apart the materials they had been inscribed onto. The dark night of Jotunheim began lighting up as the magics fought against each other, the energetic sinews of the enchantments being stretched, torn, then violently snapping as the ritual of a higher rarity and power managed to chew through.

Cracks spread along the walls, bright spider webs of broken enchantments and wood. Then the magics failed entirely, and a thin film of power was scrubbed from the surface of the walls. For the defenders standing up top, the failure of their protections was unexpected and brutal. In each of the locations where one of the rituals was directly pressed against the barricade, a surge of unchecked power rebounded through and up, creating a magical recoil that tossed anyone unfortunate enough to be caught by it over and off the walls.

The lucky ones landed inside on the freshly fallen snow and were able to pick themselves up, dust themselves off, and rejoin the defense of their Town. Those who were less fortunate found themselves outside of the walls, either being torn into by ice wraiths or cheerfully targeted by the rituals that prioritized closer enemies.

Without the enchantments slowing down the razing, the now-enchanted wood began tearing itself apart and stacking itself neatly alongside its original location. Joe and Jaxon moved at the same time, taking advantage of the confusion and much-reduced visibility to move through the breach in the wall. The Ritualist simply jumped through headfirst, somersaulting and landing in a crouched position as he looked for any nearby enemies. The Chiropractor ran up to the wall and wiggled back and forth as he came in contact with it; somehow shooting up the flat surface until he came to the still-widening hole and practically slithered into the Town.

As they had planned meticulously, no exchange of words

was necessary. They started running, not directly toward the Town Hall, but along the path that Heartpiercer had master-fully mapped out. They'd both been given *severe* warnings as to what would happen if they tried to skip over the winding sections, namely friendly fire wiping them out as the ritual effects converged on their location.

Acid, lightning, and the ghostly flames of Infernal Confla-gration were already bombarding the edges of Town. The deto-nations moved in far more rapidly than Joe had been expecting, due to the nature of Socar's formation. One of the reasons the towers and rituals would self-destruct was that the cooldown that kept them from overheating and overloading had been almost entirely removed. Before, the rituals had been cannons; now, they were semi-automatic bazookas.

Even as the world around him was burned or boiled away, even as Joe danced past crawling lightning storms that specifi-cally reached out for him and his massive mana pool, the Ritu-alist could only laugh in excitement as his and Jaxon's feet pounded against the snow. "So *this* is what my rituals can really do! This gives me so many ideas!"

"Keep your head in the game, Joe!" The Ritualist barely had time to process what was happening as Jaxon's stiff fingers shot forward, slamming into a man's neck and causing him to suck in a sharp breath and collapse. "Don't worry, young man! When the temporary paralysis wears off, you will feel twice as good as—oh, never mind. Well, he *would* have felt better."

The downed human had been swallowed by an acid bubble, the coup de gras effect coming into play to ensure he experi-enced no excess suffering.

Joe's heart was pounding in his chest as he stayed side-by-side with his companion, even as explosions tore through the town around him. The non-stop barrage of spells was doing its job extremely well, transforming the oddly decadent settlement into a nightmare of bubbling streets and burning workshops.

Jaxon proved his worth every few moments, deepening Joe's appreciation of the man and his insistence on joining him.

Every time someone charged at them and came within melee range, his fingers plunged forward to poke them in the neck, never needing more than a single blow to drop them. Each jab was precise, efficient, and—since it wasn't intended as a killing blow—managed to inflict the paralyzed debuff on the recipient each time.

Sure, then they were swallowed by ritual effects, but that wasn't Jaxon's fault. His skills were simply working as intended.

As they reached the halfway point of their path, the wind around them began to die down. At first, it wasn't too noticeable, but with every second, the blizzard waned. Joe sucked a breath through gritted teeth in annoyance, realizing that the ice wraiths had likely been taking a beating from within the Town and without. As each of the monsters fell, the strength of the storm diminished further, gradually failing entirely as the density of the creatures dropped below whatever threshold caused them to create the area of effect.

There was a cry of victory, the still air allowing Joe to hear their gasps of relief and sudden upswing in attitude. The respite was momentary for the defenders, as they began to realize the scale of the onslaught the Ritualist had set against them. Already nearly half the Town had been reduced to ruin, and the magical attacks were still ongoing. The cheerful chatter transformed into alarm as they began trying to counter the bombardment, the ritual towers having finally been revealed as the wind died down.

"It's not an invasion; it's a distraction!"

"Abyss, that didn't take them long at all," Joe grumbled as he hopped over a fallen chimney. At nearly the same moment, a bright red flare shot into the air, the spotlight showcasing Joe's lack of hair. His bald head reflected and refracted the light, turning him into a blazing beacon that drew all eyes in the area. Fully visible to the Town's defenders, Joe and Jaxon were forced to take evasive maneuvers as a hail storm of arrows and spells joined the ritual effects raining down on them.

The sprint became a ballet of evasion: each dive, dip, duck, or Omnivault needing to be perfectly choreographed to not only escape the attack coming at them but remain on the path that had been set for them. Arrows whipped past them, spells exploded around their heads and feet, transforming the snowy streets into a pothole-lined, ankle-rolling trap. Whenever Joe got the feeling that Jaxon would be unable to block or dodge in time, he threw himself in front of the attack, allowing his Exquisite Shell to bear the brunt of the blows.

Exquisite Shell: 7,816/12,002

He watched the damage accumulate, knowing that he couldn't take any time to refresh his shields. On the plus side, not a single defender managed to make it within melee range of them after they had been spotted. The density of ritual magic raining down and the area of effect inherent in each of the chosen spells imbued into them made it nearly impossible to cross the open ground without knowing exactly where to step.

Since they were taking a circuitous, zigzagging route around the Town, various buildings would block line of sight for a short while, giving the duo a few moments of respite every handful of seconds. Their goal was in sight, and Joe nearly hesitated and turned to charge directly at the open door, only to be grabbed and yanked out of the blast radius of an oversized Infernal Conflagration. "Don't skip steps, Joe! Just *skip*!"

The Chiropractor followed his own advice, hopping lightly up and down with each step, looking for all the world like they were simply going through a playful jaunt through the Town. They circled the Town Hall twice after that before finally being able to approach the building itself. Seeing as it was exactly at the center of Town, none of the rituals had yet been able to bring the structure within range.

As soon as the small group was within five feet of its walls, they were able to travel along it however they pleased. Jaxon flashed his signature bright smile at Joe. "Wow! I didn't actually see us getting this far. So, now what? Window? Smash a hole in the roof?"

Joe only shook his head and started power-walking around

the side of the Town Hall, his movement hidden by the pounding the rest of the Town was taking. Smoke was choking the air, breaking up their silhouettes and making it harder for their enemies to detect them. "Nope, in a situation like this, assume that they're planning for us to do exactly what you said. There's no being sneaky, not after *that*."

Both of them looked out at the burning Town, watching as flashes of dark lightning and detonations of infernal flames brightened the night. Then they looked up, where the flare was still tracking Joe's location. The Chiropractor pursed his lips and bobbed his head a few times, "Yeah, yep. Makes sense to me. Then... what?"

"We go through the front door. *They* still have to use the building, and anyone who's supposed to be here isn't going to be crawling through a window like a thief." They turn the corner, seeing the grand wooden doorways on the only establishment seemingly untouched by the chaos all around it.

The duo went directly to the doors and shoved them open without a moment's hesitation. The bright, consistent light inside made them blink as their eyes adjusted, and both of them dropped into a fighting stance as casual, cajoling words met their ears.

"Ah, Mr. Joe. We've been expecting you."

A half dozen Mages stood in the center of the area, each of them holding a shining, outstretched hand directly toward the entrance. Unlike the Elf, the humans' faces were masks of fury, and several of them were clearly needing to force themselves not to attack until ordered.

The Elf noticed their desires and let out a gentle, soft chuckle. "Don't worry, he'll be able to replace the damaged and destroyed structures by this time tomorrow. Joe... you've been such a *naughty* human."

As he leaned forward to study Joe with glittering eyes, the Elf moved just enough to reveal a face that was not full of anger, fear, or resentment. Only resignation.

A half-smile appeared on Joe's face, and his eyes refused to leave her downcast ones. "Hey, Daniella. Ready to get outta here? We've got this great new local coffee roaster up and running."

"You will speak when *spoken* to! *Palm of the Luminary!*" the Elf barked, a wave of glowing force erupting from his flat palm and spiraling across the distance.

CHAPTER FORTY-EIGHT

Joe and Jaxon dodged in opposite directions, the Ritualist going straight into an Omnivault and hurtling across the room at an oblique angle. He was glad they'd moved so decisively a moment later, as the glowing palm expanded out to over five feet in length and width—then slammed onto the ground where they'd been standing, shattering the quartz-speckled flooring into shards of stone and mulch.

"Celestials, I hope you can't use *that* very often." Joe didn't even realize he had gasped the words aloud until the Elf let out a knowing chuckle and a grunt of exertion, a glowing palm print erupting from his alternate hand. The Ritualist pushed back with his feet, trying to stop his momentum but ending up losing his footing and sliding under the flying palm, which hit the wall and dissipated as the magic enchanted into the structure absorbed the attack.

Joe's mind started spinning frantically, and he looked around the room for any way to find an advantage. They were outnumbered in a large square space approximately twenty feet wide and twenty feet long. There were woven-vine tapestries growing along the walls, but the floor itself was cut stone. Almost everything else had been cleared out of the space, though the center-piece of the room was Daniella seated on a chair.

The six human Mages were flanking her, each of them focused not solely on combat but keeping their backs toward each other to ensure that she couldn't be snatched out from under them. Compared to the Elf in their midst, the humans' hands were shimmering with much lesser magic, though that made them less predictable. At least the Elf would focus nearly entirely on light-based spells, where the humans might be using anything from high-pressure water to infernal summoning, making them the true wild cards in the situation.

Jaxon glanced at Joe, his left eyebrow arched in a wordless question. The Ritualist nodded, and a huge grin spread across the face of the Chiropractor as he launched himself at the human mages. With the grace of a seasoned acrobat and the slipperiness of an underwater snake, he slithered through a barrage of random spells. Ice shards, fireballs, and even grasping vines missed him by fractions of an inch as his fingers extended toward the Elven-aligned enemies.

Jaxon's hands shifted, each digit becoming sinuous and growing a T-rex head, and Joe forced his attention back to the Elf, swiping an arm overhead the bandelier on his chest and releasing all of his ritual orbs. They lifted into the air, spinning around him and reflecting the kaleidoscope of color generated by the variety of magics in the room. "Question for you. When I finish you off, are you booted off Jotunheim, or do I have to constantly watch my back for your holier-than-thou visage?"

"Ah, certainly something you will never need to worry about. Nor will you ever find out." The Elf breathed out a sharp sound, and the air around him wavered. "*Dawn's Embrace. Twilight Mirror.*"

Joe didn't wait for his adversary to power up further, though he noted the fact that the two incantations seemed to form protective magics around his opponent. By the way the air seemed to be more *real* after the first spell, and more—the only way he could think to describe it was *abstract*—after the second, the Ritualist assumed that the first spell provided physical damage resistance, while the second would either cause his magic to deal less damage or send it back at him once cast. As the dainty lips of his foe opened, Joe attempted to stuff his Ritual Orb of Constitution down the Elf's mouth.

The heart-shaped orb had been circling Joe, and at his command, it thundered through the air, only to be neatly avoided *almost* in its entirety. Only the tip of the Elf's right ear was impacted, but that was enough to cause the hostile power-house to fly into a rage.

"You *dare* assault me? That's it! I don't care how useful you are *supposed* to be, you don't tame rabid dogs. You put them down! *Luminary Lance!*" A bright tendril of light streaked across the space, but Joe had thrown himself to the side as soon as he sensed the buildup of power. The spell hit the wall, drilling through and leaving a sizzling, burning hole where it had passed. A miniature light show filled that space as the enchantments attempted to rectify themselves. "Abyss!"

Joe didn't pretend not to see the chagrined expression on his nemesis's face, instead he used the distraction to send his orbs rapid-fire at his rival from as many positions as he could. The Ritualist bounded from one side of the room to the other, each Omnivault providing plenty of power for him to catch himself against the walls, ceiling, or floor and push off without needing to pause. Soon, orbs were attacking the Elf like a swarm of angry hornets, striking from all sides, the ones bound with spells intermittently testing the magical defense that had been set up.

The Ritualist was greatly pleased that he hadn't yet attempted a direct magical attack. His first impression had been correct: at least a part of each of his spells rebounded whenever they hit, but his orbs were moving so quickly that they were gone and out of the way before the reflected magic could impact their durability. His body wouldn't have been so lucky, he was sure. Focusing intently, Joe started only using the stored spells when the rebound would be sent toward the human Mages keeping Daniella in place.

As he continued to pretend to be a human bouncy ball, Jaxon was proving himself a terror in close quarters. Each of his fingers moved independently, as though they were the prehensile tail of an opossum. The only difference was that these fingers had *teeth*. The Chiropractor let his fingertips chomp into outstretched arms, then flowed around the person, pulling on the gripped area to pull off mind-boggling feats of flexibility, forcing spells to be cast at teammates, avoiding incoming attacks without concern, and leaving his enemies with large, bleeding gouges each time he moved away.

"Mind the poison, gents!" Jaxon cheerfully called to them as the first people he had touched started to slow down ever so slightly. "They *are* young hydras, but all that really means is that they like to use up all of their venom right away. Symptoms include burning, itching, paralysis, medium-term incontinence—"

As the Elf swatted a spell away from his face, Joe sent his orb of Intelligence spiking into one of the distracted Mages, causing him to crumple as his eyes rolled up into his head, vanishing as he was sent straight to respawn.

Then he had to dodge as his main opponent, looking more frustrated, summoned a shining sphere into his hand. For a fraction of a second, the shimmering, burning sphere hovered above the gold-tinged hand, then it zipped into the air and started tracking Joe around the room. Even pushing his jumping skill to the maximum, twisting in midair, and going from a horizontal jump to a slide across the floor couldn't cause the spell to lose him. Each time the human managed to evade, the orb shrunk a small amount but moved faster. Soon, it was singeing the hair off of his Hoardling cloak, then his arms, his eyebrows, all as it came within a tenth of an inch of his face.

A rapid backflip got him out of the way just as the spell detonated like a flashbang, rattling Joe and forcing him to blink. By the time he could get his senses under control, a concentrated beam of light had hit him directly in the chest, sending him tumbling across the room and leaving a burnt cylinder through his clothes and burning his chest deep enough that his rib bones were exposed.

Exquisite Shell: 0/12,002

Health: 1,872/2,496

"Shoulda… refreshed Exquisite Shell before I came in here." Joe wheezed as he cast a quick Mend on himself, closing up the wound and reversing the macabre damage.

A crisp *smack* rang out as Retaliation of Shadows hit his opponent, sending him tumbling to the ground with a squeal of surprise. "I *despise* that little trap you have on you!"

Damage dealt: 625 dark damage!

"Slappity-slap, don't talk back!" Joe called as he sprinted across the room, strafing left in order to put the group of Mages in the center of the room between himself and the Elf. He thought he'd gained himself a moment of respite, but as a burning sphere flew in an arch over the group, Joe realized he was being naive. His adversary had literally centuries more experience in combat than he did, and something so simple as having someone in the way wasn't going to stop him from being able to light Joe on fire.

"Alley-*oop!*" Jaxon hopped into the air in front of one of the Mage guards, his legs clamping around the man's neck as he went over him. Then the Chiropractor flipped the unfortunate guard up and used him like a flyswatter to slap the blazing orb. With a cry of pain, another person vanished from the room.

"Oh, for Ascetic's sake," the Elf growled as his hands spun through the air, shaping the mana pouring off of his body. "Foul humans, even your deaths inconvenience me. *Blades of Daybreak!*"

Lights that shone so brightly that they hurt to look at directly started collecting on the leader of the Town's outstretched arms, forming into long blades that began at the elbow and scraped against the floor when he dropped his arms to the side. Two more appeared in the air above the Elf's shoulders, and Joe pulled his orbs back just as they flashed into motion, attempting to dice the metal assailants.

"Close one." Joe didn't recall the orbs, instead having them pound on one of the guards who looked as though he had a bead on Jaxon's exposed back. The man stumbled, and Joe hopped to the side—putting himself, the guard, and the Elf in a line, with those deadly light blades as far away as possible. That didn't even slow the potent Mage down. The guard was slashed into four pieces with a single swipe of the blades, causing cauterized meat chunks to rain to the floor before the man abruptly vanished. "Okay, don't know why I *wasn't* expecting that."

As the sentient blender closed in on Joe, he scrambled to think of something to do. Some way to fend the attack off or break through the defense and potent offense of his adversary.

The edge of light snapped through the air, and Joe finally forced himself to move out of the way. As he tumbled across the ground, the blades struck down around him, each aimed center mass, with the Ritualist forcing all of his muscles to work in tandem to let him thrash out of the way just before impact each time.

"Stop moving, and I'll only take your arms and your legs!" The furious combatant bellowed as he stared down at Joe with bloodshot eyes. "No? *Fine*! This is *over*!"

Two blades sliced down as the Ritualist's back hit the wall.

Instantly, the air was filled with the smell of overcooked pork, and the only thing Joe could hear was the sizzling of cauterized flesh.

CHAPTER FORTY-NINE

"Mind... the poison," Jaxon cackled weakly as his hands dropped off his arms, landing on the Elf. There, the hydra heads struck the Elf over and over, doing not much damage—thanks to the damage reduction barrier, but getting enough through to inject poison into his veins. "Now would be a *great* time to move, Joe."

Joe's eyes were wide, fixated on Jaxon barely above him in a seated wall squat. The Chiropractors' elbows were locked just below the point on their attacker's arms that were coated in light. As his hands had been cleanly chopped off; he was supporting his own arms with his knees but seemed to be quickly running out of steam. The Ritualist shifted to the side and Omnivaulted up as the blades hovering in midair came down and took Jaxon's arms off at the shoulder.

Then, contemptuously, a single swipe chopped off Jaxon's legs at the knee, and the Elf turned his full attention back to Joe. "What wonderful, self-sacrificing friends you have. Always ready to dive in and save you because they know that you are practically a helpless baby bird. What *trust* he must have in you, to put himself in my power like this."

Joe cursed at the fact that his friend hadn't just been finished off. If he were in the same situation, that would absolutely be his preference. Otherwise, just as the condescending being was taunting him, they could be locked up, or worse. "Don't worry, buddy! We'll get out of this."

"You will? How? Do tell." Something about his enemy seemed off, and Joe's magical senses started whining at him. Realizing what was likely happening, the Ritualist called a Dark Lightning Strike down on himself, taking the damage but also revealing the Elf sprinting at him while disrupting the illusion he had left behind.

Health: 1,902/2,496

The illusion in the distance faded away, and Joe shot straight up at the ceiling. With a roar, the Elf leapt at the same time. "Not *this* time, brat!"

A standard Ritual orb launched out, aimed directly at the center of a delicate-looking forehead, only to be sliced directly in half by the glowing sword.

One of your ritual orbs has broken!

Joe cursed internally; he didn't have any Characteristics bound to that orb, but it was one he needed, as it unspooled into part of the ritual circle that allowed him to summon Morsum. Now he'd need to redo the *entire* diagram to ensure it matched up properly. "Three hours down the drain. *Acid Spray!*"

Caustic fluid splashed out of Joe's hands, the pressure of the spray enough to slow down the Elf and blind him. Not because of the liquid, but because his floating swords of light swung furiously at the liquid, cutting off his line of sight and causing the acid to turn into burning gas. Joe managed to push away at a slight angle, and as the two of them fell toward the ground, the distance between them increased.

"They attack independently of him..." Joe's eyes narrowed in determination as he thought of a plan. "Got it."

"I could use a hand!" Jaxon called at him. "Two would be even better!"

"Do you know what it means to *Thesaurize*?" Jumping into

the air, Joe spun and threw two objects. The first of them was a ritual tile that was activating even as it moved through the mostly empty room, aimed directly at the pretty-boy Elf running at him. The second was the orb he had that was imbued with Lay on Hands. That one was thrown at the Chiropractor who was wiggling across the room toward him.

"Looking down on me?" The tile was ignored as it flew over the Elf's head, which made Joe smile. The first indication that the Elf had made a mistake was when he blinked and found his face embedded in the stone floor of the building, lightning crawling around him and digging into his mana pool to fuel itself.

Joe landed and leaned forward slightly, arresting his momentum as he prepared to spring again. "It means I replaced the wording of that spell with a synonym that makes it *twice* as potent!"

"*Ahhh*! Greater Dispel!" Even through his pain, the combat-hardened Mage managed to use his own power, and a wave of energy pushed out of his skin and into his surroundings. His blades disappeared, as did the lightning that was burning out his synapses. "You... have truly upset me. Your greatest chance at surviving this encounter was having my hands too tied up to work with my other spells."

The Ritualist's reply was to start tossing out handfuls of tiles, each of them primed and ready to start blastin'. Joe had planned to use these to burn down the entire Town on his way out, but this seemed like a better option. "Humans have a saying I don't think you're going to like very much."

"*Radiant Chains of the Prismatic Aurora!*" The entire room darkened as every photon in the space was pulled into the spell, and a gigantic manacle made of burning light clamped around Joe's torso. From there, smaller chains shot out, clamping onto his elbows, wrists, knees, ankles, and neck. "We Elves also have a saying. Tally not your dragon eggs before they've birthed their majestic flames. Tell me, *captive*, what was your saying again? Now that your body and magic are bound?"

"Ours is a little more straightforward." The lack of concern Joe had on his face gave the Elf pause. "There's no kill like overkill."

Before Joe could even finish his statement, the ritual circles inscribed onto the tiles sprang into full activation, releasing their effects into the enclosed space and burning through walls, flooring, and the roof. Infernal Conflagrations screamed with dark glee as they lit the tapestries aflame. Lightning danced among the Mages flanking Daniella, acid washed across the floor, pooling in low spots and rapidly reducing the durability of the building. Half a dozen Rituals of the Crawling Storm boiled across the stone toward the Elf, who watched all of this unfold with shaking eyes.

Even knowing that he was about to be fried by his own powers, Joe had a smile on his face. This was his second favorite outcome: a guaranteed respawn for himself, Jaxon, and Daniella, while the Elf would have to go through its own lengthy respawn process, likely off this world. "Only thing better would've been us living through this while he didn't."

"*Grand Dissolution of Mana!*" The Elf suddenly turned into a shining beacon of energy, his aura rapidly expanding and shoving back the active effects of the rituals. The swirling circles fought back, but the potent magic radiating off of the Elf caused each of them to fail in turn. The expanding wave struck Joe, snuffing out his bindings in an instant and causing him to fall to the floor in a heap.

Joe turned his head and coughed, a light mist of blood erupting from his mouth and splattering across the floor. He looked up, nauseated from the way his head was spinning. Everything in the room, everything *about* the room, seemed dull and fake for a few long moments. Then the Elven aura snapped back, and the standard chaotic weight of Jotunheim's ambient magic slammed down onto them. "Did you just erase the *mana* in this entire room?"

The Elf was heaving for air and half-collapsed onto a nearby charred wall. "Do you have any idea… how long it takes before I am able to cast that spell once more? No. Never mind that, this is exactly its intended purpose. An entire level in the spell from a single cast? You have my gratitude, and it makes me wonder how much power you managed to pack into those little stones of yours."

"Uhm." Joe pushed himself to his feet as the Elf did the same. "Not enough, clearly."

"Pah." His adversary was quickly recovering and already had a gleam in his eye as though he had a new plan forming. "No matter what you threw at me, the outcome would've been the same. Prepare yourself, and say your goodbyes. You will never get this far into *my* Town... ever again. Luminary–"

"Face slap!" Jaxon yelled as he spun through the air, coiling his entire body into a spring shape, then unwinding and unleashing all of the kinetic energy he could possibly impart into his attack. The Elf went corkscrewing through the air, hitting the wall and smashing right through a flame-weakened section. "Grab her and *run*, Joe!"

The Ritualist was so stunned at the sudden turn of events that he almost failed to take advantage of it. Turning on his heel, he pounced over to the center of the room, landing with both feet on the back of a guard's head just as he was starting to push himself to his feet with a groan. "Ya-*hoo!*"

Clearly having been running on the last fumes of his health pool, the final Mage guard vanished in an instant. Joe dropped down to a knee, stretching his hand out and casting Mend on Daniella, just in case she'd gotten injured in the ruckus. "Told you I'd come for you, now let's get out of here before–"

"It's not going to work, Joe." Daniella finally looked up at him, meeting his eyes as a single tear streamed from hers. "I didn't know, I *swear* it, and you know that if I swore something and lied about it, Jotunheim itself would punish me right now. So *please* believe me. Joe... that Elf? He's on the same level as Havoc. He's just been toying with you because he wants to crush your spirit. This entire Town was a trap to lure you in and force you to work for the Theocracy."

As if to punctuate her words, Jaxon went flying past the two of them, the left side of his face mangled from a return slap the Elf landed on him. When Joe's friend hit the far side of the building, he didn't just make a hole; his impact caused the entire wall to collapse.

"Haaa… why did you have to go and ruin my fun? Daniella, we're going to be working together for *years*. Eventually, you're going to have to learn to like me. But before that, all of you are going to need to learn to *respect* me. Well, if our little game is over, we might as well get on with reconstruction. No time like the present to work, and you have a lot of effort to put in if you want to be able to live through the next Beast Waves."

Bits and pieces of the Elf that Joe had been in combat with were flaking off, his original visage subtly shifting, his clothing becoming of a finer cut and quality. The golden skin that Joe had taken note of earlier in their fight began to shine with an inner light, as though a flashlight had been pressed against the opposite side of him.

A deep frown appeared on Joe's face, and as his opponent came into full view, Joe realized that he recognized him. "You're the Cleric. Not the High Cleric, but one of his lackeys. The one who activated the prison of light that contained Jaxon and me in the Elven capital city."

"Yes. In my home. Which you *destroyed*." The cleric had a benevolent smile on his face, but Joe didn't believe this person was good or decent in the slightest. "Like I said, you have a *lot* of rebuilding to do. Once we capture the bifrost, after making this Town into a fortress, a proper city, I have been tasked with bringing you back to Alfheim, where you will serve penance by replacing every single building you destroyed in your 'grand escape'. Once you are done with that and ten years of hard labor, the Ascetic may even pardon you. Well, contingent on the destruction of the Dwarven homestead you have been scraping together on this planet."

As the Elf monologued, Joe came up with a plan. A plan he absolutely hated. He was out of alternates, contingencies, and even emergencies. It was time to go with a Hail Mary. Joe turned sorrowful eyes toward Daniella and took a deep breath. "I'm sorry about this. But, do you trust me?"

"After all this?" Daniella choked on her words, shaking her head as tears glistened on her eyelids. "All you went through, for me? Just to be trapped here? Yeah. I trust you."

"Goodbye, Daniella. See you soon." Joe closed his eyes so he wouldn't see the look of shock on her face as his Ritual Orb of Intelligence penetrated the back of her skull.

Coup de gras!

Daniella's body slumped to the ground, then she was off to respawn. The Cleric sucked in a harsh, furious breath. "*Why?* What in the *abyss* is *wrong* with you?"

CHAPTER FIFTY

Instead of answering, Joe simply stared at the Cleric. His stance was relaxed, his gaze filled with watchful anticipation. "Eh, nothing. Had a bit of pent-up aggression, maybe?"

"You mean to tell me that you traveled who-knows-how-far, fought against what *should* have been insurmountable odds—" here the Elf sent a sneer at the area where the Mages he'd tasked with Daniella had stood, "and made an enemy out of me —now a *personal* enemy, instead just having a non-specific dislike of you—all so you could enact some kind of... of... petty *vengeance?*"

Shaking his head slowly, Joe maintained his stare and answered slowly. "Nope. That has nothing to do with why she's been sent away from here. To respawn. That's merely a symptom of this disease. An unfortunate necessity, perhaps we could say?"

"Then I suppose you want to surrender? You've made no additional hostile moves. No one is coming to save you?" Just in case he was wrong, the Elf started summoning his power, his hands filling with light so hot the air around his open palms shimmered. "I'm not so sure I *want* you to give up at this point."

The Ritualist shook his head, his wry smile still in place. "No, nothing like that. I'm just waiting for you to get punished. For lying and breaking your sworn oath."

"Pah, I have never done such a thing," the Cleric stated with deep conviction. "When you walk the path of light, there is no room for shadows to grow."

Blinking a few times, Joe looked around the room, over-acting as though he were searching for something, or more specifically, some*one*. "No oaths broken? If that's true, then... where's Daniella? You know, the person you swore you'd keep in the Town Hall for the next thirty days, in case I wanted to come and pick her up? I don't *see* her anywhere."

"T-that! That doesn't count, and you know it! *You* just killed her." The Cleric didn't wait for an answer and began advancing on Joe.

"For someone who doesn't think it counts, you sure do look nervous." Joe chuckled darkly as the shining lights in the Cleric's hands began to *flicker*. "Besides, I didn't swear that I wouldn't kill her, only that I'd eventually rescue her. I'm still working on that. But it looks like *your* situation is... in review."

The Cleric stopped dead, his face going white as a sheet. The light shining through his skin winked out as though someone had thrown a switch. Joe could see that he was reading something, and it appeared to be distracting enough that the Ritualist couldn't keep himself from going for the kill. His orbs were flung to his sides, the spray shifting their angles midair to start zipping toward the frozen combatant like a set of missiles launched from orbit.

"Temporary!" the Elf shouted in triumph, his eyes refo-cusing on the world around him. "A simple *penance*, as well as an offering at so much as a *shrine* will take care of this Warlock status you forced onto-"

Thud.

Joe was impressed by how each of his weapons had hit so simultaneously that only a single impact could be heard. He followed it up with as many spells as he could manage to get off while the Elf was reeling from the blows. *"Cone of Cold. Dark Lightning Strike. Infernal Conflagration!"*

Damage dealt: 2,028 (847 physical, 1,181 Magical)

The currently-powerless Cleric fell to the ground, gasping in pain from the simultaneous strikes. Seeing that the Elf was still alive, even after taking one attack from nearly every source Joe could deal it from, the Ritualist could only be somewhat impressed. "You have more than two thousand Health as a Cleric? I assumed you'd devoted everything to your mental stats to better focus on your abilities and connection with 'the light'."

Before Joe had finished speaking, the Elf convulsed from pain as a fresh wave of agony filled him. "What did you do to me? Damage over time effects? Poison from the baby hydras? My health is still dropping!"

"You won't have to worry about that for long," Joe informed the Cleric, his deadly intent shining through as an intense bloodlust that caused the Elf to look up at him with wide eyes. Already, Joe had his orbs in position, and only the desperate show that came a fraction of a second before he attacked caused Joe to stay his hand.

"Wait!" The Cleric panted in pain and fear, his eyes scrunched tightly closed as he waited for the blow that Joe had pulled. Noticing that he hadn't died, the defeated Elf let out a deep sigh and met Joe's gaze, for once not looking at the human as though he was beneath him. "Not here, not like this. You don't understand how terrible this failure will look, what it will do to my career!"

"Your… career." The Ritualist tried to think of a proper response to that but could only nod his head. "After all this, the big, bad, devoted Cleric is just a salaryman at the end of the day.

"I'm in the running to be a High Cleric by the end of the *decade!*" came the affronted retort. "Do you have any idea how huge of an honor that is?"

"Yeah, I got offered that class as a specialization and turned it down because I found something better." Joe chuckled at the stricken look on the helpless Elf's face. "What're you offering? Your Town? All its burned-up resources? Not to come hunting me a continent away? None of that's appealing to me in the slightest."

With each word that Joe spat out of his mouth, the Cleric flinched and winced, clearly having been planning on trying to strike a deal with at least some of those options. "I… will swear not to come after you or your friends. Not directly. I cannot promise *not* to attack your Dwarven settlement."

"Oh, wow, what a great deal," Joe sarcastically scoffed, sending his Ritual Orb of Intelligence spinning down from near the ceiling to nail the Elf's leg in place. His target let out a scream and began babbling at a frantic pace. Though he hid it well, the Ritualist felt queasy over his actions, though it did prove that his foe was on the verge of being sent to respawn.

"More than that! I can transfer this entire population to you. I have power of attorney for the entire guild, and I know you need people. That has to be a requirement for progressing your settlement further, right?"

"Oh, yeah, why don't I just take a huge group of people who want to destroy me and everything I've built, and everyone around me, straight to my house? It'd be fun. Like a sleepover." Joe's fingers twitched, and the Elf screamed, expecting another orb to hit him.

"They *hate* this life!" the Cleric shouted desperately. "They may not say it directly, but I know. The culture shock was so extreme when they joined us in the first place, and now there aren't even the glorious amenities of the Theocracy to keep them happy. If they had a way out, they would take it… ungrateful dogs that they are."

"You know what? Fine. I'll take your oath and your people." Joe held up a hand to forestall any rapid agreements or handshake deals. "But I'm not taking *only* that. You're going to offer me a quest. The quest is that I heal you enough not to die from bleeding out, in exchange for you not hunting me, either directly or through proxies, and I get your power of attorney over the guild here. Then I'll give you two days of time where I'm not actively looking for you. That should give you plenty of time to get to one of the other Villages or Towns."

"You want me to issue you a quest? A holy compact? You would use—*wait-wait-wait.*" The heart-shaped ritual orb stopped barely an inch from the Elf's face. "While it might be made under duress, I… I *suppose* it is no less than I have already offered. Fine, I agree to your terms."

Quest offered: The Pact of Survival. You have somehow come across a wounded Elven Cleric, a formidable foe teetering between life and death. This adversary presents an opportunity, but there is a delicate understanding to be made. If you heal them enough to prevent their death via blood loss, a pact of mutual non-aggression will be made. As a part of this agreement, they must vow to cease all direct and indirect hunting of you.

All rewards will be given to you upon acceptance of this quest. For the quest to be considered complete, you must give the Cleric a 2-day grace period for them to recover, during which time they will not be allowed to attack you or send people to do so. Failure will result in all rewards being rescinded.

Quest objectives: heal the Cleric enough that he can survive his current open wounds. Reward: Mutual Non-aggression pact. Power of attorney over the local guild. Accept? Yes / No.

"Uh, excuse *you.*" Joe scoffed at the message. "A mutual non-aggression pact? I think not. I've already proven that I can take you down. As soon as I leave here, you're all but forgotten. All the way until you do something to tick me off, at which point I'll *absolutely* hunt you down."

"*Fine.*" A moment later, a slightly adjusted quest appeared in front of Joe, and he accepted it after carefully reading it over.

As soon as he let an orb drop down and cast Lay on Hands —allowing the Cleric's cheeks to regain some color—an absolute *wall* of text appeared in Joe's vision. He could only thank his lucky stars that the Elf wasn't allowed to attack him. Otherwise, he'd be in the same helpless position that he had used to win this battle.

Wow! You used pain and fear to convince an Elven Cleric to part with his seat of power! Dark Charisma +4! For choosing to end the battle in a mutually beneficial bargain without killing the enemy you had under your control, Light Intelligence +5!

You have gained control of a player guild: The Chosen of Eternium! As the First Elder in Waiting of The Wanderer's Guild (reach Sect status to attain benefits), you may retain personal control or make them a subsidiary of The Wanderers Guild at any Guildhall.

Life or death combat against a Grandmaster has imparted greater training than usual!

Acid spray (Student 0 → Student II)

Dark Lightning Strike (Student VIII → Journeyman 0) Congratulations! This Spell has passed a threshold! As it is a spell granted by a deity, it has a branching path available for upgrade. Seek out a shrine to see the options.

Mend (Journeyman IV → V)

Exquisite Shell (Student IX → Journeyman 0) Congratulations! This Spell has passed a threshold! As it is a spell partially *granted by a deity, it has a trio of paths to choose for upgrades. Seek out a shrine to see the options.*

Retaliation of Shadows (Expert II → Expert IV)

Infernal Conflagration (Beginner 0 → Beginner III)

Combat Ritual Orbs (Exotic) (Apprentice IV→ Student 0) Congratulations! For breaking the threshold into the Student ranks, combat ritual orbs under your control now have a minor Psi barrier applied to them, allowing them to take up to 20% of their durability in damage before beginning to degrade. In order for the barrier to be repaired, you must sleep for at least 4 hours.

Battle Meditation (Passive breathing pattern) (Student VII → Journeyman 0) For passing into the Journeyman ranks, 10% of the skill ranks of this skill are added to your passive mana regeneration.

Hidden Sense (Student III → Student VI)

Magical Synesthesia (Beginner IX → Apprentice II) Oh look, you hear magic more clearly. Don't get too entitled about earning bonuses!

Omnivault (Master I → Master II) Congratulations, for increasing a Master-rank skill, you earn +5 to all stats!

Alchemical Rituals (Beginner 0 → Beginner V)

Somatic Ritual Casting (Journeyman 0 → Journeyman II)
Intelligence has reached 200! Prepare for a mental adjustment!

Everything went dark as Joe's brain shut down in order to have a proper reboot. When he came to, he wasn't entirely certain how much time had passed, but it couldn't have been more than a second. He was still falling toward the ground and managed to catch himself by rolling as though he were doing a celebratory somersault.

"Eight," the Cleric called over conversationally, earning himself a *look* from Joe. "That's the number of times I could have gotten to your unresponsive body and killed you with your own weapons, in case you are wondering."

"I wasn't," Joe stated stiffly, "Your wounds are healed enough that you won't bleed out. Get out before I take your presence as an admission that you're going to break our deal."

"Mmm." The Elf smirked as he stood and started limping away. "I'm certain we haven't seen the last of each other. Besides, I wouldn't do something like that. Breaking an oath gets me a slap on the wrist. Going back on a quest reward gets me shoved into an instant dungeon for a week."

The Ritualist had been about to goad the Elf into attacking him, perhaps taunting him and hoping his increased Dark Charisma would force the Cleric to start swinging. But he held his tongue as the injured man approached the door. He'd seen what being the target of an instant dungeon did to people, and remembering the broken people who had been spit out by the minor calamity made him queasy.

"You know, Daniella told me that you were on the same level as Havoc." Joe scoffed as the Elf stepped out of the Town Hall and scurried away through the snow, on the lookout for monsters. "Turns out *that* was a lie. I've literally seen Havoc self-destruct to win. Until you're willing to win, no matter what it costs, you'll *never* be on his level. I can only hope… that I won't be, either."

CHAPTER FIFTY-ONE

With the Cleric gone, Joe quickly put the rest of his plan into play. Taking a deep breath and steeling himself, he activated his Mass Resurrection Aura. The beautiful, esoteric streamers of darkness reached out through the room, creating a portal above each place someone had fallen. As the last vestiges of his mana left him for the next twenty-four hours, Joe sank down into the chair in the center of the room. "Ugh, that sucks just as bad as it did last time. Didn't pass out though; that's a plus."

Daniella stepped out of the portal, looking at him, then around the room, before a bright smile appeared on her face. Joe let his minor headache fade from his attention as he focused on her presence.

Six other humans stepped out of portals in the next moment, and even though Daniella started to panic, Joe remained calm. Not only had he been expecting them, he'd been *counting* on them coming back. Half a dozen spells were prepped and aimed at him, before they even bothered to take stock of the situation. "Surrender immediately, and your death will *only* be painful."

"Hold on a few minutes; I need to read Something. It's a

great book." Joe reached into his ring inventory and pulled out a thick document. As he flipped it open, he allowed the other people to see the cover.

"Our guild charter? How? You *dare!*" The leading Mage puffed himself up, greatly overacting to showcase his 'anger'.

Joe simply held up a finger to forestall them then brought it down and licked the pad of his finger before flipping through the pages. He lifted his coffee mug with his off hand, and a moment later, the scent of fresh-brewed espresso filled the room. After taking a few deep sips, Joe made a noise of appreciation as he tapped a section in the charter. "Ah-ha! Here it is. The guarantee to showcase 'genuine realism in every public situation'. Well, since I have power of attorney for your guild, I'm just going to go ahead and *scra~atch* that section out."

As he made a deft motion with his quill, the small cluster of people in front of him gasped as though they'd been physically punched in the chest. Several of them bent over, breathing heavily as they tried to move past the nausea a long-term compulsion imparted when it was finally removed. One of those heaving men was the first to speak. "You freed us? Wait, you own the guild? Did you win it in combat? Was that... is that a thing?"

Joe shrugged lightly, showcasing the fact that he didn't *need* to be serious in the slightest at the moment—and for the first time since joining their guild, neither did *they*. "It happens. Hey, you guys want to switch teams? We have a really nice Town and an absolutely massive population with a ton of luxury items and such."

"You had me at being able to slouch," another of the Mages called, getting a round of nervous laughter in reply.

The first of them who had spoken wasn't as amused. "What happens now, to the rest of us? Are you going to turn us into a mercenary squad or something?"

"Nope!" Joe waved off that line of thinking immediately. "First thing I'm going to do is make sure everyone in the guild knows that they have the option to leave if they want. I'm not just talking about the area, I mean The Chosen of Eternium. I doubt many of you will; shared struggles have a way of bonding people, and it's not like there's a huge number of options for everyone at the moment."

After exchanging glances, they all relaxed quite a bit more, and the light of gathered mana vanished. "You mean... you'd just let us walk away? To do... whatever? Even if that meant we would eventually come after you?"

"Sure, but then I'd know that you chose to do it, and I'd be way less understanding." Joe smiled to blunt the savagery of his tone, but the only thing that accomplished was making the Mages shiver in anticipation of consequences. "Look, let's go round up the survivors and have a talk. But first; Daniella, are you okay? What do you need?"

After a long moment of looking around the room, Daniella simply let out a grunt of annoyance and waved at the door. "Just get me outta here, Joe."

They stepped outside, the Ritualist leading the way, and he felt a slight *squelch* as his foot came down. Confused and slightly concerned that perhaps the Elf had left a booby trap in his way, Joe glanced down, only to see a rime frost-covered Jaxon frozen to the ground. Chuckling softly, he started moving his hands as if he were gathering his power to Infernal Conflagration. "Oh no! He's icy to the core, but the only warming spell I have is going to burn him to a crisp! I guess beggars can't be choosers."

Jaxon started wiggling away immediately, managing to get indoors and ever so slowly waiting out the 'frozen' debuff. His voice was muffled slightly, as his lips and teeth were solid ice, but Joe could still clearly make out, "Aye knoo ya fergot bout me."

"I didn't forget about you; I knew that hit hadn't killed you off. I figured you were searching the Town for reptiles or some other Jaxon-y thing. Look, you got about half an hour before I take this Town Hall down. Get warm, then come find us."

"Joe?" Daniella's call made Joe twist his head to look at her, and the nervous gesture she made into the distance. "Any chance you can call off the artillery?"

He poked his head back outside, this time his eyes focused on the horizon, and found that the majority of the Town had been reduced to a smoking crater. "Huh… yeah. Whoops. Kinda makes me wonder if the Cleric managed to leave. Maybe Heartpiercer nailed him to the wall. Either way; not my problem."

It only took a thought to cancel the active rituals, but he snapped his fingers so he could still have good *presentation*. Immediately, all of his magical effects stopped. He could only nervously hope that they were no longer required, because he couldn't reactivate them for at least a day.

As the dust settled, Joe found that their group was alone in the epicenter of the obliterated Town. Looking around and seeing the destruction that his abilities could create, sweat dripped down his forehead. Victory was sweet, but he'd been far too close to choosing to live a life where this would be the only way to progress. Not for the first time, he was thankful to his past self for not choosing a combat specialization.

"Think anyone lived?" He wanted the words to be casual, but they shook slightly as they left his mouth. A side benefit was that Daniella stepped closer to him and linked her arm in his. He paused and whispered instructions into her ear. After a momentary hesitation, she nodded and slipped around to the other side of the structure they had just exited.

One of the Mages nodded and pointed into the distance. "We have a few fallout shelters. I'll go open them up and get people over here."

"While he's doing that, hey, Jaxon! Can you go find Socar and Heartpiercer? I'll work on a shrine and… right, no access to mana for the next day. Just tell them to come over here?"

"Fine, but you owe me." As the Chiropractor walked away, Joe noticed that he was moving far slower and more rigidly than usual. Without giving it a second thought, the Ritualist sent an orb over and sent the mental command for Lay on Hands to activate. An instant later, Jaxon glowed slightly, and his form recovered greatly. "Oh? My thanks! But I thought you were cut off?"

"I... am?" Joe was as confused as Jaxon at the moment. "I guess it's because I'm not using mana to control the orbs or to cast the spell? Nice, a solid workaround."

It took a while, but Joe had nowhere else to be, so he waited patiently as more and more people gathered in the Town, many of them giving him concerned, distrustful looks. "Listen up, people! The Elf is beaten and gone for now, and for what might be the first time in a long time, you have a choice. A real choice. You can join me in Novusheim, the Dwarven Town. There, you'll have to work hard to earn your keep and earn a chance at a new start. But, it's a real offer. You'll be able to be a part of polite society again and pursue your own goals, not what's assigned to you."

He waited a few long moments, breathing in deeply and tasting the smoke-filled, dusty air. All of the remaining residents of Middle Town were quiet, save a few survivors mumbling to each other under their breath. "The other option is to leave the guild. If you can't figure out how to play nice on this world, I'm not going to risk my friends for you. In fact, I'm adding it directly to the guild charter. Anyone who plans to harm a Dwarf or Novusheim in general will automatically be booted from the guild. If you get in a fight, or something happens, the matter will be reviewed. For those of you who choose to stay, welcome back to living your own life for yourself and the people you *want* to be around."

Ending his dramatic speech, Joe turned around and waved at the Town Hall. He didn't have anything to do with the Ritual of Raze activating; he'd had Daniella get into position before he started speaking and had her wait for his signal. Still, it looked impressive to see the building at the center of the Town get ripped apart and have its materials neatly stacked next to it.

Quest complete: This planet isn't big enough for both of us. You have destroyed three Elven settlements of various rarity. Return to Grandmaster

Havoc in order to gather the blueprints for a Mana Battery Recharge Station.

"Nice," Joe whispered to himself with a smile on his face before wiping it off and turning back to the gathered guild members with a stern expression. "I need volunteers to go to the two nearest Villages and collect the fallen members of your guild. They won't be back for a few days, but don't worry about getting out of here. I set up a fast travel system that anyone with my permission can use. You won't need to brave the dangers of Jotunheim in order to find safety in some far-distant location. Just a short, hour-long sprint in the brisk morning air."

That earned him a few chuckles, and Joe could already tell that the vast majority of those gathered would be joining him. As Daniella came back into view and sidled up to him, he continued speaking. "Everyone else, let's get moving toward the shrine. It's time to get to your new home. This place is going to be overrun by beasts, so whether you're coming with me or leaving for good, now's the time to get going."

With that, everyone was either handed a map and given detailed instructions or started gathering anything of use that remained in the Town. Still, time waited for no one, and as the hours passed, they heard a roar in the distance that likely signified a gathering Beast Wave. "Time to go! Novusheim awaits!"

As they walked into the frigid world waiting for them, Jaxon slithered up next to Joe and postulated a quiet question. "Don't you think the Elf is going to give the guild members you sent to the next Village over some trouble? I can't imagine he would let them go without a fight, and you didn't make any deal to get *them* out of here."

Joe snorted at that, his cheerful expression hardening for a moment. "Yeah, about that. He didn't get far. Our deal was for me to heal him enough that he wouldn't die... from blood loss. But he was constantly burning from Infernal Conflagration to the face, and I can clearly remember one of his people laughing at me when they let me know that there were very few people who could remove infernal damage over time. If he hasn't already been sent to respawn, he will be soon."

"Ooh, using your words in a nice, specific way. I love it, the duplicitousness of it all! Say one thing, mean another, and get exactly what you wanted in all cases." Jaxon clapped Joe on the back and let out a too-loud chuckle.

"All I did was take Havoc's advice," Joe replied 'humbly'. "I simply put my full intention into my words, making it seem more formal and impressive by replacing my simpler intentions with synonyms. Better rituals, razing Towns, putting the hurt on a Grandmaster Elf? I just needed to Thesaurize."

EPILOGUE

By the time the final people from the Middle Village area trickled into Novusheim, the first hint of morning was arriving in the form of a slightly increased amount of light illuminating the massive world. Joe had decided to make everyone wait overnight at the shrine, both until he had access to his mana, as well as letting everyone that was going to join arrive. Only then did he start sending people across in waves.

Then, when the very last of them had hopped on the fast travel system, did Joe make the jump himself.

As soon as he arrived in Town, he found himself surrounded by the entirety of the Dwarven Council. Master Wrath stepped forward and had to be held back from slapping Joe to the ground. "You just *had* to take the towers with you? Do you have any idea what this last week has been like for us? Constantly fighting? Incredible stress on the population? Now you're bringing in *thousands* of people who were purposefully and intentionally working for the Elves? Have you gone rogue?"

Joe had been prepared for a confrontation; he knew that his actions were certainly going to cause some issues for people. Even so, he was slightly off-put by the ferocity of his welcome.

"Let's try that again, *Master* Wrath. First of all, the towers *aren't* supposed to be the only thing keeping the monsters at bay. They're a service I provide, and I'm happy to be informed that my absence has *shown* how much value *I* bring to the Town both as a councilman *and* as a private citizen."

Wrath scoffed at that, but there was nothing more to be said on the matter. They knew just as well as Joe did that, at any time, the Ritualist could simply leave or remove his towers, and they'd just have to deal with it. There was no agreement in place whatsoever, and he decided to take this opportunity to remind them of that fact.

"I certainly hope there's more of a reason for the *entire Council* to gather to try and lambast me into resetting the towers that I made. Wait... are you angry because they're gone or because the tax revenue they generate for you is gone? If my towers aren't killing the monsters, you aren't getting your enormous cut, after all."

"Joe..." Grandmaster Snow groaned as she put her hand on her forehead, the middle finger and thumb pressed against her temples as she tried to figure out a way to head off the situation.

"Come on, tell me. Was everyone gathered here to be impressed at my bringing us a vanguard of several thousand people that would stand steadfast in our walls in the coming conflicts? At destroying a major Elven Town, even if it was far distant?" The Ritualist looked at the stony faces around him and scoffed. "Of course not. I think we're going to have to reassess our 'deal'."

Wrath shoved a finger in Joe's face, "If you *think* you can—"

"My towers generate a massive amount of revenue for the Town. If you want them back, you're going to have to pay me for that *privilege* from here on out. As the person who sends you the raw materials *I* generate, I know *exactly* how much they bring in. Let's work out the details of how much I'm going to charge you for the use of *each tower* in the near future. Don't worry, I'll be coming to the Council with my proposition in a few days. After a nice, long, well-deserved rest. Don't worry, I won't be too unreasonable… especially if I get some nice, fat bribes before then."

He looked around at each of them archly, and Snow shook her head and let out a puff of air. "*Told* them this was a bad idea. Well, people, let's go try and figure out how to salvage this mess. Let me be the first to point out: *this* is what happens when you overrule the Grandmaster with a majority vote. If you think for a second that I'm *not* going to be making some changes to the makeup of the Council after this—"

As the group slunk away with their tails tucked between their legs, Joe deflated slightly. "Is this really how it's going to be every single time?"

"Nah, stick it to them like this enough, and they'll be way too afraid to go against you. How do you think Oligarchs are made in the first place?" Havoc chuckled as he came to a standstill next to Joe, nearly knocking the human over with the gust of wind that his high-speed movement generated. "Frankly, I think you're well on the way to being a first-class Oligarch. Got anyone you want to turn into a princess? Any utterly unreasonable demands? Not what you just sent at them; frankly, I think that conversation has been a long time comin'. You let things go too easily. Well, some things. Other things you obsess over. How *is* Daniella, anyway?"

"Pretty good, I think. I need to figure out a way to get her out of the walls and into Town." Joe and the Dwarf started walking while they talked, headed for the very walls they were discussing. "I suppose I could make that a point of the concessions I want for putting the towers back?"

"Like I said, first-class Oligarch in the making! You'll be throwing people out of windows in no time flat. Ahh… I miss Oligarch Defenestration. He didn't make it to Jotunheim." After letting out another long chuckle, Havoc retrieved a stack of documents from some storage device hidden on his person and handed them over. "There you go, the blueprints to a nice, high-end Mana Battery Recharging Station. This'll get you anything up to the Expert rank. If you want something more than that, I'll need to be paid for custom work."

"With… *money* next time? Please?" When his mentor didn't say anything in reply, Joe could only take the documents and begin perusing them with a grunt. The more he saw, the more he liked it. The designs were intricate, complex, each detail practically shouting about the capabilities of the final product. Just as expected, the design was actually three separate enchantments that were interlocked in an impressively cohesive design. "Is this modular? Can I make them one at a time?"

"Sure, why not." Havoc took a puff of his cigar and looked away. "Probably won't blow up. Anyway, you're going to have to hold off on these for a while. Don't get me wrong, it works, but the connection points between the battery and the recharge pad can't be changed without years of research. That means the final product won't be stable unless you can find a way to ease the burden the chaotic pressures of Jotunheim will put on it."

Still deep in studying the amazing enchantment he was holding in his hands, Joe slowly nodded, fully understanding the gravity of Havoc's words. "Goals are good, and I like having them. In fact, I already have a plan to adjust the chaotic flows, at least within the Town proper. As for this? A little delay won't hurt. Especially if I'm going to start being paid for my services by the Town. Hold on a second… when I asked if they'd always acted this way, you seemed pretty sure about the eventual outcome. Havoc. Are you—or *were* you—an Oligarch?"

"Heh. Yeah." The Dwarf led Joe around a trap that had been set out in the labyrinth. "Don't you remember how we met? The government asking me to do them a favor, you coming out to my private research facility, me shouting at the sky? Yeah. If you're going to be in a position like that, you need the power to back it up. I have it; you're well on your way to getting it. That's what it means to be my Apprentice."

"Is that why people were looking at me so strangely?" Several things were becoming rapidly clearer to the Ritualist. He let out a rueful chuckle as he tucked the designs safely away, and his mind turned to the future. "Looks like you have lofty goals for me, too. I'm fine with that. I've never been afraid of high expectations. At least now the path forward is clear. Fix the ambient energy and turn it into a permanent, renewable power source for us to use. Then make Novusheim the most powerful City this world has ever seen."

"Fun, right? Imagine having all the resources you could ever want, and no red tape slowing you down. One or two more events where ya prove yourself indispensable and too expensive to cross, and you'll be able to do everything you've ever wanted." Havoc offered Joe a cigar, which he immediately declined based on the fact that inhaling the *diluted* version of it was usually enough to send his Neutrality Aura into overdrive. They walked in silence for a few more minutes, until the first camp finally came into view.

Daniella was talking to someone, but she was obviously waiting for Joe to arrive. As soon as his shiny, bald head made an appearance, she made her excuses and started rushing over to them with a wide smile on her face.

"Not a terrible thing to have reasons you want to progress, huh?" Havoc nudged Joe in a slightly teasing way then started coughing as an ember shot to the back of his mouth. "Look how—*cough*—happy she is to see you—*cough*—and to be here. Isn't that a sight for—*cough*—the sore eyes?"

ABOUT DAKOTA KROUT

Associated Press best-selling author, Dakota has been a top 5 bestseller on Amazon, a top 6 bestseller on Audible, and his first book, Dungeon Born, was chosen as one of Audible's top 5 fantasy picks in 2017.

He draws on his experience in the military to create vast terrains and intricate systems, and his history in programming and information technology helps him bring a logical aspect to both his writing and his company while giving him a unique perspective for future challenges.

"Publishing my stories has been an incredible blessing thus far, and I hope to keep you entertained for years to come!" -Dakota

Connect with Dakota:
MountaindalePress.com
Patreon.com/DakotaKrout
Facebook.com/DakotaKrout
Twitter.com/DakotaKrout
Discord.gg/mdp

ABOUT MOUNTAINDALE PRESS

Dakota and Danielle Krout, a husband and wife team, strive to create as well as publish excellent fantasy and science fiction novels. Self-publishing *The Divine Dungeon: Dungeon Born* in 2016 transformed their careers from Dakota's military and programming background and Danielle's Ph.D. in pharmacology to President and CEO, respectively, of a small press. Their goal is to share their success with other authors and provide captivating fiction to readers with the purpose of solidifying Mountaindale Press as the place 'Where Fantasy Transforms Reality.'

Connect with Mountaindale Press:
MountaindalePress.com
Facebook.com/MountaindalePress
Twitter.com/_Mountaindale
Instagram.com/MountaindalePress

MOUNTAINDALE PRESS TITLES
GameLit and LitRPG

The Completionist Chronicles,
The Divine Dungeon,
Full Murderhobo, and
Year of the Sword by Dakota Krout

Arcana Unlocked by Gregory Blackburn

A Touch of Power by Jay Boyce

Red Mage and
Farming Livia by Xander Boyce

Ether Collapse and
Ether Flows by Ryan DeBruyn

Dr. Druid by Maxwell Farmer

Unbound by Nicoli Gonnella

Threads of Fate by Michael Head

Lion's Lineage by Rohan Hublikar and Dakota Krout

Wolfman Warlock by James Hunter and Dakota Krout

Axe Druid,
Mephisto's Magic Online, and

High Table Hijinks by Christopher Johns

Skeleton in Space by Andries Louws

Dragon Core Chronicles by Lars Machmüller

Chronicles of Ethan by John L. Monk

Pixel Dust and
Necrotic Apocalypse by David Petrie

Viceroy's Pride and
Tower of Somnus by Cale Plamann

Henchman by Carl Stubblefield

Artorian's Archives by Dennis Vanderkerken and Dakota Krout

Vaudevillain by Alex Wolf

Made in United States
North Haven, CT
29 April 2024

51921421R00217